# The Men
*in* Her Life

# The Men
# *in* Her Life

## MARY HOSTY

POOLBEG

Published 2003
by Poolbeg Press Ltd
123 Grange Hill, Baldoyle
Dublin 13, Ireland
E-mail: poolbeg@poolbeg.com

1 3 5 7 9 10 8 6 4 2

A catalogue record for this book is available from the British Library.

ISBN 1-84223-125-1

Typeset by Magpie Designs in Palatino 10pt /11.9pt
Printed by Litografia Roses, Spain

**www.poolbeg.com**

## About the Author

Mary Hosty has taught English for several years. She has published extensively in newspapers and in the field of education. She lives in Dublin with one husband and two sons. This is her first novel.

# ACKNOWLEDGEMENTS

This, of course, is a made-up story about made-up people and made-up events and I hope you enjoy reading it! Mostly, I hope it makes you smile.

Thanks to very many people for help, encouragement, research and friendship along the way.

To Síle Sheehy of *The Irish Times*, Mary O'Donnell and Mary Hanlon for early and dangerous encouragement. To Máire Geoghegan Quinn, Nóirín Ní Chonghaile and Ella Shanahan.

Very special thanks to a great bunch of friends: Mary Ryan, Florence Hamilton, Eoin Hamilton, Peter and Kate McGonigal, Clare McNicholas, Brigid O'Sullivan, Bairbre Ní Chiardha, Mary Earlie, Jacinta Davenport, Aisling O'Grady, Catherine O'Flaherty – thanks to all for friendship and fun and listening to my interminable rambles and for supplying yarns (e.g: the T Rex incident, the wallpaper comment, and some closely guarded lingerie secrets!).

To my dad and the extended family, in particular some great cousins and friends – Anne Marie Minhall, Susie Bush, Kevin Dever and Catherine Kelly – for some great nights in London and Kent and some top-class rugby matches – very important research!

To cousin Tom Mellett for the whale joke (a

bit rude – but hope you enjoy – it's near the end!). To Auntie Delia with lots of love.

To Macciarhos Productions – they know who they are!

To Ellen Forde for a great fruit scone recipe – try it and see!

To the Ó Ciardha family and especially to Cáit for her wonderful son.

To my colleagues for support and companionship, in particular Andrea Muckian, Colm O'Connor, Margaret Brosnan and Paul Barnes for invaluable comment. Very special thanks to John Moriarty for on-going encouragement, helpful criticism and admirable patience.

To my agent Ger Nicholl – for on-going support and encouragement, for being super-efficient, effective, and kind and for giving me the chance to drop the phrase 'my agent' at parties!

A very big thank you to Paula Campbell and all the team at Poolbeg for their hard work.

To Gaye Shortland – for vision, wit and wonderful editing, for setting high standards and gently nudging me away from chaos, and for giving crash courses in e-mailing and on-line editing.

To the following people who gave generously of their valuable time, information and insight and expertise into the areas of Health, The Law, High Finance and Public Relations:

Toni Uí Chiardha, University College Hospital, Galway, on hospitals and health matters; Beverley Turner, Taylor & Buchalter Solicitors, on legal matters; John Fanning, Managing Director McConnell Media, Carol Flynn, Managing Director McConnell Advertising, Pádhraic Ó Ciardha, TG4, and Eoghan Ó Neachtain, Public Affairs Manager, ESB, all of whom helped me immeasurably in understanding the world of advertising, marketing, PR and image making; Tom Paine, of Paine & Associates, Chartered Surveyors, London, on the development, layout and running of vast building sites; Kevin Dever, AIB London, for insight into the world of banking and finance.

To my sons; to Macdara and friends for invaluable insights into matters of teenage style, music and dialect; to Seán for dedicated Playstation research above and beyond the call of duty! Both have been very understanding about the strange notions of mothers, not tearing the house down while I was writing. But mostly thanks for being wonderful.

Lastly to office boy, best lad, key grip, spin doctor, chef extraordinaire, sommelier, advisor on media, advertising and public relations, all-round knight in shining armour, fearless critic, firm ally and best friend always – Pádhraic.

*To the men in my life:*

Paddy - My dad
Macdara (aged 17)
Seán (aged 12 and a half)
Pádhraic (aged — hardly even slightly)

With Love and Thanks

# CHAPTER 1

Lit hollered up the stairs to her son.

*"Richie! Get up! You'll miss the bus!"*

She'd already gone through stages one to four of the wake-up process. One! The gentle tap on his lean shoulder – "Love, it's time to get up!" Two! The affectionate sweeping aside of a lock of his dark hair followed by a firm but sympathetic shake – "Really, love, it's time to move!" Three! The bedroom light switched on briskly and the coolly delivered . . . breakfast. Four! The shrewish "Get out of that bed, you lazy lump! If you get the sack don't come running to me for pocket money! It doesn't grow on trees, you know!"

Despite her best intentions, she usually ended up saying the pointless, silly things she'd promised herself she'd never say. Of course money didn't grow on trees. And Richie knew perfectly well that it didn't grow on trees. He wasn't really a lazy lump either – well, not as bad as his mate Barney Ryan who over the past few months seemed to have petrified into a state of semi-suspended animation. Except for his fingers and mouth, that is, which moved and functioned with no help from

1

his brain, skilfully shovelling mounds of food into himself and at the very same time guiding Dave Mirra along his merry skateboarding way on the Playstation 2.

*"If you don't get out of that bed this minute, you're grounded for a week!"* She was screeching now. Lit the cool, Lit the highly successful, Lit who could subdue a roomful of men in Italian suits with just the merest arch of an eyebrow – routinely reduced to a squealing harridan by a relatively sweet and trouble-free sixteen-year-old.

From the lofty heights of age, experience and disinterest Dandy, her father, watched the performance and chuckled quietly to himself as he slurped his way through a bowl of steaming porridge. The name Dandy had come from the fact that Richie couldn't get his tongue around 'Grandaddy' when he was small. That was hard to imagine now. All he had managed to say then was Gandy, which then became Dandy and had stuck. Now even Lit called her father Dandy. Well, there was something strange about calling a ninety-two-year-old 'Daddy' and 'Father' certainly didn't fit the bill.

She gave up calling Richie. She munched furiously through a slice of wholemeal toast, scraped with low-fat butter and the merest hint of low-sugar marmalade, then quickly demolished a cup of breakfast tea. With another holler up the stairs, she smoothed out the creases in a totally uncreased state-of-the-art suit and slipped her dainty feet into a pair of crippling black stilettos. Then she rammed the hideous green Laura Ashley smock into a carrier bag, along with a pair of flat black pumps, the kind with a cross strap and shiny black buttons.

She glanced at the clock. If she didn't get a move on, she'd be stuck in traffic. Make-up would have to be applied in the car. Make-up was always applied in the car. She had reached the stage where she could hardly apply lipstick unless she was on the move, with her hand swaying and hovering over her lips like an alcoholic's trying to take hold of a glass of whiskey.

"What's for dinner?"

"Haven't thought about it yet."

"Don't cook that green stuff. It doesn't agree with me."

"Right."

"What's it called anyway? Disgusting shite!"

"Broccoli. And it's especially good for snarly old men like you."

She rummaged in a nest of papers and Playstation magazines, football programmes and discarded CDs, junk mail and school reports, barely used perfumes and half-worn lipsticks, photos and postcards, for her car keys. The kitchen counter was a mess – everything that didn't have a place of its own got thrown there – but she consoled herself that the mess never spread beyond the kitchen. It wasn't allowed to. Beyond the kitchen door there was a place for everything and everything was most definitely kept in its place. Beyond the kitchen door, Lit Doran's house was an impeccable series of perfectly co-ordinated rooms. They said taste. They said style. They said restrained elegance. They said money.

Dandy tutted and shook his head as he shuffled across to the big old comfortable armchair by the range. He tossed the cat unceremoniously to the floor and seated himself slowly like an oriental potentate.

"It's criminal getting paid for what you do. Why don't you get a proper job – like the civil service or teaching?"

She smiled coolly, didn't have time to engage with him, didn't see the point in explaining life in the modern world to him. So she left him to his cup of tar-black tea and David Hanly on *Morning Ireland* and his raw-onion and Calvita-cheese sandwich and his grubbily thumbed book on the siege of Stalingrad, and having hollered up at Richie one last time, she slipped quietly out the door.

Lit's house was situated off Harwood Park, in a quiet leafy road with an air of prosperous redbrick seclusion. It was detached, large and imposing, but there was a homely look about it – it was a lived-in house, with plenty of flowers, shrubs and pretty mullioned windows.

Unusually for Dublin, the weather was hot and sticky. It had become the main topic of conversation, replacing the soaring price of property and the economic boom, and the absolute and total unfairness of not having a decent GAP outlet. At eight, though, a cool and balmy mist still hung in the air over Harwood Park and the fine old redbrick houses took on an almost magical quality in the pale morning light.

In the distance were the cranes, barely visible, looming over the city, symbols of success and progress. Soon they would be busy picking over building-sites like a hundred grazing dinosaurs. Everywhere in Dublin tower-cranes loomed, their long braced jibs lifting, hoisting, swinging, rising and dipping over the city from early morning till the twilight hours, ripping out decaying and wasted remnants of the past, transplanting banks, high-rise offices, multinational hotels, apartments, conference centres, like donor organs into the city. The city of Dublin was having the ultimate makeover.

This was the time of day Lit loved best, the time full of expectation and optimism when the day ahead was still nothing but a bundle of ifs, what-ifs and maybes.

It was going to be a busy day. She liked the busy days, savoured the rush of excitement as a campaign was pronounced to be a success, or the feel of anticipation when a new client was brought in. There were morality snobs who considered the world of image consultancy and public relations to be phoney and artificial. But it had always been in existence. Jesus used the apostles to do his PR work. Cleopatra probably went through several image consultants. Henry the Eighth didn't pay enough attention to his spin-doctors. Someone should definitely have spoken to Napoleon about his taste in hats.

And it was all money: tangible, reliable, versatile money. Money invested Lit with a sense of self-worth, gave her power, ensured her the company of loyal friends. She could not remember a moment's unhappiness from the day she and her business partner Matt Shiels had begun to make serious money. It drove her on to the next day and the next challenge.

She sat into her perfectly valeted, shiny red BMW – all chrome and horsepower. She had bought it three months earlier on a whim – a hundred-thousand-euro whim. And she loved it with a passion. It was her mobile beauty parlour, cloister of meditation, bubble of solitude, temple of rock, reading-room and think-tank. She reached for her DKNY sunglasses and placed them on the seat next to her. Then she turned on the ignition, pulled out of the driveway and switched on her mobile.

"Hi, Maura! Any messages for me? OK. I'll be there in ten minutes. Can you get out the file on Conrad Budd? I have a meeting with him today. And find out what time Seán Tallon – you know, that accountant guy . . . well, I haven't met him . . . Matt knows him from school, I think. We're supposed to be meeting him this morning. Then there's the presentation for Wholesome Foods. We'll have to get the boardroom set up . . ."

The prospect of meeting Conrad Budd was both exciting and terrifying. The Budd contract was just about the most hotly contested bit of property in the PR business and Budd was an attractive and dynamic man. Even in his college days he had cut a glamorous figure – attracting the attention of lots of women, including Lit and Bonnie. Though even Bonnie with all her seductive powers had failed to penetrate Conrad's inner circle. Taking all that into consideration, it was no wonder that Lit was tingling with a warm glow of excitement that misty summer morning.

The morning sun cast a greyish light through the magnificent swathe of white muslin curtains as Conrad stirred in the bed, unfolded his limbs, and slowly eased his sleek, lightly tanned body onto bounteous feather-and-down pillows. It felt vaguely as though something or someone was in the room. In the eerie half-light, through a mist of sleep and half-remembered snatches of dreams, he scanned the vast bedroom, across oceans of maple floor scattered with Persian rugs, along walls which housed some of his small but perfectly formed collection of objets d'art. His eyes rested for a moment on the early Giacometti which stood on a granite plinth facing his bed, then slid across the Yeats, the Osbourne and the Le Broquy.

The white muslin curtains swayed and sighed gently in the light morning breeze. There was air conditioning, but Conrad rarely used it, especially at night, when he loved the feel of the breeze flickering on his cheeks as he fell asleep. Perhaps, after all, it was the noise of the curtains that had woken him. Besides, he lived in what was probably the most secure address in Dublin – a penthouse, overlooking the Docklands, above the small but very exclusive Mount Pembroke hotel, one of a number of properties in his possession. The penthouse stretched across three thousand feet of discreetly monitored space. Who could reach him here? Who could breach the walls of his castle? And besides, he had no enemies. Or none that could reach him here anyway.

He slid down between the cool cotton sheets, hoping to drift back into slumber once more. But the feeling of another presence persisted – watchful, not threatening, dreamlike and oddly real at the same time.

"Who's there?" he asked in a low voice at last.

But there was no response. He recalled a shadowy figure from his distant past. But it couldn't be. It wouldn't make sense. It must have been the aftermath of a dream, he told himself, and drifted off to sleep once more.

By the time she reached the turning out of Harwood Park, Lit had successfully applied concealer and foundation. She checked in the rear-view mirror – perfect – no nasty streaks anyway. She edged out onto Morehampton Road and into the sluggish traffic. Slow traffic was good for mobile make-up application. She reached into the glove compartment and pulled out eyeliner and lipstick.

She channel-hopped – but it was all 'non-stop' music stations with incessant talk offering more music and less talk. On the news channel, a man with a wheezy voice droned on about development and planning tribunals.

"Booooring!" she chirped airily and pushed the CD button.

The words of a Verve song blasted out from her car stereo telling her that life was "a bittersweet symphony", that she was a slave to money and that she'd die. She sang along at the top of her voice. She turned the music up, enjoying the sensation of the sound filling up the cabin of the car, drowning out the world outside.

Edging forward with her feet delicately playing accelerator, clutch and brake, she returned to the rear-view mirror to apply a discreet touch of eyeliner and shadow. Driving forward while looking backwards into the rear-view mirror was quite a simple manoeuvre really once you got the hang of it. The trick was good reflexes.

Once the eyes were done, sunglasses could be put in their rightful place, firmly on the bridge of her nose. Lipstick now – and her hand hovered and shook as the car edged forward. She just had time to apply two perfect curves of pink to her upper lip when suddenly the cars ahead of her took off in a frantic dash as the lights changed. Applying a hasty and less perfect arc to her lower lip, she rammed her foot on the accelerator and charged unevenly after them.

She didn't see the patrol motorbike, much less hear it on account of the loud music, until it pulled up alongside her and an angry-looking guard with an imposingly gloved hand signalled her to pull over.

"Why didn't you stop when you heard the siren?"

"Sorry, guard, I didn't hear it . . . I was listening to music."

"You didn't see us and you didn't hear us. That could be driving with undue care."

"What are you going to do? Ban car stereos?" she joked hopefully.

He wasn't amused. "You shouldn't have it so loud that it is a distraction to your driving or your awareness of other motorists."

"Right. Sorry, guard. It won't happen again."

She flashed him the tiniest gleam of white teeth, framed with an almost perfect set of smiling pink-frosted lips.

He wasn't impressed. Not even slightly. "And applying lipstick while in charge of a moving motor vehicle is in direct contravention of the Road Traffic Act."

She thought of removing her sunglasses and doing a little eyelash flutter and perhaps even a tear-filled eye. She thought of explaining to him that she had a ninety-two-year-old father and a son of sixteen and no husband and that this was the only time she could do her make-up. That she owned a business that required her to look immaculate and stunning almost all the time. That she was thirty-four and just past that stage where it was good for the self-esteem to be seen in the harsh light of day without the benefit of make-up. That he was lucky he hadn't caught her painting her toenails or drying her hair on the car heater. That he should go and catch some real criminals. But she didn't have time.

"You're right. It was very careless of me. I have no excuse."

"Your left brakelight is broken. Did you know that? That could cause an accident."

"Sorry, guard. I'll have it fixed today."

"And remember to drive with due care and attention. Next time I'll have to book you."

She swung the car through the narrow gateway leading into the bijoux little complex of offices nestling beside the canal. Her mobile bleeped with a text message.

"THERE'S NO TROPICANA !!!"

She smiled. Richie had hauled himself from the bed at last. She messaged back.

"TOUGH! WILL U SHAVE DANDY?"

"?? LIFE'S 2 SHORT!"

"PLEASE TRY! LUV U. C U LATER!"

She switched off. Otherwise, he would spend the day

sending her messages about his current concerns: food, money and socialising.

In the office, Maura was sorting through the post, answering the phone, drinking coffee, reviewing the notes from her evening course on marketing, checking her e-mail, watering the bonsai tree and finding one of those special black roller pens that Matt insisted on using.

She looked Lit up and down as she came through the doors of the office.

"Will you be wearing that for the meeting with you know who?"

"Who?"

"You know perfectly well *who* I mean. That Budd fellow!"

Lit picked up her post from the desk and smiled coolly at Maura. She was certainly not the kind of woman to go all gushy and throbby about any man. She never would go all gushy and throbby about any man, ever again. "Not my type," she said and changed the subject. "How's Barry?"

"Great," said Maura with a fond glimpse at his photo on her desk. "Just great." And she planted a little kiss on his framed face.

Matt, Lit's partner, flustered around the place in a state of high anxiety. That was good. He had two modes, flustered and torpid. Flustered meant his brain was working overtime and there weren't enough hours in the day to do what he had to do. Torpid meant he was depressed, full of self-loathing, frustrated at his lack of ideas, inclined to moroseness and self-pity.

"Seán Tallon is due at nine."

"Who?"

"My old mate, Seán Tallon, financial whizz kid, come

to tell us how to maximise our whatsits and minimise our thingies."

Sometimes Lit clashed with Matt, mostly on matters of taste, but she loved the way that despite their burgeoning success he absolutely refused to get drawn into that mysterious jargon so beloved of accountants and bankers. Matt knew what was what moneywise – in fact, he was surprisingly shrewd. He just would not foul his mouth with words like assets and liabilities, funds, portfolios, debts and equities.

He wasn't handsome, but he had a face that sat comfortably with his personality – a plump, freckled face – and thick curly ginger hair. His eyes were greenish behind steel-rimmed glasses. When he was in good humour they lit up with infectious joy. When he was sad, his eyelids hung at mournful half-mast, hiding his inner turmoil from the world.

They had coffee in the large functional office which they shared with Paul, a graphics wizard, Fionn the clever copywriter, Zara who did the accounts and Maria whose desk was always laden with all the paperwork that no-one else wanted to do.

"Budd seems pleased with what we've done so far. But I think he's planning a bigger profile. I've been to the site, seen the plans. It's quite an awesome undertaking. That's what he'll be sounding you out about today. Any ideas?"

"Plenty."

There was a pause while he stubbed out his cigarette. Lit raised her hand to her mouth and coughed slightly to register her disapproval. She wished he wouldn't smoke in the office. Shiels Doran PR had to be the only smoking office left in Dublin. But she didn't have the heart to make him stand in a solitary miserable huddle on the street. When he wasn't around though, she and Maura routinely opened all the windows – even on the iciest days of winter. She also kept a large bunch of stargazer lilies near his desk – much more effective than the millions of products which claimed to eliminate the nasty smell of cigarette smoke.

"Right. Just be well-prepared, that's all."

"How do you mean?"

"Budd's a hardball player. If he doesn't like us, he'll be off to the next agency like a shot."

"Don't worry – it takes more than hundreds of millions of pounds in the bank to intimidate me."

"That's hundreds of millions on paper, babe," he drawled, Philip Marlowe fashion, with another cigarette dangling rakishly from the corner of his mouth.

"Since you know so much – what is he like?" asked Lit. It didn't seem proper under the circumstances to tell Matt about the Budd-infatuation she and Bonnie had nursed through college and so she conveniently neglected to mention it.

"Don't know much about him, apart from what you see in the paper. Professional background. Very successful – Midas touch sort of a guy. Impetuous in his business dealings – I've heard. Private life – very private. Engaged to a dentist's daughter from County Meath – Angela something, I think. So I guess he won't be much interested in your charms, the fool!"

"I have no intention of wasting my charms on him or anybody else. Life's far too short to waste it on seducing men. They almost never live up to their early promise."

"How would you know? You haven't exactly any recent experience to speak from."

"Shrewd observation skills."

Matt pulled a face at her.

"I'd rather have a dog," she went on. "Dogs are loyal, don't try to have sex with your best friend, have no problems being affectionate in public, and the only silly game that dogs play is – fetch! Men are hopeless. Always excluding you, of course." She pecked him lightly on the cheek. She set up her laptop on the desk in her office and began checking through her e-mail. "So what about this Tallon guy?" she shouted out to Matt.

"Tallon? Top man!" Matt said, sauntering into her office, coffee mug in hand. "Guys like him can name their fee. We can't really afford him. But he's not charging the full rate. Rumour has it that he's on the way to being next chief thingy in Cooney/Lysaght."

"A shit-hot accountant!"

"Haven't seen him that much lately. Our lives have taken different paths, as they say."

The phone on Matt's desk buzzed and Maura's soft Mayo accent came over the speaker. "It's Seán Tallon."

"Send him in," Matt said and his face creased with a crooked smile.

"This man is not your typical accountant. I promise you."

Lit was mildly curious. In truth, any accountants she had met were frighteningly practical and excessively realistic. She always felt that they had undergone the equivalent of an imagination lobotomy.

When the door opened Matt opened his mouth to speak then stopped suddenly.

"Oh my God! Tallon . . . is that you?" he managed to blurt out finally.

# CHAPTER 2

Standing in the doorway of Lit's office was what could only be described as a man in a suit. It was a fine dark-grey woollen suit and beneath it was a crisp pale-blue poplin shirt and a sober wine-coloured silk tie, flecked with tiny grey fleurs-de-lis. The fine man in the suit stood about six foot tall, had neat short sun-bleached hair and wore steel-rimmed glasses.

Matt peered at the visitor, looking him up and down several times in disbelief. "My God . . . you used to have pink peroxide in your hair and a step! And studs in your ear! What's happened to you? You're . . ." he struggled for a word, "you're . . . an accountant!"

"The peroxide hair seems like a million years ago. Matt – it's good to see you."

They embraced and patted backs and prodded shoulders in the manner of men.

Lit observed the scene with interest. It was hard to imagine Seán Tallon with brightly dyed hair or studs in his ear. In fact he was difficult to describe at all. She supposed he was handsome, though it didn't particularly register. His eyes, hidden behind the smart steel-rimmed glasses were bluish-grey, cool eyes preoccupied with grave matters.

Matt introduced them and they shook hands. Tallon smiled but only briefly – no surveying glance over the figure, no broad charming smile. In fact he barely acknowledged her at all. While Matt disappeared briefly to get the accounts from Zara, Lit led Tallon into the boardroom and offered him a seat. She sat opposite him and instantly there was an awkward silence. She felt it would be good manners to break the ice.

"Did you have any trouble finding our offices at all?"

14

"None."

"That's good because sometimes people miss the turning."

He nodded and took a document file from his briefcase and rested it on the expansive table.

"This heatwave is amazing," she tried again valiantly.

"Yes, it is," he murmured absently and quickly immersed himself in his prepared financial review.

She felt vaguely foolish. And annoyed. Unaccountably annoyed. It wouldn't hurt him to engage in a little small talk. A little small talk was crucial in the business world. Small talk was the three-in-one oil of the business world. She watched him absorbed in his silly little world of number-crunching and she decided there and then that she didn't like him. Not one bit.

"Right. To business," he said when Matt returned.

He passed around a few single sheets of figures for their inspection. Lit read over the figures, hoping she could find something to nail him on. It was extraordinary, she thought. The man was like a machine – no inconsequential little remarks about the humid weather, or the traffic congestion, not even a request for coffee. Perhaps, she mused vindictively, he was a new form of robot accountant.

He knew his stuff though. She was grudgingly forced to admit that to herself. Seán Tallon knew everything there was to know about what to do with money so that it would make more money and how to arrange it so that the taxman saw only a decently modest slice of it. Secondly, money appeared to be the sole purpose of his existence. Life for him seemed to be nothing more than a series of assets and liabilities. House – good asset, sizeable investment in small film production company – liability, spending to be curtailed in the area of hospitality

. . . travel expenditure excessive for the scale of their company . . . plans for further recruitment sound . . . proposed move to larger premises probably a necessary evil . . . investment opportunities . . . debt and equity rating . . . and so on and so on and on . . .

"Overall, Matt, I have to say, you and Ms Doran are in fairly good shape here. But we know from past experience that this can all change overnight. You must always have financial contingency plans – the old rainy-day scenario, if you'll forgive a folksy cliché."

Matt looked slightly put out. He was still smarting from the shock of seeing his erstwhile boho friend trussed up like the Christmas turkey in a suit and tie. Even after college, Tallon had forsworn the suit and tie in favour of badly paid positions in obscure charities. Then he had headed off to Brazil to run a community centre and a soccer club for impoverished teenagers in the barrios. But now it seemed as if all that had never been. Tallon had completely reinvented himself.

Lit eyed him sharply and chipped in a little tartly. "What do you suggest?"

She surveyed him with icy distaste, sitting back in her chair, her chin tilted slightly upwards to give added haughtiness.

"Well, as I say, you're in reasonably good financial shape. But you're not completely secure. I'll have another look over the books. Then we can meet in a few days. What about Thursday?"

"Sorry, I can't." Lit had just remembered. "Going to see an aunt in London. How about the following Monday?"

Tallon removed his glasses and placed them carefully in a case.

"You could travel at the weekend. More efficient use

16

of time I would have thought."

There was silence. Neither Lit nor Matt ever counted hours. Sometimes they worked through weekends without noticing.

Lit's icy distaste for Tallon began to harden. And when she thought of sweet Auntie Florence who had been a beacon of good humour, common sense and plain uncomplicated love throughout her childhood, she felt a mighty urge to tweak his ear. What was it to him when she made her family visits? This one would be especially poignant. Auntie Florence was dying, slipping in and out of consciousness in a hospice in Wimbledon. It was quite possible that she mightn't last the weekend. And Lit had already postponed the visit twice because of work commitments. She had no intention of cancelling again, especially not for a dreary meeting with a man who was surely destined to become Director General of the International Federation of Clueless Bores.

Matt, to give him his due, looked slightly askance at his accountant friend.

"My aunt is quite ill," Lit said coolly, effortlessly covering up her inner distaste and annoyance.

"Fine," Tallon said after an awkward silence. "Monday then?"

They nodded.

The meeting had taken twenty-seven minutes, not one second of which had been wasted. Lit felt that she had spent it in the presence of some sort of computer – economical with language, tidy and precise in expression, unambiguous and direct. How would he ask a girl out? Would you consider an evening with me an asset or a liability? Can we dine somewhere which is a sound financial investment with no confusing hidden little extras? It was impossible to imagine him even peeping into the little treasure-box of love. The very idea made her feel slightly queasy!

Seán said goodbye and closed the door. Lit could hear his measured steps down the corridor. She was about to launch a low-flying but lethal barb (what Bonnie called her scud missiles) about him, when the door opened once more.

"If you're going to Wimbledon, best to get the underground to Waterloo and take a British Rail train to Wimbledon. That way you'll save time and it's more comfortable."

He said it as though the Trains Menu had just flapped down on his computer screen.

"Thanks," said Lit. "I'll bear it in mind."

"Don't get a taxi from the airport or you'll be stuck in traffic all day."

What an irritating bastard!

He turned to her again as he was going.

"Oh . . . and there's a taxi rank at the station if you need one."

He left.

"He seems a nice chap," said Lit sarcastically.

"Oh, he's not so bad," said Matt. "He has a well-ordered, uncluttered mind. Perhaps that's what you're uneasy with."

Lit didn't exactly think that having a photographic memory of the London train network was evidence of an uncluttered mind, but in deference to Matt she said no more.


Conrad set out to the site in Stoneyfield in his battered old Range Rover. He always kept at least two cars in Ireland. At the moment he had three. The old Range Rover was kept exclusively for the site, in the same way that he kept a well worn check shirt and faded corduroys and wellies for site visits. No sense in waving his wealth around on the building-site. Besides, he didn't want to wreck either of his other two cars, the S-class Mercedes for bankers and potential investors and the Convertible BMW which he kept especially for nights out.

Outside the site entrance, a small huddle of people in T-shirts and jeans waved placards half-heartedly. One placard had a picture of a big tiger chewing up people in little houses with the caption: CELTIC TIGER DEVOURS HISTORIC DUBLIN. Others simply said: DEVELOPERS DESTROY DUBLIN.

Conrad wasn't bothered. He smiled, rolled down his window and said, "Morning to you all!"

They smiled back and returned his greeting. People had a right to protest and he respected it. Sometimes when he passed them, he would clench his fist and shout out at them: "Power to the people! No hard feelings, lads!"

They had been there for weeks now and each day he arranged for tea and sandwiches to be distributed to them. It was only a matter of time before they packed up their placards and went home.

"Morning, Tommy," he said to the security man as he swung through the wide site entrance, already pitted and rutted with the tracks of heavy machinery.

"Howsi'goin', boss?" said Tommy with a deferential smile.

"The finest, Tommy. Isn't this a great morning? God's own country in the sunshine, eh?"

He passed on, the Rover bumping over the rough ground, zigzagging between mountains of timbers and plywood and girders and steel reinforcing bars and sand, miles of cable, clusters of temporary site offices, vans and trailers and labourers everywhere. In the distance he saw his right-hand man talking to one of the engineers. He beckoned him over.

Jack Kennedy was a five-foot-nothing commerce graduate from Galway. But what he lacked in stature was more than made up for in native cunning. In the space of five years, he had risen in the ranks to become a kind of Chief of Staff.

"Jack, things going all right here?"

"Fine, Conrad." Jack kept his head tilted upwards in an effort to make himself look taller.

"The crane is due in next week."

It wasn't just any old crane. It was the biggest crane in the world. The sort of crane that had never before been seen in Ireland. Conrad stepped out of the Rover and put his hard hat on.

"No problems with it, I trust?"

Jack stuffed tiny delicate hands into his trouser pockets. "Now that you mention it – it's nothing major – the engineer wants to make sure the base is solid . . ."

Conrad kicked at the dried dust with the heel of his green wellie. "Tell him to do what has to be done."

Jack hesitated. He knew the dangers of troubling his boss unnecessarily. "I think he wants to talk to you," he said eventually.

Jack could almost see the sunshine draining from Conrad's face and the brow working its way into a scowl.

"What does he want to talk to me for?"

"He's not a hundred per cent sure that this thing is safe to use on reclaimed land."

"Of course it's safe. The company we hired it from guarantee it's safe and that's good enough for me. After that it's the same as anything else – good insurance cover. Which we have."

"The thing is . . . these cranes can buckle. Last year in the States . . . we wouldn't need that kind of publicity, Conrad."

Conrad cursed. These were exactly the sort of niggly little things that he expected Jack Kennedy to deal with. He stalked across the scorched ground to the site office where Billy Hannon, the chief site engineer, was busy surveying site maps in preparation for laying down temporary cable and services.

Conrad patted him amicably on the back. "Billy, my man – what's this about the crane?"

"This is all reclaimed land here. And that crane needs a stronger base than we can provide."

"Then build a stronger base. Build it thicker! Deeper! Stick steel girders in it or whatever you have to do. The experts say it can be done."

He patted him again on the back and went off in search of the architect.

After Seán Tallon had left, Lit and Maura set up the small boardroom with video, flip-charts and story-boards in preparation for the couple from Wholesome Foods. Then Lit dashed into the tiny bathroom, wriggled out of her Donna Karan suit and slipped the Laura Ashley smock over her head. She didn't dare glance at herself in the mirror. It was too awful a prospect.

"Hey – that doesn't look bad at all," said Maura with a note of surprise.

"What!"

"The green goes well with your hair and the shift style looks the perfect cool thing for this sticky weather."

"It's a smock, not a shift."

"No. It's definitely a shift. And it's a lovely shade of

green. But the shoes are foul, I'll give you that."

Lit quickly realised that Poppy and Dara Cornwell were not run-of-the-mill millionaires when they arrived on two state-of-the-art mountain bikes, which they insisted on locking and storing in the narrow hallway between Shiels Doran PR and Henderson Career Consultants.

"Coffee?" Maura offered as soon as they were settled in the boardroom.

"No, thank you," said Dara like he had been offered a line of cocaine. "Do you have any still mineral water?"

When Maura produced a perfectly decent plastic bottle of Ballymacbarry finest spring water, he waved it away dismissively and said he was hoping for something without harmful chemicals.

Maura, whose regular daytime tipple was Red Bull (with an occasional vodka), slipped out to the corner shop where she spent ten minutes trying to find water in a glass bottle with no added chemicals. Eventually she returned to the office with two half-litres of water which had set her back more than four euros.

She placed the bottles on the table with exaggerated reverence and muttered in her broad Mayo accent, "Talk about a waste of money. Fine wather out there for nothin' and all them babies dying of the drought in Africa."

Lit gave her a look. Maura was a great worker, but she still hadn't learned that clients were in essence always right and always wonderful – even when they were totally wrong and/or total gobshites.

Dara Cornwell uncrossed long elegant legs and leaned forward like an earnest cat. He spoke with the gentle timbre of a church minister. Lit found him uncomfortably feline or feminine even, though he sported a clipped light-brown goatee beard and had astonishingly thick eyebrows (a sure sign of bucket-loads of suppressed testosterone, her friend Bonnie would say). His wife Poppy sat demurely beside him. Both were dressed in expensive natural fabrics, he in black, she in taupe and white. Her hair was pulled back into a bun and held together with a wooden clasp. Lit longed to lean forward and check it for a renewable-forest label.

Dara scrutinised the bottles before pouring two half-glasses.

"Now to business, Mr Shiels – Matt –" He addressed Matt and virtually ignored Lit. "We're not entirely satisfied with these storyboards for the TV commercial."

Matt feigned surprise and munched on an apple. He hadn't eaten an apple in years. But he thought the Cornwells might be more impressed by an apple than a Mars bar, his preferred mid-morning snack. "I'm listening." He munched on the apple, the sour taste making his nose wrinkle up. "What's the problem?"

As if he didn't know.

"Natural health foods is a serious matter," said Dara and paused. Poppy nodded briefly in agreement. "And I'm not all that comfortable with the idea of ridiculing nuns. It's a bit cheap. We, our company that is, believe that products can be successfully marketed without resorting to stereotypes which are clichéd and trite. You were chosen by us because we liked the work you did for Irish Natural Fabrics last year."

Lit was certain she could hear Matt hissing through his teeth in barely suppressed irritation. He hated evangelists.

"I understood you wanted to lighten your image," said Matt, "to appeal to a younger, more sophisticated customer. That was the brief you asked us to work from."

"Of course. But does the advertisement have to be so suggestive? The nun holding the corn on the cob and loitering lasciviously with the gardener behind a cock of hay – a bit Boccaccio surely . . . and where does the heavy metal rock band come in? What message are they sending out about natural foods and remedies? Isn't that right, Poppy dear?"

"Well, I sort of liked –" she began.

"Exactly!" Dara cut in. "You liked the Irish Natural Fabrics stuff too!"

Poppy nodded her agreement once more.

Matt sighed. He knew what young people liked: they wanted humour, subversion, sex and irony. They enjoyed being challenged, puzzled and visually stunned. But he wasn't so foolish that he was going to lose a client over a matter of taste.

"Look – I still think it's the kind of campaign you need at this time . . . but you're the boss. Perhaps you could give us an indication of the sort of thing that might – that might . . . suit . . . and we can discuss it with the advertisers."

Dara and Poppy exchanged glances.

"We like the idea of maybe a pastoral scene . . . you know, a nice-looking girl – but not too nice-looking – no make-up – roaming through a field of corn – or strolling by a stream perhaps. Some sounds – not music but the wind in the trees maybe – or surf on a beach. Perhaps the girl is doing something natural . . ."

Lit exchanged looks with Maura.

"Like picking flowers or rinsing cloth in the stream . . . or picking blackberries . . ."

Cliché, cliché, cliché! Matt wanted to scream out.

Lit could see the irritation gathering on his face like a sudden storm-cloud waiting to burst.

She chipped in. "Certainly we did look at those ideas, but we thought you might consider them a bit – how shall I put it – commonplace. But if that's the line you want to pursue, we'll be happy to have a rethink. Matt?"

Matt looked at Lit with gratitude and admiration. It was why they made a perfect team: her coolness and taste coupled with his passion and imagination.

"Yes. Indeed. We'll be in touch. Don't worry. It generally takes time for people to get their image right – to convey what they want. Of course, there'll be no charge for this preliminary work –"

"I should hope not!" said Dara sharply.

Not for nothing was he a very rich man, thought Lit.

After they had gone Matt adopted the tone of a TV announcer: "No ears of corn suffered during the making of this commercial and all the raisins were sundried humanely as stipulated under EU guidelines."

"Quite weird," added Lit. "I mean the bicycles and the clothes and all that fuss over water. Imagine being married to a man like that! She hardly got a word in edgeways. Rumour has it that he packed her off to a health farm once because he found an empty Belgian chocolate box in her wardrobe. I mean, why would any woman put up with that?"

"Lurve, my dear, lurve – she idolises him. Married him straight from school when she was nineteen and he twenty-nine. They're first cousins, you know."

"No!" Lit was shocked. "But that's incest, isn't it?"

"It's legal. I think you have to get some kind of certificate or other – but it's legal all right."

"God. She's never going to bolt for freedom, is she? Poor girl."

Lit felt a surge of sympathy for Poppy, as she did for all down-trodden wives. Why did they stay in unhappy or suffocating marriages? If they could only see the independence and contentment that she enjoyed in her life as a single mother, perhaps they would forsake their marital beds of nails.

On her way to meet Conrad Budd she reflected on the tragedy of Poppy Cornwell's marriage and the perfection of her own life. Here I am, she thought, about to do business with one of the most influential men in the country. I can go where I want, eat what I want, live where and how I want, mix with whatever friends I like. I have a fine son and a decent old father. I have great friends and all in all – the perfect life.

She had promised to meet Bonnie for a drink that evening. Lit and Bonnie had been friends since college days and though other friends had drifted away into marriages, careers and different lives, Lit and Bonnie remained close through thick and thin, almost like sisters. Bonnie practically lived in Lit's house during the long summer holidays. They called each other every day and met often.

She dialled her friend's number. "Bonnie?"

"Hi! Where are you?"

"I'll tell you in a minute. Are we still on for tonight?"

"Yeah. Café Salamanca, OK?"

Lit sighed inwardly. Bonnie always had to pick the trendiest places. Café Salamanca was a pleasant enough place to pass an evening, but it was full of posers and foreigners who had found it listed in their *Lonely Planet Guide*. Lit made a point of avoiding, at home and abroad, any place mentioned in any well-known guide book. Bonnie sensed her reluctance.

"If there's somewhere else?" she said half-heartedly.

"No. That's fine. But it can't be a late night. I've got some big stuff going on at the moment."

26

"Now tell me where you are and what you're are doing."

Bonnie loved to hear about what she considered to be Lit's life of glamour and sophistication. Relegated to an ugly 1970s community school in the suburbs, anything which happened in Dublin 4 or 6 had the aura of gracious and high living for her.

"You'll never guess who I'm just about to meet!"

Bonnie lit up like a little girl at Christmas. This was the jet-set stuff she longed to hear from her friend. "Let me see . . . George Clooney . . . Bono . . . Damon Hill . . . I give up! Tell me, please!"

"None of the above. Not show business. Not sport."

"Nelson Mandela? I don't know . . . ah, shite, Lit, tell me!"

"I suppose you could call him a blast from the past . . ." She paused. "It's Conrad Budd!"

There was a brief, almost imperceptible pause before Bonnie said quickly: "You're joking? You're joking!"

"Calm down! It's just business."

"Well, it's not fair! The only glamorous man I've met recently in the line of business is the father of Kylie Hannigan in Transition Year. And he's not really glamorous. It's just that he wears a lot of gold jewellery and has a tattoo of Madonna. Conrad will be wasted on you! Do you remember him at college? And when he played rugby for Ireland? Oh, those shoulders, those thighs! All those days I sat in Landsdowne Road drooling! And then . . . " she paused, "then he definitely became a force to be reckoned with. I imagine he's hard to resist."

"Bonnie, he's engaged! And, besides, you know I never mix work and relationships – it's a recipe for trouble. Anyway, I'll tell you all about it later."

"OK. I look forward to a full shoulder-to-thigh

report this evening."

Lit laughed. She didn't bother telling Bonnie that with close on a million pounds at stake, she would hardly be taking too much notice of the state of his legendary thighs.

Nonetheless, driving down Leeson Street, she wondered about meeting Conrad Budd. Was she dressed smartly enough? She knew only too well the importance of first impressions. In this instance, she needed to convey coolness, calmness, collectedness, intelligence, efficiency, imaginative flair and pragmatism and she probably only had half an hour in which to do it. She was glad she had changed suits before she left the office. Matt had suggested she dress down for the Cornwells, which was why she had suffered the humiliation of the smock/shift/whatever. It had made her feel like Pippi Longstocking and she hated it. But the Pippi Longstocking look wouldn't do for the owner of one of Ireland's biggest property portfolios.

After the Cornwells had left, she slipped into the little shower-room next to the tiny office kitchen, had a cool shower and dressed in a light grey suit. The grey worked well with her blonde hair and the skirt just above the knee showed her legs to good effect without posing a distraction. A pale pink silk blouse and black kitten-heeled slingbacks put the finishing touches to her outfit.

When she elegantly took the steps of the Shelbourne with her long slender legs the doorman gave her a very approving look.

"Good afternoon, madam. You look very smart today."

Ordinarily she did not encourage forwardness from hotel staff or anyone else, but today she was feeling

28

good and she gave him the benefit of a cool, disinterested smile.

For much of the year, Conrad kept a suite at the Shelbourne, a stone's throw from his offices in Merrion Square. It was more central than his penthouse in Ballsbridge and was useful for more private entertaining and meetings of a sensitive nature.

After leaving Billy Hannon to deal with matters on the site, Conrad went there and showered and changed into a light suit before meeting his London bankers and financial advisors. For an hour they talked about debt management, equities and gearing. It would not be a good idea, they felt, to float his company on the stock exchange. Current wisdom suggested that shares in construction and property companies generally underperformed.

"Large borrowings require careful and strategic debt management . . ."

So tell me something I don't know, thought Conrad to himself. In the end his brain could take no more. He adopted the line he usually took with so-called experts.

"Look. You're the money-guys. You sort it. I don't have time for all this technical crap. Just do it. But . . ." he smiled at them genially, "but, I expect you to get it right . . . " A man of his stature didn't need to issue threats or dire warnings.

He drank coffee with them, made a few polite enquiries about their return flight to London and saw them off in a taxi to the airport.

Now, Conrad, called after Joseph Conrad by his doting father, sat contentedly in the lounge of the Shelbourne Hotel. He sipped his black coffee and idly watched the pretty blonde waitress glide about the room with her tray and cloth. He eyed her midriff, briefly imagining how her tummy would ripple if she sat astride on him. Then he dismissed the thought. Those days were gone.

His mobile phone vibrated discreetly in his trouser pocket.

It was Jack Kennedy with a progress report on the financial backers.

He spoke into the phone quietly. "Jack, my boy – how did it go with Diamond?"

"They're getting a bit twitchy – not happy with the figures."

"Tell them we'll have their figures for them next week."

"These guys don't hang about, Conrad – if we can't produce the figures soon, they'll find other projects to invest in."

"I've just met with the bankers and it will be a few days before their end of things is finalised. Diamond can have half-baked figures today – or wait until next week. If they're as smart as I think, one week isn't going to put them off. They'll want copper-fastened guarantees that their investment will be safe. Use your West of Ireland charm, Jack – that's your job – you go between me and them in logistical matters – I merely provide the vision and the charisma . . . and don't set up any meetings for me with them until next week."

The people in question were an international consortium called Diamond. They were the money behind many of the major building developments across Europe in recent years. They had a reputation for only investing in sure-fire winners and they also researched their potential investments with a thoroughness that would have put the Inquisition to shame. Conrad was fully confident of the outcome. All his dealings with them had suggested mutual confidence and respect, the two intangibles of high finance. Nothing could go wrong. Nothing would go wrong and when the work was complete, he, Conrad Budd, would be the tzar of a vast property empire.

"I'm in the Shelbourne waiting to meet this Doran woman from the PR company. I like their approach – classy, professional. You should be doing this meeting with me."

His tone was slightly accusatory.

"I – well – you said you wanted – that I was to concentrate all my energies on the backers for now . . . "

Conrad could picture Jack talking into his mobile with his head tilted up into the air as if it would make him look taller. "I'll manage without you for today – but keep your mobile switched on."

He hung up, leafed laconically through his papers and glanced at the new headed notepaper which Lit Doran's advertising agency had procured for him. It featured blue and gold script-style lettering and it said: *Conrad Budd Holdings & Budd Construction International.*

Ms Doran was five minutes late. Nothing surprising in that. PR people lived in an airy-fairy never-never land. As far as he could see they didn't know what it was like to live in the real world. They rattled on all the time about image and maintaining a positive profile and capturing the spirit of the moment and hitting the pulse of the nation and getting to grips with your target audience. Advertisers could go into ecstasies about product launches and campaigns, logos and lettering, but they knew nothing about bricks and mortar and that's what it was all about – the real world – cement and sand and mortar and steel and big real machinery doing real moving and shaking.

A slim blonde woman stood at the door hesitating for a moment. Her hair was straight and swept back from her face into a bun which was precariously fastened at the nape of her neck. Conrad thought she looked like Grace Kelly, one of his all-time favourite women – beautiful, elegant and simply dressed – not at all what he was expecting. He stood up, smiled and held out his hand to greet her.

# CHAPTER 3

As soon as Lit stepped into the drawing-room of the Shelbourne, she recognised Conrad Budd and, despite her customary coolness, her heart skipped a beat. She had seen him on TV recently but he was more handsome in the flesh – broad-shouldered, with cropped dark hair and mesmerising black, black eyes.

"OhmyGod!" she murmured quietly under her breath. She composed herself, tilted her head upwards in an angle of slight hauteur and advanced across the room. She was doing quite well with the hauteur until he stood up and smiled. And it wasn't so much a smile as a blinding nuclear explosion of welcome, warmth, admiration, charm and just plain sexual magnetism. Never before in the history of Lit Doran had she ever been the focus of such a smile.

Please, God, let him be rude and horrible, she prayed as she made her way towards him. Or let him talk constantly about his fiancée. He smiled once more and held out his hand to her.

Then in spite of gallons of self-discipline and carefully

nurtured reserve, and an eyebrow valiantly attempting to arch itself to the back of her head, she felt her eyes sliding down to take in the broad shoulders and the legendary thighs.

She extended a perfectly manicured hand to him and said coolly: "Lit Doran. Nice to meet you, Mr Budd."

"Conrad. Please."

His handshake was firm, strong, with a tantalising glimpse of his forearm. Lit found herself chanting inwardly: one million euros, one million euros, he's just a man smiling and shaking my hand, one million euros . . .

None of this showed in her demeanour, of course, because Lit had long ago schooled herself in how women should conduct themselves in business: friendly but not familiar, warm but not flirtatious, cool but not distant, sharp but not suspicious.

"Won't you sit down, Miss Doran?"

Conrad had temporarily forgotten her Christian name – it was something odd and he hated saying names which made him feel silly. Jack Kennedy had a friend called Lysander who seemed to hang around a lot. Then there was a Spanish couple who cleaned his apartment – Jesus and Mercedes – addressed by Conrad as 'Howsitgoin . . . erm'.

"Thank you."

She sat down, smoothed her skirt and tucked one ankle behind the other in a way she knew looked elegant and business-like.

"Forgive me for being late. Meeting with a client ran over."

"No apology needed. I've used the time to order a bit of lunch. How about you? Have you eaten? Perhaps I can order you something? Anything you like. Please allow me . . ."

"No, thank you. Tea will be fine."

She wished he would stop being so charming. She prayed for some unpleasant mannerism to make itself apparent quickly. Making noises with his food would do it for sure. Or nasal hair might work. Or bad breath. Or dirt under his fingernails. Or shovelling his food in. But Conrad did none of these things.

She pulled urgently at her portfolio, setting out documents on the table between them with exaggerated efficiency.

Conrad poured tea and offered milk and sugar which she declined.

"Perhaps we could look at these now, Mr . . . Conrad."

"Sure. Why not? But, before we begin . . ." He smiled warmly at her again. "I'm a busy man – successful – but I know the importance of image, public consciousness, public good will. I can afford to cultivate such things seriously now. Your ideas are impressive and so far you've done a good job – but from here on we're not talking just logos and headed notepaper, we're not talking promotional videos. This is moving into the big-time, the mega-big-time. Do you think your company can handle that?"

There was a vaguely patronising tone to his question, but Lit let it go. Once more, as they leaned over the papers together, she found her eyes lingering on his thighs. She looked away abruptly and studied the wallpaper intently for a few moments. Then she sucked in her breath and responded in even tones.

"I think you'll find that, given the opportunity, we will more than meet your expectations of us. We have a proven track record. We're young, vibrant. By the time we're finished, everyone in Ireland, indeed across

Europe, will know who Conrad Budd is and what he stands for. I've brought along a few outlines of ideas for sponsorship – at present we're thinking sport, third-level education . . . but we need to stay at the thinking and exploring stage, tease out all the angles and see what eventuates. Then of course there's the official launch of the Stoneyfield site project which needs to be handled in a professional manner . . ."

Good, yes, she urged herself on. She knew she sounded good. She felt herself moving into her stride.

Conrad listened attentively, admiring her slender wrists and the graceful movements of her hands as they worked through drawings, graphs and figures. Most of all, though, he was captivated by her voice which he found light and seductive with a tiny musical catch in it.

Lit was more than pleased when their first meeting came to a close. She had made a good impression and he clearly approved. Above all, she was happy that she had remained cool, calm and collected. A man like Conrad Budd was of no real interest to her, nor she to him. It was human nature to notice an attractive man. That was all she had done. Phew, she said to herself as she left, for a moment I was afraid I was going to lose it there.

It was a short walk back to the underground carpark and she was glad of it because the day was now swel-tering hot.

Then, rounding the corner into Molesworth Street, she was confronted with a familiar face – Alice Madigan.

"*Lit! You haven't changed a bit!*" squealed Alice through collagen-enhanced lips.

"Hi, Alice! It's been years!"

"Yes. How long is it? And how is that boy you had? It was so brave of you to keep him!"

Two digs in the space of thirty seconds. Alice certainly

hadn't lost her touch in the intervening years. She looked quite remarkable in a Barbie-doll, lacquered-hair kind of way. She wore a skin-tight turquoise trouser suit which looked like it either cost a fortune or came from a bargain shop – Lit couldn't quite make up her mind.

"What are you working at, Lit? So many opportunities now for doing well. You should really think about setting up a consultancy or something. I've got some great contacts through the laundry business. We could meet for lunch sometime. I'd be more than happy to throw a bit of business your way."

"That's kind of you, Alice, but I'd hardly have time what with running a PR company, then looking after my dad and Richie."

Alice face expressed mild surprise.

There was plenty more Lit could have said to put Alice Madigan and her little sheet and towel business firmly in their place. But life was really too short.

"Well, must dash! Shareholder's meeting," Alice said modestly. "Such a nuisance. Byeee!"

As Lit sat into her car, Matt called her mobile to see how the meeting had gone.

"Good. Very good, in fact. Matt, I have a really good feeling about this."

"You can tell me all about it in the morning. By the way, what did you think of him?"

"Who? Oh, Conrad? Fine. Nothing special. Polite, I suppose. Well, quite pleasant really."

"Is that so? I've heard him described as sex on legs."

"I didn't notice. It was a business meeting."

"Get you! Sister Laetitia of Perpetual Purity pray for us!"

"That's got nothing to do with it . . . it's just . . . he's no big deal, that's all!"

"Relax! I'm just winding you up! I'm off to the pub – meeting Tallon to catch up on the lost years."

Lit could think of nothing less exciting than sitting in a pub with Seán Tallon, but she bit her lip and wished her partner a good night.

As she turned her car off Harwood Park into the quiet tree-lined road, she could make out the figure of her father leaning on the front gate. He was wearing a tweed cap, and braces held up a pair of voluminous twill trousers over big sturdy black boots. He looked like a country farmer from the 1950s, like he should have been leaning against a cock of hay and smoking a pipe. When her car pulled up at the kerb, he barely turned his head to acknowledge her. Instead he carried on chatting earnestly to young Mr Redmond from next door who was in his late seventies.

"Tell you what, Mr Redmond – old age has its compensations."

"Such as?" queried Mr Redmond sceptically.

"Well, you know . . . passions are spent. Old animosities fade. You find delight in the simple things – like the breeze playing the leaves on that plane tree over there or a bird tugging at a worm . . ."

"Dandy Doran's Little Book of Wisdom," Lit quipped sardonically as she passed the two men.

"Ah, the wisdom that comes with old age," mused Mr Redmond fondly.

"Fuck that!" said Dandy vehemently, in an abrupt change of mood and direction.

Lit glanced about her quickly, hoping none of the neighbours were about.

"Fuck that wisdom that comes with old age! What good is it? Just when a man is in the happy position that he can figure every angle, anticipate every crisis, interpret every gesture and facial expression, conceal every thought beneath the most inscrutable expression – what happens? He's too old to make any use of it. So what does he do? He sits back armed with endless resources of useless wisdom and takes a malicious pleasure in watching younger people make the same mistakes that he made. No! I say fuck the wisdom and serenity of old age!"

"Come in, Dad," Lit said, linking his arm and steering him towards the oak-panelled and stained-glass front door. "You'll catch a chill."

She did not think her neighbours – the high court judges and hospital consultants and the little old lady who was distantly related to the queen – had any interest in hearing her father's views on life.

# CHAPTER 4

Lit bustled Dandy through the panelled hall and into the kitchen where she watched him make his slow progress to the chair by the range. He had insisted on the range. He wouldn't move to a house without one. And it had to be a proper one – fuelled with wood, peat and coal – not, he said, one of those toy things run on oil.

Even on these, the warmest days she had ever experienced in Dublin, he kept the range blazing. Now he reached down to the wicker basket, took a log in his hand and shoved it into the range.

"Are you not warm enough?"

"These big old houses – very hard to heat. I can't get warm at all."

There were beads of perspiration on his forehead, but

she held her tongue. She wasn't in the mood for a spat and she didn't want to upset him. In some respects he was an awkward kind of father to have, but the house in Harwood Park wouldn't be home without him.

When it had come on the market a few years earlier, they were still living in Templeogue. That house was fine, but there were only three small bedrooms and a tiny kitchen. She needed a study. Now that she was earning piles of money, she also needed a house where she could entertain friends and clients. Richie needed a bigger room. Dandy should have his own sitting-room. They needed a larger kitchen. She told her father these things regularly on the basis that constant dripping wears a stone. It wore her down all right.

"I like it here. The neighbours are my kind of people. Ordinary decent people. What do I want with living in some posh place where no-one knows anyone? You can move if you want. I'm staying put."

At last she put Richie to work on him.

"Dandy – Mum's seen this really nice house and if we all lived there, I could be nearer my school. I wouldn't have to get up so early in the morning."

"That's great, son. Don't forget to come and visit."

"But I can't leave without you!"

Lit remembered how Dandy had grunted, the way he always did when someone said something affectionate to him.

But Dandy hadn't reckoned with Richie and actually neither had Lit. For about three weeks he kept up a constant barrage of laid-back affection and gruff cajolery. Which wasn't bad at all for a twelve-year-old.

"I mean who's going to give me shaving lessons? Show me how to put a knot in my tie? Tell me off for being cheeky to Lit?"

"Humph!"

"Yes, and as well – who's going to protect me from Lit when she gets in one of her moods? You know what she can be like, Grandad."

"Humph!"

"What if she tries to turn me into a wimp?"

"What's a wimp?"

That was a tricky one to explain as Richie had no idea what a wimp was, except that it was something that a man definitely did not want to be called. He racked his brains furiously to think of something which would make sense to his very old grandfather.

"A wimp is someone who doesn't hang out with the guys. Someone who's scared to climb trees. Someone who's not allowed to get his clothes dirty."

"Oh!" said Dandy, a look of something approaching horror sweeping across his inscrutable old face. "Do you mean a mammy's boy?"

"Yes! That's it. A mammy's boy. She'll turn me into a mammy's boy if you don't come with us. It's up to you. The choice is yours entirely. Personally I have no problem with being a wimp. I could get used to dressing up in sailor suits and being the only boy in the class without rollerblades. And having to wear a gum-shield for table tennis. I mean there are worse things."

Dandy shifted uneasily in his chair. A man should not have to deal with moral dilemmas of any sort in the closing years of his life. But Richie was the nearest thing to a son he was ever going to have now, unless some young one of child-bearing age were suddenly to take a shine to him – which wasn't all that likely to happen since he didn't get out much any more. So he had a responsibility to Richie.

"Jesus, can't a man have any peace in his twilight

years? All right! I'll move! I suppose someone has to keep an eye on you. But there has to be a range – a proper one – and a decent kitchen where a man can read his paper and have a beer in peace."

Richie hugged him. "Don't worry, Dandy! I'll see to it that you have everything just as you want it."

And that was how Lit's house came to be such a schizophrenic affair – a kitchen that was in a constant state of homely disorder under seige from the relentless money, style, taste and order that governed the rest of the house.

When she first saw the house in the paper she knew it was the place for her and Richie and Dandy. It was large, redbrick, detached and double-fronted with an Edwardian arched porch and bay windows. But it still had a warm inviting look about it.

Her heart fell, though, when the estate agent led her inside for the first time. The square hall was as big as the living-room in Templeogue and panelled in well-seasoned oak – but some obsessive-compulsive stencilling maniac had been let loose everywhere. Each oak panel proudly displayed different sorts of multi-coloured birds perched elegantly on twigs and surrounded with garlands of leaves and flowers. The floor was pink-tiled and the walls covered in a particularly strong and dark chinoiserie wallpaper – peacocks and roses on a deep green background. There were yellow sunbursts stencilled on the ceiling.

Bonnie was called in to comment.

"It's not that bad."

"Oh, please, Bonnie! Look at those stencils! I mean who in their right mind? And the pink tiles – there's an oak floor somewhere under there you know. And wait till you see the drawing-room!"

41

"It's pink," said Bonnie when she saw it.

"Yes, it's pink. The question is, can you find anything in the room that isn't pink?"

"The fireplace?"

"Look closely. It's rose-tinted marble."

"So? It's not so bad. Personally I like pink. It's an honest sort of colour."

Lit rolled her eyes to heaven. "It's just too ghastly for words. I can't bear it."

"What's the big deal? You can change it if you want to," Bonnie said a bit testily. She was still living in a rented flat in Ranelagh. She could afford to buy a three-bedroomed semi somewhere miles out of town, but what was the point of that? And buying even a small place in town was out of the question. So all in all she wasn't overly sympathetic to Lit's pink dilemma.

"The problem is time, Bonnie. Not money. I don't have the time to deal with it. I want this house, but I don't want all the hassle that goes with making it the way I want."

Bonnie shrugged and went upstairs to examine the bedrooms.

There followed six months of stripping down and ripping out and pulling up before Lit could say she had the home of her dreams – except for the kitchen, that was, where Dandy's taste reigned supreme: big ugly farmhouse chairs with faded tapestry cushions, an old white-painted dresser which he wouldn't let her strip, a telly, a sofa, a big scruffy old armchair and a basket for the cat which the cat never used.

She refused to go along with lino on the kitchen floor, and was delighted with the rich old oak floorboards which polished up nicely. But now on an almost daily basis, Dandy complained about them.

"Terrible draughts from under those plain wooden floors. Pity you didn't put the lino down."

And sometimes she was tempted to give in just to keep him quiet.

But she was proud of the rest of the house. The hall was now restored to its original unstencilled and unpapered condition, the wooden panelling stripped and polished to exactly the right sheen, the walls painted a pale duck-egg blue, with here and there some paintings she had picked up on trips to New York. Against the wall opposite the carefully restored fireplace was a perfectly proportioned early Georgian mahogany table with elegant tapering legs. It was flanked by two beechwood Shaker chairs and quietly complemented by a single art-deco black smoked-glass vase. Above all that: a painting of the New England coast.

Beyond the hall she hadn't put a foot wrong either, furnishing the house throughout with original and ludicrously expensive Shaker tables and chairs and sideboards, scattering the darkened oak floors with exquisite rugs and draping the bay windows with muted brocades. Even the rose-tinted fireplace was unceremoniously dumped and replaced by an original white late-Georgian find.

In short, the rest of the house was in such a state of perfectly balanced taste and harmony, it wasn't really all that hard to overlook the horror of her kitchen.

All in all, taking Dandy's opposition into account, Lit felt she had done well.

# CHAPTER 5

Richie would have liked to spend the summer of his six-
teenth year just hanging out with his mates, but Lit
insisted he take a job in the local supermarket for three
days a week. It was all part of her 'money doesn't grow
on trees' campaign. The work was tiring – hauling
boxes, wheeling trollies and stacking shelves. The only
minor excitement in each dreary day was the prospect of
spotting a shoplifter and placing bets against himself as
to whether they would get away with it or not.

It was now seven o'clock and he was still hauling and
stacking. By the time he got off work, he knew he would
be too tired to go to Barney Ryan's house, where Barney
and his mates would sit around watching videos and
playing Playstation games well into the night.

Lit was probably home now, eating dinner and skir-
mishing with Dandy about something really important
like shop-bought apple-tarts. By the time he got home,
Dandy would be ready for bed and his mother working
late or out with Bonnie and he would have to fend for
himself. More and more in recent times, Richie found
that he had to fend for himself, while his mother continued with the business of making piles of money.
Sometimes he even had to fend for Dandy as well. He
didn't mind so much, but sometimes he wished Lit was
more like Barney Ryan's mother who was plump and
old-fashioned-looking and always seemed to be on
hand with generous supplies of home baking and roast-
beef dinners. She always welcomed him with a big smile
and said, "It's open house here, Richie. No need to stand
on ceremony with us." She was secretary of the Ladies'
Golf Club. She organised the fund-raising table quizzes
and fork suppers for Barney's rugby club. She was

chairperson of the Residents' Association and she took part in a monthly reading club with her friends. Barney's house was always packed to the gills with his friends and his sister's friends and Mrs Ryan didn't seem to mind at all having droves of unidentified teenagers skulking around the corners of her large and welcoming home. Richie lived under a sterner regime. He could have as many friends in as he wanted – as long as Lit was there. Which wasn't often. Barney Ryan had a den in the basement of the house that he could wreck as much as he liked. Richie had to be content with his own room. It was large but too nicely decorated – too many classy, minimalist boy's-bedroom-style furniture and drapes. Lit had spent a fortune on it, he knew. Built-in cherry-wood shelving was specially designed to house his computer, his Playstation 2, his TV and video, his cherished model crane. She had ordered and waited six months for the most expensive captain's bed available from Heal's in London. There was even one of those stylish stainless-steel mini-fridges so that Richie could keep a store of cold drinks and snacks in his room. The floor was stained in a super trendy shade of dark green and there was a very expensive, specially commissioned hand-made rug depicting the green and white crest of Celtic Football Club. And it seemed a churlish and ungrateful thing to say but sometimes he longed to have his old battered boxroom in Templeogue back, where under the bed was a treasure-trove of cardboard boxes filled with half-forgotten books and magazines, where the doors of the wardrobe had to be held together with twine, where the bed was so small that, even when he was only twelve, turning in it required careful planning to avoid falling out.

He mused pessimistically on these thoughts as he

once more made his way to the storeroom with his trolley. He went to the shelf and slid off three large boxes of cat-food tins. He should only take one and his mother would say he was carrying a lazy man's load. But he was tall and athletically lean, the tallest in his class. He could handle a couple of extra boxes. He made his way blindly to the trolley, but instead of touching up against the metal frame, he felt his hands come into contact with something soft and warm. He lost his precarious grip on the boxes and one by one they tumbled to the ground leaving him face to face with Janet Byrne, the supervisor. Janet was about twenty-five, full-lipped, pink-cheeked, plump, with a big bosom and an expansive bottom. She wore a lycra-patterned dress that was too tight and she had a brassy walk, with her chest pushed out and her head thrown back.

"Sorry, Janet," he murmured and bent to pick up the boxes, colliding as he did so with her ample bosom.

"That's a fine broad pair of shoulders, Richie," she said, resting her hand lightly on his upper arm.

His face coloured a deep purple and he stood up, staring into her uptilted face in terror. He opened his mouth to say something, he knew not what, but all that came out was a sort of backward swallow and an "nggh" sound.

"Ya can kiss me if ya like," she said in a soft and suggestive way. "You know you want to."

The awful thing was that it was true. Janet Byrne was really sexy and Richie had a bit of a crush on her.

She pulled him towards her and parted her lips so that he could see the glistening pink tip of her tongue sliding out ominously towards him.

"Sorry," he muttered eventually and thrust himself away from her. "It's my tea break." And somehow he got himself out of the storeroom.

For weeks now he had been fantasising about his first sexual encounter and how he planned to be definitely-not-a-virgin on his return to school in September. Most of all he fantasised about Bonnie. But Bonnie wouldn't look at him because he was too young and by the time he was mature, she would be too old. It was a hopeless dilemma to be in.

Now, suddenly, he went off the whole idea. Kissing Janet Byrne seemed an OK sort of an idea in the abstract, but the reality of it was quite different. Perhaps he might postpone losing his virginity. Perhaps he should wait for Bonnie.

It was eight thirty in the evening and Seán Tallon was still in his office. With his left hand he clicked away at the computer keyboard, writing figures on paper with his right, while speaking to a colleague on the phone. He enjoyed that feeling of doing three things at once, each of them requiring him to test his mental skills to their limits. He planned to work until ten.

Home held few pleasures for him. He had no sense of place and the fact that he was being paid large amounts of money did not change that fact. He lived in a small apartment along the seafront. It was more a studio than an apartment, chosen simply because it faced onto the strand. Whether it had been a mansion or a tenement he would still have used it in the same casual fashion. A place to live was a roof over your head. So long as it was warm and dry and in a reasonably quiet area, he was happy.

He had been in a few relationships. Only three years ago he had been on the point of getting married to Helen, a doctor, who was pretty and capable and awesomely efficient. Friends and family, including his mother, had said what a perfect match they made. And they made a handsome couple: Helen – tanned and blond and terrifically athletic, Seán – tall, lean, sandy-haired, with blue-grey eyes – "just like Steve McQueen's" his mother used to boast, much to his embarrassment. When he and Helen moved into an apartment together, everyone including themselves believed it would only be a matter of time before they tied the knot. They played tennis and golf together. They enjoyed the same people, read the same kind of books, liked the same places for holidays.

"A match made in Heaven," his mother was fond of remarking to her neighbours. And so it might have been. Seán would never know now.

One night, he and Helen made love and she fell asleep in the bed beside him. He couldn't sleep.

He watched her in the half-light, her beautiful blonde hair cascading down on the pillow beside him, her perfect face the picture of contentment and peace. He surveyed their large bedroom of polished beech-wood and white linen drapes. Then he climbed out of bed and walked barefoot into their living-room. It was perfection. There were his and her desks, oriental rugs, rare Edward Hopper prints on the walls and a glass-topped table resting on an exquisitely carved scaled currach. The kitchen was stainless steel and granite, everything hidden behind doors, not even so much as a toaster on the counter. In the corner, a small alcove housed two sets of golf-clubs and two tennis-rackets. On the shelf above were two pairs of golf-shoes and two sets of gleaming white trainers.

Magazines formed neat little piles on the glass coffee table in the living-room – *Business & Finance*, *The*

*Economist, The New Yorker, Vogue, Vanity Fair* and *Empire*. On the table too were wedding catalogues, a wedding list for Brown Thomas and a selection of fine properties from estate agents. He saw his life ahead: the fine house in Ballsbridge, the golf club, the tennis club, the children, the private schools, the other couples they would befriend. And he panicked.

First he took down an Edward Hopper print of a lighthouse from the wall. He had always liked it very much – the strange Cape Cod light, a calming blue cloud-scudded sky, a stretch of sea he could almost hear, the artist's use of shadow, the swaying grass. He had bought it in Provincetown with his last two hundred dollars when he was a student and it symbolised something that he hadn't quite figured out yet.

He removed it from its hook and stored it near the door of the apartment. Then, slowly, methodically and quietly so that he wouldn't wake Helen, he moved about the room gathering up his things and packing them into suitcases. By morning he had almost completely disentangled his life from hers.

Helen was upset. He suffered agonies of guilt about the hurt he had caused her though he knew it would have been worse to marry her and not make her happy. Then one day he told himself that at least it was good that he felt bad about hurting her. Pretty quickly he recognised that as vanity of the most insidious kind and instead vowed never to hurt any woman again. If that meant living as a bachelor, so be it.

Now he took the Shiels Doran file out once more. He was doing his friend a favour, but favour or not he scrutinised the file with the same attention to detail he bestowed on his most lucrative accounts. He studied the list of clients, noting the income they brought to the company and the outlay for each project. There was no doubt that Conrad Budd was the big fish. Projected income from his company dwarfed almost all the other clients put together. But the company would also be spending more before they saw any profit from him. It spelled risk. Doran Shiels were about to put virtually all their financial eggs in one basket. He punched out his friend's phone number and waited for a reply.

"Matt, it's Seán – I'm still at the office."

"Hey, Tallon – it's half past eight – what are you playing at?"

"Afraid I'll be here until about ten. I'll meet you then."

"OK – see you in The KGB – ten o'clock."


"Did it ever occur to you that we might be a bit old for a place like this? I can't see a woman here that's over twenty-five," said Seán. He looked around at the decor of the trendy northside bar which overlooked the river. As its name indicated, The KGB had a Russian theme, though the letters stood for the owners, three brash young commerce graduates – Kenny, Grant and Blaney – who had bought the premises before property prices rocketed. There were lots of little wooden alcoves, each with a Russian theme: spies, communism, vodka, Tolstoy, Yuri Gagarin, Mir, Lenin. The place was brimming with groups of twenty-somethings drinking the hundred different drinks you could make with vodka. The barmen were all from Eastern Europe.

"I like it here. I feel at home. Your problem is that you're ageist," retorted Matt.

"No – I'm just realist."

Matt nodded to some passing friends. "I have to keep in touch with what these people are into. It's important for business. You should understand that."

"Put like that it makes a certain amount of sense, I suppose. But sitting in bars people-watching isn't going to increase your business in the short term. You need to build up a bigger portfolio of clients. Your present position is quite high risk."

"There's a lot of competition for business out there. And we do work hard. Twelve-hour days mostly. Ready for another?"

Seán had noticed how quickly Matt downed his pint but said nothing. "Just a glass for me – I'm driving. As a matter of interest, how did you and your partner set up together? You seem an unlikely pair."

"Don't you approve of Lit? Most of the guys I know turn to putty when she's around."

"I've hardly met the woman so I've no opinion about her. I'm just curious. That's all."

In truth, he couldn't remember much about her. Perhaps she had nice eyes though he wasn't even sure of that.

"We were working for the same company. Decided to go it alone," said Matt.

Seven years earlier both Matt and Lit worked in a big PR firm in Ballsbridge. Lit was in bad shape in those days, but he wasn't going to tell Tallon any of that. Richie was eight and she was struggling to rear him on a meagre salary. Some weeks she hardly had money to pay the woman who minded him after school. She put in for a raise but was told that she'd have to join the queue.

Harry Menton was a large feature of her life at the time and Matt remembered how she might go weeks on end without seeing him and then he would turn up from New York with a great welcome for himself, expecting the VIP treatment. Sometimes Matt would come across Lit snuffling quietly in a corner of the office.

"Man trouble?" he plucked up the courage to say to her one day.

Then it all tumbled out: how she had been having an affair with Menton for three years, how he was married, how every time she tried to finish it, he would protest his love loudly and shower her with attention and gifts for a few weeks, before abandoning her again for his wife and family in New York.

Matt was shocked. She was by far the most beautiful woman in the office. All the guys fancied her and she could have had her pick of them.

"You have to give him up," he said to her eventually.

"How?"

"First of all – why? Because he's a selfish bastard who gets his kicks from knowing someone like you is pining for him all the time. That's why he love-bombs you when he thinks he's going to lose you. If he really loved you, he'd want your happiness."

Lit had never thought of it that way before.

"And because you can do much better."

She didn't seem convinced.

"*How* you do it, is: don't finish it. Just don't be around when he calls. Don't respond to messages. Don't call him. Find out when he's going to be in town and arrange to be away."

"That's a lot easier said than done. If only I had a more challenging job then it might be easier to forget about him."

A few days later, Matt's boss hauled him over the coals for an advertisement that had been commissioned for butter. Matt knew that the butter ad was brilliant. But he had also known it would get him into trouble. He wanted to get into trouble, wanted to be thrown out of his job, so he was busy dreaming up offensive storylines and captions. The plan was that he would get the sack and then cajole the brilliantly talented and utterly wasted Lit Doran to go into partnership with him.

He'd started mildly enough with an advertisement for a healthier eating campaign which was captioned *Nine and a Half Leeks*. But the director didn't quite get the pun and had simply dismissed Matt's idea as "not catchy enough for the young people". There followed *Pornflakes* and *Night Porter – The Erotic Stout!*

But the butter commercial took the biscuit so to speak. The chief executive of the creamery was a deeply conservative man with strong views on sex. The ad, set in a grocery shop in a small Irish town, showed various suggestive and soft focus shots of a man and a woman and some butter with the caption *Last Tango in Borris.*

Matt tried to look a bit upset when the boss roared at him. But it was just the sort of kick in the arse he needed to make him change jobs.

"I mean whatever next, Shiels? This is still a Catholic country. I'm putting you to work on the semi-state organisations. It's for your own good."

Matt's ideas for Aer Lingus were the last straw as far as Lit was concerned. If the boss saw them, Matt would never work in this or any other town again. She relented and listened to his business proposition.

"How about it? You and me? Shiels Doran or Doran Shiels PR. I don't care. We'll do the whole range of services: image consultancy, marketing, advertising, media, profiling. Think about it. Independence. Artistic freedom. Clients of our own. A real coffee machine. We can hardly earn less than we earn here. And we've built up good contacts."

Lit had to admit all that was true. Still she was cautious.

"It sounds great on paper. But neither of us knows anything about running a company. What if we fail? What if nobody wants to do business with us? And it's not good business to pick and choose clients. It's all right for you with no dependents. But I've got Richie. And there's my father. And what about raising capital?"

Instantly Matt knew she was the perfect partner. Already she was thinking it out in her head, addressing the practicalities. Then he played his trump card.

"If you want to forget Harry Menton, you'll join me."

"I'll think about it," she said finally.

Two days later, they both handed in their notice.

Lit and Bonnie sat in the gloomy atmospheric Cafe Salamanca in Temple Bar. It was long and narrow with elaborate dark stucco work. Large paintings of matadors and flamenco dancers and cancan dancers adorned the walls, and the music was Francoise Hardy, Jane Birkin and Marianne Faithfull. A group of Englishmen held forth at the bar, consuming vast amounts of drink and occasionally looking around to watch the women.

Lit sipped from a glass of chardonnay and Bonnie toyed with her Vodka Martini. Between them on the table was a bowl of succulent, glistening green olives.

"So. Out with it!" said Bonnie, spearing an olive and biting into it enthusiastically. She was anxious to hear every detail of Lit's encounter with Conrad.

By now, Lit had entirely composed herself and felt confident enough to discuss him dispassionately. But she wasn't going to spill the beans just yet. She wanted to tease Bonnie, whose favourite subject was men – getting them and getting rid of them.

For Bonnie, there was never simply a man. He was always beautiful or irresistible or illicit or dangerous or preferably all four. There was never a casual date. It was always a union of souls, a coming together of kindred spirits. And there was never just sex. It had to be a grand passion, one long continuous ecstasy, forbidden practices, the earth moving. It was tedious when Lit wasn't in the mood, but mostly she found her spirits lifted in Bonnie's company. They always seemed to laugh a lot, the abandoned giggling and cackling that girls get up to when they're free from the restraints of having to appear elegant and dignified and ladylike in the company of men or older disapproving women.

Bonnie realised she would have to play the waiting game and changed the subject.

"How's Dandy?"

"Not bad."

"And Richie?"

"Working. I made him get a summer job."

"Poor fella! Probably thought he had a summer of sex and sleeping ahead of him."

"I don't want him to be spoilt. I want him to know the value of money and how hard he has to work to earn it."

"God, you sound just like my mother."

"Bonnie. You have no idea what it's like to be a parent – the responsibility for another person, the constant worry about giving them the right values. Worse, worry about drugs and the mad things teenage boys get up to. I'd far rather he was working in the supermarket for a pittance than hanging out with his friends in town for the summer."

"You're right. I haven't a clue what it's like to be a parent. But you'll have to let him have some sort of holiday before he goes back to school. It's only fair. He has to grow up sometime – you know, girls, parties, sex . . ."

Lit had mixed feelings about Richie growing up. On

the one hand, she longed for the time when he would be an entirely self-sufficient human being. On the other, she longed for the days when he was a little boy and would sit curled up in her lap telling her he loved her more than anything in the world.

Bonnie decided it was time to raise the subject of Conrad again.

"So then. You met Conrad Budd."

"Yes."

"And?"

"And I met him. That's all. We met, discussed business, shook hands and arranged to meet again. That's all that happened."

Bonnie rested her glass on the table and scrutinised Lit's face for signs of hidden tension or excitement. But there were none.

"Where did you meet him?"

"In the drawing-room of the Shelbourne."

"How did he look?"

"Fine. He looked just fine."

"Still the same dark, dark eyes? Shoulders? Chest? Thighs?"

"Yes! Eyes. Shoulders. Chest. Thighs."

Bonnie thought she detected just the slightest tremor in Lit's voice when she said the word 'thighs'. She decided to adopt the negative approach.

"Not as good-looking in the flesh these days then?"

"Oh no! Much better – I mean – you know, smart suit, crisp shirt –that sort of thing."

Bonnie smiled triumphantly. She leaned forward and looked directly into Lit's cornflower-blue eyes. "You were gagging for him, weren't you?"

"That's awfully crude. And, no, I certainly was not at all inclined in that way." Lit sipped rapidly from her glass and added: "Anyway, he's engaged and I'm not interested."

"You're mad. He's not married yet. Handsome guy, attractive bank balance, all's fair in love and war. Fuck him and chuck him – or not – what does it matter? He'd go for you big-time."

Lit's mobile purred discreetly from her bag. "Sorry. It might be Richie wondering if I'll come home and make his tea."

She pushed the button and waited for the voice. But instead of a voice she could hear a squeaky door creaking and what sounded like a man breathing heavily and moving about.

"Heavy breather?" enquired Bonnie.

"I don't think so. I have an idea what this is. Listen."

There was the sound of a lid and some whistling and then the unmistakable irregular stacatto sound of a man urinating into a toilet bowl. Then the line went dead.

Lit keyed in a number and waited. "Matt, hi – your mobile is switched on again."

"Oh, shit! Sorry – I was just . . ."

"Yes, we know! How many pints have you had?"

"Oh no . . . well, at least it wasn't –"

"Bye, Matt."

Lit switched off her mobile and turned to Bonnie.

"Bonnie, can we drop the Conrad Budd thing now? A joke is a joke, but I am not interested. Harry Menton was positively my last experience with a long-term relationship. And he taught me all those things that up to then I didn't really know about men: that they are self-obsessed, vain, two-dimensional, emotionally retarded, narrow-minded, judgemental, lacking in any sort of understanding or empathy, sanctimonious, hypocritical, psychotic . . ."

"You just haven't met Mister Right. Harry Menton could be President of the International Federation of Gobshites but he is an exception."

"OK. I know lots of good men – Dad, Richie, his father David – Matt – probably even Conrad – it's just that with the exception of David, I've only ever dated pricks – and if they're not a prick starting out, they soon turn into one. Conrad Budd is a 'ride', as they say, but that's it. Beyond an occasional dalliance, men no longer interest me. I have the perfect life. I have the perfect job, the perfect home, the perfect car and the perfect designer wardrobe. I have it all and I don't need Mister Right to come along with his muddy shoes to spoil it all."

Bonnie munched on an another olive. "Mmmm! These are just yummy. Anyway, you're wrong. I know it's rarely said in polite society nowadays – but I really like having men around. And it's not only about sex. Life is just plain dull without them."

"And what about you, Bonnie? Is there a latest man of your dreams?" Lit couldn't resist the little dig.

Bonnie didn't mind. Finding the perfect man was like searching for the Holy Grail. There was probably much more fun to be had in the search than there ever could possibly be in the possession, should such a person prove to exist.

"Not at present," she said. "But I have plans." She smiled like a child considering a newly opened box of chocolates.

"I'll introduce you to Conrad if you like."

"Thanks, but no thanks. Anyway, I think I've had enough of flings."

"Do tell," said Lit.

"All right. But this is wicked. I mean this is shocking. Actually I don't think I should tell you this, Lit Doran,

58

because you might never speak to me again."

"Oh, stop being so dramatic and just spit it out!"

Conrad's solicitor, Fergus Cunningham, and his wife Rhona were celebrating their tenth wedding anniversary and Conrad had promised to put in an appearance. The Cunninghams lived in a fine house on Amalfi Terrace in Dalkey and the party consisted of a barbeque on the long back lawn which sloped down to the rocky seashore.

More than a hundred people milled around the Cunningham's garden, sloshing champagne and grazing on trays of sushi. It was a fairly upmarket barbeque, with several tuxedoed waiters in discreet attendance and a band on a bandstand playing middle-European folk jazz.

Conrad didn't plan on staying long. The truth was most people bored him. Few of them could match him for power and influence. Even the women at the party were either gushing or aloof towards him.

He chatted to a few acquaintances and then sought out Fergus.

"Everything going according to plan?" enquired Fergus as he led Conrad into the bright south-facing drawing-room.

"So far. Money, planning permission, plans, everything seems fine. But I'll be a relieved man the day that first sod is turned. No turning back then."

"What about these objections? I saw something about protesters."

Conrad laughed scornfully. "Fine bunch of people. Perfectly within their rights. We live in a democracy, Fergus. Anyway they have no clout."

"Are you sure?"

"There are five of them: a schoolteacher, a retired bus

conductor, a university lecturer, a shopkeeper and one of the long-term unemployed."

"Not much of a turn-out for the neighbourhood, is it?"

"No-one's interested. The working people are too busy making money and doing up their houses and going off to Spain for their holidays."

Fergus changed the subject. "How's the engagement working out?"

"Couldn't be better. Don't know why I didn't get engaged years ago. Angela's just perfect."

The two men had hunted together in the old days in Leeson Street. Now Fergus was neatly stitched up with three children and a wife who kept careful tabs on his every move.

Fergus moved over to the window looking out over the garden. "Plenty of sport out there for a single man." He looked at Conrad pointedly, but Conrad just laughed and shook his head.

"See her," continued Fergus. "The one with the long legs and the short black dress and the brown hair blowing in the breeze."

"What about her?"

"How old is she? Jesus, man, I could be her father probably."

"I'm sure she's older than she looks. Nice though, isn't she?"

Conrad was aware of his immense charm and attractiveness with the opposite sex. Women regularly threw themselves in front of his carriage though he didn't allow himself to be vain about it. Like many successful men, he seemed to draw them to him without even knowing it. He knew that at any time he could amble casually into the crowded garden, make contact with the girl with the long brown hair and have her screaming in ecstasy before the evening was out. The question was – why would he do it? He certainly was no saint, particularly before his engagement to Angela. In his twenties he had sampled from the five continents and from the teens to the forties. But a man must put aside childish things and besides he didn't have time.

Fergus went to answer the front door and Conrad strolled into the cool evening air to say goodnight to Rhona.

The girl with the long brown hair was sitting alone on a garden seat, looking out to sea.

"Hallo," he said casually.

"Hi. I'm Lara."

"Pretty name – Lara. Excuse me. I'm looking for Rhona."

"She's not here. But I'm here. You want to sit down?"

She held his eyes with all the innocent allure of the sixteen-year-old, tucked her feet under her like a little girl and patted the seat for him to sit down. Conrad hesitated. Then he reasoned that he wouldn't stay long and besides he didn't want to hurt her feelings.

"OK," he said, easing his big frame down onto the seat beside her. "I'll just finish this beer and then, sadly, Lara, I must be off."

"Why?" she said, curling up languidly beside him so that her bare feet brushed lightly against his thighs.

"Work. Business. I shouldn't even be here . . ."

Dandy sat in a chair by the range. Richie was reading to him from *The Irish Times*.

Richie liked being with Dandy. His grandfather gave off this air of having seen it all. Nothing would surprise him. His pale-grey eyes gazed into the middle distance as his grandson read aloud about the latest box-office hit.

"This is a film about revenge and it takes its subject matter by the throat. The viewer is taken on a roller-coaster ride of suspense and excitement as Denn (a very creditable perform-ance from a sometimes lacklustre actor) seeks out the man who murdered his wife in a fit of road rage."

"Road rage?" enquired Dandy.

"It's a media buzzword for people who have no man-ners when they are driving."

"Buzzword? You'll have to speak in old-fashioned English, Richie. Couldn't you translate into my kind of English as you go along? Like – say – the man who murdered his wife in a fit of bad manners when he was driving."

Richie smiled. He wondered what words would have become bandied about and cliched by the time he got to be ninety-two. 'Buzz' after all used to be a thing that bees did. 'Wicked' used to be associated with women in black stockings and suspenders who drank the night away with other women's husbands. Saying someone was a ride used to be an insult, now it was a compli-ment. Perhaps he should draw up a dictionary for Dandy, a handy ready-reckoner of contemporary English usage. No, that wouldn't be any use. Dandy's sight was failing and anyway he had no interest in learn-ing anything new. Mostly he liked talking about the past and sport. The only contemporary thing which occupied his thoughts was film.

"Get me a cup of tea and make sure it's strong."

Sometimes Lit took offence at her father's directness, but Richie understood – well, at least he thought he did. Manners, saying please and thank you, pass the milk and excuse me, were really invented to keep children in their place. Old people had no intention of being kept in their place. After all, what did saying please actually mean? Perhaps it meant something like: 'If it's not too much trouble I would like you to get me a cup of tea. And if it is too much trouble, I am still asking for it anyway. And if I grovel slightly perhaps you will give it to me.'

Manners weren't high on Richie's list of priorities at present. Wicked ladies in black suspenders, now that might be different. Then he blushed suddenly, remembering the embarrassing encounter with Janet Byrne earlier in the evening.

"Is it made yet, or are you day-dreaming about naked women again?"

How could his grandfather possibly know what he was thinking about?

"Time enough for that. You should still be only thinking about sport and things like that. Look at you! You haven't even got a proper beard yet."

"Did you think about naked women when you were sixteen, Dandy?"

"Ha! My father made me have a cold shower anytime he ever saw me giving myself over to lustful thoughts, as he used to call them. But I still thought about them. Couldn't stop sometimes. Now, I still like to admire a pretty woman with a nice figure . . . but . . ." He paused and gazed into the mid distance.

"But what?"

"But I wonder now what all the fuss was about."

"All what fuss?" asked Lit as she came in.

Richie jumped.

"Oh, nothing," said Dandy. "Going to dances. Where have you been? I need to get ready. I have a doctor's appointment in the morning."

"Don't worry. We still have an entire twelve hours," she said with a hint of sarcasm.

"Anyway, I've changed my mind. I don't want to see the doctor. Pack of gangsters. What are they going to tell me at ninety-two? That I'm dying? Only a gangster would take money from an old man for telling him that. Or else they'll tell me to go away and not to be bothering them because they have plenty of people under the age of eighty to be worrying about, thank you very much."

"Well, I'll have to cancel the appointment. They may charge for it anyway."

"Tell them I feel weak and can't come. Well, it is the truth. I do feel weaker."

# CHAPTER 6

The Stoneyfield Residents Association had its headquarters in a small room above The Cobbler pub. In contrast to the cosy paint and bare-wood simplicity of the bar beneath, the walls of the upstairs room were draped with frayed red velvet curtains and the whole place smelled of stale beer and tobacco because at night-time it was used as a music venue.

Originally the association had mounted a large campaign against the development of Conrad Budd's site, but over the three years members had fallen away as each new planning appeal was rejected in Budd's favour. Now that work on the site had begun in earnest, the locals had lost heart. People were no longer interested in their plight. Reporters no longer looked for interviews. Financial contributions had all but dried up. They had gone from a budget of over twenty thousand pounds at the start of the campaign to a derisory one hundred and seventy-three euros.

Pat Sullivan, history lecturer and chairman of the SRA, waited despondently in the gloomy room for the stragglers in his legion. For three years, he had been the driving force in the fight to stop Conrad Budd erecting his monstrosity in the historic heart of the city. He had devoted every spare moment to the cause – researching, writing, phoning, lobbying, petitioning, marching, picketing, compiling newsletters.

Into the third year, his girlfriend Ciara had decided enough was enough and told him that he was a man on a mission and she had no interest in the missions. She packed up all her stuff from the little two-room artisan cottage in Corbawn Street and went home to her mother. Pat was surprised and quite hurt at the time because, the way he saw it, he was only trying to preserve a future for his children and maybe even his and Ciara's children.

But now he told himself it was almost time to call it a day. One last skirmish and he would return to researching his doctoral thesis on the history of penal institutions in Dublin during the eighteenth century.

Miss Dillon was the first to arrive. Though the weather was sweltering, she wore a little black beret and a long woollen cardigan. Miss Dillon used to run the corner sweet shop in Stoneyfield, but now she was retired and had lots of time to spend on important causes. Sometimes Pat wished Miss Dillon would find some other cause to attach herself to, but he couldn't exactly tell her that. And besides, he needed all the support he could get.

"Miss Dillon. Always on time. If only everyone were as punctual as you!"

"Nothing else to do, dear. That's my problem. If only I

had one of those hectic schedules where I always had to arrive late and leave early, like film stars, then everybody might pay more heed to what I had to say."

Pat was wondering what he might say to that, when the rest of the group arrived – Old Tom McNally who was one of the first ever bus-drivers in Dublin, Gearóid Magill a flashy young primary teacher from County Sligo, who was intent on saving the inner city and its children single-handed, and Fidelma, who had introduced herself to the group with the words: "Hi, I'm Fidelma and I'm unemployable."

Pat thanked them all for coming and passed around a plate of sandwiches and a pot of tea.

"This is the end of the road for us," he continued. "We will soon be just a little footnote in Stoneyfield history. It is only a matter of weeks to the official turning of the sod. I'm therefore proposing that out of a sense of honour and perseverance we maintain our picket at the site up to and including that day. After that – well, all we can say is that we truly did our best."

"If only there was something else we could do," said Fidelma. "You know what? I'd love to give that Conrad Budd a good kick up the arse, the way he drives past us every day with that grin on his face."

"Fine-looking man though – gorgeous, like Anthony Quinn and Gregory Peck rolled into one," said Miss Dillon. "Personally I'll miss seeing him driving by every day."

"Miss Dillon," snapped Gearóid, "Conrad Budd is the enemy."

"But he's always so pleasant – you know, all the tea and sandwiches –"

"Those are the nastiest of all – those sort, the smarmy ones, that play on the vulnerability of naive little old ladies with nothing better to do than –"

"Let's just stick to the plan for the next few weeks," Pat interrupted and gave Miss Dillon a reassuring smile.

Gearóid had put a great deal of personal energy into the campaign, but Pat did not particularly like him. He was sleeping with Fidelma, though he claimed that love was an invention of women to trick men into marrying them, and was rude to Miss Dillon. And though Miss Dillon was tiresome there was no call to be rude to her.

The little group huddled around a calendar and a sheet working their way through a roster for the coming weeks. When all the dates were fixed and agreement was reached on spending the remaining money on a few press releases and a few new placards, Pat decided it was at last time to adjourn.

He was just on his way down the gloomy stairs when his mobile phone began to flash.

He wasn't expecting any calls. All the reporters, politicians and lobbyists had long forgotten about their lonely little cause, Ciara never wanted to see him again and most of his friends were away on holidays.

He pressed the green button. "Hello? Pat Sullivan."

"Pat. Brendan Browne here."

In the first eighteen months of the campaign, Brendan Browne, the local government TD, had been one of the Stoneyfield Residents Association's biggest public advocates, making it known early on that he would be doing everything in his power to stop the Budd development going ahead. Then suddenly he had dropped the whole project. Said it was inappropriate for a man like him to be seen to take sides. Said that progress was progress and why couldn't a part of Dublin be developed like so many other historic cities – like Canary Wharf or like Manhattan. It was when Browne withdrew his support that the Residents Association had begun to lose heart and Pat Sullivan disliked him for that reason. More to the point, he didn't trust him.

"What can I do for you, Brendan?"

"I feel I've been neglecting this whole Budd thing lately. I'd be interested in having you fill me in on the latest developments."

Pat was not cunning. In fact, cunning was one quality he detested. All the same, he was smart enough to realise that Brendan Browne could find out quite easily what was going on in Stoneyfield without talking to him. "There's nothing much to tell. In fact, in a few days we'll be winding down. It's only a few weeks to the official opening. Then Stoneyfield is history."

He could hear Browne's wheezy smoker's breath on the end of the line.

"All the same, I'd like us to meet," Browne said finally.

"I'll meet you here in The Cobbler tonight."

Again the wheezy breath. "Not The Cobbler. Not the constituency. Somewhere on the southside. The Bayview in Killiney at nine. It's closing down for refurbishment. We'll have the place to ourselves."

The line went dead before Pat even had time to reply.

Lit was trying very hard to come up with ideas for re-working the Wholesome Foods project, but she was distracted by the news from London. Auntie Florence was sinking fast. Lit felt helpless and terribly sad. There would be no question now of postponing her visit. She only hoped she would make it in time to say goodbye.

Aside from which, Maura was behaving very oddly. She kept lifting things up and banging them down in foul temper. Though Lit generally tried not to get involved in other people's business, it was difficult not to notice that her secretary was extremely unhappy about something. And when Maura was unhappy about something she did not like to suffer in silence. In fact, suffering in silence was entirely alien to her nature. The words stoicism, endurance and martyrdom did not form part of her vocabulary. She was not the sort of girl to grin and bear anything.

Lit had figured that something fairly nasty was brewing when Maura acknowledged her with only a mumbled snarl in the morning. Then she'd spent ten minutes snipping quite unnecessarily at the branches of her bonsai tree. When Matt asked for yet another of his favourite pens she'd told him to go and find one himself and did he think she was a "fecking doormat". Lit watched her as she pulled a bunch of files from a cabinet, slammed the drawer and dropped the pile unceremoniously on the floor. Then, as though she was looking for a particular file, she picked them up one by one, examining each one and then ramming it back into the drawer and slamming the drawer shut, each time more viciously. Lit who prized harmony and calm, couldn't take the noise any more.

"Something up, Maura?"

"What do you mean? Nothing's up. Can't a girl just have a bad-hair day without everybody askin' her what's up?"

"I'd say it's more than a bad-hair day."

"And how would you know what a bad-hair day feels like? You're always the same – cool, calm and collected."

Lit laughed. "Is that what you think? I have to be that way at work and it's easier to be that way at work – but you should see me at home!"

"I'm not interested in hearing about your home-life and anyway I don't believe you."

"Believe me. Richie says I'm psychotic or schizophrenic or something. One day I got so mad at the mess in his room that I got all his stuff and threw it in the bin. He didn't speak to me for a week."

Maura eyed her with disapproval. She was very fond of Richie and didn't like the idea of him being subjected to such wanton acts of cruelty. Lit wished she'd kept her mouth shut. But there was no point in turning back now.

"Of course I apologised to him afterwards," she added.

The truth of the matter was that one day when he was at school, she had gathered up a pile of old Playstation magazines, a few discarded discs, some old posters that he kept under his bed, a worn-out pair of trainers and a pair of pyjamas that he'd outgrown, slung them all in a black sack and quietly put them in the wheelie-bin. He'd never even noticed they were missing. She'd exaggerated the story to make Maura feel better. But now Maura was mad at her as well as being really mad about something else. Perhaps she should just change the subject.

"How's the love of your life?"

Lit thought she heard the word 'pisshead' though that couldn't be right. Maura loved Barry. Maura talked incessantly about Barry. She called him every day. He wanted to call her but on his sound technician's wages he couldn't afford to make too many calls on his mobile. Sometimes, when Maura was in a sentimental mood, she would look longingly at wedding dresses in magazines and wonder if Barry would like her in a particular dress. Last year she had saved two thousand pounds to go on a holiday to South America but made the supreme sacrifice at the last minute because Barry had just heard of a really brilliant sound-engineering course that he really should do if he was to get on in his career. Now she was calling him a pisshead?

"So what's up?"

Maura sat down at her desk and pulled his smashed and crumpled photo from the rubbish bin. She laid it out on the desk, flattened it with the palm of her hand and then stabbed at it angrily. "Gobshite!" She was rigid with anger, her pretty round face contorted with the sort of rage that only a man can arouse in a woman.

"What's he done?" Lit tried to sound surprised that Barry might have done anything of the gobshite variety. But up to now, about the only person in the world who didn't know that Barry Owens was a gobshite was Maura.

"What's he done? What's he –" Maura was almost beyond speech.

"How about a coffee?" asked Lit.

"OK."

They often exchanged confidences over a coffee when Matt was out of the office. They were good mates as well as colleagues. It was Lit who had encouraged Maura to take a marketing course at night school so that she could move into a bigger role in the company. She was already dealing with a number of clients and Matt had agreed that once Maura had her qualification, she could start working with one or two of the bigger accounts. Lit had to work hard to convince him of Maura's worth because he argued that they needed her as an administrator. Lit knew that if they didn't recognise Maura's obvious talents, she'd be off to work with a rival company as soon as she qualified.

Lit poured the coffees and led Maura into her own

office where they could talk in peace. Maura shoved her coffee around on the table, did a bit of hissing, glowered at a few pictures on the wall and then began in the tone of someone making a police statement.

"On Saturday night, when I was down in Mayo visiting my parents, he went and stayed over in Ciara Norton's apartment."

"So?"

"So – do you know Ciara Norton? She's only the biggest man-eater this side of the Atlantic. She can't look at a man without flirting with him. You know the sort – always showing off her boobs or her legs or her back or her midriff or something! Someone should weld her legs together. Anyway, I know he's always fancied her because every time we meet her, he goes all funny – you know, blushing and saying stupid things like he has potatoes in his mouth – like a feckin' teenager. Lit, do men ever grow up?"

"They never grow up – they only grow old. Maybe that's why some women only date younger men – they figure that at least younger men can perform better in bed."

"Do you think that's true? Did you ever date a younger man?"

"I gave up dating five years ago. You know that. I have no need for that totally useless item commonly referred to as 'a man in my life'. Maybe an occasional holiday fling – but that's all. Anyway, back to Barry. Maybe he didn't sleep with her."

"I'm not an eejit."

That was the understatement of the year. Maura could buy and sell her for shrewdness. Maura was pretty, like a plump Julia Roberts and, boy, she knew how to use it!

"I came back to my apartment on Sunday night and he

wasn't there. Then he turned up around half ten, freshly showered and smelling of Tommy Hilfiger Freedom which he doesn't own – you know, not reeking of sweat, fags and beer like he usually does. Now why would a fella turn up late on Sunday night smelling so sweet, I asked myself. Where've you been, I asked him. There's something I want to tell you, he says, and I'm telling you because we agreed on total honesty between us. Before he said it, I had it figured out. The horny little bastard!"

"What did he say?"

"He said 'I spent last night and all of today in bed with Ciara Norton. I had to do it, Maura. I had to get her out of my system.' He says. 'I couldn't stop thinking about her and about having sex with her. But you know, it's great. It really worked. It was such a let-down – not at all like what I'd imagined. I never want to even see her again. Yep! Been there! Done that! And got the T-shirt!' He says. All proud of himself like he had just given up the beer for ever."

"The bastard!"

Ordinarily Maura would have leaped to her beloved's defence, but this time, she didn't. "T-shirt! I'll show him feckin' T-shirts! Do you know what I did? I went to his wardrobe, flung all his clothes on the floor and picked out his absolute favourite T-shirts."

"He has a wide selection?"

"Oh, you should see them! Some of them are collector's items: a black one with *Sound Engineer Robbie Williams Slane* on it, a *Live Aid at Wembley Stage Crew* one that he got from his big brother – that's like nearly an antique now. A rare U2 one – oh, and one from Madison Square Gardens for a Mohammed Ali fight – he says that one is worth about five hundred pounds."

"What did you do?"

"I used to make costumes for an amateur drama group before I started the evening classes. I had all this dressmaking equipment including one of those big scissors – you know, the ones that make the zigzag pattern. I just picked his three favourites – and chopped out the writing and the pictures on them – and I said 'Got the feckin T-shirt? Then you won't be needing this lot, will you?'"

Lit laughed. How she wished she could show her anger like Maura! She thought back to her own relationship with Harry Menton, the awful pain he had caused her and how she had never, ever told him. Five years later, she still longed to pulverise him, decimate him, tear him to shreds, reduce him to a quivering blob of jelly. But she never had.

When she and Matt still worked in Devlin Satchwell PR, Lit came to work one morning and as soon as she sat down at her desk, she began to feel unwell. She struggled through until lunch-time, but by three o'clock there were spots in front of her eyes and she could hardly see. The glaring lights of the office hurt her eyes and her limbs were aching.

"What's up?" Matt asked her.

She could hardly see him and his voice seemed strangely disembodied. She stood up to go for a glass of water and collapsed on the floor. When she came to, it was several days later and she was in the hospital. A doctor examined her.

"You're very lucky to be alive, young lady."

"What do you mean?"

"Meningitis."

"Meningitis!"

"And you'll be able to walk."

"Walk? I don't understand."

"Sometimes people lose limbs. Sometimes their eye-sight. You've been very lucky."

Lit asked the nurse if there had been any calls or visitors.

"An old man – your father, I think. He's been here every day with your little son. A chubby man – Matt maybe? A girl called Bonnie – she sat with you all night the first night you were here."

"No-one else?" she enquired plaintively.

The nurse shook her head.

Lit plunged into depression. She might be dead and Harry Menton wouldn't even know or care less. Then she reasoned that perhaps he didn't know. After all, how would he know? When Bonnie came to see her that evening she asked her to make a call for her.

"If it's Harry Menton, I've already called him."

"What did you tell him?"

"That you were very ill, dangerously ill. That if you did come round which was looking doubtful, a bunch of flowers or a message or even a visit might be good for your recovery."

"What did he say?"

"That he was sorry about you being ill. That if he wasn't married to Ludabell or whatever her name is, he would be instantly kneeling at your bedside. Unfortunately, he had promised Ludabell that he was taking her to the races in Paris for her birthday and he couldn't get out of it."

Lit sank into the bed, filled with self-loathing and even deeper despair. But she wasn't letting the side down.

"Her name's Annabel," she said, defending her lover's territory, "and I'm sure he was telling the truth that he couldn't get out of it. I know he'd be here with me if it were humanly possible."

Bonnie looked down at her best friend. She had been so relieved when she discovered Lit wasn't going to die that she had promised herself not to make any more disparaging comments about Harry Menton. But she could hardly bear to see the emptiness and despair in her friend's face.

"I shouldn't say this because you're still very ill and we've all been very worried about you and I promised myself I wouldn't. But here goes. What sort of a man gets news that the woman he claims to love is seriously ill in hospital and doesn't even bother to send her a bunch of flowers?"

"He does love me, Bonnie. He just doesn't believe in all those tacky gestures. You know – flowers, birthday cards, presents. He believes those things are only a racket for making money. He believes that you don't need to tell a person you love them more than once. And he does sometimes send me flowers on my birthday."

"When you remind him."

Lit ignored that. "I'm sure he's thinking about me. I'm absolutely sure of it."

Bonnie said no more. But she knew that Harry Menton wasn't losing any sleep over Lit's illness. Most probably he'd completely forgotten about it by the time he'd woken up the next morning.

Lit didn't hear from him for six weeks and by then the pain of his neglect had turned to anger. One day he called out of the blue and asked if she could fly to Paris for the weekend. He had a business meeting there.

"I'm a bit tired still," she said by way of a gentle reminder about her illness.

"Oh, come on! That doesn't sound like you? Tired? Why would you be tired?"

It took some time for the truth to sink in. Harry

Menton had completely forgotten that she had been at death's door only six weeks earlier. Clearly it wasn't something that he had fretted too much about. She briefly wondered if he would have even noticed had she actually died. The anger welled up inside her. She wanted to claw his eyes out, scream at him that she had wasted four of the best years of her life loving him and for what? Instead, she laughed light-heartedly and said she really couldn't get to Paris that weekend because she was taking Richie down the country to see his cousins. Then Matt had approached her with the offer of setting up in business and Harry Menton had just quietly faded away. But the anger stayed.

Conrad went to his office overlooking Merrion Square for about an hour every day. He didn't always manage to get there and, in truth, he hated sitting at a desk. That was why he had gone into the construction and property business. He liked meeting people, doing things, getting out on the site and getting the mud on his feet. Occasionally, though less often in recent years, he would don the hard hat and shovel cement with the men or operate the heavy plant machinery. It was all good for the image. Now he sat restlessly in the office, signing documents which his secretary had been begging him to sign for days.

The phone rang.

"Budd."

"Brendan Browne here."

Conrad was silent for a moment.

"Brendan. What can I do for you?"

"I thought you might like to know about some people I've been talking to today."

"Who?"

"The Stoneyfield Residents Association."

"And?"

"Well, it seems they have reservations about your development plans."

"Yes, and they've been protesting as is their right. I pass their pickets every morning at the site gates. But we've made whatever changes they requested within reason, including increasing the greenspace allocation from forty-five to fifty per cent. And we've made ample provision for community development initiatives. All planning appeals have been rejected and the train is now leaving the station. Can't put the clock back, Brendan."

"They're going to lose their community environment, whatever you say. Three thousand apartments full of young trendies and affluent students – no community can withstand that sort of invasion."

"Your concern for the people of Stoneyfield is admirable, but it's over. An acceptable compromise has been reached. I have all the planning permissions I need, so there's no more to be said really." Conrad's voice was low and menacing.

Brendan changed direction. "Diamond Consortium . . . impressive backing . . ."

"What of it?"

"Sensitive area – financial backing . . ."

"Meaning?"

"Meaning scandals can make financial people edgy – especially where public opinion is involved."

"I hate to disappoint you, Brendan, but this project, along with all other projects of Budd Developments is squeaky clean. You, above all people, know that. Thank you for your interest though."

Conrad replaced the receiver quietly, picked up a Waterford glass paperweight and flung it at the wall.

Then he picked up the phone.

"Catherine, could you tell Jack Kennedy I need to see him in here. Immediately. Oh and get Doran Shiels on the line in about fifteen minutes. They're about to start earning their money."

# CHAPTER 7

In the office Lit was having a busy day working through a back log of phone calls and correspondence. She dealt with the most pressing ones and then, anxious to get cracking on Conrad's sponsorship programme, she called Dermot O'Driscoll, her contact in the Irish Rugby Football Union.

"I've got a client offering a good sponsorship deal to a high-profile sports organisation, Dermot – any interest?"

"Could be. Allied Building Society are blowing hot and cold. Who is it?"

"Best not to get into names for the moment. But this client is well disposed and will be a more than generous sponsor if things work out . . ."

"Sounds interesting."

"I'll see if I can set up a meeting and call you back."

Lit was pleased. That sounded like a positive result.

Maura was working through Matt's correspondence with all the thoroughness of an avenging angel. Her humour had improved slightly, but every so often she would make another observation about the male of the species.

"And that's another thing I can't understand," she said now.

"What's that?" asked Matt, who was leaning on her

79

desk and signing letters for the evening post.

"Why men are gay." She tore venomously at the brown envelopes with the letter-opener. "I mean I can understand why women are gay . . . because men are just such a let-down. But men? I mean men must know what gobshites other men are. I mean, you're a man, Matt – you tell me."

Lit observed the scene through the open door of her office and shifted uncomfortably in her chair.

Matt looked up over his glasses. "So, Barry Owens has finally shown his true colours."

Maura nodded dolefully and was suddenly on the verge of tears.

"I'm sorry, Maura." He went and put his arms around her and gave her a big squeeze.

"I loved him!" She sobbed into the keyboard on her desk. "He was so . . . so . . . complex."

"But look – he was only a second-rate sound engineer so don't feel so bad about it." Matt felt that the best way to console someone was to tell them not to feel bad. "You can do much better than him. I heard it from a few production companies that they wouldn't even look at him because he was so unreliable and, if he did turn up, all he did was grouch and complain and try to stir up trouble. Do you know he completely wrecked the sound system in Temple Manor Productions? He's a jinx, a nasty –"

"Matt!" Lit hissed, swiftly bolting to his side and fixing him with a meaningful look. Maura didn't need to hear any of this, no matter how true.

"Oh right," he said, the penny finally dropping. "And as for the gay thing . . . all sex gets in the way of drinking. That's my view for what it's worth."

The switchboard was flashing and Maura raised her

tearstained face from the keyboard to answer it. She immediately sat bolt upright and began to make exaggerated gestures at Lit.

Lit thought Maura might be experiencing delayed signs of post-relationship traumatic stress disorder until she realised that she was mouthing the words 'Conrad Budd', making a rather leery expression with her eyes.

Lit returned to her office and picked up her phone. "Conrad, what can I do for you?" she asked with cordial efficiency.

"We need to deal with the press."

"What's up?"

"It's a small matter. A little protest group. Fine people from Stoneyfield exercising their democratic right to protest. I respect that."

"And what's the problem?"

"There's no problem as such. But I want to make sure that the public knows everything here has been done right."

He reminded her about the greenspace allocation, the community initiatives, his significant contribution to the local schools and youth clubs, his compensation money to the people who lived in the row of houses likely to be most effected by the development.

"Do people know about all this?"

"Didn't think to make much of it at the time, but perhaps I made a mistake. Can you come over to my office?"

"Of course. I have a few appointments this afternoon, but first thing in the morning . . ."

"Tomorrow's no good. I'm travelling to New York. It has to be this afternoon."

She hesitated for a moment. "I'll be there in an hour," she said finally.

If Conrad had been a less substantial client, Lit would have put him off. It never looked good to be available to clients at a moment's notice. But Conrad had to be cultivated. For the time being, he would have to take precedence over other business.

"Why were you making that funny face when Conrad was on the phone?"

"What face?" asked Maura with feigned innocence.

"I have to go to his office in Merrion Square."

"Have fun."

"Don't call me on my mobile. It's an important meeting and I don't want to be disturbed."

"She doesn't want to be disturbed."

"Maura, will you stop that! This is business. Professional stuff. That kind of innuendo is – is – inappropriate."

"Don't forget to touch up your lipstick – oh, and put on some of that nice Bulgari perfume – it's light – perfect for the business meeting . . ."

That did it. Lit had been on the point of reaching into her bag and doing just that. But now she just grabbed her bag and bolted for the door.

As soon as her car was safely out of sight of the office, she held the steering wheel with her right hand and rummaged around in her bag until she found her lipstick. Stopping at the traffic lights, she applied one coat and blotted it with a tissue. At the second set of lights, she applied a second coat and blotted it once more, this time sucking on her little finger for a moment to prevent any colour from accidentally straying onto her teeth. There was nothing more potentially embarassing than having a smear of pink grease across a perfectly polished white front tooth. Then she quickly applied a light splash of perfume.

She found a parking space on Merrion Square and made her way to the office of Budd Holdings.

Jack Kennedy shoved his hands in his pockets and looked out across Merrion Square from Conrad's expansive office.

"What's the problem, Conrad?"

"I had a call from Brendan Browne."

"I thought we'd sorted him out."

"Apparently not. He's been talking to the SRA again."

Jack gave a derisive snort. "I'm quaking in my boots," he said sardonically.

"Now see. That's the difference between you and me, Kennedy. You think this is a minor detail. I know it's important."

"I don't get it, Conrad. What can they do? The planning permission is there. What can Browne do?"

"Finance . . . backing . . ."

"That's all in the bag, isn't it? Isn't it, Conrad?"

"Of course. But all these contracts have a walk-away clause. That's how these people do business. As I see it, I need to raise my media profile a bit . . . highlight some of the good work I've done in Stoneyfield . . . and ensure there's no scandal . . ."

"What scandal? There isn't going to be any scandal. I've been through every single document concerning this development with the lawyers – not once but several times. If Brendan Browne is looking for a scandal he'll be disappointed. There's nothing there."

"Naturally there's nothing there. By the way, Lit Doran is on her way over. She's going to work on this with us."

"Lit." Jack gave a little snort. "What sort of name is that? Probably some silly college nickname. Lit? Does it mean 'little'?"

Conrad shrugged.

"Literature?" said Jack. "Litigation? Litmus? Litter? Ah, what's the use? Maybe we can ask her. Lit – Lit – Clit – Clitoris . . . Veuve Clitoris . . . maybe her da was a champagne-lover. What's she like?"

"Good ideas. Practical. Intelligent. I think they're the right company for us."

Conrad liked practical women. He was especially drawn to intelligent women. If they were both beautiful and intelligent, he could barely resist them.

Jack persisted. "Lit. Sounds like a lesbian name. She's not one of those big butch women with cropped hair, is she?"

Conrad didn't even smile and Jack wondered, as he often did, if his boss had any sense of humour at all.

Lit arrived at Conrad's office exactly on time. She introduced herself to the pretty receptionist at the desk and then took the elevator to the top floor where his private suite of offices was located. She sat on the sofa in the lobby outside and made small talk with Catherine, his personal assistant. Catherine was a no-nonsense woman in her late forties with a relaxed warmth about her and Lit took an instant liking to her. What tales might she be able to tell about Conrad Budd? While Catherine disappeared to make coffee, Lit looked around her and admired his collection of original paintings. She was mildly curious about his office. What would it be like? She imagined it would be a reflection of himself – ordered and tasteful. Then she turned her mind to the business in hand, collecting her thoughts, prioritising the points she would make. After about ten minutes the door of Conrad's office opened.

"Thanks for coming at such short notice," he said as he held the door open for her.

Lit suppressed a gulp. Conrad had removed his jacket and the sleeves of his shirt were rolled up. The shirt was a fine white poplin material and beneath it she could make out his lightly tanned chest and the broadness of his back. The collar was unbuttoned and his tie was thrown unceremoniously on his desk.

Conrad introduced her to Jack Kennedy.

"Hi," said Lit, extending a slender, perfectly manicured hand.

"Lit . . . unusual name . . . what does it mean?" asked Jack.

She sat facing Conrad across the desk, opened out her folder and extracted a pair of designer glasses from a case. She perched them primly on the bridge of her nose.

"It's short for Laetitia," she said curtly. She turned to Conrad. "How would you like to do this?"

"I'll show you everything I've done for Stoneyfield. Then we'll discuss a strategy to publicise it in the most positive way." He handed her a folder containing documentation of his work for the people of Stoneyfield.

Lit took her time, scanning each document for the essential information. "This is good stuff." Eventually she turned her attention back to Conrad. "We can arrange an official opening of the school computer room . . . with TV and press . . . what about a newspaper or TV profile of you walking Stoneyfield and showing the various things you've done there . . . there's bound to be a child we could do a colour piece on . . . you should come across as a practical and successful man but with a strong sense of community. Nothing too syrupy."

Conrad shifted uneasily in his chair. "I'm not all that keen on the limelight. This kind of thing doesn't come easily to me."

"What are you afraid of?" Lit asked.

"I don't understand?" Conrad was taken aback at the question.

Jack Kennedy laughed scornfully. It was a naive question to ask a successful man. Perhaps, after all, she was just a dumb blonde.

"Everybody is afraid of something," said Lit. "Losing power, rejection, being ridiculed. Often, very successful people seek out the help of PR companies to allay these fears."

"I see what you mean. It's a smart question. I suppose the answer is losing power. But maybe it's all three."

"OK. Perhaps you don't like the limelight because you're afraid of being ridiculed?"

"It's possible," said Conrad non-committally.

"But you may need to risk ridicule if you want to be sure the Stoneyfield project reaches completion. That's the priority. Besides, you won't be ridiculed. We'll see to it. That's our job."

Fine." Conrad was absentmindedly sliding the mouse around the pad as he listened.

"I'm just guessing here," Lit continued. "This is partly about reassuring the investors, right?"

"Meaning?"

"Meaning that for Doran Shiels PR to work successfully for you, we need to be on a fairly honest footing. I'm not being cynical, but your contribution to the Stoneyfield community was most likely motivated out of self-interest."

"I'm a pragmatic man. As you said."

"Nothing wrong with that. But we need to be clear about it so that no-one can accuse you of self-interest later on. If you openly admit self-interest, then that's fine. Also . . . if there was any reason why financial backers might lose interest, it would be helpful for us to know now so that we could put the right spin on it and allay any fears they might have."

Lit noted the slight pause and the brief exchange of looks before Conrad fixed his deep, deep black eyes on hers and said with the merest hint of admiration: "You're sharp. Damn sharp."

She could feel herself melting. A strange jellylike feeling at the pit of her stomach threatened to overcome her. She thought she might like to lean across the desk and rub her finger along the moist part of his lower lip. There was also an attractive little triangle of chest showing where his collar was undone. I could kiss that, she thought. Just lean over and plant one brief moist kiss there that would leave him burning with desire for days.

"And you haven't answered my question," she said, coolly rebuffing his compliment.

Conrad buttoned up his poplin shirt and pulled the loosely knotted tie over his head. He fixed the knot firmly in place and reached for his jacket.

"There's nothing else," he said. "No little skeletons in the cupboard, no corruption, no fears to be allayed. All I want you to do is steer us through the next few weeks and any little surprises the Residents Association might throw at us. It's that simple. Jack will see you out."

He extended his hand across the desk. "Good to see you again. Talk to you soon."

"One last question," she said as she put Conrad's papers into a neat stack for her briefcase.

"By all means."

"This isn't likely to get dirty, is it?"

"Couldn't you handle that?"

"I can handle it. I'm just not sure if I'd want to.

Goodbye, Mr Budd."

The prospect of seeing Lit Doran out of the office was too much for Jack Kennedy, or rather not enough. He offered to walk her to the car.

"No, really. Goodbye." Lit didn't like him very much.

"I'm going that way anyway. Besides I wanted to ask about an item in your last invoice."

God preserve us from accountants, Lit thought.

Jack Kennedy had to lengthen his stride to keep up with her as they walked down the east side of Merrion Square.

"You mentioned an artist's fee. But I haven't seen any artwork yet. No videos, no posters . . ."

"That's for the logo."

"Ten thousand euros?"

"You're getting it cheap. The guy we used generally gets six-figure fees."

Jack was fiendish with the books. It was one of the reasons Conrad placed so much faith in him. He never worried Conrad about the nitty-gritty, but he accounted for every penny as it came and went. That was partly his reason for wanting to get her alone. And it was nice to be seen walking along Merrion Square with a beautiful woman like Lit Doran. He was well able to keep a conversation going with her.

"Don't you think this whole business of logos is getting out of hand?"

Lit said nothing.

Jack continued. "Every bloody backstreet businessman in the country, every Mickey Mouse charity and pressure group has to have a logo now. Imagine living in a society where people are paid huge sums of money just to draw three letters into a fancy shape with colours!"

Lit retrieved her keys and counted the number of cars

that she would have to walk past before she could escape the obnoxious little drone.

Jack was well into his stride now. He knew that women liked intelligent men, men who could make interesting conversation.

"Last week United Bank of Ireland paid out a seven-figure sum to a PR firm just to have something fancy done to the letters UBI. I mean, what is the world coming to? Ten thousand euros – I suppose it doesn't seem so bad. Just had to check. Doing my job."

They had reached Lit's car.

"If you have any further queries about money, by all means contact the office," said Lit. "Our accountant will work through them with you. Goodbye."

She sat into the car, put on her sunglasses and turned on the ignition. Cocooned in air-conditioned bliss, with Santana's 'Smooth' thumping out loudly, she sped away and dismissed him from her thoughts.

Back at the office, she began putting together a preliminary press release concerning Conrad's work in Stoneyfield. She called his office and asked for more photos to be sent over. Only rarely did Lit or Matt shut the doors of their offices which faced one another and now she could see across to him, through the open doors, puffing his way through a PR initiative for one of the health organisations. He was bored out of his wits, but it was a very lucrative account so he had to give it his all. Maura was drawing up a guest list for a forthcoming charity benefit dinner. In between times, she scoured the net for tips on how to get revenge on Barry Owens and called out the best suggestions.

Matt stubbed out his cigarette, drained the last of his tenth mug of Italian coffee that day and ambled across to Lit's office.

"I was thinking . . ." he said.

"What is it you'd like me to do?"

"Dinner party?" he said tentatively.

"Why? What for?"

"Entertain clients and all of us. You've got the house for it."

"Why not bring them to the races, or a box in Croke Park. Or golf in the West? Or take a room in the Coq Henri?"

"Nah. People are sick of all that. *Dinner party, dinner party, I want my dinner party!*"

He stamped his foot playfully like a little boy having a tantrum. Matt often got hung up on the whole idea of human contact in business. He thought that people met at corporate weekends and sporting events, but that they didn't really connect.

"I hate that Coq Henri," Maura chipped in. "The last time we were there, it was full of dry auld sticks."

"Who do you have in mind? How many?" Lit asked.

Matt settled into an easy chair and began warming to his theme.

"Well, all of us . . . you, me, Maura, Zara, Dave and John over there . . . then our top clients . . . Budd for starters and some of his crew . . . the health organisation . . . Northern Lads . . . Seán is encouraging us to be more 'proactive' in pursuing business so then some other prospective clients I have in mind. There's a bank and a new computer software company . . . the Wholesome Foods people. And Seán. We do owe him, I suspect that we may be very indebted to him if his advice pays off."

"The weather's too hot. I don't want to, Matt."

"It's networking. We need to do it. Look. It's simple. Caterers, staff – you have a piano . . . a bloke sitting quietly in the corner playing the piano . . . sit-down meal or outdoor buffet . . . people like that . . . they get to connect . . . and your house is the perfect venue . . . thirty or forty people . . . it's a doddle!"

Anything Matt didn't have to do himself was always a doddle. And she knew that thirty would quickly become fifty or even sixty. But she had to admit that there was a certain amount of sense to the idea.

"What do you think, Maura?"

Maura was cackling nastily and not really listening to Matt and Lit.

"Maura?"

"What? Party? Great idea. What about this for an idea? I could go to his flat when he's away for the weekend, dial the speaking clock in New York and leave the phone off the hook. Or I could spray his carpet with water then sprinkle cress seeds or bean-sprout seeds into the pile – or hide a few pieces of fish in the lining of his mother's curtains. It's all here – www.boyfriendrevenge.com. I could paint his stupid old car pink . . . send him a letter addressed from the sexually transmitted diseases clinic . . ."

She shook her head. None of the options seemed vindictive or cruel enough for Barry Owens. She needed something that would strike at the very heart of his being, something to reduce him to grovelling despair, something from which he would never recover.

She stared off into the distance, her eyes narrowed as she anticipated the pleasure of seeing him utterly decimated, rightly annihilated, completely obliterated, bolloxed for all eternity.

"Thanks for your input, Maura," said Lit sarcastically. "When you're finished fantasising about taking a cleaver to Barry Owens, you might like to draw up a guest list."

Later that evening, Lit sat in her back garden with Bonnie. The six wall fountains made a pleasant rippling-water sound, blocking out virtually all traffic and back-ground noise.

"How much did this lot set you back?" enquired Bonnie.

"Ten thousand."

"Just for a few little fountains! Jesus! You are making serious money."

"How much did you spend on that trip to California last year?"

"Five thousand pounds."

"I don't have time to take long expensive holidays like that. You're time-rich. I'm money-rich. Anyway water fountains give great privacy. They soak up the sound. Elizabethan spies used to always have their clandestine meetings beside fountains because it drowned out the sound of their voices. The Viet Cong used to sneak up on the Americans near water to drown out the sound of their movements."

"Fascinating," said Bonnie with a big yawn. "So any Conrad sightings today?"

"A meeting this afternoon. It was mostly strategy and stuff."

"Sod that. How did he look?"

"I didn't notice."

"Liar."

"As I said, I am not interested and besides he's engaged."

"So? I mean, engaged – it's not like married. Sometimes you're such an old-fashioned prude. Nobody gives two hoots about that any more."

"That's not true. The kind of circles he mixes in – an engagement announcement is still a major step.

Anyway a guy who's engaged and fools around with someone else . . . well, he's a slimeball . . . that's my view and I'd have no interest in a rat like that. And I'm not completely sure, but I don't think Conrad Budd is a slimeball."

"Don't you think he might be entitled to one last fling?"

"Not really," Lit retorted. But she sat quietly in the dusk considering the issue all the same. Perhaps Bonnie was right and she was being a prude. If a person had one last fling before marriage, did that make them utterly undependable for their entire married life? Wasn't it a bit like having that last extra five fags on New Year's Eve before giving them up for good, or like going on one last shopping binge before tearing up your credit card?

"I'm just not very interested in flings or one-night stands. And that's all that Conrad would be offering."

"Ah!" cried Bonnie triumphantly. "So you have thought about it!"

"Truthfully, I haven't."

"Then your subconscious has thought of it!"

Lit couldn't really think of an answer to that.

# CHAPTER 8

The following morning Lit decided to assign one hour to arranging Matt's dinner party. Maura took on the business of organising the caterers and staff and Lit made phone calls. The first person she called was Conrad. Her list was alphabetical.

He was on his mobile, travelling to the airport. She

could quite easily have called his secretary but she reasoned that his secretary would probably only have to call him anyway to confirm. So in a sense she was cutting out the middleman or woman. She planned the call. It would be brief and cordial. She shut the door to her office so that Maura would not hear.

"Conrad. Lit Doran here."

"Lit . . . good morning."

It was the first time he had used her name – and did she imagine a lowering of timbre, a softer voice as he said it? Ignore it, ignore it, she scolded herself inwardly.

"I'll be brief. The company has an informal dinner party each year. It's something Matt likes to do. This year it's in my house."

Was she babbling? No. So far, so good. She weighed her words carefully. "We're thinking next weekend. Would Saturday suit for you and your associates?" She paused. "Perhaps your fiancée as well?"

"Just let me check my diary."

She felt impatient and a bit fluttery. She realised that she would be very disappointed if he couldn't come.

"Nothing that can't be rescheduled," he said finally.

"Fine. We'll post a formal invitation."

"I look forward to it. Talk to you soon. Bye."

Lit's heart lurched unreasonably in several directions. It was possibly the very soft way that he said "Bye", but she couldn't be sure. Or perhaps it was the way he'd said that he'd talk to her soon. Down, silly hormones, she scolded herself once more and immediately dialled the Cornwells as a distraction.

"I'm sure we have no other engagements that evening. It's quite good of you to invite us. By the way, both Poppy and I are vegetarians . . ."

"That's no problem," said Lit. "Thanks for letting us

know, though. Look forward to seeing you. Bye."

She called the bank, the software firm, the health organisation and she called Dermot O'Driscoll from the IRFU, who said that he would be delighted to come but that he wouldn't be bringing a partner because he and his girlfriend of five years had just split up.

Last on her list was Seán Tallon. She cursed and dialled his office number.

She was surprised when he answered the phone directly.

"I hope I'm not disturbing you. I thought I'd get your secretary."

"This is my direct line. Who is this?"

"Lit Doran."

"Who? Oh yes, Matt's friend – eh, partner." There was a pause. "Had your trip to London yet?"

She could hear the impatience in his voice, the striving to be polite and the annoyance at being interrupted at whatever he was doing. "Tomorrow morning." It was like having a conversation with the talking clock or one of those ubiquitous touch-tone answering services.

"Well . . ."

There was another suffocating pause as he ransacked his brain for some bland social comment – the kind that he seemed to have so much difficulty with. "Safe journey. So what do you want?"

What a charmer, thought Lit. She wondered what Bonnie would make of him. Probably short work, she thought.

"Matt asked me to call. We're having a dinner party in my house – the company, that is. Matt would like you to come."

"Oh, I see. Where do you live?"

Lit didn't quite see the connection. "Harwood Park."

He let out a low whistle. "Nice! Edwardian houses, built on land originally owned by the Earls of Pembroke, houses sold in 1905 for £800. You must have big repayments on a house like that. One sold in the paper last week for two million pounds. I'm impressed. That's quite a property investment for a single woman."

Well, how dare he! The pure and utter cheek of the sad creature! First he implied that she was wasting company time and now he had more or less implied that she was living beyond her means!

"Yes. Isn't it. Luckily I got it cheap a few years back because it was in such bad condition. I did most of the interior work myself and Matt's brother helped with the more structural work. And – yes, the house is worth millions now. Quite a bargain when you think about it. And I don't, as it happens, live alone."

That showed him, the pompous prig!

There was a pause. Then he said, "Like you say, a solid investment. Thank you for your invitation to dinner. I accept."

"Please feel free to bring a friend," said Lit glacially. She almost added – if you have any friends.

"Thank you. Goodbye."

Men! Always trying to tell you how to improve your life, always showing you a better way – their way.


Seán was flummoxed. Lit had sounded annoyed. He needed to know where she lived if he was going to dinner there. Perhaps he shouldn't have mentioned the value of the house, but it was his work after all. He spent his entire day reviewing other people's assets and encouraging them to shift their money around for the best possible return. He hadn't meant to be offensive and he hadn't realised that she didn't live alone.

Perhaps her husband had an equally lucrative job.

He had to confess that he found it hard to understand women. They astonished him. They were like emotional diviners, magically capable of finding vast wells of feeling, nurses who could draw out the festering pus of buried wounds. How did they know these things? If he ever had a hunch about a character, it was generally wrong. So he never allowed himself to rely on his instincts. Instead, he negotiated the world with logic, problem-solving skills, mathematical certainty and practical concern for his fellow man.

There were women in his life, of course, but since his experience with Helen he was careful not to become involved and always made his position clear. He would never hurt a woman again, whatever the cost to himself. Dating, of necessity, became an intermittent pastime like tennis in the club and sailing on Sunday mornings – a pleasant pursuit which enriched the fabric of life but meant no more than that.

He knew he had annoyed Lit Doran. She had made it quite obvious. He hadn't intended to annoy her. In fact, the thought made him vaguely uncomfortable, but he couldn't fathom it.

He tapped absentmindedly on the keyboard, allowing his mind to ramble for a rare moment of reverie.

What did she look like? He couldn't remember. Slim, he thought. Fair – or was she brown-haired? Fair, he decided. He returned to his work and thoughts of Lit Doran slipped quickly from his mind.

Pat Sullivan waited for Brendan Browne in the back lounge of the Bay View Hotel. He was the sole customer. Pat didn't like hotels. There was something seedy about even the best of them. Mostly though, he was uneasy at the prospect of meeting Brendan Browne. Browne was an independent TD, a lone wolf who occasionally rented his soul to the highest political bidder. Rumour had it that he had lost interest in the Stoneyfield controversy because the outcome wouldn't affect his Dáil seat one way or the other.

Pat sipped his glass of beer and absentmindedly shuffled through the pile of papers he had built up since getting involved in the Residents Association. He sighed. His vision of a vibrant thriving Stoneyfield community was fading fast. Instead would come the rat packs, the glitzy young tigers, the fat cats from across the globe, and Stoneyfield would become just another soulless hub of trendy affluence.

Browne arrived punctually, bought a mineral water and joined him in the lounge.

They shook hands, exchanged pleasantries about the heat and the traffic and then Browne placed a large brown envelope on the table and leaned forward, holding Pat's gaze.

"Do you want to stop this development?"

Pat shrugged. It was like asking a pacifist if he wanted world peace. "Of course."

"Then this envelope will interest you." Browne slid the envelope further across the table.

Pat glanced at it briefly but didn't move. "What's in it?"

"Open it and see."

"Why don't you tell me what's in it first?"

Browne sighed, breath wheezy. "This will stop the development – if that's what you really want."

"I want nothing to do with anything nasty. This has been a very clean campaign – something we're proud of."

Browne indicated the envelope. "That's the truth in there. Can the truth be that nasty?"

Pat desperately wanted to look in the envelope – out of basic human curiosity if nothing else. But a brown envelope from a politician could contain anything. He changed the subject. "Why are you so interested all of a sudden? Where have you been for the past two years when we needed your support? And why this envelope now after all this time?"

Browne gulped down some of his mineral water, then smiled coldly. "I'm here now. That should be good enough for you. Look, I have to go. I'll call you tomorrow."

He stood up and turned to go. "There's a price to be paid for everything." He wheezed cryptically and left.

Richie sat at the computer in his bedroom, compiling his dream soccer team. There would have to be Pele, George Best, Cantona, Ronaldo, Gullit, Schmeichel, Larsson, Keane, Beckham. . . maybe . . . Michael Owen . . . yes, no – indoor, outdoor which would be best? Half the fun of it was having to make all the choices. The game at the end was great, but he liked the feeling of being like a manager and combining the talents of certain players. His summer project work for school could wait.

His mother knocked on the door, asking if she could come in. This was a relatively new trend. He never knew where adults got their notions from. All those articles in newspaper supplements about how to cope with awkward teenagers, he supposed. About six months ago she had decided it was time to start knocking on his door and saying things she had never said before like 'Excuse me, Richie, I hope I'm not disturbing you?' It made him feel uneasy as though she was preparing herself for the time when she would really have to treat him like an adult. Or even as though she thought he might be up to something naughty in the solitude of his room. Couldn't she give him credit for being a bit more discreet?

"Come into the lair of the seriously deranged," he called out, "but do so at your peril!"

"Hello, love . . . I hope I'm not disturbing you."

She walked over to him and gave him a hug. Wrapped her two arms around him from behind and kissed him on the back of the head. Dandy had warned him never to refuse his mother a hug because it was a small thing to ask for and a small thing to give. 'She'll be shocked but pleased if you buy her presents; annoyed but impressed if you start trying to help around the house; amused if you try to play the role of confidante to her. But a simple hug will never miss the target.'

Richie didn't quite see it. But he was onto a good thing and he knew it. Other guys in his class had to do stuff like mow the lawn, clean the gutters and tidy the shed. He figured his mother wasn't getting a very good bargain but that was her problem.

"I thought you were working on some school project?"

"Later. I just have to finish putting this team together."

"Don't spend too long at it. Dinner is in twenty minutes."

He grimaced with the left side of his face so that she wouldn't see him. Dinner with his mother and Dandy could be a bit like sitting in no-man's-land between the Germans and the Allies. The crossfire could be lethal – long-dormant mines could suddenly explode with devastating consequences. Sullen moods could hang over the table like invisible poisonous gasses. Then there would come an uneasy truce followed by a peaceful settlement that might last for months before some diplomatic blunder hurled the pair of them into open conflict once more. For the past few weeks they seemed to be languishing in the uneasy-truce phase where they largely managed to remain civilised and restricted their conversation to safe subjects like the weather or television. That meant that an explosion was almost certainly in the offing – any day soon.

Down in the kitchen, with Lit gone to make a phone call to the hospice in Wimbledon about her Auntie Florence, Dandy took a notion to give Richie some seduction instruction.

"You know, Richie, some day some young one, some pretty girl – what do you call them now? Dolls? Chicks?"

"No – that was in my mother's day – now it's 'babes'."

"Some babe is going to be sitting alone with you somewhere. Let's say on the bank of a river."

"Nobody does that any more, Grandad."

"Oh. What do they do? Or more to the point – where do they do it?"

"Well, we have a number of options: friends' houses, friends' brother's college apartments, cars, the holiday home . . ."

"I give up," said Dandy impatiently. "Anyway, let's take it that the butterflies will be fluttering by. The sun will be shining and this baby or chicklet or whatever you call them will be wearing something so light that you can see bits of her you mightn't have seen before. Mysterious, alluring bits . . ." He spoke the last three words in tones of sacred reverence.

"Like the posters on my wall."

"I haven't seen the posters on your wall."

"Supermodels, Hollywood babes . . ."

"Yes, that sort of thing!" Dandy snapped.

He was growing impatient with the interruptions. He wanted to pass on his store of sexual expertise to his grandson. After all, who else was there to tutor him? Dandy himself had achieved one hundred per cent success with the ladies when he was single. Women used to throw themselves at him all the time. I'll take you to the peaks of ecstasy, he used to promise them. Or was that 'ultimate heights'? He couldn't be sure any more.

"You'll feel warm and full of confidence that you're with such a pretty girl. Then you'll want to kiss her . . ."

"Snog, Grandad."

"What?"

"Kissing is called snogging now."

"Yes, well . . . you'll want to smog her and to touch her. You'll kiss her probably and then without knowing it you'll find yourself wanting to touch every bit of her. But you have to always be a gentleman, Richie."

"A gentleman?" Richie wasn't sure he liked the sound of that.

"So never smog or touch a chicklet-babe if she doesn't want you to. Of course, if she touches you first – well, that's another lesson entirely. So . . . what you have to do is to learn timing – life is all about timing – remind me to tell you about that sometime. The secret of romance and seduction is timing . . . and when the moment is right –"

"What? When what moment is right?" Lit enquired as she returned from calling the hospice. Florence was still conscious and looking forward to seeing her.

Dandy appeared to ignore her. "There may be – a – tug on the line. Don't do anything. Let that trout play himself out. Give him plenty of line . . ."

"You silly old man! What do you know about fishing?

Sit up at the table."

Richie led his grandfather to the table, and helped him ease down into the chair, then folded his own long, lean frame into another chair.

"Well, how's my baby sister?" barked Dandy. "Don't I deserve to know?"

Richie was fascinated at how Dandy changed in the presence of his daughter.

"I thought you might be upset." said Lit.

"Since when do you decide when I'm going to be upset? I'll pick my own moments, if you please."

"The nurse I spoke to on the phone said she's comfortable."

"Is she going to die?"

"Oh really!"

Lit struggled to get dinner on the table. She didn't like cooking. Left to her own devices, it would be Marks & Sparks microwaveable low-calorie, organic dinners for one. But Dandy would have none of it. Every evening he demanded meat and two vegetables with gravy. Often she tried to cheat by passing off a ready-made meal as her own creation but it rarely worked.

"What's this, Laetitia?" he would enquire with feigned politeness.

"Fillet steak and gravy."

"Ah. You don't know what's in them ready-made foods."

"But it's not ready-made!" she would protest.

How was it that she could bamboozle and spin and concoct and conceal from some of the greatest minds in the country and she couldn't get Tesco's steak dinner for two past her father?

"I'm not hungry. The cat will eat it."

Then he would watch sternly as she and Richie polished off the dinner, peppering the meal with helpful comments like, "I see in the paper that additives in meat give you mad cow's disease", or "Did you know you can get cancer of the colon from eating white bread?"

The very thought of a colon was enough to make Lit lose her appetite. So she supposed the only good thing about having her father at the table was that he contributed to her slim figure.

This evening, she had managed to find enough time to grill lamb-chops and bake some potatoes. She had chanced frozen broccoli.

"What do you call this vegetable?"

"Broccoli."

"Never heard of it."

"Yes, you did. You've been eating it for years. You like it."

"No, I don't. Don't cook it again."

Richie was beginning to think he should just go to the army & navy stores and buy some sort of protective combat gear. Dandy chewed a piece of meat with alarming jaw movements and then dispatched it to his stomach. For the rest of the meal, Lit tried to steer the conversation into safer waters: the long dry spell of weather, the new neighbours at the bottom of the road, the flowering plum tree at the bottom of the garden. Dandy and Richie talked football while she produced dessert. But it came back to death in the end.

"I want to talk about Florence," Dandy said, now tucking into some rhubarb crumble. "You think at my age I'm going to pussyfoot around the subject of death? I might be off to infinity and beyond myself tonight – I liked that film, Richie – any moment I could be gone. I could be sitting in my chair, lying in my bed, on the toilet even – and the Almighty, whoever he might be, could decide my number is up. Then I'm dead too. It's alright for you. Death is still a vague and future prospect for you."

"Auntie Florence has cancer. It has spread. She's been ill for almost a year. You haven't a thing wrong with you. Dr O'Connor said you'd probably live to be a hundred."

"You could always get your body frozen, cryogenically," Richie said, pushing a lock of chestnut brown hair back from his face and winking at his grandfather, who latched onto the suggestion with malicious glee.

"Yes. I wonder if you could do that? Laetitia, you might check it out. I believe there's a cryogenics outlet somewhere out in the Tallaght Industrial Estate now. After it's done, maybe you could keep me in the shed down there. I've enough money to pay for it."

Lit rolled her eyes to heaven and began clearing away the dishes. Richie and Dandy always ganged up on her. There was no point in rising to the bait. Men were born with a teasing gene. Good-humoured banter, slagging, just taking the mick, just winding you up, just having a laugh, they liked to call it.

The phone rang and Richie answered it.

"Hello? Hello?" He hung up. "No-one there. It's Zoe Delaney. She's stalking me."

"Don't be ridiculous," said Lit. "You don't know what stalking is."

"I'm telling you, ever since that night I went with her at Dave's party, she's been following me around."

"You wish."

"Mum, why do you never take me seriously when I talk about girls? How come Zoe Delaney always happens to be in the café where I hang out with my mates? How come she walks past my school about twice a week even though it's not on her way home? And what about those birthday cards and the red rose that was delivered to the school on Valentine's Day last year? You said yourself that there are no nuisance calls when I'm in school. I'm telling you, she's stalking me. Next thing she'll be e-mailing me and sneaking into the house and stealing my underwear."

Lit could feel one of her post-feminist lectures coming on.

"Stalking is a serious crime and you shouldn't be making fun of it. What you're describing is just a nice girl with a silly crush. Next week she'll no doubt fasten her attentions onto someone else. It's a million miles away from people being pestered, harassed and threatened and being in so much fear for their lives that they find it hard to go about their daily business."

"What's stalking?" enquired Dandy who had retired to the armchair by the big range with his mug of tar-black tea. "I've never heard of that."

"It's a girl that you snogged once at a party eighteen months ago, Grandad, that won't leave you alone."

"Anyway, I don't know what you're being so precious about," said Lit. "Zoe is very pretty. I would have thought she was just your type."

Richie snorted derisively. "Zoe Delaney! Pretty! She's alright-looking, I suppose. But . . ."

"But what?"

"But she's a complete yawn."

"Yawn?" enquired Dandy.

"Yes. Yawn. As in she makes everyone yawn. She's into horse-riding and when she's not trying to ride me, she's riding horses."

"I give up," said Lit and returned to checking her post.

There was a card from a friend in the States, the usual

bills and a note from Dr O'Connor asking her to bring Dandy to see him about the results of some tests. She would bring him when she got back from London. There wasn't much point in mentioning it now because he would only start grousing and then he might refuse to go altogether. With her father, the element of surprise was crucial. She rarely told him about important impending events until the last moment, a strategy which gave him enough time to get angry but not enough time to change his mind.

After dinner, while Dandy stayed on in the kitchen to watch TV, she played a half-hearted game of cards with Richie. She knew she should be grateful for the fact that he would still even deign to sit in the same room as her. But she was tired, all her energy spent on the business, the clients. Then Richie slouched, feet up on the sofa and watched *The Simpsons* and *The Sopranos*, while Lit sat demurely in the sofa opposite, trying desperately hard not to think about work. When it was time for *Friends*, she made her excuses and retired to the study to work on a press release.

Once more, Seán found himself sitting in The KGB with Matt.

"I'm not really interested in going. I've something else on. I hate socialising. All I ever seem to do is to sit glumly in a darkened corner, nursing a drink and looking at my watch. Socialising is superficial, a lot of people getting together in an artificially enhanced environment, chattering about the issues of the day, laying out the stalls of their informed opinions, social status and material success, inventing friendships where there really aren't any."

"No change there since college days!" Matt retorted.

"Look, it's just a bunch of people – some family, friends, business associates, clients. You qualify on two counts. What's so important that you can't cancel? What's wrong with you? I practically had to beat you up the aisle with a stick to give your sister away on her wedding day. I recall you didn't even go to your own graduation ball. You can't be saving yourself for the good times. These are the good times. We're thirty-five. Most of our mates are married – parents. We're richer than any of our forefathers – more educated, sophisticated, confident . . . do I have to go on? It won't get any better than this . . . why not enjoy it while you can?"

"I think you're confusing enjoying life with socialising."

"Yeah. Whatever. See that girl over there? She's been throwing the glad eye at you ever since you came in. She's pretty and friendly-looking. Why not buy her a drink? No, you won't, will you? It might just smack of spontaneity. But there was a time, Tallon . . . there was a time . . ."

"I have to go soon. Late night tele-conference. Look, I'll come to dinner. Just don't expect me to be the life and soul of the party. And don't tear strips off me later on because I wasn't."

"It's a deal," said Matt.


# CHAPTER 9

Pat Sullivan lived in a Victorian terraced house in Stoneyfield. It was compact – but perfect for a single man. His neighbours on the left were the Meehans, an elderly couple who had lived and worked all their lives in the area. In the house to his right were an actor and his artist wife. Beyond them lived a gay couple – Brian and Leonard. They all watched out for each other.

Last year it had been Pat's turn to host the Christmas party and about a hundred neighbours crowded into his two-bedroomed house. Ancient natives sat drinking side by side with exotic blow-ins from the four corners of the globe. The sing-song took in everything from The Dubliners, to Miriam Makeba to The Village People. He loved the place. He loved the people and he loved his house, packed to the gills with books and disks and historical journals and music magazines.

Now he sat in the middle of it all, sipping a glass of wine and trying to concentrate on the heavy book which rested in his lap. But, for some reason, *A History of Prison Regulations* didn't hold his attention. His eyes roved about the untidy room and he promised himself that when the business with the site was over and done with, he would embark on a Feng Shui weekend – clearing out all the clutter from his life. His eyes rested for a moment on the unopened envelope which he had tucked in behind a clock on the mantelpiece.

Perhaps he should start on the Feng Shui now. He jumped up and began pulling at a pile of old magazines – those to be binned to the left, those to be saved to the right. After ten minutes, the pile on the left consisted of one very old DIY magazine left behind by the previous tenant.

So much for Feng Shui. And when he thought about it, Pat wasn't sure he agreed with the idea anyway. He would feel very stressed out and alienated if he wasn't surrounded by comforting piles of books and reassuring mounds of academic work in progress. He replaced the magazines on their shelf and stared once more at the envelope.

He lifted it out from behind the clock and tapped it absentmindedly against the knuckles of one hand.

He could open it. For one shameful thing, he was curious. He couldn't help speculating about it and Browne had muttered a few potentially libellous things about Budd. Wouldn't it be better to open the envelope and find out the real truth? Perhaps it wasn't as bad as all that? He could simply examine the contents and burn them if he so wished. But what if he was honour bound to reveal what he read? He felt a sudden burst of sympathy for people like Pontius Pilate, people who didn't want to grapple with complex moral dilemmas but were forced to. He could put his scruples to one side and commit this one distasteful act to save Stoneyfield. Or he could wash his hands of the matter and return the envelope unopened to Browne and nobody would be any the wiser and he wouldn't have the worry of having a man's destiny resting on his shoulders.

He picked up a biro and wrote *For The Attention of Brendan Browne TD* on the front of the envelope. Then without even thinking, he slipped the biro beneath the flap and tore open the envelope. He took a deep breath and slid the contents out onto his desk.

It was past midnight when Lit finally trudged up the stairs to bed. First, she looked in on Dandy who was fast asleep, lying on his back with his hands thrown outwards. He looked almost babylike. She rubbed his grey old head lightly with her hand and pulled the sheet up over his chest.

Richie was stretched on his bed fully dressed, with headphones and a pile of music and sports magazines strewn across the duvet. He was deeply immersed in one of the magazines.

She bent and kissed him lightly on the cheek. "I'm off to bed, love. Night."

"Night, Mum." Without raising his eyes from the page, he put his arm about her and gave her an absent-minded hug. "Love you," he mumbled fondly as an afterthought.

She asked herself the same questions every night when she kissed him. Where had the sixteen years gone? How was it possible that she was the mother of this boy on the verge of manhood?

Lit had lived the wild life in college for a while – parties, drink, the odd joint, holidays in Spain and Greece with the fun crowd. Together, she and Bonnie planned to cut a swathe through any eligible males on campus. They were both seventeen. Bonnie insisted they draw up a list. One afternoon, instead of attending lectures, they sat in a corner of the student bar sipping Madison on Ice and munching Tayto crisps. In the background The Human League were singing 'Everybody Wants To Rule The World'. In the far corner a bunch of black-clad students plotted the downfall of Ronald Reagan and Maggie Thatcher. It was the era of glasnost and the Iran-Contra affair. Joan Collins was bitching it up in *Dynasty*. Meryl Streep had a farm in Africa. Bruce Willis was moonlighting. Madonna was living in a material world. Glen Close was boiling bunnies and Indiana Jones was everybody's hero.

"The list," said Bonnie with a sense of purpose. "The list will fall into four categories: Category 1: Fuck 'em and Chuck 'em. This category includes: the more handsome and well-endowed members of the more high-profile sports teams, hunks with money, dangerous white-trash hunks with no money (known as 'the bit of rough'), any known hunky flirts, mean hunks, younger hunks with crushes on us (one year age gap is the absolute limit),–"

"In short, hunks of any kind," Lit said.

"No," said Bonnie. "It also includes less attractive but incredibly witty and clever blokes. Now, Category 2: Meal Tickets. This category includes nerdy guys from the States with lots of money, any well-established rich Irish nerds, guys with good connections – connections must be bona fide and checked out first . . . "

"Define 'meal ticket'."

"Meal Ticket equals anyone with the money to bring us to the cool places – good parties, holiday homes around the globe – without of course expecting to avail of our irresistible feminine charms . . ."

"Be realistic!"

"Well, at least free beer and Chinese takeaway." It was the grim eighties when a Chinese takeaway was still considered the height of luxury in student circles. "But no sex."

"Agreed."

"Category 3: Not With A Ten-foot Barge-pole: This refers to all nerdy guys with no money and no brains and no sense of humour. Anyone who likes Kajagoogoo. Anyone who tries to look like Kajagoogoo. Communists, any other ists, anyone from Roscommon . . ."

"Bonnie, that's not fair!"

"Sorry. I can't help it. I know it's an entirely irrational and silly prejudice. But a guy from Roscommon beat me to a summer job once and I just can't help it."

"But still though . . ."

"Category 4," Bonnie cut in then paused dramatically, pushed the long black plum-streaked fringe from her forehead and took a significant breath. "Dangerous/Potentially Lethal/This Man Can Seriously Damage Your Health. This is an extremely small but deadly group including anyone you find yourself fantasising about at the nine o'clock lecture on Monday morning, anyone whose address and phone number you know off by heart even though you've only said hello to them on the way from the library to the coffee bar . . ." Bonnie fixed her eye accusingly on Lit at this point. "I think you and I both know who I'm referring to . . ."

"You're the one who stole his gum-shield from the changing rooms," Lit countered defensively.

"I only did that to stop you from doing it. I have to save you from yourself."

"Save me!" Lit was indignant. "I don't have enlarged photos of him bending over a scrum with thighs from here to eternity. I did not accidentally on purpose attend engineering lectures and sit in the back row drooling for three months until the lecturer got suspicious. I did not loiter around the canteen like a scavenging rat, waiting to pounce on his empty Coke can. I did not fortuitously faint in the carpark when a certain person was driving by and had to stop and transport me to the college medical centre!"

"You're just jealous. Anyway he's Category 4 and definitely off limits. And besides, he probably doesn't even know we exist. Every time I see him he's with a new blonde. And they're always *those* type of blondes."

"Meaning?"

"Meaning – big hair, big tits, big lips – small IQ, small waist, small nose. We're OK-looking, but compared to that lot, we're plain Janes and we look our age – seventeen. They all look like they're twenty-five or more. There's one consolation though."

"What?"

"We will come into our prime!" She said it like
Maggie Smith in *The Prime of Miss Jean Brodie*. "And
when we're in our prime in our mid-thirties, they'll look
like tired old slappers. Their hair will be destroyed from
all the dye. Their skin will be ruined from all the stuff
they plaster on it. And gravity will have played hell with
their big tits. We on the other hand will be elegant,
sophisticated, svelte, praised for our style and prized for
our intellect. And when Conrad Budd meets us in ten or
so years' time, it is not we but he that will be drooling!"

"What do you think he will be like when he's thirty-
five?"

Bonnie shrugged dismissively. "Probably bald and fat
with a nasal-hair problem."

But he didn't turn out like that at all.

Bonnie's list didn't last long, at least not as far as Lit
was concerned. In the first term of second year she met
David Morris. He was quite handsome, very intelligent,
witty and popular. Lit thought he was a nice enough
guy to lose her virginity to and she did to the strains of
George Michael singing 'Careless Whisper'. In a matter
of weeks she found herself bringing him home to meet
Dandy. Home in those days was that nice quiet road in
Templeogue. Having dragged home a number of sad
spectacles in her day, Lit was proud that at last she was
hitched up with David. Her father liked David. He
mucked in around the house, always showed respect
and wasn't a smart-arse. David was a dream come true
and everyone envied her.

"I needn't worry about you as a rival any more. Now
I can work through the list on my own," Bonnie said
gleefully.

"What do you mean?"

"You and David. That's kismet. That's perfect unity and harmony. He's divine. Together you make the perfect couple. You'll never meet a better guy. End of story and they'll all live happily ever after."

Lit's heart died a little when Bonnie said that, but she kept her feelings to herself.

Then in August, disaster struck. She discovered she was carrying David's child. He had just qualified with a first-class honours degree and was working in one of the new software firms in a nice new industrial estate on the southside.

"We'll get married. I was going to ask you anyway. I love you. We're a pair. Let's get married. Say yes! I'll soon have enough money for a deposit on a house. We'll buy a little starter home and then when we're on our feet, we'll move to wherever you want."

"I can't even think about that now. Please, David, don't put me under extra pressure. We'll talk about it when the baby is born."

Lit felt like the world was closing in on top of her, her life mapped out for her before she even knew what she wanted – the little house, the family, the mortgage. A terrible image of hanging out nappies on a windy day and cooking shepherd's pie dinners and wearing fluffy slippers and sitting next to David on a pink dralon sofa, flashed in front of her eyes.

Coming to terms with the idea of becoming a mother was scary enough. She felt like she was standing on the edge of an abyss – tumbling into an unknown and frightening world. Babies were ugly little things that screamed and kept you awake at night. Any house with a baby that she had ever been in smelled of puke and sour milk. Women who had babies lost their figures, went grey overnight, got stretch marks that they could store their jars of Sudocream in, and frequently went mad. All this was made even scarier by the fact that she had no mother, no map to navigate from, no-one to reassure her when things went strangely.

She dreaded breaking the news to her father. Even then he was elderly – in his seventies. The shock might affect his health. Besides they weren't what might be called close. They were at that stage in the parent-child relationship which psychologists imaginatively call 'the breaking of attachment bonds'. Between Lit and Dandy it mostly consisted of him avoiding her as much as possible and her dumping a major door-slamming tantrum on him about once a week. Telling him she was pregnant was the first really grown-up thing she'd had to do in her life thus far.

When she did tell him, he responded in typical Dandy fashion.

"And what the hell do you know about bringing up babies? You couldn't even look after the dolls I used to buy you!"

Apart from that, he was mercifully silent on the subject.

Auntie Sheila, who had reared seven children and knew all there was to know about every conceivable subject under the sun, was sent for. Each month Auntie Sheila would take it upon herself to familiarise Lit with the business of birth and motherhood. By the seventh month, Auntie Sheila had succeeded in driving her into a state of advanced panic over the trials and tribulations of parenthood.

First there was the birth. Auntie Sheila knew a woman who had lain in labour for five days before being delivered of her baby. Auntie Sheila knew another neighbour who had given birth to a twelve-pound baby who had to have stitches halfway up her back. And then terrible things could happen to the baby in childbirth. He could strangle on the umbilical chord. His brain could get squashed. There were forceps deliveries and stirrups and Caesarean sections.

If Lit and the baby did come through the ordeal of birth relatively unscathed, there was all the stuff that happened afterwards. If Lit didn't breastfeed the baby he might become malnourished and need counselling. If he was a boy and he wasn't breastfed he might become gay. Breastfeeding had to be done, but Lit could say goodbye to her shapely breasts. By the time she was finished breastfeeding, which she would have to do for a year at least, her nipples would be hanging down to her waist like two raisins in two crushed brown-paper bags. It was also true that Lit's hair was going to fall out and that her face would be wrinkled beyond repair from screaming her way through the birth. Added to that her teeth would begin to rot and fall out. But wouldn't it all be worth it? Lit would also have to guard against the baby blues, which Auntie Sheila said would surely turn into serious post-natal depression when there was no husband on the scene. If Lit got post-natal depression, she would most probably be suicidal, homicidal and would do awful things to her baby. Mrs Brannigan's daughter had got post-natal depression and started thinking she was the Blessed Virgin or was it Diane from *Cheers*?

Lit might have started early with pre-natal depression if it hadn't been for Bonnie. Each evening, Bonnie would call over with a chop suey from the Chinese takeaway. Together in Lit's bedroom, they would discuss the latest development while Lit guzzled down the chop suey at an alarming rate. Sometimes Bonnie was dispatched for a second helping.

"Piles – that's disgusting! I thought only old men got piles!" Bonnie was horrified.

"Don't you remember the nuns saying that we shouldn't sit on the radiators because it would give us piles? Well, they were right."

"What does a pile look like?"

"I don't know. I haven't looked and I'm not going to. Now have I told you about the foot cramps?"

By the end of the nine months Bonnie had reached breaking-point.

"Jesus! Piles, cramps, migraines, chilblains, backache, swollen feet, swollen ankles, swollen everything as far as I can see, exhaustion, cleaning fits in the middle of the night, heartburn, indigestion, flatulence – I am never getting pregnant and I will never, never ever have sex again – without using a safe method of contraception."

Lit realised she would have to take drastic action. Each month, she saved every penny of her allowance and the money she earned from her part-time job in the advertising department of a daily newspaper. She was good at saving when she put her mind to it. Anyway, what could she spend money on? She couldn't drink or smoke. She couldn't buy nice clothes or even go anywhere exciting because as the months went by she felt increasingly ugly. The movies were out because even the most tacky schmaltzy films made her cry and comedies made her feel like vomiting. There was no point in buying books because her normally astute brain seemed to have deteriorated into congealed porridge. The best she could manage were the magazines in the hairdressers with articles about how to make the perfect creme caramel and when to plant herbaceous perennials.

My life is over, she thought. Perhaps I should just marry David and be done with it. At least he loves me.

And there are worse things in life than a windswept line of washing and a pink dralon sofa.

Still, she kept rigidly to her savings plan and by the eighth month, she had almost a thousand pounds saved. Her plan was simple. She rehearsed it every night throughout the last six weeks of her pregnancy, in between avidly devouring all the drawings and descriptions of babes in the womb that she could lay her hands on and eating whole blocks of banana ice cream.

Once the child was born, she would stay in the hospital long enough to recuperate then go home as planned. When the child's health and wellbeing were well established, she would go to the long-haul travel agent in town and book a single one-way ticket to Rio de Janeiro. She would pack two suitcases. A little one with all the baby's favourite things and the white cardigan Auntie Sheila had made her knit to keep her mind occupied, then a big one, with her things, including some photos of the baby.

She would wait until dark, when the baby was fed and clean and sleeping and she would sneak into Holles Street and deposit him somewhere safe and warm with his little suitcase. Then she would set off for a new life in Rio.

It seemed a perfectly simple and logical plan. The baby deserved someone better than her. She deserved better than to be a mother at nineteen. Strangely, the thought of adoption had never entered her head. The plan to run away to Rio seemed the only option – a fact that now made her realise how very young and immature she was then. Or how very trapped and desperate she felt.

But she never got to Rio. Instead of a five-day labour, Richie was delivered without forceps or stirrups after six hours and an epidural. She had no stitches, not even a sore bum. She watched in sympathy and horror as the other women on the ward perched themselves on cushions shaped like large inflated polo-mints and heard them squeal in agony in the toilets as they tried to relieve themselves.

Richie was a perfectly normal and healthy eight pounds and five ounces, not twelve pounds, and when she examined her face in the mirror, two days after he was born, she was relieved to see that although she looked tired and drained there were no grey hairs and no wrinkles at all. Most of all, she loved her baby's funny little face the minute she saw him and it was that little face more than anything that put paid to her plans for Rio.

"I will never abandon you," she whispered into his tiny little ear when the ward was quiet and everyone was asleep. "From now on, everything in my life takes second place to you."

She did get depressed though. After the initial excitement, after Bonnie examined his willie and pronounced him a future contender for Category 1 of The List, after Dandy came and patted her hand and told her that it would all be fine and wasn't he the grandest little chap, after watching David lovingly cradle his new son, after all that, the depression came trundling in like an unstoppable train. She went from joy and love and dreams of the future with her baby, to a pit of despair where it frightened her to think beyond the next hour, where she fretted when the baby was awake and worried when he was asleep.

She kept it to herself, putting on a brave face when visitors called to the house, presenting herself as a cool, calm and collected mother, outwardly serene, inwardly fearing for her sanity.

And despite Auntie Sheila's vast knowledge and experience of everything pre-natal, peri-natal and post-natal, it was not her but Dandy who first recognised his daughter's distress.

She was sitting in the garden, ferociously guarding Richie as he slept in his carry-cot, like a cat watching over her kittens.

He sat down beside her.

"Going to be a big lad," he said.

She nodded.

"He'll be spoilt rotten. Do you think he'll be a hurler or a footballer?"

She shrugged apathetically.

Then he patted her hand. A pat on the hand from Dandy was the equivalent of ten treacly hugs from Auntie Sheila. In fact it was probably more potent.

"I'm sorry your mother isn't here, Laetitia. I'm not much use. I'm old and I don't know the right things to say or even the right questions to ask."

The tears welled up inside her, great heaving gasps that she had no control over. It was the one thing she hadn't talked about to anybody. But becoming a mother herself had brought her own motherless childhood back with a vengeance. To his credit, Dandy had seen it when no-one else had.

"Is there anything that you'd like me to do?"

She looked down at Richie who was sleeping peace-fully and sucking his fist. What am I afraid of, she thought to herself. If this old man beside me could rear two girls virtually single-handed, then I sure as hell can manage one boy.

"There is one thing," she said. "Send Auntie Sheila home. If I hear one more horror story about cot deaths and babies choking to death on unattended bottles and having to have skin grafts on their bottoms because of neglected nappy rash, I think I might just strangle her."

# CHAPTER 10

Lit was relieved that her only luggage was a briefcase when she saw the tangled mass of travellers huddling around the baggage belts in Heathrow. She passed swiftly through customs and strode purposefully across the arrivals hall to the taxi rank. The visit to Auntie Florence would be harrowing enough. Why make it any worse by arriving at the hospital stressed out and frazzled from the London Underground? She was disconcerted to see a long queue at the taxi rank though cabs were pulling up at regular intervals. She made a quick calculation and found that her wait wouldn't be longer than ten minutes. That would still be less time than finding the underground and getting a ticket and finding the right platform.

She called Maura to check for any messages and spent the remaining time scanning through a few press releases.

After about seven minutes, she found that she was only third in the queue. She slipped the papers into her briefcase and then it was her turn.

"Wimbledon, please," she said, sliding into the back seat of the cab.

The hackney driver looked at her as though she had asked to be taken to Area 54. Perhaps he hadn't understood her accent.

"Excuse me," she said more slowly. "I said

Wimbledon. Can you take me there?"

"You're joking me, luv."

"No. No, I'm not joking. What do you mean? Is there a problem?"

"'Aven't you 'eard of The Tennis? This is Tennis fortnight – today's the quarter-finals!"

Lit raised one eyebrow slightly and looked coldly down her nose at him. She surveyed him for a moment with withering disdain. "I'm sure the next man will be more obliging . . ." She slid out of the taxi quickly and turned to go.

"Look, luv, no offence – but no 'ackney's gonna bring you to Wimbledon. They'll all tell you the same thing." His eyes were seeking out the next person in the queue.

Lit's annoyance was growing and it wasn't just at the taxi-man. These were the sorts of things which sent her temper flying off the Richter Scale. She could take death, birth, single motherhood, illness, broken love affairs, even losing a big contract in her stride. But minor frustrations like the vacuum cleaner losing suction or her Beauty Flash Balm going missing before an important function, or having to take the train instead of a taxi – minor frustrations like that could push her over the edge. She longed to lay her hands on the person who had first said those oft-quoted words '*It is better to travel than to arrive*' and wring every bone in their body before depositing them in Heathrow Airport for a week.

"Tell you what you should do . . ."

"What?" she said, pouting like a teenager who has been told to make their own way to school on a cold wet morning.

"Take the Underground to Waterloo . . . "

"Yeah . . . yeah, thanks."

She stood back from the queue and watched furiously

123

as a happy-looking young couple took her place in the cab. But there was nothing for it. She trudged off to the Heathrow Underground station and studied the map there for a good ten minutes. She thought about Seán Tallon's suggestion of going to Waterloo and taking the fast train from Waterloo to Wimbledon. But when she looked at the map, that didn't make any sense at all. Surely it was taking her miles out of her way. It would be far quicker to go to Victoria, on to Stockwell and get the Northern Line to South Wimbledon.

Delighted that with a little time and logical thought she had figured out a much less time-consuming route, she boarded the train. She changed at Acton for a train to Victoria, but the train was going northbound and she ended up in Paddington and had to retrace her steps. When she got to Victoria, the southbound Victoria line was closed for essential repairs so she had to go on to Embankment to link up with the Northern Line.

By the time she reached South Wimbledon tube station, she was very grimy, very sticky and very cross. Who did Seán Tallon think he was? The Sherpa Tensing of the London Underground? Perhaps he was a trainspotter. That would make sense. She imagined him sneaking out of his house on Saturday mornings in a green anorak with a little wireback notebook and a pair of binoculars, sipping from his flask of tea and drooling at the mouth every time he saw a high-speed locomotive. Some people lead such sad lives, she thought, as she stepped out of South Wimbledon Station to hail a cab.

But that was the final ignominy because the cabs didn't even think it worth their while to stop at South Wimbledon – which she discovered was some two miles from the main Wimbledon Station where the nearest taxi rank was.

The grimy 1930s station housed an even grimier newsagent's. She bought a *Daily Mail* because it was the only paper with headlines smaller than three inches. She bought a large bag of peanut M & Ms because she was cross and she bought a bottle of tepid still water. She trudged off once more trying to look cool and walk elegantly in the stifling heat. The soles of her black slingback kitten-heel Manolo Blahnik shoes stuck uncomfortably to the base of her feet. Her designer suit clung stickily to her skin. The strap of the leather handbag that Bonnie had brought her from Bergdorf Goodman in New York cut into her shoulders. She vowed that next time, she would travel in a light cotton track suit with M & S terry-lined foot-gloves and a little canvas rucksack.

In between popping peanut M & Ms and sipping from the bottle of tepid water she cursed the humid heat of the city, the person who had invented high heels and Seán Tallon because he seemed like a good person to curse under the circumstances. At this very moment, he was probably sitting at his desk unable to work because of the venomous curses Lit was raining down on him. At the very least, his ears must be burning.

After what seemed like a century, she found a bus stop and stood shifting from one sticky-sandalled foot to the other, moving her bag from one shoulder to the other, waiting for a bus to come along. This time she was lucky and, in a matter of minutes, she found herself at the main station taxi rank.

"Perhaps I'm getting spoilt," she said to herself as she ate a small feta-cheese salad with no dressing (a self-imposed punishment because of the M & Ms) in a quiet little café near the station. Once upon a time the thought of taking a taxi anywhere would have seemed like outrageous indulgence. And even five years earlier the very idea of owning a pair of Manolo Blanik sandals would have been unthinkable. Cursing them now seemed like heresy somehow. Instead of cursing, she should be counting her blessings.

When Richie was small, neither she nor he ever owned anything new. His toys were second-hand and invariably had bits missing. She used to wonder if it would affect him psychologically to always have things with bits missing – train-sets minus a vital bit of track, jig-saws minus a vital three pieces, books with the last pages torn out. The only complete toys Richie ever had were from David, and Lit used to get so anxious about these wonderfully complete toys that she would hardly let him play with them. Once David had brought Richie a big state-of-the-art Meccano crane with a motor and full working bits. When it was finally assembled, she insisted that he put it up on the top shelf in his room and issued dire warnings that he was never to take it apart.

As for Lit, she learned to make do and mend. When Bonnie and her other friends turned out for graduation in puffball skirts and big shoulders, Lit had to endure the humiliation of appearing in an old pink Laura Ashley skirt and blouse. She couldn't even afford to go to the graduation ball. And besides no-one on Bonnie's List had much interest in being seen with a single mother in those days.

Five years later, when she packed Richie off to school, Lit was still wearing the same old clothes. Bonnie, now in her first job, had started wearing power suits and lethal-looking stiletto heels. Although, looking back, it was a blessing to be poor in the eighties because she had been saved the humiliation of plum-streaked fringes down to the chin or equally ghastly frizzy perms, of frills on everything, of wearing high heels with leggings or stonewashed jeans, of making sure her shoulder-pads didn't slip embarrassingly down the sleeve of her jacket.

For five years she and Richie survived on a meagre welfare allowance. She refused to take a job. She refused all but the smallest help from David because she did not want to feel in any way obliged to him. Dandy helped out whenever he could, but he too was surviving on his pension and the few savings he had put by. Bonnie contributed with little treats to the cinema or the occasional weekend away. But, all in all, for the first five years of Richie's life, they lived on the poverty line.

The big emotional break from Richie, the moment that she had been dreading since the day he was born, finally came seven weeks after his fifth birthday when he was packed off to primary school. For weeks beforehand, Lit wouldn't talk to anybody and nobody except Richie could talk to her. For five years, he had been the centre of her life and she of his. She had never experienced such fierce love, such an uncomplicated bond between two humans. Richie brought her daisy-chains from the garden, painted pictures of her, brought bowls of dry cereal to her bedroom in the morning. Every night when she tucked him into bed, he would wrap his small arms around her neck and say: "I love you, Mammy. When I grow up I'm never going to get married. I'm going to stay here and look after you, and get a job that pays lots of money – like driving a crane – and buy a big house with a moat around it and castle walls – and we'll drive around in the biggest car in the world and –"

"Of course you will!"

On his first day at school, Bonnie and Dandy stood at

the school gates with Lit as she fought back the tears and reluctantly nudged her son off into the big bad world.

"Give 'em hell, Richie!" said Bonnie and she slipped a cherry-flavoured lollipop into his satchel. "And remember – anybody messes with you, I've got five big brothers – all over six foot four! Have fun."

Richie studied her earnestly as she made her little speech. He swung an old plastic carrier-bag which contained his books and his lunch by his side.

Dandy leaned forward and shook his hand and patted his head. "Make sure you get picked for the hurling team."

Lit fought back the tears as she took him by the hand and deposited him with Miss Casey, his new teacher.

"Bye, Mammy."

"Bye, big man."

At home she sat at the kitchen table sipping weak instant coffee and sobbing inconsolably. Bonnie was less than sympathetic. "What's this? Tears? Get a grip, woman!"

"You don't understand. You don't know what it's like to be a mother. I've lost him! It's over."

Bonnie poured herself a cup of coffee. "Got any biscuits?"

"We finished the packet last night. No more until I do the shopping on Friday."

"Right!" Bonnie barked. "Time to stop this martyr business! I hate it when you do the martyr and you've been doing it for five years now. Time to start living your own life again. Time to get a job, Lit Doran! Time to get a man!"

"There are no jobs – at least not for people with my qualifications."

"Then do something else!"

"Who would give me a job? What man would even look at me?"

"No. You're right. You just stay here all day making shepherd's pie with cheap mince meat and assembling Rice-Krispie buns, and running out of Yellow Pack Fig Rolls, and making pots of tea with reused tea bags, until Richie is eighteen. Yeah, and those green leggings and moon boots should last for another ten years at least. And as for a man – you're right. No man would have you!" She looked Lit up and down. "Look at you! You're pathetic. Your hair's a mess. Your posture is gone to hell. Your skin looks like an old turnip. And to be honest, you've turned into a right old bore!"

"Meaning?"

"Meaning – all you ever talk about is Richie. Richie's uniform, Richie's runny nose, Richie's food allergies, Richie's tooth cavities . . . there's more to life than motherhood! When was the last time you read a book that wasn't *Thomas the Tank Engine*? When was the last time you went to a movie? I bet you don't even know who Tom Cruise is."

"Do so," Lit replied sulkily.

"Do you know the Berlin Wall is down? Do you know communism is collapsing all over Eastern Europe?"

"I do watch the news."

"The point is that you have to get back into the swing of things – before it's too late. You're only twenty-four for God's sake, but you're carrying on like you're sixty-four. I'm surprised you're not moaning about osteoporosis and cystitis!"

"Now that you mention it –"

Bonny cut in swiftly. "Come on, Lit! Fate dealt you a cruel blow. You handled it magnificently. But now it's time to face the world again."

"Bonnie. I'm scared. I haven't ever really worked. I have no confidence. I know on paper I have a good degree. But that was five years ago. And there aren't that many jobs about. And as for a man – that doesn't even bear thinking about. I don't even know if I could . . . well, you know . . ."

"No, I don't know. What?"

"All the stuff you do with men – the flirting, the eye contact, the body language, dating . . . sex . . . that sort of thing."

Bonnie rolled her eyes to heaven. "It's like riding a bicycle! You never forget. Just get up there and ride like the clappers. But first things first." She reached into her handbag and pulled out an envelope. "This is towards your self-esteem fund. Don't refuse it. I intend to make good on my investment."

Lit opened the envelope and found three hundred pounds inside. It had been years since she had seen so much money together. She was so astonished and touched she could hardly speak for a few moments.

"Self-esteem fund . . . what do you mean?"

"Hairdresser. Beauty parlour. Eyebrows, leg-wax – you can't wear leggings forever. Facial, manicure. Suit, shoes and handbag."

"I couldn't possibly –"

"Ah, ah!" Bonnie was at her bossiest. "No refusal, remember? Any money left over will be spent on a night in Leeson Street."

"Bonnie, I haven't been outside the door in five years, except to Cathy Brennan's wedding. I don't think I can do that any more."

"Course you can. You wouldn't believe the hunks that are about town these days."

"It wouldn't be right . . . Richie . . . I'm his mother. I just can't go clubbing and . . ."

But it was no use. The next day when Richie was dropped off to school, Lit was carted off to town and they spent the day on essential body maintenance, as Bonnie called it.

When Lit went to collect Richie, he hardly recognised her at first. Her hair was stylishly cropped with little blond streaks. Her face was lightly made up and her nails neatly manicured and polished. She was wearing a plum-coloured suit with black cone stilettos that put an attractive swagger in her walk – a far cry from the old moon-boots she had shuffled about in for the previous five years.

"You look different," he said appraising her changed appearance as they walked home in the warm September sunshine.

"I'm going to get a job, Richie. Is that OK? Then we might be able to have little treats now and then . . . maybe even a holiday by the sea."

His eyes lit up. "When can you start?"

Bonnie knew of a company who were looking for someone to man the phones and type a few letters. The office was in the ground floor of a large ugly building in Baggot Street. They were a small American company trying to sell car-phones. It didn't seem to Lit like much of a business, but she went for the interview anyway.

Mr Butler, the manager, interviewed her. He had a smooth red face with glasses that made his eyes seem bigger. He wore belted trousers which he hitched up so that they folded into the cheeks of his bum.

"Can you type?"

"I can learn."

"We're looking for someone who can type."

"It's only pressing buttons. How hard can it be?" said Lit, desperation and embarrassment making her defensive. "I've learned much harder things. What's the big deal?" Oh God, she shouldn't have said that – it made her sound cheeky and difficult.

"Do you know how to lay out a business letter?" he continued.

"I can learn that too."

He sighed. "Have you ever worked in an office? Worked at reception? Operated a switchboard? Used a filing system?"

This was hopeless. Lit stood up and gathered up her bag and the CV that Bonnie's friend had typed for her. "It's obvious from my CV that I haven't done any of those things," she said. "I have a first-class honours degree in Marketing and Languages. I have raised a son on a small income and never got into debt. I care for an elderly parent single-handed. I can mend a washing machine, fix a boiler pump, change a plug, clean gutters and replace an element in a kettle. Oh and for your information – I can make a cup of coffee."

Mr Butler was gobsmacked. He watched her turn angrily on her heel, stalk out and slam the door.

He pulled open the door and rushed after her, shouting, "Wait! When can you start?"

"I don't understand." She thought he might be making fun of her.

"I mean you're hired. A hundred pounds a week after tax. I know it's not much – but it's a start."

Lit almost ran back and kissed him. But she didn't. She straightened herself up and composed her face. "Thank you, Mr Butler," she said coolly. "I think you'll be quite happy you hired me."

With her first wage packet she bought Richie a

Teenage Mutant Ninja Turtles schoolbag and a matching lunchbox. She also bought him the complete (meaning all pages intact) works of Roald Dahl.

At Hallowe'en, she rented a small house in Rosslare near the beach. Together, they travelled to Wexford on the train and took a taxi to the little house, which was made of tin and old wooden sleepers from a ship wrecked many years earlier. Every day they walked the beach and explored the sand dunes and the rock pools. Even though it was cool and breezy, they managed to have a swim, or at least a paddle, most days. In the evening, she cooked dinner with lots of Richie's favourite treats for dessert – Arctic Roll ice cream, chocolate fridge cake, fudge brownies. At night she tucked him into bed and read to him from *Charlie and The Chocolate Factory*. Then she would pour herself a glass of wine and look out at the sea. It seemed as though the world was slowly opening up to her. She had never been happier in her life, she concluded.

She had been working for Mr Butler in Motorphone for almost a year when he informed her that one of the directors from the parent company in Newark was due in Ireland. There was to be a round of high-powered business meetings because the company was expanding. It all sounded very important. Lit would have to attend meetings in banks and hotels and take notes and type up minutes, and look after the visiting director. She would have to book his accommodation in the Shelbourne Hotel and organise some entertainment for him during his month's stay in Ireland. Mr Butler suggested a weekend in Ashford Castle because the director was a keen angler and his ancestors had come from County Mayo.

Bonnie was enthralled with the glamour of it all.

"What's he like? This director fella? Do you suppose he's married? God. He's probably one of those tall handsome preppy Yanks with a sexy Boston drawl and a loft apartment in Manhattan. This could be your big chance."

"I imagine that he's small and pudgy with a bald patch and glasses. He probably has a daughter my age. Besides, this is business, Bonnie. If I get it right, Mr Butler has promised me a salary increase – maybe even a more administrative role. Now where should I bring him in Dublin?"

Bonnie was full of ideas . . . theatre for the new Brian Friel play, a trip to Powerscourt and Glendalough, a round of golf in Portmarnock, perhaps the races or an international rugby match.

Lit was dispatched in a taxi to collect her charge from the airport. She sat in the back of the taxi feeling proud of herself and her achievements, feeling important and successful. When the taxi pulled up she walked smartly to the information desk. By now she had perfected the high-heeled swagger and she was able to swing her hips just enough to look elegant but not enough to make her look like she was seeking attention. She felt a bit like Alexis Carrington. And despite the way that she and Bonnie used to snigger at *Dynasty*, she realised it wasn't such a bad feeling at all.

"I'm meeting a passenger from JFK Airport – the eleven thirty flight."

"Name?"

"Mr Harry Menton."

Lit finished her coffee and hailed a taxi outside Wimbledon Station to bring her to St Theresa's Hospice for the dying.

"Is it anywhere near The Tennis?" she enquired.

"No, luv. Opposite direction. Otherwise you'd have to walk, I'm afraid."

In the quiet bedroom of the Hospice, she held Auntie Florence's hand as the old lady struggled to make some acknowledgement of her visit.

"Thank you for coming," she finally wheezed.

Lit squeezed her hand.

"You've a good heart. Dandy brought you up to have a good heart. Not like that other one."

Florence was referring to Lit's much older sister Azelia, who had run off to Argentina with a bankrupt horse trainer and never been seen or heard of since, except for a card at Christmas. Florence had gone to the trouble of putting on lipstick. It looked to Lit like a gash of scarlet on a faded monochrome portrait.

"Dandy sends his love. He says you're still his favourite little sister and you still owe him for all the schoolwork he forged for you."

Aunt Florence managed a weak smile. "Somehow, I can imagine me dead, but never your father. He's too full of life. He always was."

"I'll tell you the truth about my father. He's a cantankerous, lecherous, contrary, sly, spoilt ninety-two-year-old. He drives me crackers. He gangs up with my son against me. He says the work that I do is meaningless and cheapens everything. He flirts with my friends when they come to call. He drinks far too much and he smokes horrible cigars which stink out the house."

"*Age shall not wither him . . .*" smiled Aunt Florence. "How's little Richie?"

The last time Aunt Florence had seen Richie he was seven and making his first communion.

"Little Richie is big. Bigger than me. He has nice brown eyes, broad shoulders and girls ringing up and pestering him. He's working in a supermarket for the summer."

"Sponge my neck, Laetitia dear," Florence whispered.

Lit found a white facecloth, held it under the tap and squeezed the water from it. She pressed it gently to Aunt Florence's neck. "Is that better?"

Florence nodded and squeezed Lit's hand and they were quiet. An hour passed and Lit thought she might be asleep. It was time to be going if she didn't want to miss her flight back to Dublin. Gently, she tried to move her hand but Aunt Florence gripped her with quite surprising strength.

"Laetitia. Thank you for coming. For making the effort. I had been longing to see you. Goodbye, dear."

She patted Lit's hand and pushed it away. It was time to go.


# CHAPTER 11

The return journey to Heathrow from Wimbledon via Waterloo was swift and painless and, sitting in the departure lounge, Lit wondered at the sort of person who could be as socially inept as Seán Tallon but yet so practical. She imagined that he was the sort of person who could save the planet before breakfast but who couldn't string two entertaining words together on a date. Like the Clark Kent of the banking world.

There were several messages on her mobile which she listened to before deleting the unimportant ones. A message from Bonnie to say that she would collect Lit from the airport was deleted. A message from the graphics artist confirming an appointment was stored. The last message was from Conrad Budd. Lit's heart insolently skipped a beat when she heard the voice.

*Hello, Lit. Conrad here. I'd like to firm up on a few things about this newspaper article the Gazette are doing. How about lunch tomorrow at the Valmont – one o'clock? Call if this is inconvenient. Look forward to seeing you.*

The last sentence was said with a softness that shot through her like a bolt of very pleasant lightning. Little goose-pimples shot up the back of her neck and she felt a delightful warmth in the pit of her stomach.

Instantly she dialled up his number to confirm the appointment but stopped at the last digit. He had said: *Call if this is inconvenient.* Then she shouldn't call if it was convenient. She ransacked her brain for any possible pretext on which to call him.

No, that wouldn't do. She was being pathetic and it would have to stop. She wasn't attracted to him, never was and never would be. It was just Bonnie whipping up a romantic storm for the fun of it. It was important not to confuse Bonnie's fantasies with her own more realistic appraisal of the situation.

She redefined the situation in her head as the plane prepared for take-off. Lit Doran was a successful owner of a PR company. Lit Doran was reasonably attractive. Conrad Budd was a successful entrepreneur. Conrad Budd was reasonably attractive. Business had temporarily brought them together. It was as simple as that. And besides, Conrad Budd was engaged. And despite what Bonnie said, being engaged was akin to being married.

By the time the plane touched down in Dublin, Lit had firmly uprooted any tender succulent feelings for

Conrad Budd and cast them ruthlessly aside. Nothing in the world would make her have feelings for him.

Armed with a new sense of purpose and a pride in her own emotional discipline, she made her way smugly to where Bonnie was waiting in her car. She sat into the rusting orange Toyota Corolla and hugged Bonnie. The engine spluttered reluctantly to life and jerked and stalled a few times as Bonnie revved and cursed. At last she coaxed the car out of the carpark, through the ticket barriers and they made unsteady progress onto the dual carriageway. Traffic was heavy, moving at a nerve-jangling five miles per hour.

Bonnie swerved suddenly into the hard shoulder, swiftly overtook about ten cars and indicated to get into the right lane again. A man in a black Ford Escort beeped his horn and gave her the two fingers. She rolled down her window and shouted at him.

"Fuck off, wanker!"

"Bonnie! Don't!" Lit pleaded. "You don't know what he might do. Leave it."

Bonnie rolled up her window and said dismissively, "Probably can't get it up. Stupid prick."

"You did try to cut in front of him."

"That's not the point. He should have more manners. I might have been in the wrong lane by accident. How is he to know I'm not a tourist who's just not used to driving in Dublin?"

"Are you coming to my dinner party?" Lit asked to change the subject.

"If I don't get a better offer. Who else is going? Should I bring a bowl of coleslaw?"

"It's not that sort of party. It's formal . . . caterers, waiters, a pianist probably . . ."

"Are you sure you want me there? I might do

something silly."

"Like what?" Lit enquired nonchalantly though she knew precisely the sort of thing Bonnie could get up to at parties.

Discreet sex with one single and available man was the very least that Bonnie might get up to. Her men were rarely single or unattached and usually the entire house knew if Bonnie was engaged in having 'a right good shag' as she liked to call it.

Bonnie giggled conspiratorially. "Do you remember the time you found me in bed with the guy from the American football team?"

Lit grimaced at the sordidness of it. Bonnie's eyes, on the other hand, glistened with fond remembrance.

"You're very promiscuous sometimes, Bonnie. Do you know that? You should be more careful. What if you got a bad reputation or some horrible disease – like Sally Flaherty who got those awful warts and had to have them burnt off. It's disgusting."

Bonnie scoffed dismissively. "Do you know what I read lately? I read that promiscuous women are far happier and more mentally stable than women who are monogamous or celibate."

That was about the silliest thing Bonnie had ever said. Lit knew for a fact that if a woman was promiscuous it was because her father hadn't loved her enough and that if she was going around trying to sleep with every Tom, Dick and Harry, it was a sign that she was deeply unhappy and unfulfilled – like Marilyn Monroe or Vivien Leigh. Happy contented women didn't need to sleep around. In fact, happy contented women could manage quite nicely without men.

"Well, what if you got AIDS?" she countered. "It hasn't gone away, you know."

"Lit Doran, you are such a prude. Sex is just sex. Why do you always make such a big deal out of it? It's just another means of human contact – like conversation or dancing. I can talk with whoever I like. I can dance with whoever I like. I can have sex with whoever I like."

"Say what you like but men still don't like women who sleep around."

"Oh, you're very wrong there, Laetitia dear. Men absolutely love women who sleep around. They just don't want to be married to them. And I'm not interested in marriage. So there!"

"Then you're going to end up a sad old slapper in a little flat in Sandymount – you'll be like Blanche Dubois and the schoolboys – a mad old nymphomaniac. You'll have to pay gigolos to have sex with you and they'll steal your savings and then you'll end up on the street without a penny to your name – offering your body for a swig of watered-down meths!"

Bonnie was quite amused by Lit's doomsday scenario. It was like one of her mother's dire warnings on what happened to loose women. "So am I good enough to come to your wonderful dinner party or not?"

Lit disapproved of Bonnie's behaviour sometimes, but she also knew only too well that Bonnie was generally the life and soul of any party. Bonnie would talk to anybody and made everybody she talked to feel as though they were the most wonderful remarkable people in the world. Unless she didn't like them.

"Of course you're coming. I need you there to break the ice. And besides, Conrad Budd will be there – that is, if you're interested. I may have a problem about him being engaged – but you don't."

Lit was quite pleased with this last suggestion. It was sure proof that she had completely quashed any lingering attraction to Conrad. Bonnie had a thing about him – so why not let her get it out of her system? It wouldn't mean anything to Lit. If Bonnie wanted to shag Conrad Budd's brains out she wouldn't feel jealous about it. And if he did make a play for Bonnie, then in a way that would prove him to be a love-rat – not capable of remaining faithful this girlfriend.

But instead of being excited and delighted at the prospect of a night's flirtation with Conrad, Bonnie slipped her a strange sidelong glance and said nothing.

"Matt will be there and Maura who has just broken up with Barry the Bastard Owens. The Cornwells will be there. Lots of people – about twenty-five in all. Dermot O'Driscoll from the IRFU . . . some boring health people, Manus from Northern Lads . . . oh, and Matt's friend Seán Tallon."

"Who's he?"

Lit yawned. "Our financial advisor."

She was very tired now. She longed to be at home, wallowing in a big warm bath and listening to Classic FM. She had a regular music routine – loud contemporary rock music in the morning, undemanding pop music in the afternoon and in the evenings soft jazz or classical music – Myles Davis or Mozart – nothing too precious or demanding. She yawned again. They were at Baggot Street Bridge.

"I can walk from here," she said half-heartedly.

"Crawl, more like. You must have had a tough day."

"I did," she said and recounted the long rigmarole about Seán Tallon and the taxis and the trains.

Bonnie laughed. "Jesus! You are one stubborn woman! Why didn't you just do what the guy said?"

"Because I don't like him particularly," said Lit coolly.

"Why? What's wrong with him?"

"See for yourself at the party." Then she added crossly. "And I defy you to find anything attractive in Seán Tallon. If you end up fancying him, then you should seek counselling. It would be like fancying the FTSE or that statue of Daniel O'Connell in O'Connell Street."

"Why? Is he ugly? Old-fashioned dress sense? Wear a hairpiece? What?"

"No. He's not ugly I suppose. He dresses unremarkably and has a full head of fair hair."

"What then?"

"I'm not one to judge . . ."

"Yes, but, and?"

"But, I think the man has a severe personality disorder. That's all I'm saying. It wouldn't be fair to make any other comment."

"And Conrad Budd – are you still gagging for him?"

"I am not. These days there's nothing special about him at all."

Bonnie swung the car into Lit's road and parked crookedly outside her house.

"I've still got the photo."

"What photo?"

"You know . . . calves, thighs, shoulders . . . I know! I'll bring it to the party. We can have a good laugh."

Lit was horrified at the very idea. It would be suicidally embarrassing if Conrad Budd discovered that she'd had a silly teenage crush on him in college. It might even affect their business relationship. She had spent the past five years cultivating a serious professional outlook and projecting the image of a capable and successful businesswoman. Anything which might make her look ridiculous could not be tolerated.

"Bonnie, you can't! You mustn't! That was all a hundred years ago. We were kids. Please don't!"

"Why are you so worried? If it was just a business thing, you should see the joke. So would he. I'll bet he sees the joke anyway. Bound to be flattered and amused. I might even be able to dig up his old jersey."

Lit was horrified at what Bonnie might get up to. "I don't want him to be either flattered or amused. And if you're going to be so childish perhaps you'd better not come. You know I don't approve of that kind of behaviour."

"Ouuuh! Get you! Touchy, touchy . . . I'm only winding you up. I promise I will not produce a photo of Conrad's butt at the party. Is that OK? Or his jersey. Or tell him that you used to cycle past his house on your way home even though he lived in entirely the opposite direction."

"I did not. That's a lie. That was you!"

"Was it? I can't remember. Anyway, cross my heart and hope to die, I will not embarrass you in front of Conrad Budd."

"Thank you."

"Or any of your other guests," Bonnie added wickedly.

# CHAPTER 12

In the morning Lit prised Richie out of the bed and pointed him in the direction of the shower, the fridge and the bus. She could only hope that he would stay awake long enough on the bus not to miss his stop. Now she turned her attention to preparing her father for his visit to the doctor. When they had moved into the house, she had a specially large shower installed so that there was room to put a slatted garden chair into it. This was especially so that Dandy could have a sitting-down shower.

Getting Dandy to remove all his clothes took all her diplomatic and persuasive skills. Finally she resorted to threats.

"If you don't take off those long johns, I won't cook any meals for you for a week."

"Fair enough. You're an awful cook anyway. Richie will cook for me."

"Suit yourself. But Richie can only cook stuff that's frozen or for the microwave."

"That's intimidating and threatening behaviour to an elderly person. There must be something like Childline for old people like me who are being abused by their children. I think I'll phone them."

"Tell them you're calling because your daughter wants you to have a shower before she brings you to a doctor. I'm sure they'll send the police around to arrest me without delay. Now get those long johns off! I'll hold this towel up so I won't see anything."

Dandy slowly and awkwardly did as he was bid and sat on the slatted chair in the shower, like a naughty schoolboy in the dunce's chair.

An hour later, he was combed and dressed and sitting in the hallway muttering to himself. "I feel like a fucking Christmas turkey."

"Don't be vulgar. And don't be rude to the doctor. He's only doing his job."

"Thieves and vagabonds – the lot of them. Right, let's get going. Let's see what fate has in store for me today."

Dandy's humour didn't improve as they sat in the waiting-room. Lit thought enviously of Bonnie's dad who was only sixty-two and still working part-time in the bank. He played a round of golf most mornings and travelled abroad with his wife several times a year. He was always clean and smartly dressed and had pleasant easy manners. Lit had never heard him being cranky or vulgar.

"I don't want any whispering behind my back with the doctor."

"All right."

"And another thing, you're not to tell anybody I've been here."

"Fine."

"It's nobody else's business. They'll only start visiting me to see how bad I am. To see if I'm dying."

"True. Did you watch *North by Northwest* last night?"

"No, I didn't. Those old films are rubbish. I don't think I'll watch them any more. They're all waiting for me to die because I'm a lot older than them. But I won't give them the satisfaction. So you're not to tell them. Especially if it turns out that I am dying. Oh and by the way, if I do happen to die unexpectedly, there's a copy of my will in a locked box under my bed. The key is in an envelope under the carpet. And the deeds of the house in Templeogue . . . "

Lit was relieved when the door opened and Dr O'Connor called her father in. She sat in the waiting-room, leafing through *Hello* magazine, marvelling at the way celebrities cheapened themselves and their families to make a few quick bucks, pleased that she never wasted money buying it for herself. She allowed herself a few moments of looking forward to lunch with Conrad.

The Valmont wasn't exactly her favourite place though work occasionally took her there. It was full of old politicians on the take and young women on the make. It was the sort of place that certain journalists frequented, sniffing out and dishing out scandal, sitting in dark corners composing self-righteous articles about the outrageous villanies of other men. But it would be a chance to discuss the forthcoming article with Conrad. She could show him the draft press release and finalise a meeting with the director of the TV programme. She would just have time to shower and change after dropping Dandy home. She planned to wear her navy Ralph Lauren jacket and beige skirt, which were smart/casual New York chic.

After about ten minutes the door opened and Dandy reappeared. She tried to read his face but it was expressionless. Like a stone – like an ancient monument – full of history but yielding nothing.

"Mr Doran, I would like to speak to your daughter."

"Well, do it some other time. I'm not going to sit here like some naughty little schoolboy while you two discuss my innards and decide what detention you're going to give me."

"Fair enough. I'll call you on Monday, Lit, if that's OK."

"Thanks."

She held her father's coat and slid it up his arms. She turned down his collar and did up his buttons. There was a slight dribble at the corner of his mouth and she dabbed at it with a hankie. They walked in silence to the car.

Inside, she tried to put on his safety belt.

"Don't bother."

"Well, it's safer. Besides, it's the law."

"Safer. Safer than what? It's like having a boa constrictor across your chest. I drove for fifty years of my life without any safety belt. As for the law, what are they going to do? Arrest me? Ha! Besides . . . " He stopped.

"Besides what?"

"You might as well know. It appears that the doctors have finally found something wrong with me."

"How do you mean?"

"Apparently, having pooled the combined knowledge of about five different experts, having between them what – forty years of university education, they have come up with the startling conclusion that I'm dying."

"Oh nonsense! You're always dramatising things. You're just winding me up."

The car was in gear and jerked forward suddenly before coming to a halt. She shifted the gear into neutral and started again.

"Not nonsense. I have something in here I'm not supposed to have." He patted his stomach.

"A swollen liver probably."

"No! Some stupid bloody cancer or other. I can't actually feel it, but according to our learned friend, it's there all right. They say it's about the size of a mandarin orange and that it will grow to the size of a melon . . . but that it started out more grape-sized. If they had got it at the grape stage, then it mightn't have become a melon . . . but since it is now a mandarin orange there is simply no way of stopping it becoming a melon. He read out the report to me. I have to go and see some other specialist who'll no doubt tell me exactly what sort of a melon it's going to turn into . . . let's hope it's cantaloupe and not watermelon . . . and tell me I have even less time to live and charge twice as much."

"Stop it. Stop it!" Lit shouted.

It couldn't be. Dandy was going to live forever. Even Auntie Florence had said it. Dr O'Connor had said it. *He'll outlive us all. He'll live to be a hundred.* That's exactly what he said.

Dandy could see her brushing the tears from her face.

"Stop! Stop the car! Look what you're doing! You're going to hit that wall!"

She stopped. He put his gnarled, wrinkled, bruised old hand on hers.

"I'm sorry, I shouldn't have blurted it out like that. It was cruel. I'm so used to being at death's door that I think everyone else must see it in the same cavalier fashion. I'm not scared, Laetitia. Not at all. I just don't want you to be sad about it. After all, I've done a lot better than some Holy Joes. I'd like to be here with Richie for a while more, but it can't be helped."

The tears flowed freely now. He gave her his crumpled-up hanky.

"What else did the doctor say?"

"Maybe if I was lucky . . . six months. Oh yes . . . this'll make you laugh . . . when would I be ready to start chemotherapy? I told him he could take his chemotherapy and shove it up his well-padded arse!"

Lit smiled and the smile became a little laugh and before long both were laughing helplessly.

Back at the office, after phoning a tearful Azelia in Argentina to tell her about Dandy, she threw herself into a flurry of paperwork. It was the best way to deal with bad news. There was no point in dwelling on it. Not now at any rate. The best plan was to go on with life as normal and pretend nothing was wrong. Besides, there was nothing she could do. By mid-day she had set up preliminary meetings with two new clients and organised a function and press releases for a publishing company about to launch a new celebrity magazine. At ten to one, she suddenly jumped up in horror.

"Oh my God!"

"What in the name of Christ is wrong with you?" Maura exclaimed.

"Lunch – the Valmont – I have to go. Maura, get Conrad Budd on the phone! Tell him I may be a few minutes late. No wait! Tell him I had to bring my father to the doctor. No! No, don't tell him that!"

Maura folded her arms and asked, "Well, what would you like me to tell him?"

"Say I understand that he's a busy man and that I'm very sorry that I'm going to be a few minutes late and that of course if he'd rather cancel or reschedule I'll understand. Say that I'm sure he's the sort of man that's not used to being kept waiting and that . . . ."

Maura was transfixed. "Jesus! If I didn't know you better I'd say . . . well, I won't say . . . "

Lit knew exactly what Maura was implying and was quick to defend herself. "I'm all confused."

"I can see that."

"No. You don't understand. I've just had my dad at the doctor. And . . . the thing is, he's not that well."

"Sorry. I thought – no, but that would be silly. Going to pieces like that over a man . . . that's not your style."

"No. No, it's not. Now I have to go. Please call Conrad Budd and tell him that I'm on my way. Bye."

She swept out of the office and hailed a taxi.

Pat Sullivan had a proposition to put to the Stoneyfield Residents Association. And with this in mind he called a last-minute meeting in the upstairs room of The Cobbler. As usual Miss Dillon was ahead of time and the remainder turned up in dribs and drabs.

"What's this all about?" Gearóid demanded. "It better be important enough to drag all of us away from picket duty."

"Take your time, Pat dear," consoled Miss Dillon, patting his hand.

Pat placed the brown envelope on the table, took a deep breath and began. "The other night I met with someone who suggested that there might be a way of putting a stop to Conrad Budd's development."

"I'm all ears," chirped Fidelma. "Anything to cut that bastard down to size."

"Anything?" repeated Pat.

"Anything. And I mean anything. OK."

Pat shook his head. He had spent another disconcerting half hour with Brendan Browne and he came away oddly disturbed. Browne had put into his hands the means to defeat Budd. The two documents in the envelope were absolute proof. Pat Sullivan should have danced jigs all the way home. But he didn't. Instead, his mother's words danced in his head: *If you can't say something good about a person then keep your mouth shut.*

Brendan Browne had plenty of bad things to say about Conrad Budd, most of them libellous and unprovable and nothing to do with the proposed development.

Pat glanced guiltily at the envelope and took another deep breath. "Suppose we were to find out that –" He couldn't bring himself to say the words. "What if we discovered that Conrad Budd . . . that sums of money . . . that it is rumoured . . ."

With a swift move, Gearóid laid his hand firmly on the envelope. "We get the picture," he said briskly and snatched it up. "Someone with a vote took a bribe from Budd. Can we prove it?"

Pat eyed the forsaken envelope, sorry that he had allowed it slip so easily into the hands of a crude operator like Gearóid. "I'm not sure I can do this sort of thing.

Legitimate protest sure. But we're talking about a man's reputation here, a man's livelihood. Perhaps two livelihoods."

Gearóid ripped the contents from the envelope, scanned them briefly and allowed himself a small triumphant smile.

"You're not serious," snapped Fidelma. "If there's a way of stopping Budd that doesn't actually involve a clear breach of the law – well, I'm up for it. My house is going to be destroyed by this monstrosity. I'll probably never see daylight again. It's OK for you to be noble and fair-minded. You live in a road that won't be affected. I have my children to consider."

"I didn't know you had children, Fidelma dear," said Miss Dillon. "How nice."

"I don't have children. It's just a figure of speech. But I might have children. And why should they grow up in a house that has no daylight?"

"Fidelma's right," said Gearóid. "We can use this. I suggest we take a vote."

Pat shrugged. The Stoneyfield Residents Association was a democratic movement. He was only one of five remaining voices.

"Right then," continued Gearóid. "All those in favour of following up on allegations of corruption with regard to Conrad Budd's development of the Stoneyfield site, raise their right hand."

Fidelma, Gearóid, and Tom McNally each raised their right hands.

"All those against?"

Pat and Miss Dillon raised two forlorn hands.

Suddenly Gearóid was like a man possessed. He waved the envelope above his head in a gesture of victory.

"This will raise the morale of the troops! You just wait and see. This time tomorrow night, the room here will be packed. People know when their democratic rights have been infringed. People have a nose for corruption. You cannot put a stop to a people's right to self-determination – let the powers beware – we might even get a tribunal out of this – what a pleasure it will be to see this tyrant developer destroyed –"

"Give it a rest, Magill," Pat said wearily. "It's a small man that takes pleasure in destroying another's reputation."

"He's done it to himself. And if you got down off your high moral horse, you'd see that."

Pat regarded Gearóid with world-weary sadness. "I resign. I want no part in this. I'll do my picket duty and that's all."

He stood up and turned to leave.

"I'll do the same. If you don't mind," added Miss Dillon with frail dignity and together they walked out.

"Right, down to business," said Gearóid when they'd gone. "Tomorrow morning we'll go on a consciousness-raising tour of the streets. There's three of us. Let's each of us agree to guarantee ten people at the meeting tomorrow night. And each of those another ten and so on. Fidelma, will you take the minutes . . . oh and I want photocopies of these documents . . . ."

"Can we see them?" enquired Tom McNally hesitantly.

"No! Later – when I've decided what I'm – we're going to do."

Three hours later Gearóid and Brendan Browne sat hunched over two pints of Guinness in the Bayview Hotel.

Gearóid wasn't stupid. He had good insight into people. He wasn't a fool and though he was delighted with this new ammunition in his arsenal, there were one or two things about the whole scenario that didn't quite add up.

"I'll get straight to the point, Browne," he said stridently. "Why are you doing this? It doesn't make sense."

Browne's bloated face creased up into something approaching an inscrutable smile. He gave a short wheezy laugh. "You and I, Gearóid – we're men of the world. I won't insult your intelligence by lying."

Gearóid was glad they had got that much straight.

"I'm not well. Bad health. Let's call it clearing out the desk before I leave. Putting the record straight. Whatever you like."

"And you're prepared to admit that you took a bribe from Conrad Budd so that he could get on with his despicable monstrosity."

"I am."

"Even though your reputation will be in ruins."

Browne nodded and continued calmly. "You see, Gearóid, at the end of the day, to a politician like me, the people of Stoneyfield are more important than my reputation. What am I? One little man who had a moment of weakness! What is Stoneyfield? It's a whole history. It's generations of families. It's future generations of families. It's a community. It's a microcosm of mankind."

"Nice rhetoric but why don't you publicise this yourself? Why don't you go to the DPP? Why don't you go to the press? Why don't you take Conrad on yourself?"

Browne nodded with patient understanding. "I knew you'd ask that. And the simple answer is that I haven't the heart for the fight. Let the press or the courts do what they will. At least I will go to my grave knowing that I have redeemed myself by saving Stoneyfield after all. Better late than never, eh?"

Gearóid could think of nothing to say to that and so he drank deeply from his pint for a few silent moments.

"Think of me as the sinner on the cross who repented at the eleventh hour. Think of me that way and it all makes perfect sense."

"What's the next step then?"

"Oh, that's entirely your business. I have put the loaded gun in your hand. It's up to you where and when you shoot it off. Just one thing, Gearóid . . ."

"What's that?"

"Make sure it doesn't backfire."

# CHAPTER 13

The main reason that Lit wasn't keen on the Valmont was that Harry Menton used to take her there and as the taxi-driver dropped her off just outside the elaborate brass art-deco doors, she experienced a terrible sense of déjà vu, a sinking feeling in the pit of her stomach that her carefully constructed world of business success, financial security, status home in Dublin 4, elegantly restrained early Georgian and genuine Shaker furniture, size 10 figure and carefully co-ordinated wardrobe was about to start slowly crumbling about her ears. She knew that meeting Conrad Budd for a business lunch was an entirely different situation from meeting Harry Menton but, all the same, the restaurant brought back bad memories. And besides, despite the fact that she tried very hard not to think of Dandy, she was already in quite a melancholy mood.

While she had waited for Harry Menton at the information desk in Dublin Airport, Lit hoped that he wouldn't be too American. She liked Americans, but sometimes they didn't adapt well outside their own surroundings. Would Harry Menton be one of those awful people who had to trek around the country in search of his roots? Perhaps he'd be like John Wayne in *The Quiet Man* and say ghastly stupid things like "Woman of the house, where's me tay?" and "The hell I will!". She was quite worried about these things because she was to be his personal assistant and would have to spend a lot of time with him. He might have daughters called Colleen Erin and Kelly Shannon who did Irish dancing and wore dancing frocks which cost thousands of dollars.

She needn't have worried. Though when she first saw Harry Menton, he didn't strike her as anything special. He was tall, lean, fit-looking though his hairline was receding slightly which made him look older than his thirty-four years.

"Mr Menton? I'm Lit Doran. Mr Butler asked me to collect you."

She held out her hand and he shook it warmly and smiled pleasantly at her.

Looking back over it all, Lit realised now that she must have been a sitting duck. Harry Menton was the first man that had smiled nicely or appreciatively at her since her time in college with David. So though he wasn't strikingly handsome or delightfully witty, though he certainly wouldn't have made Category 1 or 4 on Bonnie's list, she was drawn to him straight away simply because she was flattered.

"It's a great pleasure to meet you, Lit," he said, grasping her hand for a fractional moment longer than necessary.

"I've arranged for your luggage to be sent on to the Shelbourne. Our taxi is outside."

"I'm completely in your hands," he said with a warm twinkle in his eyes.

She led the way, being extra careful that her high-heeled swagger suggested classy broad not sassy ride because she knew instinctively that he was observing her closely from behind. For a few moments she agonised about her bum. Then for a few moments longer she agonised about her shoulders. Bonnie had a big-bum complex, but Lit's rear-view worry was always shoulders. Were they straight enough? Did they droop? Bums didn't say much, but shoulders said a lot.

Mary Dempsey, the woman in accounts, had a perma-nently defeated expression in her hunched shoulders which hung down as though she carried the weight of the world on them. Mary Dempsey's deflated shoulders reflected her dismal character. Lit dreaded asking her how she was because there was always some impending catastrophe like the kitten having to be spayed, or the shopping to be done, or the plants to be watered, or the ink cartridge in the printer having to be replaced.

So Lit avoided Mary Dempsey and her droopy shoul-ders like the plague. Sometimes she fretted that she might develop a dowager hump like Auntie Sheila who Bonnie unkindly referred to as Aunt Quasimodo.

Harry Menton held the door of the taxi open for her and closed it before he moved around to take his own seat. He held up the buckle for her seat belt and pulled down the arm-rest so that she would be more comfort-able.

"I'm looking forward to being in Dublin again for a while," he said. "When I heard about this assignment I just had to have it."

Lit noticed that his accent was more Dublin 4 than Harvard Yard. "You've been to Dublin before, then?"

"My family are Irish. Of course that doesn't mean much in the States. Sometimes people whose family left five or six generations ago still consider themselves Irish. But I am Irish. I was born here before my family moved to Boston. Then I was sent back here to school and I chose to do my degree in Trinity."

"So how did you like it?"

"Great. I'm looking forward to visiting some of my old haunts." He listed off a number of pubs which were definitely Dublin and not on the tourist trail. "Perhaps, if you're not busy, you might be my accomplice."

Accomplice. She liked the word. It had a seductive ring to it, as though there was already a bond between them.

"I've drawn up a list of things which you might enjoy during your stay," she said. "That is, of course, if there's any time – what with meetings and everything." She was determined to be businesslike – friendly but not familiar.

"But we must make time. You can only work to capacity if you play to capacity. I'm not a workaholic. If I think things are getting on top of me, then I just quit for a while and go fishing or something. So what do you have in mind for me?"

"There's a couple of good race meetings, a new play opening at the Abbey. Mr Butler thought you might enjoy a stay in Ashford Castle. He says they have good fishing."

"Would you like to come to Ashford Castle with me?"

He looked at her directly when he said it and Lit couldn't make out if he was just teasing or genuinely serious. She didn't know what to say. It would be impolite to refuse but reckless and sluttish to accept.

"I don't know the first thing about fishing," she said finally. "Besides, I don't think Mr Butler plans for me to be idling the time away in the West of Ireland."

"Probably wants to keep you to himself. I would if I was him."

Lit was horrified at the very thought that Mr Butler in his hitched up trousers might be lusting after her. And though she was beginning to really like Harry Menton because he had instantly made her feel so special, she still thought he was being forward. Besides, she knew for a fact that he was married. And that was a road that she definitely didn't plan to travel. In those days, she hated having to be assertive but the situation called for it. It would not be right for Harry Menton to get the wrong idea about her.

"I must tell you, Mr Menton –"

"Harry – please –"

"Harry. I work very hard for Mr Butler and he in turn is respectful and encouraging to me. It's simply part of my job to look after you and show you around in your spare time. Within reason! And I'm getting paid good overtime for it which is useful because I have a young family."

As soon as she mentioned the family, she noticed his eyes focus quite deliberately on her very unringed left hand.

"Forgive me," he said lightly and laughed. "Well, just look at yourself, Harry Menton! The first pretty girl that comes along and you're wading in like there's no tomorrow. You'll have to forgive me. I'm just a bit of a romantic. And I wasn't expecting . . . well, I wasn't expecting someone like you." He flashed her a smile of open and sincere admiration.

Lit longed to remind him that he was married and that he had no business being romantic about her or anybody other than his wife. But she remained silent and basked instead in the warmth of his compliments. She knew it was wrong but couldn't help herself. For nearly seven years now, not one man had paid her a compliment. She had begun to feel invisible like they say you feel when you're middle-aged. Now, in just a few moments in the back of a taxi, she felt as though she was blossoming into a real woman for the first time in her life.

In a matter of weeks Lit and Harry became firm friends. He wouldn't go anywhere without her. When he arranged to meet his old college mates, he insisted that she come along. When he needed to buy a new suit, he dragged her into Louis Copeland as his style counsellor. He asked her all about Richie and turned up one day at the office with a gift of an expensive Hornby train-set. Then, because he had bought a present for Richie, Lit had to bring Harry home to meet her son and her father.

She introduced him as a business associate and he turned his back on her and tramped upstairs after Richie to assemble the train-set. She sat in the tiny sitting-room with her father who was watching *Charade* with Audrey Hepburn and Cary Grant.

"Who's that gobshite?" her father enquired.

"Ssshh! He's one of the American Directors." She said his title reverently as though he was the reincarnation of Christ or Mahatma Ghandi.

"Smarmy Yankee bastard. What's he doing upstairs with Richie? These fellas can get up to anything. You shouldn't leave your son unsupervised with a stranger."

"Don't be ridiculous. He's a very important man and

159

a very decent man."

"How do you make that out? Important doesn't necessarily mean decent."

Of course Dandy didn't see the Harry that she had come to know and respect and like, the man of integrity, the man who loved the simple things in life – a bag of chips, a day's fishing, a quiet pub in the backstreets of Dublin.

"Don't bring him here again. I don't like him. Do you hear?"

"I'll bring whoever I like. And I don't give a hoot what you think of my friends."

"Friend now, is he? Hmph!" Dandy grunted and returned to watching Audrey Hepburn.

Later that night, Lit had dinner with Harry. He took her to a smart secluded restaurant off St Stephen's Green, a place where it was virtually impossible to get a table, and made her feel like a princess. It was the Valmont. She wore a little black dress that she had bought in Next. She couldn't afford anything more expensive, but she knew she looked good in it anyway. Harry couldn't take his eyes off her.

"I probably shouldn't say this but you look beautiful," he told her and she blushed warmly at the compliment.

"Thank you." She was about to add 'This old thing!' but didn't.

"What should we eat?" he asked.

Lit hadn't a clue. It was the first time she had ever eaten in a really posh restaurant.

"Why don't you order?" she said helplessly. If Bonnie had been there she would have kicked her mercilessly under the table.

He ordered crab claws and a main course of wild

salmon in a dill sauce, the most expensive things on the menu. Lit didn't even know what dill was. They drank a bottle of champagne while waiting for the meal and by the time the starters arrived, Lit was feeling quite light-headed. She hadn't had so much to drink for a very long time. And the only time she had tasted champagne was at Rose O'Dwyer's wedding and that wasn't really champagne but Spanish sparkling wine at six pounds a bottle. Harry had ordered Veuve Cliquot and asked the waiter for the vintage. She had no idea what it meant, but it sounded impressive.

All the other women there were dressed in glittering Versace or tailored Karl Lagerfeld. They oozed money and style. Beside them, she felt gauche and faded. Harry sensed her mood. He cast a baleful look around the room.

"Some people can try and try and never get it right. You don't try at all and you have more style and elegance than any woman in this room."

It wasn't strictly true that she didn't try at all. She had spent a whole two hours mincing in front of the mirror in various stages of undress, trying to match the walk to the shoes to the dress to the face to the hair. She had never worn make-up apart from a little eyeshadow and lipstick. Now she shamelessly plastered on foundation, concealer, powder, blusher, mascara, lipliner, several layers of lipstick and something which claimed to magically keep lipstick in place all night. (By the time they reached the end of the champagne, she had bitten most of it off because it felt like wet glue on her lips.) She had washed and blowdried her hair twice before she was happy with the result.

They talked about everything – childhood, school, college and Richie. Harry told her about his extended Irish-

American family in Massachusetts, stories about his college pranks and the summer jobs he had on the buildings in Boston and later as a tour-boat guide. She laughed her head off eagerly when he told her the story of how he picked up the wrong notes on his first tour of Boston harbour. And while the Japanese tourists were busy snapping photos of the site of the Boston Tea Party, Harry was earnestly regaling them with tales of the South River on the other side. She banged the table with gusty approval when he told her how he had once impersonated a priest in the confessional so that he could hear the sins of an Italian girl that he fancied.

Starting on the second bottle of wine, Lit realised that she had never felt so close to anyone in her entire life. It was like they were looking into each other's souls. She thought she would happily spend the rest of her life with this man – this man who was kind and thoughtful and intelligent and good-humoured with impeccable taste and manners.

"Well, just listen to me droning on like I'm the big cheese. I'll be up for culpable homicide – for boring beautiful Lit Doran to death!"

"No! No. I'm having the best time." She beamed eagerly at him.

"But you can't be having the best time! Not yet! You're going to have the best time when we go to Ashford." He was silent for a moment and then added softly: "I like you very much, Lit."

Her face clouded over. Inside, she was a storm of conflicting emotions – fear, lust, guilt. By now she had to admit to herself that she wanted to go to Ashford with Harry Menton more than anything. She'd been thinking about it quite a bit, all the time in fact. It was only a fantasy of course and she was intelligent enough to recognise the difference between a fantasy and the realities of life. The reality was that he had a wife in Boston, someone who loved and trusted him and waited loyally for him to return. On the other hand he liked her – very much. And she liked him – very much. And when fate threw together two people who had so much in common, it might seem a little churlish to fate to calmly stroll away from such an awesome union of mind, soul and of course body.

While she thought all these thoughts she tried to compose her expression so that nothing would show on her face other than mild interest and the merest hint of disapproval.

But Harry seemed to have a special gift for divining her thoughts. "There's something you should know perhaps. I don't know if it will make any difference. But here goes."

Lit quickly ran a number of possibilities through her head. My wife doesn't understand me. If only I'd met you first – we could be married now. Another time – another place. We got married too young. My wife is in a mental institution. We have an open relationship. We live separate lives. My wife is a lesbian. We're staying together just for the kids. And Bonnie's personal favourite: don't get me wrong – I love my wife – but you I could die for.

Lit never dated married men, but Bonnie had amassed quite a comprehensive collection of the sayings of married men engaged in the act of seduction. In fact, she was planning to publish a list for the unwary single woman called *The Little Book of Pricks or Men Who Bullshit Too Much*.

So Lit waited in trepidation, wondering what Harry was about to say. If he said any of the above, then she knew exactly what she would say. She would smile graciously, thank him for his invitation to Ashford and decline on the grounds that she couldn't possibly leave Richie for a whole weekend.

He took a sip of wine, swallowed it, took a deep breath and swallowed hard again.

"My wife has filed for divorce. That's it. That's all I wanted to say."

"I'm sorry. I'm so sorry," Lit managed to blurt out finally. "When?"

"About two months ago. That's the real reason I took this job."

Bonnie urged extreme caution.

"He's a love-bomber."

"What?"

"He'll keep calling and buying you presents and bringing you places until you're utterly seduced. The minute he knows you're hooked, bombed into submission, blitzkrieged – call it what you want – then the bombing campaign will stop. Then you'll see the real Harry Menton. I've seen it happen."

"He's not like that. Anyway, he hasn't bought me any presents."

"He's bought Richie a Hornby train-set. That's even more insidious."

"Bonnie, what does insidious mean? I wish you wouldn't always use those big words!"

"It means sneaky and nasty. Nasty and sneaky. He knows a train-set for Richie will create a bigger sensation than a bottle of Giorgio Beverley Hills for you."

But Lit wouldn't listen.

Two weeks later, she found herself thrashing around feverishly with Harry in a huge bed in Ashford Castle.

Not counting the diminutive news reporter with the tiny tackle at Bonnie's birthday party, Lit hadn't been with a man in the proper sense since David. And looking back on it, she couldn't really describe her relationship with David as sexual. It mostly involved fumbling and rubbing and in one sense it was a miracle that she had managed to get pregnant at all from a bit of fumbling and rubbing.

But there was no doubt about it: Harry Menton was all man in every perfectly throbbingly endowed department and a skilled and generous lover with it. He knew the places to touch her so that she felt she might explode with desire. He knew all sorts of positions that Lit hadn't even imagined. They might be sitting in a crowded room somewhere, and he would lean over and whisper something suggestive into her ear which would turn her into a seething mass of lust on legs. All in all Lit spent the weekend in Ashford in a permanent pre-orgasmic or post-orgasmic state.

After making love on the first night he leaned up on his elbow and looked down at her, stroking her face gently.

"I love you. You know that, don't you?"

"I love you too, Harry."

Lit wanted to cry with the joy of it all. Harry probably wouldn't return to the States now. It would make perfect sense for him to transfer to the rapidly expanding Dublin office. It would probably be a promotion for him. Then they could be together and begin to make plans. He was, after all, a man who enjoyed simple pleasures. He was made to live in Ireland.

On their last night in Ashford, after several hours of marathon thrashing, gallons of sweat, muscles used which she didn't even know existed, he lay back contentedly on the pillow and said: "I'll always love you, Lit."

Always. She wasn't sure she liked the sound of that. Like someone might say: "I'll always love that old car of mine that I'm about to send to the scrapyard."

Back in Dublin, she waited like an eager puppy for his visits to the office. But he was much busier now and when he did come to the office, there was little time for those pleasant little snatched moments that she had anticipated might happen. He was so busy, in fact, that he could not afford the time to see her on weekday evenings. They would have to confine their meetings to weekend. Harry was working hard on advancing his career and Lit was intelligent enough to appreciate that she would be most helpful to him if she didn't cramp his style. So she made no demands, hid her disappointment when he cancelled a date and dropped everything when he suddenly found himself available. Very occasionally she would plan to make herself unavailable just to keep him on his toes. But it never worked. Somehow he was never able to reschedule his time to accommodate her.

Anyway, it didn't matter, she told herself. He loved her and she loved him – a real grown-up love affair – with no silly adolescent sulks or misunderstandings or unreasonable demands. She still stayed over in the Shelbourne. They still had romantic candlelit dinners. They still shared their innermost thoughts. It just didn't happen as often as before.

One night in the Valmont, he ordered the most expensive bottle of champagne – hundreds of pounds' worth. They had pan-seared scallops and lobster and a special white Bordeaux which couldn't be got anywhere. Lit knew he was building up to something special. There were long, warm and meaningful silences, affectionate little glances across the lobster and the Bordeaux. She could hardly breathe with the excitement and she congratulated herself that she had never nagged him into seeing her when he was busy and that she had never put any pressure on him to speed up the divorce proceedings.

Finally, he gazed into her eyes and held her hand across the table. "You are one beautiful gal, Lit Doran." He pursed his lips in a rueful smile.

She nodded. It seemed pointless to disagree and in his eyes she was beautiful – that was the most important thing.

"There's something I want to say," he went on with the pursed rueful smile.

She nodded encouragingly, anxious that she might scare him if she said anything.

"I've been putting off telling you, but I'm going back Boston in a few days."

That was it? He was going to Boston for a few days. No. That was just the prelude. It was a typical male thing to start talking about something entirely inconsequential like the weather. *'God, isn't it awful humid altogether and I was just wondering will you marry me?'* Or *'I'm thinking of changing the car and I was just wondering if you'll marry me?'* Or *'I'm going to Boston for a few days and I was just wondering if you'll marry me?'*

She continued to nod and smile encouragingly at him.

"I'm not coming back."

She tried to make sense of the words. "But – but you said . . . " Then she realised what he had said. 'In a few days', not 'for a few days'.

He must have good reason – his job, perhaps a father's natural yearning to be near his children.

So that was what he wanted to say to her. He was

167

going back to the States and he wanted her to go with him.

But what about Dandy and Richie? Richie might take quite easily to life in the States, though she had a fair idea how her father would react. Still at least it meant that Harry loved her and meant for them to be together. That was the important thing. She could bring Dandy round in time. She felt sure of it. All these thoughts raced through her head in a matter of moments. But when she scanned his face the cold, horrible truth quickly dawned.

She could feel the tears welling up in her eyes. So this was what all the champagne and the expensive food was about!

"You never said . . . "

"You never asked. You must have known I couldn't stick around here for ever. Gotta keep my eye on the bigger picture."

"You said you loved me!"

"I'll always love you, Lit – like I said. But surely you don't expect me to stay here? Dublin is – is on the edge of nowhere really."

"Maybe I could come with you?"

"That's not an option, I'm afraid."

"Why?" Tears of frustration welled up inside her. "Why is it not an option?"

"I'm going back to my wife."

"What! But you said she had filed for divorce!"

"She got sense. Look, we'll still see each other, Lit. I just don't see why a marriage should be wrecked here. I've seen too much of that. Call it the Irish Catholic in me, but I really do believe that marriage is forever. I'll be here every month. We can go on as before."

And for a while she was pathetically happy with those

miserable little crumbs he threw her.

Bonnie said he was the most despicable kind of snake.

"He's not a snake, Bonnie. I love him. He loves me. In his own way he does. You don't know him like I do."

"He's a first-class wanker who doesn't give a shit about anyone's happiness but his own! The Yankee shit-face!"

"You've been out with much worse than Harry Menton!"

"That's because I can handle people like him. I don't fall in love with them. Use 'em and lose 'em! Fuck 'em and chuck 'em, remember? You broke the golden rule. You went and fell in love."

"I couldn't really go to bed with a man I didn't love, and actually enjoy it."

"Oh, please! Lit, we're not innocent little teenagers any more. The world has changed. The rules of engagement have changed. Men don't need to hang around any more. And neither do women. There's no need to fall in love. That only complicates the issue. You can have sex, fun, someone to bring to parties and you don't have to wake up to them farting and snoring and trying to run your life for you. It's the new give and take."

"You're only saying that because all your relationships fail."

"Am not!"

"Are so! You can't keep a man so you don't want any of your friends to have a long-term man either."

Lit knew it was a nasty hurtful thing to say, but she couldn't help herself. And in a way it was true. If Bonnie knew so much about men, how come she could never hold onto one for long? Lit suspected it was because Bonnie scared them away. As far as she could see, men still liked coy, giggly women who didn't understand the offside rule, who never looked under the bonnet of their car, who were appreciative and impressed and a little mysterious. Bonnie's idea of a little mystery was to make them guess what sort of sexy underwear she had on.

One day, about a year later, Lit returned from seeing Harry off at the airport. They had spent three hours and ten minutes together, an hour for lunch, an hour and a half in bed, a quick shower and change and the drive to the airport. The lunch was rushed. The sex which she'd spent weeks longing for was mechanical and, she could hardly bear to admit to herself, dull, tediously dull. The most enjoyable part of Harry's visit was the quick shower. Still, she felt like the guts were being wrenched out of her when he disappeared into the departure lounge.

"You know I love you. I came all this way to see you."

It wasn't strictly true. He had business in London and it suited him to make the little detour to Dublin. But she wanted to believe it and so she did. On the other side of the Atlantic, she thought, is a man who loves me and thinks about me when he lies in bed at night. That's more than Mary Dempsey with the hunched shoulders has. That's more than Bonnie has. She made the best of a bad situation.

In the foyer of the office block, she hovered, reluctant to face her colleagues in Motorphone. Then someone tapped her on the shoulder.

"It's you! It is you! Oh my God, it's you! The one with the baby. Breastfeeding in the canteen at lunch-time!"

Lit turned around and came face to face with Matt Shiels, all ginger wavy hair and twinkling green eyes. She hadn't a clue who he was.

"Of course you don't remember me. I was a year behind you. I used to defend you when the league of decency made complaints about your breasts. How is your baby?"

Lit smiled and laughed. "My baby is eight and thinks he's Indiana Jones."

"I'm working upstairs in Devlin Satchwell PR. I look after advertising. And you?"

Lit shrugged. Suddenly her job seemed not just dull but demeaning. Here was a guy a year behind her in college who had a glamorous job in advertising. She, on the other hand, spent her days typing and answering the phone and making travel arrangements and dreaming about a man who lived three thousand miles away. And somehow this chance meeting with a virtual stranger brought it all into horrible stark reality. She began to sob.

"Oh God, I feel just awful!"

Matt fished out a hanky and passed it to her. "Here. By the way, I'm Matt Shiels. Can you take five minutes and walk this off? You really should."

She nodded pathetically and followed him out of the foyer into the cold February air.

"I'm sorry. I don't know what's come over me. Just having a bad day, I suppose. As well as that your job sounds so interesting and I'm stuck down here in Motorphone doing stuff I can do in my sleep. In fact, I do do it in my sleep."

"Then you need to stop. That's no work for a brilliantly gifted woman like you. Did you know your work was always whispered about with grudging admiration by some of us blokes? We all wanted to get our hands on your essays so we could cog them. Other blokes – well, they wanted to get their hands on other stuff as well. Not me though. I worshipped in the purely aesthetic and intellectual sense."

Lit laughed. It was the first time she had laughed in

days. She felt she had discovered a new friend quite by accident.

"In the department where I work, one of the girls is leaving to work in London. I don't think they've advertised her job yet."

"Oh. Thanks. But I couldn't do that kind of work. I wouldn't know how. I mean I have no experience –"

"Who needs experience? One look at you and the whole department will be drooling. Oops! Sorry! Shouldn't have said that. I suppose that's sexual harassment. I'm never quite sure. I mean do you feel in any way diminished or threatened by what I just said about the department drooling?"

He was comical and charming which was probably why his comment didn't at all feel like sexual harassment. He was friendly and not threatening and not trying to seduce her, just trying to do her a good turn. It was as if she had caught a little gust of fresh air. She thought of years sitting in the office next to Mary Dempsey and years of her impending disasters involving the washing being rained on or the chimney needing to be swept, years of answering the phone and typing letters and making coffee. If she kept on going like this, she would be doddering around the office in thirty years' time with a dowager hump that would put Auntie Sheila to shame, sipping gin from a flask under her desk and reduced to fluttering her eyelashes at Mr Butler. But beyond all of those things was a new start, a chance to end things with Harry Menton at last.

"So?" Matt enquired chirpily.

"OK," she said finally. "I'm up for it."

172

# CHAPTER 14

So when she thought of Harry Menton as she passed through the lobby of the Valmont, it was not so hard for Lit to suppress any lingering, quivering, shivering little frissons of anticipation about meeting Conrad Budd. It was very much a case of once bitten, twice shy. No man had breached her formidable defences since. Plenty had called, but none were chosen.

Conrad watched her idly as she walked towards him and then stood up casually as she reached the table.

"Lit, good to see you." He held out his hand and she shook it briefly before taking her seat across the table from him. She was determined to maintain a cool and professional courtesy throughout their meeting.

She produced a slim folder of papers for discussion and rested them on the table. Conrad glanced quickly through them and set them to one side. A waiter was hovering discreetly, but hovering all the same.

"Let's order some food. I like to work as I eat. The sole is good."

She was about to say that the sole would be lovely, when she remembered Harry Menton and the salmon in dill sauce.

"I'm not all that keen on sole. Just a salad for me. No dressing." She pointed at random to one of the salads on the menu and smiled charmingly at the waiter. "Thanks."

"Wine? They do a very nice 1985 white Bordeaux . . . "

"No, thanks. Water for me. I'm driving."

"Fine. Just two mineral waters then, please."

Conrad settled back in his chair and idly observed Lit as she produced the press release from her folder. She certainly wasn't the most beautiful woman he had ever seen – but there was something extra fine about her all the same.

Lit had spent hours getting the press release right and was proud of the result.

Conrad read and re-read the heading. *"Building a Better World* . . . mmm . . . does that sound vain? I don't want to sound vain. I do what I do because it's what I like to do."

"Yes, but you have to spell things out sometimes. It's like a sound-bite, a simple formula that people can remember. For instance, what word comes to mind when you think of Volvo?"

"Safety."

"Right! Now what comes to mind when you think of Rolls Royce?"

"I do understand what you mean –"

"So what does come to mind when you think of Rolls Royce?"

"Big petrol bills."

Lit was about to throw her head back and laugh eagerly at Conrad's silly little joke, but just in time she stopped herself and smiled fleetingly instead. "The answer people generally give is 'luxury'."

Conrad rapped his knuckles with a fork. "So: Conrad Budd . . . Better World!"

"Quite."

He shook his head and fidgeted with the folds of his napkin. "Thing is . . . Lit . . . it all sounds a bit, you know . . . as I said, I'm a fairly modest man . . ."

"Modesty has nothing to do with it. You want to impress the investors. You want to appease the Stoneyfield Residents Association. You won't achieve either of those aims, particularly the second, by maintaining a dignified silence. You hired my company. Now let me earn my salary."

He nodded and looked down through the list of his contributions to Stoneyfield.

"So where do we go from here?"

"*TV Features* are running a programme on the area – you know, history, old characters, changes down the years, the new development. I've been speaking to the producer. He's interested in doing a feature on you."

"Don't like the sound of that."

"You have to do it, Conrad. It's a chance to present your side of things to a wider public. You can be sure the Stoneyfield Residents Association will get plenty of air time."

He shrugged and straightened his tie. "Well, I guess I'm in your hands."

Lit bristled and fixed her eyes steadily for a moment on Conrad's tie. Harry Menton had said that to her the first day they met: 'I'm in your hands.' It was all part of the 'hapless male needs to be taken in hand by the strong woman' strategy. It was time for some arctic eye contact. She lifted her vivid blue eyes to his of deep, deep brown and raised a withering eyebrow, which she softened only slightly with yet another fleeting smile. "We'll need to spend an hour or two coaching you for the programme."

Conrad looked sheepish. "Do you think I'll be that bad?"

"On the contrary. But there's a formula – a way of making your point even when people don't want you to and a lot depends on the format of the programme . . . a discussion panel could be tricky."

She said the last bit just to frighten him and was rewarded with the sight of his jaw tightening ever so slightly.

"What's the formula then?"

"Basically: be prepared, stay calm, know what you want to say and say it, don't be side-tracked and keep your cool – it's easy."

"How long have you been in this business?"

By now he was busy tucking into his large grilled sole with the head still in place – which Lit found vaguely disgusting. She nibbled on minute slivers of black olive and an occasional piece of sun-dried tomato.

"About seven years. Matt and I worked together. Then we decided to go out on our own. The first eighteen months were tough."

"And now?"

Lit could feel his keen interest across the table. She looked up from her salad and caught his eye lingering for a split second on the nape of her neck.

"And now, things couldn't be better," she said. She wondered if he was fishing for information about the company or just interested in her. It was hard to tell.

He turned the sole over on his plate with a single deft movement of knife and fork and waited for her to tell him more.

"Our assets are far greater than our liabilities," she said at last, irritated at how she seemed to be echoing Seán Tallon's clinically precise assessment of their worth.

"Each week we bring in at least one new client . . . not all of them as significant as yourself . . . " She could have shot herself for saying that. It sounded smarmy and would only make him think he had the edge in finalising a fee. So she added a bit hastily, "Of course we give all our clients, no matter how small, a very high level of service."

"Of course. Naturally. I know nothing about public relations and marketing and advertising and cultivating an image and all that stuff . . . but I do know about bricks and mortar. And that's real. That site in Stoneyfield, it's been just sitting there for – well, forty years – with little hucksters using it for mountains of rusty scrap metal or car parking during the Christmas rush. It's been a hangout for junkies and dealers, a dumping ground for everything from old bicycles to dead bodies. Three women were raped there last year in the space of two months. It's home to the homeless. It's bang slap in the middle of one of the most historic parts of the city and it makes the place look like a third-world country. I want to take that wasted, abused, neglected scrap of land and turn it into something that Dublin can be proud of . . . "

"It's an admirable dream."

"Yes. It is a dream. I like to dream. If men didn't have dreams the world would be nothing. I also like stories with happy endings."

"Will this one have a happy ending?"

"Of course! A happy ending for everyone."

He sat forward in his seat, alive with enthusiasm for his plan, convinced of its proper worth, gazing into a future happy ending for all concerned.

For Lit this was a dangerous moment because up to now, apart from his thighs, his chest, his shoulders, his neck, his chin and his deep deep brown eyes – she had found very little in Conrad Budd's personality to arouse her interest. After Harry Menton, she had half-heartedly dated a successful hotelier for a few weeks, but he drove her to distraction with boredom and from that she naturally concluded that all rich and successful men were self-obsessed and power-fixated, focused on five-point plans and seven-stage strategies. She sincerely hoped that Conrad Budd wasn't going to suddenly turn interesting and fascinating on her. Still, she couldn't help herself. His enthusiasm was catching. His vision was inspiring.

"When I bring you down there, all you'll see is acres and acres of scorched grass with the odd old derelict warehouse and bits of corrugated iron thrown about the place. You'll see massive cranes and diggers and vast piles of concrete slabs and miles of steel bars and cable. I see something else. I see a glass and steel conference centre to rival the Sydney Opera House. I see hotels grander than the Ritz, I see imposing offices, shops to rival Fifth Avenue or Bond Street . . . that's the inevitable march of progress. How can anybody suggest that thirty acres of scorched grass, junkies and corrugated iron is better than my plan?"

Put that way, Lit found herself firmly convinced of the rightness of Conrad's cause. He was, after all, really engaged in building a better Ireland. Still, it was important to understand and respect the residents' point of view if she was going to tackle them and win the publicity battle. She asked her next question with all the diplomatic skill she could muster.

"Why do you think the residents are up in arms then?"

Conrad's brow clouded and he frowned antagonistically across the table at her.

"I'm just being devil's advocate, you understand," she added hastily. "We need to know how they're thinking if we want to keep ahead of them."

Conrad removed his jacket and loosened his tie. Lit forced herself to look at the painting on the wall behind him. She took a few rapid sips of water. Conrad didn't seem to notice her discomfort. He drew out a folded drawing from his briefcase.

"This is a reduced scale model of what I'm planning . . . see . . . "

He passed the sheet to her and she spent several moments examining it. Until now, she hadn't really had any clear idea about the size or proportion of the development. In her mind it was a vague mishmash of a couple of hotels, a few shops, offices and apartments. And when she studied the scale of it in relation to some of the tiny surrounding streets, she couldn't stop herself exclaiming:

"My God! It's huge! I had no idea. I mean, I've glanced at the file in the office – but – oh, my God . . . "

"The residents say that it is excessively large. As a matter of interest what is your view?"

Lit didn't think it was her place to have an opinion – especially if it didn't concur with Conrad's. The complexity of the situation was slowly dawning on her. On the one hand she admired his vision but, on the other, she wondered how she would feel if such a development were to loom over Harwood Park. But of course that would never happen because the residents of Harwood Park would never allow it to happen.

"Um . . . em . . . it's very impressive."

"They say that the high-rise buildings will dwarf the retained historic buildings like the old medieval church. But high-rise, if it's done properly, complements older buildings. That's the way they've gone in other cities – London, New York. They're also objecting that their houses will be in shadow for a lot of the time. But that's the price you pay for city life. Do you think the citizens of Manhattan worry about shadow and sunlight? See, Lit, people here don't know what they want. They don't want urban sprawl and they don't want high-rise either. But in a modern growing city it stands to reason that you must have one if you don't have the other. They're on about the increased volume of traffic because of offices and shops and that is another one of the prices you pay for progress. The Golden Mile in London is chock-a-block with offices and people travelling to and from their jobs – but the city provides a decent public transport service . . . sorry, this is all very boring."

"No!" Lit was quick to reassure him. In fact, she found the whole subject quite interesting, more interesting at any rate than Wholesome Foods or computer software or most kinds of sport. "It's very interesting – even if I wasn't your PR agent."

"I know what!" Suddenly Conrad was standing and putting on his jacket and straightening his tie. "I'm going to take you to the site and drive you around Stoneyfield. Then you can form your own opinion."

Lit's jaw dropped. This was definitely not in the plan – an unscheduled visit to the site – another two hours at least in the company of Conrad. At first she was annoyed. Who did he think he was, assuming she could just traipse around after him at the drop of a hat? Didn't he realise that she had other important meetings and phone calls and reports and proposals and presentations for other equally important clients? Did Conrad Budd think he could just click his fingers and the whole world would come trotting after him? And he hadn't even offered her an after-lunch coffee.

She opened her mouth to give vent to some of these pressing questions, but then she thought better of it. She should have thought of the idea herself. She knew Matt had been around the site, but now the project was largely in her hands. A visit there should have been one of the first things on her agenda and it was really annoying that he had suggested it first. On the other hand, if she had suggested going to the site, he might have thought she was sticking her nose in where it didn't belong. All in all then, after about thirty seconds, Lit decided that a visit to the site at Conrad's suggestion was absolutely the right and professional thing to do. But then she looked down at her dainty lilac kitten heels and her classy preppy outfit.

"I'm not dressed for this. Perhaps tomorrow. That's a better idea. If it suits you. I can wear my jeans and trainers to the office. I'm not seeing clients in the morning – and then we could –"

She stopped abruptly, realising she was babbling for Ireland. Next, she'd be telling him the make of her jeans and why she didn't really think trainers were comfortable at all, it was only that they looked comfortable and appearing comfortable was half the battle . . .

Conrad was gazing down at her speculatively. "May I make a thoroughly improper suggestion?" he said slowly, in a deep and intimate tone.

Lit was astonished. Surely he couldn't be about to suggest – what she thought he was about to suggest – and with such abrupt and startling candour? Of course she wasn't even going to entertain it such a notion. It didn't matter if he was one of the richest men in the country. It didn't matter if she once had a mad crush on him in college. It didn't matter that she didn't have any important meetings in the afternoon anyway . . .

"Let's go to my suite in the Shelbourne," he continued when she didn't respond, "and then –"

"Certainly not!" she croaked and began busily tidying away papers into her briefcase, going through the pretence of checking that they were all there. She finally looked up to find Conrad surveying her in some amusement.

"I think you misunderstand," he said disarmingly. "I merely meant you could go to my suite in the Shelbourne and borrow something of mine. It's just around the corner from here. And I always keep spare wellies in the boot of the Rover for visiting – VIPs."

Yeah, right, she thought. He gets me into his room and pretends not to be bothered and then, while I'm changing, he accidentally comes into the room and then he just starts with the light finger on the shoulder and the little feel of his breath on my hair. Then he just slips his finger beneath my bra strap and slides it gently down my arm. Then he runs his strong, lightly tanned hands down my back. Then he starts unbuttoning his shirt . . . oh God . . .

She almost gasped at the warm churning feeling in the pit of her stomach and the overpowering sensation of her skin tingling and wanting desperately to be touched.

Conrad fished a key with a number-tag attached from his pocket.

"Here's the key," he said. "You go on ahead to the Shelbourne and I'll meet you there in the foyer in ten minutes."

Lit thought she might be having a hot flush. But it couldn't be. She was only thirty-four.

When she didn't show any signs of taking the key, he slipped it into the side pocket of her Mulberry handbag.

"Oh! Thanks. Ten minutes – in the foyer," she finally managed to blurt out breathlessly, irritated beyond belief that her disappointment was far greater than either her embarrassment or her relief.

# CHAPTER 15

Lit called Matt from Conrad's suite and told him she was on her way to the Stoneyfield site.

"Good thinking, Watson."

She didn't tell him it was Conrad's suggestion.

"Anything your end?" she asked.

"Not much. Martinex Software are involved in a fairly major takeover bid. I've started working on the publicity. I also heard on the grapevine that one of the luxury car companies are opening up an outlet here. I'm checking out if it's worth our while pitching for that."

"Sounds good."

"The Cornwells are a bit happier with the new stuff, but he's still haggling about the fee."

"Tight."

"As a duck's arse!"

"Have we got any leverage?" Lit was generally good on negotiation.

"He's given us a deposit of five thousand euros which barely covers the paperwork. After that he's insisting we don't get a penny more until he is a hundred per cent happy with our stuff."

"So we have nothing to bargain with."

"You could say that. Yes."

"Insist that we want more money up front. The way things stand, he can just walk off and say he's not satisfied and he's not paying."

Matt sighed. "That's the uncertain business world, I'm afraid. Don't worry – he'll cough up. If I have to approve the yuckiest, most treacly stuff to get paid – then so be it."

Lit was silent, partly because she was fretting about Dara Cornwell and partly because she was trying to make herself look half-presentable in a pair of Conrad's navy jog pants. She rolled them up at the waist and the ankles and slipped a large white cotton shirt on.

"Hasn't he signed a contract?"

Matt sighed in exasperation. "Doesn't believe in them. A gentleman's agreement – all that crap."

She surveyed herself in the mirror . . . not bad, she thought . . . in a Ralph Lauren, preppy, lounging on the yacht sort of way. She pulled her hair back and tied it up in a loose knot which she knew would hold for half an hour at the most.

"Then make him sign one. Say we can't continue to act on his behalf unless he signs a contract."

"It's not that simple, Lit. He won't sign and that's that. If we back away now, he'll be off to some other hungry agency and we won't see a penny. Wholesome Foods is too big a client for us to lose."

Lit suppressed her exasperation. She'd warned Matt against taking the Cornwells on in the first place. She wasn't sure why – just a gut instinct. Big clients or not, with all the effort the Cornwells were demanding, Shiels Doran could successfully have handled four other clients, clients who might appreciate their efforts. Matt had wonderful imagination, but his problem was that he wanted to be all things to all men. He found it very hard to say no to anybody, even Dara Cornwell. It was Lit who brought in most of the really big clients – the sports organisations, the American software firm, the film distributors – and Lit who was a cut-throat when it came to hammering out deals. Though all of that counted for nothing when she remembered that it was Matt who had landed the biggest catch of them all – Conrad.

"I have to go. "

"Don't worry about the Cornwells."

"OK."

"I mean it. It's not going to be a problem. Bye!"

But she would worry about it. She was cool, she was smart, she was efficient – but she was also a worrier. She was prone to knots in the stomach, tense headaches, bouts of sleeplessness, not being able to relax, even on her days off which were few and far between. However, as in many other areas of her life, she'd taught herself to counter anxiety by always planning ahead and being well prepared and being very careful with how she organised her time. But the Cornwells were a bit enigmatic, as Bonnie might say, and the very fact that she couldn't quite get a handle on them made her worry. Conrad and his billions and his breathtaking vision of happy endings for everyone did not worry her half as much because he was a straight dealer, paid his money up front and simply expected the best available return on his investment. In that respect alone, as far as Lit was concerned, he was the perfect client.

She looked down at her lilac kitten heels. They spoiled the preppy look completely. She ought to be wearing a nice pair of ridiculously expensive deck shoes or Prada pumps. Conrad had offered wellies, but she certainly didn't intend to stamp around the Stoneyfield site in a pair of someone else's wellies. Maybe no-one would notice her lilac shoes.

Conrad could barely suppress his amusement when she appeared in the foyer wearing his shirt, rolled-up jog pants and a dainty little pair of heeled shoes which would probably last about ten seconds on the rough terrain of the site.

"Right?"

"Perhaps I'll just stay in the car after all."

"Oh, no! You're going to see the whole picture. How

can you do my PR otherwise?"

"But I look like a street urchin – in stolen designer shoes."

"You look . . . very fetching," he said softly, almost under his breath.

Lit had taken the precaution of having a quick cold shower while she was in his suite. The humid weather – and her hot flush – called for it. Now she was glad because it had dampened her ardour for Conrad completely. She was pleased to note that his half-whispered compliment barely had any effect on her at all. She was all breezy business once more.

"That's fine then," she said briskly, shattering any hint of intimacy and warmth. "I'm ready."

First he drove her around Stoneyfield to see the narrow winding streets, terraced rows of little redbrick houses with brightly painted windows and expensive new doors and satellite dishes, old redbrick schools and churches, corner shops and shops selling bicycle parts and electrical goods. She had never really explored this area of the city before. Little permed grey-haired old ladies pushing shopping trollies, groups of squealing excited children, working men and men in suits, mothers out pushing buggies, all mingled on the busy streets. Here and there she spotted the odd intrepid tourist, mostly of the younger backpacking variety. Stoneyfield was not mentioned in most of the guide books because it didn't have any famous writers to boast of, or Georgian fanlighted houses, or medieval churches or even a park like Stephen's Green to sit in. But she was genuinely surprised by the simple charm of the streets and houses and the cheerful ambience of the people there. Of course the sunny day helped, but there was definitely a warm continental atmosphere with cosy lit-

tle cafes under striped awnings, one or two rickety-look-
ing second-hand bookshops and a few bustling pubs.
There was a tiny Chinese restaurant and a North African
one right beside it.

On the corner at the end of the main street she saw a
sign for the Greek Orthodox church. Outside a
Byzantine style building, a large group of olive-skinned
people thronged around an elaborately dressed young
couple who had just married. Lit felt a twinge of envy
for the bride – young and beautiful, her whole body
alive with pride and happiness to have found such a
handsome husband. Lit had never harboured the marriage dream. In her twenties, she was too busy taking
care of Richie and trying to make a living for both of
them. Now there didn't seem any point in marriage for
someone in her enviable position. If she did even
decide, as Bonnie repeatedly urged, to test the man-
waters again, and even if she did find a man to love,
what would be the point of marrying him? She was
financially self-sufficient so there was no need for the
legal security of marriage. And she didn't intend to
have any more children either. If she ever did test the
man-waters again, it would be simply to find a companion of the opposite sex, someone to have an occasional dinner with, someone to play an occasional game
of golf with, someone to have sporadic sex with.

So if it wasn't an option, why did she feel that niggling twinge of envy for the bride? In the past, whenever she and Bonnie came across a wedding, they
talked with masses of rather smug sympathy for the
plight of the hapless young bride and all the awful
trouble and strife that awaited her as she struggled to
build her happy-ever-after dream, with a husband who
more than likely was gearing up to live out his life as a

couch potato – and not the loveable Homer Simpson variety of couch potato either. Yet here she was, icy celibate Lit Doran, driving along in a car with the most eligible man in Ireland, and feeling pangs of envy and longing for the married state. She cast a sideways glance at Conrad, her stomach doing a little somersault in the process. What was Angela like, she wondered. Why had Conrad chosen her above all others? Was she prettier, smarter, classier than the other women he'd come across? How would wedded bliss be for Angela and Conrad? He wouldn't be a couch potato for sure, but he would certainly bring other challenges. Holding onto a handsome, successful, intelligent and charming husband of his calibre must rank as a grade A marital challenge, the Mount Everest of the wedded state. Then she stopped herself. It was none of her business. Conrad was none of her business. His future marital stability was definitely none of her business. She turned her attention once more to the streets of Stoneyfield. She felt herself warming instinctively to the place and the people in it.

At the far end there was an old army barracks which was being converted into a transport museum. Conrad pointed it out to her.

"Half a million," he said casually.

"Sorry?"

"For that project alone, I donated half a million."

"But why? Does the Residents Association know?"

He shrugged.

"Why did you do it if you don't want people to know?"

"Seemed like a good idea at the time and they needed it. You know I stand to become an even richer man when this development is complete. A few million now will seem like nothing then. And the people here can get rich too."

"How will they get rich?"

"Good jobs on their doorstep – the value of their property will rocket, shade or no shade – money makes money."

"Still though, where will the kids play?"

"There's going to be a landscaped park, with a playground and tennis courts."

"That will be great for the people in the apartments – but these kids . . . "

"You're meant to be on my side, remember?" Conrad said, slightly annoyed.

"*The prince must be a fox to recognise the traps, and a lion to frighten the wolves,*" Lit replied cryptically.

"What the hell does that mean?"

"It means that first you must put yourself in their shoes, be the devil's advocate – remember? We used it in an ad campaign for sports trainers a few years back."

Conrad surveyed her sideways as he drove towards the gates of the site. She could be quite an exhilarating woman, he concluded.

The Stoneyfield Residents Association had mounted their daily picket at the gates, though even at a distance Conrad noticed instantly that there was something different about them. He slowed the jeep down and took a closer look. The little old lady in the woollen hat who smiled and waved at him every day wasn't there. And the group was larger. Instead of three or four harmless-looking individuals basking in the warm sunshine, about thirty angry-looking people stood guard at both sides of the entrance. When they saw his jeep approaching, they started to chant: *Budd! Budd! Budd! Out! Out! Out!* with their fists clenched and raised in the air. One or two banged their fists loudly on the bonnet of the jeep.

He rolled down the window as usual to exchange pleasantries with them.

"Good morning to you all! Fine day again."

"Fuck off! Parasite!" Fidelma shouted viciously at him. Gearóid had urged her to be more proactive in expressing her views about Conrad. Conrad was quite taken aback. "Your development sucks, Budd! You'll never see it built. We're going to see to that!"

Lit felt uncomfortable as she rode past the picket in Conrad's jeep. She wasn't one of life's protesters, but she hated having to pass a picket all the same. Perhaps some of Dandy's half-baked socialism had rubbed off on her after all. Once on a weekend to New York, she refused to pass a picket on The Museum of Modern Art, even though seeing the paintings there was to have been a highlight of her trip.

"What's the difference? They're not going to come after you with a big stick," her American associate had said.

"People only picket when they feel they have good reason," she had replied, taking herself off on a bus tour of Haarlem instead.

Now, she felt decidedly ill at ease. And intimidated – this crowd were mean-looking, not at all as Conrad had described them.

Conrad parked the jeep inside the gates and jumped out, slamming the door behind him. "Wait," he said curtly. "I must talk to Tommy Russell – the watchman."

"Conrad!"

But he was heading for the watchman's hut.

She quickly hid her kitten heels and, despite her earlier protestations, valiantly slipped her slim legs into the pair of size eight wellies. Then she shoved her hands in the pockets of the jog pants and strode purposefully after Conrad. She arrived at the hut to find him confronting the watchman rather belligerently.

"But why wasn't I told?" he was demanding.

"Boss, they only turned up about ten minutes ago – there was no time to tell you!"

"Has any of them threatened you? Any intimidation?"

"Not as such. But I was used to that little old lady bringing her knitting and that other man who supports Chelsea – same as myself. We used to have great chats over the tea and sandwiches. That lot out there aren't in the mood for chatting though. Wouldn't say a word to me. They've got maps of the site, plans, mobile phones and some fella from the radio is coming to interview them in the afternoon. They arrived in a mini-bus, and someone else has provided them with refreshments."

"Right. Any of them sets foot on the site – that's trespassing. I'll call security – get you back-up."

"Conrad," said Lit from the doorway, "could I have a word with you?"

He glanced over his shoulder at her. "Be with you in a moment! I'm kind of busy here."

She stood waiting quietly as he called Jack Kennedy, his right-hand man, who was due to fly to Cork in the late afternoon.

"Kennedy, get that security firm on the line. We need a few reinforcements down here on the site. There's trouble brewing . . . I'm not sure but the crowd of protesters is bigger and they seem more aggressive . . . No, don't cancel Cork, just sort out the security. Leave the rest to me."

"Conrad!" said Lit with added urgency as he put down the phone. This was her territory – what he was paying her for. She wanted to tell him that he was quickly backing himself into a stand-off situation. That would look bad in the media: *Tycoon Sets The Dogs On Inner City Residents*. She knew only too well how the press would make mincemeat of him.

But he continued to ignore her and, by the time he had made a few more calls, it was too late.

She stepped forward. "This needs to be handled very delicately," she proposed tactfully.

"Too fucking right it does!" Conrad snapped. "Somebody, and I can guess who, is winding up that mob out there."

His mobile rang again.

"Conrad. Fine! I'll be here!"

He turned to Lit and shrugged apologetically. "I wanted to show you my dream – and instead I drive you straight into this nightmare."

"It's hardly a nightmare."

"Peaceful protest is fair enough – but this is intimidation. I'll call you a taxi. There's no point in you hanging around here now."

Lit retorted quickly, "You need me here. I can help."

"And what do you suggest?" His tone was bordering on the sarcastic.

Lit marvelled at the way in which people would suddenly change mood and even personalities when large sums of money were at stake. But she reckoned if she had millions and millions of pounds at stake she might be a bit edgy too.

"Are you asking for my opinion," she asked, "or just being sarcastic?"

He didn't reply.

"I suggest you don't get involved in a confrontation with these people," she said. "The media will only have a field day with that. You may be overreacting. It's worth considering the idea of sitting down and listening to what they have to say – jaw-jaw better than war-war."

He glared at her impatiently. "That's it? That's your suggestion? Talk to them? I spent eighteen fucking months talking to them – making adjustments to the plans, financing their schemes – forget it!"

Lit would not be put off that easily. "Then why are they suddenly back on the warpath again? You said yourself that it was a token protest, a matter of principle only."

"Maybe they're all back from their holidays in the Canaries – I don't know. They must think they have something on me."

"Like what? What could they have on you?"

"Don't know. You can go through the paperwork, the applications, the appeals, the finances, everything – it's as clean as a whistle."

"What about your private life?"

He scowled at her again.

"Is there anything in your private life?" she persisted.

"I'm no saint – but there's nothing which would affect business."

Outside the chanting resumed, this time even more loudly.

*Budd! Budd! Budd! Out! Out! Out!*

"Now what's happening?" Conrad looked out the window and to his horror saw a couple of news reporters with microphones and a photographer. "How did they get here?"

"Some clever person called them," Lit said thoughtfully.

"But why? This isn't news. A small picket on a building site . . . "

"It's the silly season, don't forget – no big news stories or disasters happening for the reporters to get their teeth into. So they're stuck with the job of trying to make news out of nothing. You know the sort of thing – *Small Earth Tremor In New Mexico, Nobody Dead Or Even Slightly Concussed*." She was trying to lighten the oppressive atmosphere. "Anyway, we have to deal with it now."

"Meaning?"

"Will you talk to the reporters or not?"

"I don't have anything to say. I'm not good at this sort of thing, Lit. I told you that."

Despondently, he settled his large frame on the edge of Tommy Russell's battered metal desk.

There was something of the Little Boy Lost about him. Lit felt dangerous pangs of caring, nurturing, consoling motherly instincts. Lust could be quenched with a cold shower, but the caring stuff was a lot harder to suppress and potentially much more lethal. She found herself thinking – why don't they just leave him alone? If they only knew the kind of wonderful man he really is – the man I feel I'm getting to know.

But such thoughts weren't helpful and she tried to dismiss them from her mind.

"Right! Bear with me for a moment," she finally said quite brusquely. "It would be best if you talked to the reporters."

"No!"

"Is there someone that you would like to speak on your behalf?"

"You could do it."

Lit shook her head. "No. That's not my function. But your solicitor perhaps or your assistant, the Kennedy guy . . ."

Conrad shook his head. "Fergus Cunningham is in

court. And as for Kennedy - he's my eyes and ears – but definitely not my mouthpiece. Besides, he's on his way to Cork for a meeting."

"Then I suggest you go out there and say that you absolutely respect people's right to peaceful protest and that you have no further comment. When you're pressed say that your company will be issuing a statement. When pressed again say 'no further comment and thank you for your time'."

Conrad was deeply sceptical. "You honestly think that will work?"

She faced him head on. "Just do as I say – nothing less and definitely nothing more – and it will give us a bit of breathing space."

He nodded doubtfully.

"Oh, and I nearly forgot," she added. "Body language."

"What? You're winding me up. I'm not modelling a suit!"

"Look grave, but not desperate. Stand straight and solid, but don't go out there looking like cock of the walk who owns the place. You should smile briefly at the reporters, but don't give the impression that you're taking the matter lightly."

"Jesus – is this what the makeover is going to be like?"

Lit shrugged. "Go on. You'll be fine." She patted him lightly on the shoulder and he rose to his feet. She followed closely behind him as he went out to face the little knot of people.

"Mr Budd! Mr Budd! Have you anything to say?"

Conrad smiled amiably and, ignoring the chants and the taunts of the crowd, walked straight up to the reporters.

"Good afternoon, gentlemen."

"How do you feel about the residents protesting now?"

"I absolutely respect people's democratic right to peaceful protest and I have no further comment at this time. That is all I have to say."

"So, you intend to enter into further discussions with them?"

Lit, standing slightly behind him, muttered quietly, "Don't answer that. Remember – no comment and a statement at a later stage."

Conrad bit his lip and smiled pleasantly once more. "As I say, I have no comment at this time. The company will be issuing a statement. Thank you for your time."

He turned to leave. But the pushier of the two reporters shouted out again so that the assembled crowd could hear quite clearly.

"Mr Budd, are you aware that certain allegations have been made about you?"

Conrad's affable smile froze as he swung round. He observed the reporter coldly for a few moments.

"Allegations and rumours and scandals – that's how you earn your crust. Bricks and mortar – that's how I earn mine. Now if you'll excuse me . . ."

Lit wished he had kept his mouth shut. He'd done so well and now he'd ruined it all by rising to the reporter's bait. But there wasn't much she could do about it now except hope that the reporter wouldn't mention it in his article.

Conrad made his way back to the jeep and held the door open for her. "I'll drive you back to the hotel."

"No, really. There's no need. I can call a cab."

"I insist."

Back at the hotel once more, Lit went up to the room, showered once more and changed her clothes. Then she rejoined Conrad in the foyer.

"Drink?" he asked brusquely. "I need one."

He was slightly ruffled, disconcerted by the chanting and hostility at the gate, angered as he saw it, by the taunts of rumour-merchants with nothing better to do than stir up trouble for the sake of a cheap story in a newspaper.

Lit never accepted a drink at the drop of a hat from anyone. It looked bad, as though she had nothing better to do. Generally, if she was invited by a man for a spur-of-the-moment drink, she would claim a prior engagement. But she had to remind herself that this wasn't simply a man asking a woman out for a drink. This was her client needing her support and advice. Conrad had just had a close encounter of the mob kind and he did not seem to have the sort of common touch which could appease an angry crowd. She needed to make him more media-friendly.

"OK. Just the one. I have to get home."

He led the way into the bar and propped himself up on a stool at the counter. "What would you like?"

She hesitated. A Ballygowan, she thought. Anything else might be risky or frisky. Bonnie could drink any man under the table and frequently did. Bonnie was equally at home with creamy pints of Guinness or with champagne or Pimms, quite comfortable with Bloody Marys for breakfast. Once or twice, Bonnie had stayed up drinking all night and walked to work the next morning, still drunk as a skunk. But Lit couldn't hold her drink at all. One glass of wine and she was warm-hearted and friendly. Three glasses and she was highly confident, though still just capable of walking a straight line to the loo in high heels without accidentally tripping on a perfectly innocent piece of carpet. Into her fourth glass, if she had to visit the loo, she made very slow and exaggerated progress, as if the ground might fall away at any moment. After the fifth glass, she was quite capable of seducing a perfect stranger or sharing her unbridled admiration for Johnny Depp with anyone who would listen. After that it was generally downhill all the way . . . slurred speech, plates of pasta which slivered down her chin and which she sucked in, making plughole-type noises, and deep discussions about the impossibility of romantic love and the silliness of marriage, the non-existence of God and the need for a tax on plastic bottles. So if Lit wanted to drink herself into a pleasant fog of sleepiness she generally only did it with Bonnie in the comfort of her home where she could rhapsodise over Johnny Depp and suck pasta to her heart's content.

Should she have a Ballygowan or a fruit juice? Or one of those peach-flavoured cordials that smelled like a bunch of flowers?

Conrad ordered a pint and waited for her to complete her deliberations.

"Glass of white wine, please."

Sometimes it was best to have one drink with a client. Sometimes clients didn't like to talk business with teetotallers. Not having a drink sometimes sent out the wrong signal. A person might think she was an alcoholic or pregnant or something. It was amazing the conclusions people jumped to sometimes. And Dublin was the rumour-capital of the world and she didn't want Conrad Budd thinking she was either an alcoholic or pregnant.

"Bottle of 1986 Chablis Grand Cru, Jim."

Lit gulped. A bottle was definitely not on the cards. A bottle would bring her way past the Johnny Depp stage into plastic-bottle territory. "Oh. No. I meant, you know, one of those little bottles – a Chardonnay or something . . ."

Conrad looked horrified. It was as if she had told him she was happy to drink meths.

"But you can't drink that stuff! It's in a screw-top bottle! Do you have any idea of the chemicals – ah – here we are . . . "

The waiter uncorked the wine and poured a drop into her glass for tasting.

She sipped and nodded. It was a nice wine. Very nice! Crisp! Enticing! The waiter filled up her glass and she took another sip. Mouth-watering!

"Do you like it?"

"Mmm! But I really will have only one glass. I wanted to ask you . . . what did the reporter mean by allegations of corruption?"

"You know what they're like. Rumours – like I said – it's their stock and trade. At this stage I've heard more scurrilous rumours about myself than I can even remember."

"Such as?"

"The usual . . . sex . . . drugs . . . there was a rumour going round last year that I was John F Kennedy's love child. Course my highly indignant mother phoned the papers and informed them that I was born over three years after the assassination – which put an end to that theory. Why do you ask?"

"Just doing research so that I can package you for the TV programme."

Conrad grinned warmly showing a nice set of teeth. His good humour seemed restored.

"A package. What sort of package will I make?"

She fiddled with the stem of her glass for a few

moments. "A successful man with a social conscience .
. . a privileged man who wants to help the less privileged . . . a man of vision who wants to make the city a
better place for everyone. Then more personal stuff . . .
friendly down-to-earth character, active healthy
lifestyle, man of the people who likes a pint and a flutter at the races . . . responsible engaged man with a simple lifestyle . . . you know the kind of thing . . . "

He shrugged and smiled modestly. Then he sat forward, topped up her glass and looked directly into her
eyes. "That's enough about me. What about you? What
sort of package do you make?"

Lit had consumed only one glass of wine and was still
able to muster up the slightly withering, fleeting smile.
She held his gaze for a few moments because she had to,
but she did not intend to get personal.

"Fortunately I don't have to package myself for the
public."

"But if you did . . . "

There was more dangerous eye contact. But she held
her own.

"Successful . . . single mother . . . efficient . . . cool . . .
grace under pressure . . . that sort of thing . . . " That was
OK . . . nothing too personal there.

"But I would have said all those things and
added . . . "

The deep brown eyes bored into her and Lit studied
the rim of her glass intently.

"I don't really think there's anything much to add to
that," she said with what she hoped was a dismissive
note.

"Oh, but there is. Beautiful, sensitive, intelligent, sense
of humour, excellent taste . . . exhilarating . . . "

Lit blushed, much to her annoyance. Conrad was

flirting with her, shamelessly flirting and it wouldn't do at all. Well, he could flirt all he wanted, but she would maintain a friendly distance. It was time to change the subject and remind him of a few relevant details.

"Tell me about your fiancée."

"Angela is Angela. What can I say? We've known each other for years. The wedding is set for next year. The reception will be here in the Shelbourne. Then on to Mauritius for two weeks' honeymoon." He trailed off, clearly uncomfortable talking about it. While Lit got stuck into another glass of wine, he talked instead about his family, his schooldays, how he got his first break in business. He talked easily and she was good at asking the right questions – so that the evening began to pass quite pleasantly and the wine flowed.

"And what about you? I want to hear all about you," he said finally, his dark eyes boring into her.

"September is a lovely time to get married. It all sounds perfect. You must be so excited," Lit persisted, determined to remind them both of his unavailable status.

From his expression, it seemed that while Conrad got excited about derelict sites and architect's plans, the thought of walking down the aisle with anyone did not appear to inspire him with any feelings other than mild dismay.

"And you?" he asked. "Is there someone special in your life?"

Now he was being very forward. But then she remembered that she had asked him about his fiancée first so it would be rude not to tell him something. But what? If she said 'no', he might think she was a sad and lonely and embittered scrap of humanity. If she said 'yes', he might lose interest in her. Not that she wanted him to be interested, and in any case 'yes' would be an outright lie.

"I'm kept very busy at work. But there is someone I see occasionally." Brilliant! She ought to have given herself a clap on the back for that.

"He's lucky!"

She smiled noncommittally and began sipping rapidly from her third glass of wine.

The Chablis was the most delicious wine she'd ever tasted and she emptied it in double-quick time. It barely felt like she was drinking alcohol at all. But she was fast approaching the stage when things which would have been ludicrous and totally out of bounds half an hour earlier suddenly seemed quite acceptable and reasonable. Would it be so wrong after all to have a few hours of unbridled passion with Conrad? She was sure in her mind that all she felt for him was lust . . . that was why she had tried to avoid looking at various parts of his anatomy. So if it was just lust, maybe Bonnie was right and she should go for it? After all, who would know? And the thought of having a pair of thighs and a set of shoulders like that bearing down on her was becoming almost too much for her. The effects of the cold shower had worn off hours ago and the pleasant wobbly little ache at the pit of her stomach had returned. Now, in between sipping wine and hoping that her lipstick hadn't worn away altogether, she was experiencing little erotic flashes in her head – nibbling on his ear – running her hands along his inner thighs – having her neck lightly bitten – having her nipples gently sucked . . .

And it wasn't as if he was actually married.

There was a tense silence for a few moments then Conrad blurted out: "I suppose I shouldn't say it . . . but . . . Lit, are you listening?"

"What? Yes . . . something you shouldn't say . . . " she croaked.

"I shouldn't say . . . I want to kiss you."

He was leaning forward across the little table and Lit found her face zooming slowly in to meet with his, utterly oblivious to her surroundings.

"I want to kiss you too," she murmured.

"I know I shouldn't, but I can't help myself," he muttered as his lips fastened on to hers for the briefest of kisses.

"No. We really shouldn't," she whispered and kissed him back, parting her lips and savouring the wetness of his mouth and the closeness of his skin and the feel of his breath on her face.

He ran his fingers lightly across her face, brushed his mouth against her ear, her hair. Her whole body was tingling with desire. Every little nerve from the top of her head to the tips of her toes seemed to be screaming sex, sex, sex at her.

"Let's go upstairs," she croaked. She could barely get the words out.

"It's up to you . . . I know I really want to . . . Jesus, the minute you walked in the doors of the foyer that first day . . . phew!"

"Yeah . . . me too. I want to . . ."

"Sure? We don't have to . . . it's just nice to get to know you . . . "

"Come on," she said, standing and picking up her bag. "Before we change our minds."

Five years of celibacy and clean living erupted out of her like the proverbial volcano. She could hardly contain herself. If he hadn't been six foot three and fourteen stone of smooth muscle, she might very well have flung him to the bed and ravaged him on the spot. But she was

203

tiny in comparison and almost half his weight, so there was nothing for it but to bide her time and savour his slow and achingly delicious undressing of her. He undid the buttons of her silk blouse, his hands lightly glancing off nipples which were screeching to be touched and kissed. She felt the skirt slide past her slim hips to the floor. Then somehow he had her slender frame naked against him. He caressed every part of her, kissed her passionately with sweet lingering kisses, and murmured into her ear that she was so beautiful. She'd forgotten what it was like to even want to feel a man inside her – but now it all came flooding back with a ravenous vengeance. Outwardly, she was relatively restrained and demure, returning his passionate kisses with teasing little bites and pecks. Inside, though, she was screaming: *Fuck me senseless this instant, you great big absolutely awesome hunk of manhood!*

Finally, when she thought she couldn't bear it any longer, he led her to the bed. Even then he denied her, stroking along her thighs with his fingers, parting her light pubic hair with the gentlest of touches, and bringing her almost to howling point with his tongue and his lips. At last he was on top of her, his lips on hers, finding his way deep into her, their bodies drenched in the sweet scented juice of desire. She called out for him, lost in the great power of him almost wrenching her open, drowning in his strong thrusts until they could hold off no more.

Afterwards, he held her in his arms and kissed her many times and stroked her hair.

"You are exhilarating! Amazing! What a woman!"

What a man! Lit thought to herself, but said nothing. Perhaps everyone should try five years' celibacy if that was the reward at the end of it. She could feel her eyelids getting heavy, the muscles in her body loosening. She longed to sink into his arms and fall into the traditional post-coital slumber, to wake up beside him in the morning and do it all over again . . . and again.

But she didn't.

"I have to go," she said, sliding from the bed and dashing to the bathroom, suddenly bashful about her naked body.

"I'd love you to stay."

"It's a nice thought. But best not." She shut the door of the bathroom, to prevent further persuasion on his part.

When she arrived home from the Shelbourne, Richie needed her undivided attention about a new game he wanted for his Playstation. He insisted on outlining to her in great detail just how *Graveraider V* was a vast improvement on *Graveraider IV* – in terms of graphics and levels and sound effects. For an hour, Lit half-listened with the sort of patience that is only granted to guilt-ridden mothers.

Dandy had to be helped into his night things and tucked into bed and of course she'd felt terribly guilty that instead of sitting at her father's side, she'd been in Conrad Budd's Shelbourne suite having the most amazing sex she'd ever had in her entire life. At last Dandy sent her away and she lay on her bed fully dressed for a long time, considering the complete folly of what she had done. In a few days' time, Conrad and his fiancée would be at her house for the party. How could she face them? How could she work for him now? How could she work for him ever again?

Alone in the perfect pale-colour harmony of her New England style bedroom, on her vast designer art deco-style bed, she shuddered and blushed with shame – for having sex with another woman's man, for having sex with an important client, for having sex with anyone when her father was so ill. And she trembled with guilty pleasure for having enjoyed it so much.

# CHAPTER 16

Setting up the house in Harwood Park for a sophisticated dinner party was relatively easy. The large front living-room opened into an even larger dining-room which in turn opened onto the patio and the large, landscaped, cobble-docked, terracotta-urned, timber-decked and perfectly manicured garden. Lit had a lady who cleaned three times a week, so the house – apart from the kitchen – was always pristine. The caterers arrived in the morning, established their nerve centre in the kitchen and began setting up trestle tables in the garden.

Dandy was not impressed. He stuck doggedly to his chair by the range and rattled his paper ominously each time a stranger dared to enter his domain where he lived, sitting by the fire, expounding on this life and speculating on the next one.

A few days had passed since her night of lust with Conrad and Lit had valiantly struggled to put it all behind her, vowing that never again would she entertain even a mildly erotic thought about Conrad Budd. From now on it would be purely a business relationship. She'd satisfied her carnal curiosity about him. It was time now to put the silly business behind her. She succeeded in part because she was kept so busy with work. Then she spent every spare hour fussing over her father and trying to ease her guilty conscience about him.

She especially regretted ever having agreed to the party.

"I can cancel this dinner. I'm sure the guests will understand. You're not up to it and it isn't fair."

"What are you going to tell them?"

"I'll just say you're not well."

"No, thank you. Then it'll be flowers and cards and well-wishers at the door. Besides, I feel perfectly well. There's nothing wrong with me. They probably made a mistake – those doctors. It happens all the time. No, you just carry on. Don't mind me."

Lit fretted. What was the right thing to do? On the one hand, she had to make a living and entertaining clients was an important part of that. On the other hand, her father was dying. It seemed inconsiderate somehow.

"No. I really think I should cancel. You're – well, you're – "

"Dying? Is that what you want to say? But I've been dying for years. Don't fret. It's not likely that I'll cause you the embarrassment of toppling over tonight. I'm not going to lean over one of your important swanky friends and say – excuse me, I think I'm going to croak now – I hope it doesn't put you off your food."

"Now you're being silly. It's got nothing to do with embarrassment. I'm thinking of you."

"Hmmph!" he grunted.

He always grunted when she said something nice to him. It was, she had discovered after years of thinking him a heartless old grouch, a genuine gesture of appreciation.

The caterers disappeared until the afternoon and Lit and Dandy sat in companionable silence for a while. She generally tried to devote Saturday mornings to her father and though he was an irritating old bastard, she

207

quite enjoyed spending the time with him all the same. It was a time for pottering in the kitchen, wrestling with the pile of debris on the counter which didn't have its proper place, for listening yet again to the story of how he was chased across the fields by a Black and Tan unit when he was a young boy, for talking and speculating about Richie and how he might turn out. It was a relaxing time when she tried to put all thoughts of image-making and public relations and marketing and logos and advertising campaigns and money and planning and traffic jams and the new pair of turquoise Jimmy Choo kitten-heeled mules with the pink butterflies that she absolutely must have as soon as she got the time to go shopping, completely out of her mind.

She made scones. It was the only thing she could bake and she loved the warm baking smell and the little ritual of rubbing the butter into the flour, adding a fistful of sugar, a pinch of salt, a scattering of sultanas and the baking powder, binding the mix with egg and milk, cutting out the rounds and brushing them with egg and milk. It was Lit's version of the Japanese Tea Ceremony – Lit Doran's Irish Fruit Scone Ceremony – a time for quiet reflection and spiritual renewal and family togetherness. And now with the news of her father's illness, she felt a sharp poignancy about these special moments together. The scones only took a few minutes to bake and then they were produced at the table with a bowl of soft butter, a jar of blackcurrant jam and a pot of strong black tea.

Dandy tucked in hungrily like a hardy working man – not at all like a man who was at death's door.

As he prepared to demolish a second scone he asked her, "Have you called Azelia?"

"Yes."

"She'll be home on the next plane no doubt!" he said, a trace of uncharacteristic bitterness in his voice.

"I'm sure she'll call tomorrow. It's her day off."

"Have you said anything to Richie?"

Lit shook her head.

"He's not to be told," said Dandy. "There's no point in upsetting him."

"He'll be more upset if I don't tell him."

"I don't want him knowing and that's final. I don't want him tip-toeing around me afraid to be himself. You know the way people get when you're sick – suddenly acting like Florence Nightingale and not talking about certain things like going to the pub, or cursing, or having a win on the horses – in case the patient gets offended. If you tell him, I'll cut you out of my will!"

Dandy's will consisted of a few thousand euros and the house in Templeogue which was rented out to a young hairdresser and her husband. As far as Lit was concerned, it wasn't much of a threat. Still she had to play along and humour him.

"I won't tell him until I have to. How's that?"

"It'll do. You haven't phoned Sheila?"

"I haven't yet."

"I suppose you'd better phone her or we'll never hear the end of it. And if she's planning to visit me, tell her I'm too ill for visitors."

"But –"

"Tell her the doctor said I can't take phone calls either – "

Lit arched an eyebrow.

"I read in the paper the other day that phones cause cancer in the brain."

"That's mobile phones."

"What's the difference? Anyway I don't want to talk

209

to her. She'll only want to come and discuss my symptoms and make me get anointed."

Auntie Sheila had a thing about Dandy being anointed. For the past fifteen years she called Lit at regular intervals to warn her that at his age death could come at any time. She wasn't a religious maniac or anything, but not being anointed was as bad as not being baptised.

When Dandy travelled to Australia on his eighty-fifth birthday to see his brother in Melbourne, he had received a plenary visitation from Auntie Sheila and her partner in crime, Father Michael Muldoon.

"We've got a special dispensation to give you the Last Rites before your journey on account of your great age, Bernard. A man of your age may not survive the ordeal or the plane might crash or you might get food-poisoning. That's fatal in an elderly person, Bernard. Best to be prepared. And you'll have great comfort knowing you've been anointed."

Dandy looked from his sister to the priest and then to the jars with the oils and the candles and felt one of his periodic bouts of despair at the human condition. His sister Sheila seemed to have bypassed the 'wisdom and serenity of old age' stage altogether. Wisdom and serenity were two words he definitely did not associate with her and wasn't it an awful state of affairs that a woman could reach her mid-seventies and still be the stupidist woman on the planet? Still, it was no surprise. She was born stupid and it was a quality she had developed and nurtured throughout her busy life – like others cultivate a musical ear or an artistic eye.

"It's very thoughtful of you, Sheila dear," he said to her finally. He only called her 'dear' when he wanted to rip her head off and disembowel her. "But I wouldn't like to tempt fate. If God saw the Anointed Me flying around the globe he might decide it was time for me to die and that would be most unfair on the other passengers."

Now Lit had to make the dreaded phone call. More planning and rehearsal went into a phone call to Auntie Sheila than any business call. She could seal a deal for hundreds of thousands of euros in the space of an hour, but the mere prospect of having to speak to Auntie Sheila for five minutes turned her into a watery jelly. If Lit ever ended up having a nervous breakdown or suffering from clinical depression, it would be because of her aunt.

She rehearsed her speech:

'Auntie Sheila – it's Lit here – how are you? Good. And all the family? That's great. The thing is Dandy has been to see the doctor and I'm afraid he's not that well – something in the stomach – no, I'm not sure what – the doctor says he's to have complete rest so I'll send him your best wishes and I'll keep you informed about his progress. Give my love to the family. Nice to talk to you, Auntie Sheila. Bye – "

That sounded fine, but Lit knew she'd never get away with it. In the rehearsed conversation, she was failing to factor in what her aunt might say. She lifted the phone and dialled the number. It rang out a few times and then she could hear the sweet crackly little voice on the end of the line.

"Hello?"

"Hello, Auntie Sheila – it's Lit here – "

"Lit! I was just saying to Joe that you haven't been in touch for ages!" Her tone of voice hinted at slightly hurt feelings, hurt feelings which she had of course overcome on account of her innate generosity of spirit and her towering strength of character. But yet a silence hung in the air, a silence which could only be filled with an apology.

"Yes. I'm really sorry, but it's been a really busy few months and I really don't know where the time goes. Really."

Even though Auntie Sheila always expected an apology about something, she then generally took the aristocratic line that other people's apologies should for the most part be ignored.

"Of course I've been very busy myself. I'm taking psychology in the Open University now. It's really fascinating. I've discovered so much about people. Job still going well, dear? That's good. You just keep going at that. The psychologists say it's perfectly natural to project all your ambitions into your work-and-esteem needs if your love-and-belongingness needs are in a mess – it's called transference, dear – "

"That's very interesting, Auntie Sheila – "

"Yes, it's all to do with this man called Maslow – apparently he went to see the Pyramids and it gave him the idea about human needs – "

The most disturbing aspect of talking to her aunt was the fear that she might end up like her – lecturing Richie on the horrific diseases he might catch from water sports or the psychological tasks of adolescence which he would have to carry out if he didn't want to end up being gay. Lit earnestly hoped that if such a catastrophic state of affairs was to arise, Richie would have the good sense to tell her to fuck off.

She had to interrupt. It wasn't easy. Auntie Sheila would adopt a hurt wounded tone. She would be sad that Lit didn't have the time to listen to her any more. She would mention the months she had sacrificed, selflessly steering Lit through pregnancy and young motherhood.

Lit struggled to regain control of the conversation. "Auntie Sheila. I have some bad news."

There was silence. Then a hesitant little question laced with a quiver of excitement. There was nothing like bad news to send Auntie Sheila's pulse racing.

"Is it your father?"

"Well, yes, he –"

"I'm so sorry, Lit. But it had to come. Death the Leveller. He comes to us all – princes and paupers, old and young. We'll be there as soon as we can. If there's any – "

"Auntie Sheila, the thing is, he's not dead – "

"Not dead? But you said 'bad news'!"

"He's not well. The doctor says – a large growth." Lit swallowed, hardly able to say the words. "The doctor says – weeks rather than months."

"You poor child! That's terrible!"

"Yes, he –"

"Where does he have it?" In hushed, sacrificial tones.

"The abdomen somewhere," Lit replied.

"Ah! The abdomen. It won't be pretty, Laetitia dear. You'd better prepare for the worst. It's probably got in everywhere – Billy Doran, our youngest brother, had it in the stomach first and then of course it spread – right through him – in the end it broke out and he –"

Lit cut her off before she could go into further horrible details. "I have to go. There's someone at the door. Bye, Auntie Sheila, I'll keep in touch." She replaced the receiver.

She felt numb suddenly. Telling Auntie Sheila made it real somehow. Having to put words on it made her realise that it would soon be only Lit and Richie. Big tears welled up inside her. She wanted to stop them, but couldn't.

When Bonnie arrived minutes later, she was puzzled to find Lit alone in the drawing-room, huddled up on the sofa sobbing her heart out, at first in so much distress that she couldn't speak. Between sobs, the story of Dandy's illness finally tumbled out and Bonnie too began to cry. She'd known Lit's father since she was a child, loved his gruff humour, his decency, his insistence on plain speaking, his fierce protective loyalty to his family.

"When did you find out?" she said at last.

"Few days ago."

"I'm so sorry, Lit."

"Thanks."

"Does Richie know?"

"Dad doesn't want me to tell him."

"That's understandable. But such a strain on you! Why didn't you cancel the dinner party?"

"Because he doesn't want me to. I suppose he doesn't want to miss any fun. He's not in pain or anything so maybe it's best to just carry on as normal."

"There's a lot to be said for that."

They sat on together for a while, Lit sobbing away and Bonnie patting her hand and telling her that having a cry was just about the best thing she could do.

Much later, when the afternoon sunlight shone directly onto the cobble-locked patio they took themselves out to the garden, threw off their shoes and basked in the heat. Mad dogs and Englishmen might not go out in the midday sun – but this was Dublin and you collected sunshine with much the same sense of life or death urgency as people around the equator gathered rainwater – any way you damn well could.

"So," said Bonnie, her eyes shut and her head tilted in the direction of the sun. "Have you seen Conrad lately?"

Lit shifted uneasily in her deckchair. "Eh, yes."

Through one half-open eye, Bonnie noticed that her

friend's toes were wriggling a bit – quite an ominous sign. "Anywhere nice?"

"The Shelbourne. Why do you ask?"

"No reason. Just making conversation."

There was a long silence as Bonnie sipped her glass of Australian Chardonnay and idly cast her eye over Lit's garden. Lit nervously wondered how long it would be before Bonnie prised the whole shocking episode out of her.

Once again the full impact of what had happened with Conrad hit her. She felt her face flame with embarrassment when she thought of how disgusting she was – practically drooling across the table at him when he said he wanted to kiss her. It was too horrible to think about. The worst thing was that she would have to face him in less than four hours – with his fiancée – and to face Conrad having lain naked with him only a couple of days before was almost more than she could bear.

"Was it a work-related evening?" Bonnie enquired at last.

"Yes. Quite. You know – about press briefings – that sort of thing."

There was another brief silence, broken only by the sound of water splashing in the fountains. Then Bonnie sat up straight, wide-awake now, eyes alert and sparkling. "You went and shagged Conrad Budd rotten! Didn't you?"

Lit couldn't look her in the eye.

"You said you wouldn't! You said you couldn't! And then as soon as my back is turned you go and rip the pants off him and assault him!"

Lit slouched in the deckchair, trying to feign composure and disinterest. "I really must trim back that scented jasmine."

"You don't have to answer. It's written all over you – that strange rash on your cheek – slightly swollen lips – the contented 'I've been shagged rotten' look in your eyes!"

Lit was indignant. How dare Bonnie be so vulgar? It wasn't at all like that and there was no point in explaining. Something beautiful – something passionate had happened between her and Conrad – it was electric – exquisite – elevating. But wrong. So wrong. So shameful! So – unethical! "I'm just tired. You're letting your imagination run away with you, Bonnie." And she yawned pointedly for effect.

"No. I don't think so," Bonnie replied. "And I want to hear all about it right now."

Lit nodded weakly. There was no sense in denying it any longer. She knew from past experience that Bonnie would keep pestering her until the whole truth came out. Although, in a sense, she couldn't wait to tell about her night of passion with Conrad. After all, she and Bonnie had shared their admiration of him for many years. And after five years of celibate living, the hours with Conrad would rank as the most unforgettable sexual hours of her life. Even if they were absolutely never going to ever happen again.

She settled into her chair, and told Bonnie all about lunch in the Valmont, the trip to the Stoneyfield site, the pickets, the reporters, then drinks in the Shelbourne afterwards.

"And?" said Bonnie.

"And – well, you can guess the rest. But I promise you it was definitely a one-off – it will never happen again."

She really meant it.

There really was no need for Bonnie to be looking at her so sceptically.

## CHAPTER 17

When Bonnie's avid curiosity was eventually appeased, Lit set about overseeing a flurry of linen tablecloths, glasses, crockery and furniture moving. Luckily the baby grand piano didn't have to be moved. It was next to the patio doors in the dining-room and was the ideal place for Tony Napoli to tinkle the ivories for the guests.

She put fresh clothes out for Dandy which nearly caused World War Three.

"But I only changed my shirt the other day."

"Yes, I know, but now you need a clean one. You want to look smart for my friends, don't you?"

"Not especially. Who's coming anyway?"

"Well, Bonnie is here."

"Bonnie won't mind how I look. I think she kind of likes me."

Lit pursed her lips and fastened his buttons with brutal efficiency.

"It's only you, fussing and making me get dressed and undressed like a tailor's dummy. I have got cancer, you know."

Lit felt a mixture of nerve-jangling irritation and all-consuming guilt.

"Could you stop the light-hearted banter – it's getting on my nerves. There are one or two very important clients coming. So please, Dandy – for my sake – behave yourself."

She recalled some of his earlier party performances. There was the time he took his teeth out at the table because a bit of bone had lodged somewhere. The time he had told Matt's mother that she had a fine pair of tits. And the time Harry Menton had come to dinner. Lit still

217

blushed at that one.

Dandy asked him if the baldness was hereditary in his family and he'd suggested that it would probably take a few years before Harry went fully bald, but that there was a great old shop in the city centre that specialised in hairpieces for the sophisticated man about town. Lit remembered Harry struggling valiantly to keep his composure and succeeding, until her father added his coup de grâce. "Of course," he said nonchalantly, "it's a bit embarrassing when it starts to fall out down below – if you know what I mean, Harry." Then he'd given Lit's American lover the benefit of a dirty conspiratorial grin and a sympathetic pat on the back. Harry never came back to her house after that.

Richie came barging into Dandy's room, sneezing loudly. "Mum, have you seen my black T-shirt? And I can't find the hay fever remedy. Oh – and don't forget to ask Conrad if I can have a go in that massive crane sometime. It's my only dare-devil ambition."

Lit pulled a face. "I'll ask, but don't hold out much hope – safety, insurance and all that."

"Please, just ask anyway. Did you say Bonnie was bringing a karaoke machine? Well, what do you say, Dandy? A duet – you and me – we'll sing 'We Are The Champions'!"

While Richie did a Freddy Mercury impersonation to keep Dandy busy, Lit slipped on his fresh shirt and tie. Then she shaved him with the electric razor which he hated and which made him snarl at her like a mangy old dog. Lastly she combed his hair and slipped his arms into a nice tweed jacket she had bought for him in Foxford Woollen Mills.

"What's this?" he growled sullenly.

"It's the new jacket I bought you. You remember – you

said you wanted a heavy tweed one – that it would keep you warm."

"I'm bloody freezing. This isn't proper tweed. I told you not to buy me any more clothes!" He fingered the cloth scornfully. "Where's my old jacket?"

"In the bin."

"Well, get it back for me."

"I can't. The binmen took the rubbish this morning."

The tension in the air was palpable. If Lit was wearing boots, she might very well have quaked in them. As it was she simply had to hold her ground and make herself a cross between Nurse Ratched and Florence Nightingale.

"It's a lovely warm day. Why don't you sit out in the garden and take the sunshine?"

That was entirely the wrong thing to say. He glared up at her, fixing the piercing grey eyes on her accusingly. "Isn't that why I'm in the mess that I'm in?"

"What do you mean?"

"The sun – the cancer. It doesn't take a genius to figure that out."

Lit was all patience, but it was running out – very fast. It was time to be Nurse Ratched. "Nonsense. You don't have skin cancer. Now out into the garden with you! You can sit in the shade under the oak tree."

Richie took him by the hand. "Come on, Dandy. Boy, you look good! The babes will be hot for you tonight."

"What does that mean? Is it good?"

"It means the ladies will be throwing themselves at you."

Dandy grinned boyishly and allowed himself to be led into the garden by his grandson.

At seven thirty Seán Tallon stepped into the shower. He

shampooed his hair, and lathered his smooth body beneath a powerful stream of warm water. Then he turned the water to cold, rinsed the shampoo from his hair and the lather from his body. He stepped out of the shower at seven thirty-three. By seven forty-five he was shaved, groomed and dressed in navy chinos with a white shirt and Italian leather moccasins.

Matt arrived at eight.

"My, my, Tallon! Some woman's going to sweep you off your smug feet one of these days."

Seán tried to catch his friend's eye. It was hard to know when he was being ironic.

"Me, I never can get it right," said Matt. "I mean I have a wardrobe full of clothes, all good quality. And I still manage to look like I just got out of bed."

Matt had donned a very expensive John Rocha linen suit in olive green with an even more expensive cream speckled silk shirt. But somehow, with pockets full of cigarettes, filofax, notebooks and scraps of paper, with his lax waistline and lumbering wrestler's gait, the clothes hung shapelessly on him.

"How long do we have to stay at this?" Seán was checking the faxes and e-mails on his laptop.

"Well, it is sort of my party – so you'll have to stay for a decent while."

"Bloody hell, Matt, you know I hate these things. I mean I can barely remember what your partner looks like and I'm not going to know anybody else there. I'll just stay for the meal, then make my excuses and leave."

Matt sighed like a mother trying to humour a sullen teenage son. "Look, they're nice people. Lit's a decent human being. And it will look good for our clients to meet you. Now tidy away your little toys, boy, get your keys and we're off."

Seán smiled wryly at his friend, folded away his laptop and slipped his mobile phone into the breast pocket of his jacket.

"And turn your mobile phone off! The entire money market will not collapse if you're out of contact for just three hours in the year."

Lit and Bonnie spent an hour upstairs getting ready. Bonnie had brought along a tight-fitting black jersey slip-dress and a pair of lethal-looking black leather stiletto sandals.

"Are you sure they count as footwear?" Lit enquired with more than a hint of irony.

"What's wrong with them?"

"Nothing! There's just very little shoe – I mean two straps that will hardly last the night."

"Never mind the shoes. I have another real dilemma."

Bonnie couldn't decide on a bra. She had brought along six different sorts – balcony – T-shirt – padded – Wonderbra – backless – strapless – and one she had bought in Spain with see-through plastic straps.

Lit was impatient. "Bonnie – it's a party – not a boobs contest."

"Yes – I know that. But if my boobs aren't right – then I can't relax. It's as simple as that."

Lit never understood what Bonnie's problem was. There were a couple of days in her own cycle when her breasts swelled magically to a thirty-six B and she would swagger around the office like a Baywatch Babe. But for the rest of the month, she fell firmly into the poached-eggs department. This was fine because most daytime fashion is designed for women with less frontage. But Bonnie was a regular thirty-six D – all the time! She looked only average in an office suit, but when she slipped into a slinky evening number men were frequently rendered speechless – reduced to gulping and swallowing and offering up prayers of thanks.

"So wear the balcony one," Lit said. She didn't even own a balcony bra. What was the point of having a balcony with nothing to display on it?

"But it's very uncomfortable. It kind of rides up and I have to keep hitching my boobs up like Les Dawson used to do. I think I should just go for the plain old Wonderbra –"

She put on her Wonderbra and slipped the slinky black dress over it.

"Perfect!" said Lit.

"No, it's not! You can see the straps."

"I thought it was OK to see straps now – like a fashion statement."

Bonnie heaved a sigh of suppressed annoyance. She continued patiently and slowly for Lit's benefit. "In some situations, it is OK to have bra straps showing – like if you can afford Lejaby, which I can't, or in a retro, post-post-modern, mock-ironic, kitsch-fun sort of way. But this is a classy LBN."

"LBN?"

Bonnie sighed and rolled her eyes to heaven. "Little Black Number! How are you so hopelessly behind in matters of fashion?"

"I'm not. I just don't have the time to devour *Vogue* magazine from cover to cover. It's OK for you teachers – "

"Here it comes – " Bonnie said in tones of near martyrdom, unable to stop herself. She began to mimic her friend, adopting a soft interviewee voice laced with false humility. "'I'm just so busy, Gerry. There just aren't enough hours in the day for me. But I'm so lucky because I enjoy my work as a PR executive and image consultant. You know, Gerry – I'd do it for nothing and that's the truth!'" Then she did the interviewer's voice – deeper and with tones of exaggerated respect and admiration: "'So, Lit – ladies and gentlemen, we are fortunate to have multimillionaire Lit Doran with us in studio today – Lit, take us through a typical working day.'

'Well, Gerry – of course I usually get up at about four thirty – and do my yoga exercises – then I jog backwards to the office and generally I'm at my desk by six am. Well, I find that I do my best work between six and eight – what? Breakfast? Oh yes – of course – some fresh berries and yoghurt – and a glass of hot water with a slice of lemon in it. My day is very busy – meetings – presentations – stuff you wouldn't really understand, Gerry – I might still be at my desk until nine o'clock at night. Then a light supper of grilled tomatoes with a lime dressing, followed by ten minutes quality time with my son, followed by bed –'"

"Why don't you just give it a rest!" Lit snapped, when she finally got a word in.

"I'm sorry." Bonnie instantly felt bad when she remembered the bad news about Dandy. "I didn't really mean all that. Trust me to shoot my mouth off. Friends?"

Lit humphed and sashayed her way into the marble-tiled, free-standing-bath-with-claw-feet-on-a-glass-plinth, white-monogramme-towelled bathroom – with designer stainless-steel radiators, white freesias in a black smoked glass by Kennedy and handmade soap by someone in Chelsea.

"Let me tell you one thing," she said, coming back to glare crossly at her friend. "Richie gets much more than ten minutes' quality time with me every day."

Bonnie opened her mouth to say something to defuse

the situation, but Cool Hand Lit had quietly shut the door of the bathroom and was washing away her niggling guilt beneath the powerful water-jets of her stainless-steel and glass-tiled shower unit.

# CHAPTER 18

By eight thirty the party was almost in full swing. Toni Napoli was tinkling Burt Bacarach tunes on the piano (as ordered by Dandy) and occasionally sang along with a rakish Dean Martin drawl.

The evening was balmy and in the garden about forty guests mingled and chatted, sipping champagne and nibbling on tiny intricately constructed delicacies – panini, goat's cheese in filo pastry, black olive paté on bruschetta, smoked-salmon parcels, a selection of sushi . . .

"What ever happened to good old-fashioned cocktail sausages and crackers and cheese?" Bonnie enquired as she tried to balance on her stilettos and look elegant at the same time.

Walking on the grass was out because of the heels. She was annoyed that she hadn't thought of it because there were some interesting-looking people clustered at the bottom of the garden who seemed to be having a great time. She might have to consider going barefoot.

"If you're going to spend the evening passing comments, you might as well go home now," Lit snapped under her breath. She wondered if their friendship, already under considerable strain, would survive the evening.

"I only meant . . . these are lovely. Really. I won't say

224

another word," Bonnie murmured.

She joined Dandy who was sitting in an armchair on the patio. He had a glass of wine in one hand and a canapé of some sort in the other.

"Dandy, how are you doing?" She bent down and pecked him on the cheek.

His eyes lit up when he saw her and he pulled himself up straight in the chair.

"You look lovely Bonnie. If I was a bit younger – I'd take you out to dinner and give you the time of your life."

"And I'd be happy to be your companion," she said, settling into a chair beside him.

He smiled off into the distance, then turned his attention to the canapé. "This muck tastes like toasted chicken-shit."

"Would you like me to make you a ham and mustard sandwich? Better than chicken-shit anyway."

"Thanks for the offer, Bonnie. But I'm not all that hungry anyway. Did I ever tell you about the time I was chased by the Black and Tans?"

"No!" said Bonnie who'd heard it at least a dozen times before.

"Then I'll tell you now."

Lit wandered about the house and garden, mingling with her guests and making introductions, the very picture of a calm and gracious hostess. Only those who knew her very well would have recognised that she was in a state of very high anxiety. She wanted everything to go well, wanted everyone to have a good time, wanted people to leave with a good opinion of her and Matt. Most of all she wanted to maintain their image as a much sought after, successful, ambitious and stylish company. So the most prestigious clients had been invited along with high-profile friends from the media and film world, and low-profile but influential people from banks and large corporations. She had invited some of the neighbours as well in the interests of harmonious relations. The best wine and champagne had been ordered. The most expensive and stylish caterers in the city had been hired. The most exotic menus had been prepared.

She bustled about introducing clients to one another, setting up meetings between interested parties, maintaining a discreet but watchful presence.

But she fretted about Dandy. Would he be up to the rigours of all these people milling around and would he behave himself? Would people be courteous and nice with him? She was relieved to see that he was deep in conversation with Bonnie. But that wouldn't last. As soon as Bonnie got some hapless male in her sights she'd leave Dandy and start moving in for the kill. Lit had arranged with Richie to keep an eye on her father and steer him out of trouble. She hoped he would take himself off to bed early. She wasn't ashamed or embarrassed of him, but some of her business associates seemed to think that like children, old people should be seen only briefly, and most definitely not heard.

And she also fretted, full of guilt and embarassment, about Conrad. How could she face him? She had spent weeks cultivating the ice-maiden image with him, and had ruined the whole thing, foolishly and impetuously, after a few glasses of Chablis Grand Cru. In bed in his suite, she had behaved like a sex-starved nymphomaniac for about three hours and she knew that now she would forever be imprinted in Conrad Budd's mind as Lit Doran the sex-starved closet nymphomaniac image consultant.

In an attempt to compensate, she had dressed very demurely for the party in a chiffon silk dusty-blue knee-length dress with only the slightest hint of a vee at the neck. But she didn't think it would change his opinion of her. Then she was also going to have to act all welcoming and friendly to him and his fiancée when she really needed to be arctically cold and distant, to regain a precarious hold on their business relationship. What worried her most was that he might no longer want a business relationship.

Matt arrived with Seán Tallon in tow and quickly began working his way through the crowd. She watched her partner moving happily around the garden, a man of substance, a man of influence, oozing confidence and success if not style, and she remembered the time when they had barely enough to eat.

About six months after Lit and Matt set up in business they had only three clients, two of whom had come with them from Devlin Satchwell. They were a small confectionery company and a TV presenter who was desperate to re-invent herself for a younger, sharper audience. The third client was a German film producer who was in his own words a close personal friend of Coppola, Tarentino, Altman, Jordan and some European directors that Lit had never heard of. He disappeared after about a month's strenuous hard work on their parts involving some vaguely mentioned film work and without paying his bills.

They had rented a tiny office in an alleyway near the Ha'penny Bridge. The office consisted of a room with orange-painted brick walls, two dinged grey metal desks, a rickety filing cabinet with dodgy drawers and a couple of chairs. There was a sinister-looking carpet which they lifted and because they didn't have much work to do at the time they stripped down the floor – which turned out to be old oak – and polished it.

After a few weeks, they realised that all their work on the floor was in vain. Nobody came near them. Nobody wanted them. It was as though they didn't exist. They had no money coming in and a big city rent going out.

They hadn't been very rich in Devlin Satchwell, but now they were on the starvation line. Matt moved in with Lit and Dandy and Richie in Templeogue because he had no money to pay rent. For lunch they ate thinly sliced picnic ham sandwiches with no butter and watery instant coffee. Lit became obsessed with the free offers on supermarket receipts and would walk miles with Richie just so that he could get a free burger and chips. Matt even began to lose weight.

But he jollied them along.

"We only have to stick it out. All companies have a lean start-up time. This time next year, we'll be turning them away."

Lit didn't think so.

They trawled the city for business, but there was none. No-one wanted to hire a company they had never heard of. No-one wanted to know them. Richie was dispatched around town delivering leaflets after school. Then the printer ran out of ink and they had no money to replace the cartridge and that was the end of the leaflets.

Lit's friends advised her to give it up, to be sensible and think of Richie.

One rainy November afternoon she sat down with Matt to review the situation over two black watery instant coffees.

"I could get another job," Matt offered. "Then you

could hold the fort here until things pick up and my salary could pay the rent on the office. I'm still hopeful. It's only a matter of time. And besides it's the least I can do."

Lit wasn't so sure. The idea of sitting alone in an office day after day, staring failure in the face didn't really appeal to her.

"Perhaps we should both call it a day. Take out a loan. Pay off the rent we owe and get proper jobs."

Matt was devastated at her suggestion. He leaned his head on his arms and cried for a solid half hour. Then he stood up and blew his nose.

"Right then! I'll get a job. You stay here for another month. Then we'll call it a day. Agreed?"

They shook hands in solemn agreement across the battered old metal desk.

Two days later Matt got work doing tele-sales for a new computer firm and Lit forced herself to sit alone in the office each day, waiting for clients. She felt like someone from a Beckett play, alone in her dingy little room, waiting pointlessly for some unknown person to show up and change her life. Only no-one turned up. She made phone calls which were never returned. Sent out brochures which were ignored. Set up costly lunch dates with contacts who never managed to show up.

To pass the time, in the afternoons, she strolled around the narrow cobbled streets of Temple Bar. It seemed that each day a new business was opening up and she consoled herself with the knowledge that they would never take off. Who in their right mind could make a living from a shop which only sold skateboards or clothes for Goths? Then, what seemed like only days later, her spirits would sink lower as she came across throngs of pre-teen boys queuing to get into the skateboard shop and even bigger throngs of Goths milling around the Goth Shop and emerging with shopping bags packed with merchandise. It got so depressing watching these strange new enterprises setting up and taking off, their proprietors pulling up in flashy sports cars and popping in and out of ludicrously expensive restaurants for champagne lunches, that she stopped rambling through Temple Bar altogether. Sometimes, if the day was fine, she would go and sit in the little square and nibble half-heartedly on a thin Bovril sandwich. But mostly she stayed in the office, reading library books about highly successful entrepreneurs and how they had survived the lean times. She avoided the chapters about how they had made their fortunes. It was too disheartening. And anyway she didn't want to make a fortune. All she really wanted was enough to pay the bills, go on the occasional holiday and put Richie through school. It didn't seem like a lot to ask.

A week before the day that she and Matt had nominated as their last day, Lit was trawling through the situations vacant columns in the newspapers. There were plenty of office jobs and jobs with computers – nothing she even vaguely liked. But it was a case of taking what she could get and she began half-heartedly drawing circles around ones that she might have to apply for. She even considered calling Mr Butler in Motorphone and asking for her old job back. It would mean sitting next to Mary Dempsey and her catastrophes and support stockings for the next thirty years. But it would be a job and there was Richie to think of.

Then a sudden knock on the door made her jump. She knew it couldn't be the landlord looking for rent because they were paid up – if only until the end of the week. She quickly pushed the newspaper and the library books into the drawer of the desk and said as coolly as she could:

"Come in!"

The door opened and a funny little man put his head around the door. He was in his forties with a bald patch framed by a circle of grey crinkly hair. He wore a smart sports jacket and trousers that were too long for him and buckled at the ankles.

"Hello," she said.

"How're you doing?" His accent was northern – Donegal, she supposed.

"What can I do for you?"

"I'm looking for someone to handle a bit of publicity for me. Could you do that?"

"That's us. That's what we do. Won't you sit down?"

He sat into the chair and watched her intently for a few moments.

"See, I'm launching a new product so I am."

"A new product?" Her heart jumped. This could be the dream ticket. A new company – a new product – no baggage.

"Yes. A new product and people are going to laugh at me and say I'm just a loser."

Her heart sank. "Why would people say that?"

"Because sometimes I am a loser. I've set up more businesses and ventures than you can think of – plastic milk cartons – disposable track suits – them wee things you pin on your dashboard to hold your electric razor in – some of them work – a lot of them don't."

Lit was now experiencing a plunging feeling in the pit of her stomach. Of course he was a loser. Why else was he in her office? He'd probably been around all the other big agencies and been laughed out into the street. Still, she had nothing better to do – so she heard him out.

"Anyway, that's the sort of thing – a monster truck racing-track in Leitrim – an ostrich farm in Mayo and so on. But this one is different."

"How's that?"

He pulled a photo from his jacket pocket and passed it across the desk to her. Lit studied the blurred image of five young lads.

"Your family?" she enquired.

"Not at all! They're the boy band." He beamed proudly at the photo like a man possessed.

She tried hard to conceal her amusement. No-one had ever heard of an Irish boy band back then. Across the water there were highly successful slick professional acts who were cleaning up on the music scene – but here in Ireland, it just wouldn't happen. And if it did happen, it certainly wouldn't be because of this tubby little creature in the chair in front of her.

"The name's Oliver Doherty by the way."

"OK then, Oliver – bring me up to date on what's happening and we'll take it from there."

Oliver began his story about seeing the five lads singing in a local talent contest in Inishowen and being really, really impressed and how he approached them and offered to act as their agent and how they had jumped at the opportunity. So far they had performed at the Mary of Dunloe Festival and the Carndonagh International Carnival amongst other places. This week they were due to sing at a big international gathering of the O'Donnell clan in Gweedore.

"Can they sing?"

"They're the best." He beamed proudly across the table.

"Do they dance or any of that stuff?"

"Aye, they're getting the hang of it."

232

"Are they pretty – I mean do you think they'd look good in front of a TV camera?"

"They're fine young men. The finest. Tell you what – why don't you come and see them playing in the studio tonight. They're recording a demo-tape around the corner from here."

"OK." Lit had nothing better to do. And for all she knew Oliver Doherty had discovered the next Beatles.

She called Matt and later that evening they sat in a dark grimy studio that smelt of beer and dope, watching the five lads – Cal, Joe, Packy, Donal and Shamie – run, or rather stagger through their paces. Cal was reasonably good-looking if you discounted his stained teeth and pimples. He could also sing as long as the notes fell within a certain narrow range. But he couldn't dance to save his life. Joe had frizzy long hair so it was hard to see what his face was like. He had been an Irish dancer and was quite nimble on his feet. But he didn't seem to have a note in his head. Packy and Shamie were good-looking in a boy band sort of way, but they didn't do much of anything. And Donal, who had been drinking vodka and coke all day, sported a fine beer belly and had all the co-ordination of a deranged octopus.

Oliver Doherty beamed at them encouragingly, nodding any time their movements demonstrated any rhythm at all or when Cal attempted to hit a high note. Their chosen songs were 'Leaving on a Jet Plane', a slow number made famous by Peter, Paul and Mary, and a song which at first Matt couldn't identify but eventually turned out to be 'Take it to the Limit' by the Eagles.

Matt buried his head in his hands and Lit suppressed a few sniggers. She had reached that stage of desperation when the only sane response to their dreadful plight was to laugh dementedly at each new catastrophe.

"What are we going to do?" she asked finally and then began answering her own question. "I think we should just thank Oliver for offering us this golden opportunity and tell him that unfortunately we're not really experienced in the music business."

Matt was aghast at her suggestion. Doherty might be a no-hoper but he must have some money. And at least they'd get paid for working for him.

"Beggers can't be choosers – let's see what he has to say. At least there's a free pint in it."

Over drinks in the Clarence, Doherty outlined his scheme – appearances on television, magazine features, a single to be aimed at the number one slot, maybe a film soundtrack, a European tour, an album for the Christmas market . . .

Matt was mostly absorbed in savouring his first pint in six months and hardly listened to Oliver Doherty's grandiose schemes.

"I'll pay you a straight percentage – two per cent. How's that?"

"Certainly not," Lit cut in, convinced they would never see the man or his little boys again. "If we are to get involved in marketing – what did you call them again – Northern Lads – if we are to get involved in promoting Northern Lads – we want a fixed fee. Five thousand pounds. Up front."

Matt tugged at her elbow. It was all academic anyway, but it would be fun to engage in a little haggling. It would be practice for the real thing.

"Let me handle this," he said impressively, straightening himself up like Laurel or was it Hardy, and pulling out a pen and filofax. He made a show of doing a few calculations. "What my partner means is that we need five thousand up front. After that – we want fifteen percent and a five-year contract."

He was delighted with himself. It was a great game – and he could afford to be as pushy as he liked because Oliver Doherty and his Northern Lads were nobodies and would never see the light of day – ever.

"Ten per cent!" said Doherty.

"Done!" said Matt and they toasted the deal.

Matt felt as chuffed as if he had just signed up U2, REM and Madonna all in one go.

Doherty stood up to leave.

"I'll be along with the paperwork tomorrow. And if you don't get them on the *Late Show*, the deal's off."

Three weeks later, Lit and Matt sat with Doherty in Lit's sitting-room, watching the full excruciating horror of Northern Lads appearing on the *Late Show*. Lit had pulled out all the stops to get them on it.

The host was patronising and made sneering eye contact with the cameras. The audience sniggered nervously. The cameramen zoomed in on the lads' pimples and their uncoordinated footwork. The clothes which looked fine in rehearsal looked ill-fitting and cheap under the studio lights. Cal wasn't able to hit the high notes and the others couldn't keep in key with him and when they finished their first number 'Take It To The Limit' the audience didn't even clap. It was like all their jaws had locked open simultaneously.

For the second number, Cal fell out of step with the others which made him nervous and made him sing out of tune. Packy's pants ripped at the back and so he couldn't do the elaborate twirls that the dancing teacher had practised with them. When the camera zoomed in on Donal, he leered drunkenly at it, like a man about to keel over.

Lit pressed the mute button and they watched the

remainder of the performance in silence and in a state of gut-blasting embarrassment.

When it was all over Matt stood up and shook Doherty's hand. Enough was enough. Northern Lads had no future – well, not in show-business anyway.

"No hard feelings, Oliver. We did our best. Got them on the *Late Show*. They just don't have it. The deal was five thousand up front for expenses one way or another. So I guess it's pay-up time."

But Oliver wasn't giving up that easily.

"Ah give them a chance, lads. The audience and the lights and the cameras – they were a bit shaky! I'm going to see this thing through – and when they're number one, you'll get your five thousand – "

"But we agreed – "

. "You'll get your money!"

It was an appalling state of affairs, but there was nothing for it but to continue their association with the daft Donegal man. They needed the five thousand pounds to pay off their debts. So for three months Lit and Matt plugged away with press releases, interviews with teen magazines, appearances at charity functions and rock concerts, weekly abject letters of apology to the producer of the *Late Show* for the unusually disappointing performance of the normally electrifying Northern Lads and reminders of their forthcoming single.

"I'll get my fucking five grand out of Oliver Doherty if I have to squeeze it out of him," Matt would chant every day.

Doherty grudgingly paid up two thousand pounds and reiterated his promise of the ten per cent fee and a five-year contract if Northern Lads made it to number one.

At Lit's insistence, he took the lads to elocution classes, dancing classes, singing classes, deportment classes, dental hygienists, dieticians and style consultants. Matt began referring to him in sinister undertones as Svengali O'Doherty.

By some piece of freakish good luck, hard graft, favours pulled in by Matt and sheer pigheadedness, Northern Lads got a second bite at the apple – play-time and an interview on a morning radio chat show. Lit and Matt tuned in, more out of morbid curiosity than anything else. They hadn't even bothered to go along to rehearsals. What was the point? Northern Lads were setting themselves up for the biggest humiliation of their lives. The host on the *Late Show* was a cuddly spaniel compared to the ruthless Doberman who did the radio show. Lit was trawling the situations vacant page again. Matt was thinking of moving to Australia and idly browsed through leaflets from the Australian Embassy.

The day of the group's second interview arrived. Lit and Matt sat in their office huddled over a crackly old radio.

"So, lads – a boy band from Donegal – how do you fancy your chances? Your performance on the *Late Show* was – slated," Gerry O'Brien enquired with a hint of his lethal irony.

Cal spoke first. "The band has been hard at work for the past few months – rehearsing – voice training – "

"That's right, Gerry," chipped in Donal who sounded – sober! "We've been living like monks – only not having as much fun. No drink, no girls, no drugs – not that we would anyway – "

"And you were telling me earlier that you've lost two stone, Donal?"

"Yes, Gerry – a healthy diet, no drink as I said and

two hours in the gym every day. The killer of it is that all these babes are now making up to me big-time – but I just don't have the time." Donal laughed with modest pride and a new sexy kind of husky Donegal catch in his voice.

Lit and Matt exchanged glances. Could this be the same five teenagers who were barely capable of saying "vomiting vodka in the back of the Volvo and a packet of cheese 'n onion crisps, please" when they went to the bar, and whose idea of a hard day's work was getting to level four on the Playstation and not having the money to order in chips in curry sauce.

Then came the song – 'Leaving on a Jet Plane' – sung in perfect harmony, with Cal having added about ten higher notes to his repertoire and Donal singing two lines of the chorus unaccompanied, his voice pure, melodic – in tune!

"Wow!" Gerry O'Brien gushed when they had finished. "Wow! And double Wow! Northern Lads, folks – write it down – because you'll be hearing a lot more of these lads – sensational harmony, folks – lovely old song given the Northern Lads treatment – hurry out and buy it – now here's their beautiful rendition of that old Eagles classic – 'Take it to The Limit'."

Six weeks later they were number one in the British charts and Lit and Matt got their ten per cent and their five-year contract. The deal which they had laughingly carved out with Oliver Doherty earned them several hundred thousand pounds.

"Who's the guy with Matt?" Bonnie asked Lit.

"Sorry. I was a million miles away. Where?"

"There – the guy with the sun-bleached hair and the cool Steve McQueen eyes. Just introduce me – don't worry, I'll be on my best behavior."

"But I can't see any fair-haired guy – just Matt and Seán Tallon."

"That's Seán Tallon?"

Lit nodded vaguely. Her eyes darted around, searching for Conrad, wondering where he might be. Perhaps he wouldn't come at all and she reasoned that it would be for the best. Who wanted embarrassing little post-coital frissons at a party anyway?

"You never said he was so handsome. You said he was dull and boring and it would be like falling for R2D2."

"No – I said like falling for the FTSE. And he is – the dullest creature under the sun. Come on. I'll introduce you. But I warn you – he's an alien life form. It's life, Bonnie – but not as we know it. Think Mr Spock - and then take away the personality."

"What you mean is that Seán Tallon didn't give you the once-over like most men and your pride is hurt. You think any man who isn't instantly stunned by your beauty and elegance is dense."

"That's crap and, if you don't believe me, see for yourself. And don't expect him to notice your balconied boobs. He'll probably think they're for resting his drink on."

"We shall see," said Bonnie as she teetered behind Lit, her heels occasionally sinking into the turf beneath.

Seán Tallon sat on a garden chair nursing a glass of beer and brooding darkly. Probably fretting about the NASDEQ or whatever it was that taxed the sad little brains of tedious people like him, Lit concluded.

"Bonnie Ballantyne meet Seán Tallon," she declaimed as though she was introducing Cindi Crawford to a dung-beetle.

Tallon stood up and Bonnie shook his hand, beaming

like a cat about to pounce.

"Lit tells me you're very boring. Is this true, Seán Tallon?"

Oh God! Bonnie was in one of her shit-stirring moods. In spite of her dislike for Tallon, Lit cringed slightly, waiting for the inevitable ourburst from him. Why had she introduced them? Why had she even invited Bonnie? It was clear she didn't have any grasp of the social graces left at all. No! Their friendship definitely wouldn't last the evening.

Tallon frowned and dipped his head. "Probably!" he said.

And Lit was astonished to see the merest hint of a smile flicker across his face. Or perhaps it was a dodgy circuit! Either way, the awkward moment seemed to have passed and now perhaps Bonnie would stop being so tactless and impish and start talking about the weather or the FTSE or something.

"So what do you think is your most boring feature?" Bonnie ploughed on recklessly.

Never again! She would never ever invite Bonnie to any important event ever again. It was just too risky. Perhaps, after today, she might never even speak to her again.

He kicked at the dusty earth, then looked up at Bonnie and smiled, a broad friendly smile. Bonnie seemed to find him fascinating..

"I suppose my most boring feature is that I hate parties."

"So do I," said Bonnie sympathetically. "I mean Lit had to practically drag me here tonight. I'm only doing her a favour. Usually, I'm a simple stay-at-home kind of girl. I'm most happy curled up on the sofa with a good Russian novel and a bottle of Chablis Grand Cru."

Lit observed how the lifeless robot almost came alive and she thought she noticed something like a flirtatious, mischievous glint in his eye. She figured it was probably just the evening sun reflected in his irises but, all the same, he did almost appear animated.

She wanted to blow the whistle on Bonnie's ludicrous claim that she was happiest with a Russian novel and a bottle of Chablis. A Russian sailor and a bottle of massage oil was closer to the truth.

Bonnie chattered on, and Lit was surprised and relieved to see that Tallon seemed quite taken with her outspoken friend. Now that a crisis was averted, she was able to turn her attention to the other guests once more. There was still no sign of Conrad and it was almost ten o'clock. Of course, she had no right to be fretting more over his arrival than anyone else's, but she did all the same. Somehow the party seemed dead. Somehow the people seemed dull. Even though she didn't want him there. Even though she would never have a wicked thought about him again.

She went in search of Matt and found him in the kitchen reassuring Poppy and Dara Cornwell that there was indeed a vegetarian selection of food.

"I quite understand if you haven't taken us into account," Dara was saying. "We're used to discrimination. Please don't worry on our account."

Matt felt like saying 'It's precisely your account I'm worried about', but bit his tongue.

"No really!" he said, knocking back a glass of wine like water. "We're sorted. Vegetarian Roulade with Roasted Aubergine and sun-dried pepper and tomato – served with – now let me see – served with – ah, some kind of thingy – "

"Thingy?" enquired Dara.

"Lit, there you are! What is the word I'm trying to think of – the red watery stuff that they drizzle around the edge of the plate – "

"Raspberry coulis?"

"The very thing. Raspberry coollee. Glass of wine?"

"We're teetotal."

"Ah! Wise. Good for the liver. No wonder you two are in such good shape."

"I appreciate your sentiment, but we seek inner beauty. We do not wish to be judged by our external physical appearance."

'Ah, fuck it then!' Matt wanted to say. 'You've come to the wrong fucking place altogether. We're a drinking, swearing, meat-eating, sexually deviant, totally superficial kind of a company who spend all day worrying about the length of our dicks or the size of our bums.' But instead he expressed his complete agreement with Dara Cornwell, smiled warmly at Poppy and told Lit that there was someone he had promised faithfully to introduce her to down at the really far end of the garden.

"Jesus! They're like the fucking Sisters of Mercy, the Poor Clares, the Amish, the Mormons, the Moonies, the Jehovahs all rolled into one – but without the humanity or the sense of humour," he mumbled as he followed Lit out into the garden once more.

"Shh!" Lit hissed.

"Anyway, the important thing is I got him to agree to put a bit more money up front."

"How?"

Matt cocked his head to one side and smirked. "I just told him we wouldn't do any more work for him until he paid us our due."

"Liar! That wouldn't work on him! How did you do it?"

Matt bowed his head sheepishly. "I promised him a discount."

"Jesus! Matt!"

"What would you have done?"

Lit shrugged. Now was not the time to scold Matt about a job badly done.

"Never mind!" she said. "Look at your cryogenically frozen friend."

"Who?"

"Who do you think?"

Matt followed her gaze to the seat at the bottom of the garden and saw Seán Tallon talking earnestly to Bonnie, his arm draped casually across the back of the seat.

"And your point is?" he said to Lit.

"Well! It's obvious, isn't it? He's had his sex microchip installed. I'm impressed. You know, from here, it almost looks like the real thing. I mean – Bonnie laughing and smiling like that. It's some kind of Kryptonite hypnotism thing."

"You're all wrong about Seán. The money thing – it's just a shield. He's rolling in the stuff though you wouldn't think it. He drives an old Renault and lives in a simple little apartment."

"Where's that? Mars?"

As far as Bonnie was concerned, the main requisites in any man were those which were visible or potentially visible to the naked eye. And she figured that Seán had those qualities in abundance. She had accidentally dropped her lighter into his lap and, in trying to retrieve it, was able to make a brief but effective examination of the inner thigh area. Firm and ample, ample and firm. And as well as that, she felt comfortable enough with him to kick off her shoes and hitch up her bra without having to go to the loo. He seemed to think her jokes were funny and he insisted on lighting her cigarette though he didn't smoke himself.

It was as good a way of measuring a man's worth as any. Because Bonnie had met men who couldn't cope with women who kicked their shoes off, or women who needed to adjust their underwear, or women who smiled and seemed to enjoy life or women who liked their food, or smoke or drank or swore, or women who had more than a few brain cells – or for that matter, women of any sort, apart from naked women with boobs the size of airbags.

She curled up comfortably beside him on the seat, glowing with the prospect of his admiration and aching at the possibility of sex with him.

Toni Napoli played 'This Guy's In Love With You'. The waiters carried platters laden with food to the long tables in the garden. The waitresses moved among the crowd refilling glasses and telling people that food was now being served. The red sun glowed warmly on the horizon. The guests smiled and laughed. And already Matt had clinched two new lucrative deals. Even Dara Cornwell had found someone tolerably interesting to talk to. Poppy stood demurely by his side for a while and then excused herself.

"Now behave yourself, darling," Dara said to her pointedly.

"I'm just going to the bathroom," she replied, wounded.

Out of sight, in the house, she dashed into the kitchen, and grabbed some leftover smoked salmon and brown bread, stuffing it into her mouth like her life depended on it. She looked disapprovingly at the foie gras and opted for some succulent-looking honeyed chicken. As she wiped the warm sweet syrup from her chin she spied Matt out of the corner of her eye.

"Don't mind me," he said. "Here, have a glass of wine, why don't you?"

He poured her a glass of white and she tackled it eagerly.

"Steady on! You should sip wine."

"You won't tell?"

"My lips are sealed." He smiled reassuringly at her.

"Thanks," she said shyly, knocking back the last of the wine. Then she grabbed a stick of raw celery and returned demurely to her husband's side.

"Hmmm!" said Matt to himself.

Dandy sat in his chair on the patio surveying the scene like an ancient Chinese mandarin, inscrutable and unimpressible.

Maura was in high spirits. She was well over Barry Owens by now, well past the stage of constantly playing 'I Will Always Love You-u-u-u' by Whitney Houston and had moved on to a non-stop frenzy of 'No Woman, No Cry', 'I Will Survive' and looking at new car brochures. Buying a new car was a fail-safe way of confirming that a relationship was over. She chatted effervescently to Dermot O'Driscoll from the IRFU who seemed more than happy with the attention.

The only person who was definitely not in the party mood was Lit. A few times, she had found herself sneaking looks at the door. Twice she told Richie that she thought she heard someone knocking and made him check. Then Jack Kennedy turned up alone and her heart sank further. Conrad had been too embarrassed or too disinterested to come himself and had sent his tedious little mosquito of an assistant.

She decided to turn her back to the house and the door

altogether. It was an awkward sort of arrangement because sometimes she found herself doing a strange dance around her guests so that at all times her back would be to the door and she would be facing the row of trees at the end of the garden.

Jack Kennedy sidled up to her.

"Great party."

"Thanks."

"Pity Conrad can't be here. Still – here I am – his able lieutenant at your service."

She wondered if it would be an awful thing to stand on his tiny feet or just push him into the bushes and spray him with insecticide. Then she realised what he had said: 'Conrad can't be here.' So that was it. The whole night was a disaster. She had intended to feel icy and dispassionate, to repel any advances he might make, to rebuild the boundaries of professional competency. Instead, she was experiencing awful flushes of rejection and neediness. And even if she never intended to have anything other than a business relationship with him in future, she still felt stung that Conrad hadn't considered it worthwhile coming to her party. He had been all over her the other night – in every sense. And it was obvious now that it meant nothing.

She wondered why she was surprised. Just because she had been out of the dating game for a couple of years didn't mean that all the bastards had gone away. Now that she thought about it, they were probably even more advanced now – it was like Leaving Cert results. Now a bloke probably had to have a PhD in bastardy to qualify as a bastard at all.

She met Bonnie who was carrying second helpings for Seán Tallon.

"Seconds?" she said a trifle cattily.

"It's for Seán."

"You mustn't feed him. It'll interfere with his circuits," said Lit waspishly.

"Just because you're in a huff doesn't mean the rest of us can't have a good time."

"What a sad life you must lead!"

"Look! Lay off! If you screwed Mr Megathighs and he hasn't even had the decency to turn up at your party – that's your problem. Seán Tallon is handsome, witty, good-mannered and I bet he's dynamite in bed."

"If you're into electronic sexual aids, I'm sure he's just the thing."

Lit turned on her heel and went to talk to a couple of newspaper columnists.

Watching Bonnie and Seán Tallon together out of the corner of her eye, she experienced a twinge of jealousy. That was her a few nights before. She too had basked in a man's admiration and attention just like Bonnie was basking now. She too had glowed with warm feelings and the prospect of things to come.

She chatted to the newspaper men until they had to leave. Then she sat with Dandy for a while and introduced him to some of her guests. When he settled into a friendly argument with Dermot O'Driscoll about whether Gaelic or Rugby was the better game, she was happy to leave the pair of them to it. Once again she rambled down the lawn and once again found herself in the company of Bonnie and her attentive companion.

"I was asking Seán earlier what time in history he would like to have lived in," said Bonnie. "Tell Lit, Seán, while I go and top up our drinks."

It was hardly a riveting topic of conversation, thought Lit. But she was stuck with him until Bonnie returned, so she might as well make the most of it.

"Well?" she said, not even bothering to feign interest in what his answer might be.

"I'd live in the nineteenth century and be an explorer." He looked directly at Lit. "What about you?"

"I've never given it any thought," she said coolly and then, vaguely regretting her rudeness, added, "Well, no other time actually. Now is the time for me. Now is the only time so far in history that I can do what I am doing. In the past women had a dreadful time."

"Probably – in some respects."

She resisted the urge to hiss at him. "Probably! If I was alive two hundred years ago, I'd certainly be dead by now."

Tallon smirked. "Yes, I see what you mean!"

She decided to ignore his sarcasm. "I mean that I'd be prematurely dead from childbirth, from disease, from malnutrition. And I'd be powerless to do anything about it. Now I can live to a ripe old age and make a difference in the world as well."

She knew she sounded harpy-like and strident, but she couldn't help herself. Suddenly it seemed vitally important to win this silly little argument, to get the better of Tallon. She continued. "I have a chance to use my real strengths in the modern world."

Bonnie returned with drinks and with Matt in tow.

"For instance?" asked Tallon.

"For instance, women tend to be less confrontational. I find that's helpful in the business world. And it's also a good thing in government, don't you agree?"

"Nonsense," he said. "You must have confrontation. Otherwise, how do you tease out all the angles on things? If everybody agrees to agree then vital points may be overlooked. Look, let's say, for instance, a man stands up in the Dáil and says he's going to give free housing and excessively generous tax allowances to unmarried mothers – well, that's a matter to be teased out. It would be quite wrong to accept such a notion without confrontation." When no-one responded to this declaration, he continued in an attempt to clarify his point. "Because, of course, society can't survive in a situation where women are rewarded for bearing children out of wedlock – a society made up of single mothers isn't a society at all."

Because he was someone who lacked the vanity of needing to see how his character impacted on others, Seán didn't even notice the awkward silence which followed his little lecture.

Lit wasn't much offended for herself. In fact, she wasn't even surprised by the vehemence of Tallon's words. It was probably something his microchip had programmed him to say. It was when she glanced over at her son that she felt her chest filling up with anger and motherly indignation.

She raised her withering eyebrow and beamed a look of mild contempt at His Robotship.

"Excuse me!" she said softly and then with her most charming and gracious smile she added, "I have important guests to attend to."

She had barely turned to go when Bonnie, now quite pleasantly awash with copious amounts of alcohol and sexual chemistry, suddenly exclaimed a little boozily, "Oh, my God!" Then, quickly regaining her composure, she tugged at Lit's demure blue chiffon dress, led her to one side and whispered in her ear. "Don't look now! But some other guests have arrived. Oh my God! Could you not have tied him to the bed and kept him there as your sex slave? I mean, it's a sin that a man like him is at liberty to roam the streets! He ought to carry a government health warning. Lit, he is still the most beautiful man I have ever seen!"

Lit trembled and took a deep breath. "Where is he?"

"Halfway towards the house on the left. Talking to some squirty little guy."

"That's his chief executive. What's *she* like?"

"Who?"

"His fiancée? Angela?"

"Well, how the hell would I know?"

"Does she have a good figure – legs – you know – compared to me?"

"I'll have to go and check the house, but Lit – I'm almost a hundred per cent sure – Conrad Budd is in attendance without his future bride."

Once more Lit and Bonnie were buddies, the closest of friends, partners in crime, Thelma and Louise, Elizabeth and Jane Bennett, the entire cast of *Friends*. Bonnie tottered across the grass, not caring now about the damage to her high heels and ridiculously expensive sheer tights, and went in search of the elusive Angela.

Lit fixed Matt in front of her. "Don't move!" she ordered him.

"Is it a wasp?"

Seán watched in confusion and some amusement. First he had said something which seemed to cut all conversation stone dead. Now Bonnie had staggered off abruptly and Lit was engaged in some sort of symbolic disembowelment of Matt.

"No, it's not a wasp. I just wanted to say – I just think that . . . it was a good idea, the party."

"Right."

"And – and – Maura is happy with her new clients. Which is good for her self-esteem and her sense of belonging to the – "

Matt cut in. This was not an aspect of Lit that he was familiar with – the aspect of her dishing out bland comments about the niceness of everything. "Isn't that Conrad over there?"

If she could have stapled her arms to her side, she might have done, but there was no stopping the automatic flight of the hand to the hair at the mention of his name and the little patting and fixing of the curl behind her ear.

"Oh! I hadn't noticed. Will you look after him?"

Matt raised an eyebrow. "What's got into you?"

"Nothing. He's probably more of a man's man, don't you think? Well? Go on."

The downside of dispatching Matt to look after Conrad was that she was now left alone with His Alienship. But he was firing on all the cylinders tonight. All his circuits were connected. He glanced at her briefly, recognised a hostile force in the atmosphere and strode off in pursuit of Bonnie.

# CHAPTER 19

It was a case of do unto others as they would do unto you – only do it first. Before Conrad got the chance to make his rueful little 'another time, another place' speech, before he could utter the words 'Things got a little out of hand the other night', before he could say the words 'Angela' and 'engaged', she would cut him dead. For much of the evening, Lit had felt morose and ill-tempered. But now the prospect of ignoring Conrad and putting him in his place (subtly, of course) put a sparkle in her eyes and a spring in her step.

She tripped lightly past him, her nose slightly in the air, her eyes smiling and fixed on Richie and Dandy. She patted Dandy lightly on the shoulder.

"Bearing up?"

He nodded. She could see he was tiring.

"Now don't pack me off to bed yet. I don't want to miss anything."

Out of the corner of her eye, she could see Conrad turning away from Jack Kennedy and striding purposefully across the grass towards her. She didn't want to engage in combat just yet. She wasn't ready.

Quickly, she ducked into the dining-room, past Tony Napoli. She could hide in the study, but that was probably the first place he would look so she took the stairs two steps at a time and bounded into her own bedroom. She sat at the dressing-table talking to herself.

"Lit Doran, when you leave this room, Conrad Budd will be nothing to you. You will not think about him any more except in a business sense. The past, meaning the other night, is history. You wanted sex. He wanted sex. It was just lust. Nothing to be ashamed of. Be cool, calm and collected. Be friendly and polite. Be interested but distant. Deep breath . . . deep breath . . . "

She applied a new coat of lipstick and another light splash of Thé Vert. She stood in front of the full-length mirror and smoothed her dress. Shoulders back, head high but not haughty, elegant graceful steps to the door. Then she stopped in her tracks. She could hear footsteps outside and then a knock on the door.

"Lit. I need to talk to you. I want to talk to you."

Conrad. He sounded pleading, sincere.

"I'll be down in a moment. Just freshening up. Why don't you get the waiter to serve you up some food while you're waiting? And your fiancée!"

"She's not here and I'm not hungry. I'd really like to talk to you alone."

"Damn!" she muttered to herself in the mirror. It wasn't meant to happen this way. How could she be cool, calm and collected with Conrad in her bedroom? Alone with Conrad in her bedroom. It would take the willpower of a saint. She took a deep breath.

"OK then. Come in." She tried to sound slightly irritated, as though it really wasn't convenient. She busied herself rummaging in a drawer and made a point of not looking up when he came into the room. Though she couldn't resist taking a peek at him in the mirror.

"Just a sec. There's something I have to find."

"Perhaps I can help."

Lit thought furiously of something that she might be looking for. A letter – a ring – a photo – a fresh pair of stockings . . .

"Here we are!" she exclaimed, pulling out an old address book and brandishing it triumphantly in the air. There was an awkward silence – the kind that needs to be filled. She stood up and forced herself to turn and face him. He was sitting on the edge of her bed, studying the floor with – with what? She couldn't decide. Was it sheepish embarrassment? Was it contrition? Was it disapproval of her?

She patted the address book fondly. "Looking for an old address for Bonnie."

"Bonnie?"

"Yes. We're old friends from way back."

He nodded, and there was more of the 'silence which must be filled' while he surveyed her coolly from head to toe.

"I really must get back. The guests," she said finally. "Excuse me."

"Lit. Please. Don't go. There's something I need to say. It's not easy."

"Save it, Conrad. Don't waste your breath. If it's about the other night – that was no big deal."

He began to speak, but apparently thought better of it.

"You know," she continued, getting into her stride, "sex is just sex. That's all it was. No need for either of us to feel bad about it. Personally I quite enjoyed it. So that's that!"

She was amazed at how cool she sounded, how clinical, how matter of fact.

He stood up suddenly and put his two hands firmly on her shoulders and looked down at her.

"Sex? That wasn't just sex. That was passion – real passion. It was great – and it's demeaning to both of us to say it was just sex!"

Lit shrugged and gave him a slight dose of the eyebrow. "I think we should just leave it. Don't you? The past is history. You're about to be married. Let's not waste our energies dwelling on a few hours of fun in the Shelbourne."

She hated saying it. He was hurt. Visibly hurt, stunned by her iciness, rebuffed by her indifference, humiliated by her dismissal. She slid away reluctantly from his beautiful strong hands and made for the door.

"Lit!"

She stopped without turning.

"I really want to see you again."

"You will see me again. I'm your PR agent, your image consultant, remember? We'll be seeing lots of each other."

"Not like that. I mean I want to take you out to dinner. I want us to get to know each other."

"And how might your fiancée feel about this?"

Conrad dipped his head as though she had inflicted a mortal blow. "Look! All I know is – the other night – that was something – something I've never experienced before. You can't just walk away from that. I have a very warm feeling about you, Lit, as though I've waited for you all my life, as though some empty place inside of me has suddenly filled up. That's all I can say."

Lit smiled ruefully and threw her eyes to heaven. Then it was her turn to look him straight in the eye. It was difficult because when she looked into his eyes she remembered how he had caressed each bit of her with such tenderness, how his lips had slid gently over her breasts, had taken her nipples into his mouth, how his tongue had flicked and licked her until she could barely remember who or where she was, how his hands had slid across her belly, beneath the silken fabric of her panties and wet his fingers and rubbed her until she could barely catch her breath, how he waited until just the right moment and slid into her, moving with her until they both came together in wave after wave of orgasm. How afterwards, he had held her in his arms and lightly stroked her hair with his hand and told her she was the most beautiful woman he had ever met.

"You'll get over it," she said into his deep, deep brown eyes. She pecked him lightly on the cheek, turned abruptly and went off to see to the guests.

"I think I'll take to the bed, Richie. You don't mind?" said Dandy. He was tired. Looking at all the people had been interesting for a while, but now he was weary of them. He'd seen it all before – the flirtations, the struggles to impress, the pecking order, the little cliques, the factions – now there was only one new experience left to him.

"Wait another while, Dandy! Bonnie's getting her karaoke machine."

"OK," Dandy agreed reluctantly. "Who's that grand-looking chap – the tall man?" "Which one?"

Dandy pointed a shaky, bony finger in the direction of Conrad Budd. "That one. The one my daughter has been avoiding all evening. Is he someone important?"

"He's Conrad Budd – a big property developer. Big client."

"What's she ignoring him for if he's a big client?"

"Who knows!" shrugged Richie.

"I know what it is!" said Dandy.

"What?"

"She wants to – well, he'd be a fine catch. Builders are tough men. He'd take no nonsense from her."

Richie chortled. "The man isn't born who'd take no nonsense from her. You know that."

# CHAPTER 20

It was past midnight and the last few remaining guests had drifted inside from the chilly night air. Dandy was tucked up in bed. Richie was nervously expounding to Conrad about his ambition to climb to the top of a crane.

" – and I read in the paper the other day how the biggest crane in the world, a Lampson Tranis-lift 3, is being assembled on your site –"

Conrad half-listened, admiring Lit as she bustled about the house overseeing the clearing-up operation.

" – it's 500 feet high, can lift 1500 tons – it's set on a reinforced cement pad – has over a mile of cable – "

Richie babbled on and Conrad nodded tolerantly.

Bonnie and Seán Tallon were sitting on the sofa in the large bay of the drawing-room, heads close together, his arm resting lightly behind her. They were deep in conversation. Lit saw Seán giving Bonnie his card and Bonnie writing what was presumably a phone number on a piece of paper for him. She watched in disgust as Tallon leaned forward and kissed Bonnie fleetingly on the lips, then pulled away. Bonnie pulled him forward once more and began to kiss him passionately. There was certainly no accounting for human taste. Lit thought that she would far rather kiss her computer screen or fondle the office shredder.

Matt and Toni Napoli leaned drunkenly on the piano discussing how Dean Martin was a much better crooner than Sinatra. Then Matt broke into 'That's Amore' accompanied by Toni. Together they made an awful racket.

Lit had reached exhaustion point. She wanted everyone to go home so that she could go to bed. She threw her eyes to heaven and shook her head. Matt was well capable of working through the entire Dean Martin repertoire and the worst of it was that he hadn't a note in his head.

"Sing 'Li'l Old Wine-drinker Me'!" Bonnie called to him.

And he did. Then he sang 'Volare' and 'Gentle On My Mind' and 'Ain't That A Kick In The Head' and on and on and on.

She was reaching desperation point. Why didn't they all just go? Bonnie wouldn't go because she was staying over – but the rest of them!

Conrad was the first to move. He stood up, shook Richie's hand and prodded him approvingly in the shoulder.

"I have to go, Lit. Early start."

Her heart plummeted. "Yes, of course! Thanks for coming."

When she was telling herself that she wished they would all leave, what she really meant was that she wished they would all leave apart from Conrad. It wasn't that she still fancied him or anything. It was just that she was really looking forward to him waiting around until the all others had left and making one last play for her. In fact, she positively expected it. And she planned to play it out until she was on the point of succumbing. Then she would draw herself up and with lashings of virtue and restraint would inform him that there could be no further personal contact between them. And she would affectionately take his hand in hers and tell him that she looked forward to remaining firm friends and business associates.

Now he had gone and ruined it all by just getting up and saying he was leaving. She didn't like being deprived of her little heroic gesture.

She walked to the front door with him.

"Thanks again. See you on Monday for the packaging." He smiled down at her.

"Packaging?"

"Remember? You're going to package me – make me over."

"Oh yes!"

"I look forward to it." He grinned appreciatively at her.

She was on the point of putting out her hand for him to shake, when he bent down and planted a soft, moist kiss on her lips.

"Good night, lovely Lit," he said and then turned and closed the door behind him.

258

For several moments she stood in a daze staring at the door. Then she stamped her foot and cursed. The kiss wasn't meant to happen. She planned the handshake or at the most very briefly offering her cheek for a peck. The kiss had set her back to square one, tingling skin, wobbly feelings in the pit of her stomach, flashes of Conrad naked and her naked and . . .

She stormed into the dining-room and scowled viciously at Matt who was now rasping his way through 'Memories are Made of This', eagerly but haltingly assisted by Richie who had a glass of wine in his hand.

"Give me that!" she said.

"Loosen up, woman!" said Matt garrulously. "A glass of wine isn't going to turn him into an alcoholic!"

"How come I can drink wine with Sunday dinner but I can't have a drink now?" said Richie.

"Because I say so!"

"Control freak!" he grumbled and took one last long and insolent slurp from the glass before she whipped it from his hand.

She was completely mortified to discover that Seán Tallon was standing behind her the whole time, watching the scene intently with a slight smirk on his face. She didn't care what he thought of her, but of course it would confirm all his worst suspicions about single mothers and the children of single mothers. She could almost hear his disapproving words – teenage drinking, dysfunctional families, single mothers, blah – blah – blah!

Tallon gave a half-smile and jangled his car keys noisily. "Matt, we should be going. What do you think?"

"Just one more song. Do you always have to be the pooty-parper?"

Richie sniggered and Lit glared at her son again.

"Maybe our hostess is tired. Come on, Deano." Tallon put his hand firmly on Matt's shoulder to steer him towards the door.

"No! I have to say goodnight to Poppy."

Lit thought he must be very drunk to want to say goodnight to Poppy Cornwell. In any case, she'd long gone. Dara had found her crouching behind a clump of rare and perfectly divine bamboo, tucking into a bowl of profiteroles in a rich chocolate sauce. And that was the end of Poppy's little bamboo adventure. Dara whisked her off home where she would be safe from all the temptations of the flesh.

"Poppy's gone home ages ago."

"Pity!" he said and lurched sideways.

Matt had reached the stage of drunkenness where his head seemed to be wobbling quite fluidly on his neck. Lit thought if it wobbled any more, it might just roll off.

He took a couple of drunken steps and then stopped with exaggerated suddenness. There was a sudden and urgent need to embrace everyone and he hung on to Toni for a precarious few seconds to say his fond good-byes. Then he hugged Richie fondly before practically crunching Lit into smithereens with a brotherly embrace.

Tallon turned to Lit.

"I'm over the limit so I'm going to walk. I'll collect my car in the morning if that's all right with you."

Lit shrugged. "Whatever you think," she said with barely disguised rudeness. "I'm sure you're OK to drive." She smiled nastily to herself, thinking that if he drove home, she would definitely call the guards and tip then off that there was a drunken driver in the neighbourhood.

"It's a warm night. I'll walk." He held out his hand

and shook hers, firmly.

"Thank you for the night. I mean, good party – good house – good investment – goodnight!" He half-smiled at her, then quickly turned to Bonnie.

"Great to meet you. I'll call you." He smiled broadly at her and kissed her warmly on the cheek. Lit exchanged cynical eye contact with her friend as if to say I told you so. But Bonnie didn't see or else chose to ignore the message.

"Come on!" said Bonnie when everyone was gone, leading Lit into the kitchen.

"I'm tired!" groaned Lit. "Please, Bonnie – no post-mortems tonight!"

"It has to be tonight – when it's all fresh in our minds. What happened with Conrad?"

"Nothing. Whatever little thing was going – I finished it."

"Why?"

Lit sighed impatiently. "We've been over this. Engaged – client – there's no more to be said."

Bonnie was about to say something, but Lit cut across her rudely. "I'm going to bed."

She turned on her heel and strode off.

"Suit yourself!" said Bonnie. She was well used to Lit's periodic bouts of rudeness.

"So I take it you're not interested in whether I got a hot date with Seán or not?"

"Not in the slightest!" said Lit as she hauled herself up the stairs to bed.

Matt and Seán ambled home along the canal. Matt was making exaggerated expressions with his face, scratching his head in an effort to figure something out.

"Something I wanted to say. Can't remember.

Something to do with you – you wanker!"

Seán laughed and waited patiently for the missiles to start firing. Any time Matt called him a wanker, it was usually followed by a barrage of other insults.

"You're up your own arse, Tallon, you know that?"

Seán shrugged and nodded. There was no point in arguing.

"That's it. That's what I wanted to say. You're up your own arse – you're anally retentive. But I can't remember why, except that you are. Anyway I was right to drag you along tonight. You had a great time in spite of yourself."

"It was OK. Bonnie's good fun."

"So?" Matt always relished the details of other people's affairs.

"So – nothing!"

"Well, did you ask her out?"

"None of your business."

"What did you talk about?"

"What's it to you?"

"Tallon – don't be so touchy! You spent practically all night sitting at the bottom of the garden with Bonnie, while I dashed about trying to keep my customers amused. I'm bound to be a bit curious."

"Well, I don't know. I can't remember – work, family, people – just stuff."

They walked in silence for a while and because the cool night air had sobered him up, Matt suddenly remembered what it was he wanted to say, why it was that his friend was a wanker.

He stopped dead and glared at Seán.

"Lit's not married. You stupid fucking prick!"

Seán was astute at most things, but the labyrinthine workings of his friend's mind sometimes confused even him. Matt said Lit wasn't married and that he was a prick? What on earth was the connection? Was Matt trying to pair them off? Was he supposed to have spent the evening talking to her instead of Bonnie? Had he inadvertently mentioned her husband? Was there some tragedy that he didn't know about? But she must have been married at some point. After all, there was the son. Perhaps she was divorced.

"But the son?"

"I'm telling you she's not married. She's a 'single mother' – to use your daft phrase from that prissy lecture on marriage in the garden earlier. I mean think about it – 'single mother'. It kind of implies that other children have multiple mothers!"

So that was why Matt was angry. Seán blanched at the thought of his tactlessness. But it wasn't his fault. How was he to know?

"Why didn't you tell me?"

"I sort of thought you knew and that you were just being your usual tactless self."

"No wonder she barely said goodnight. This is exactly why I hate going to dinner parties, Matt. It's your fault. You made me go. I always put my foot in it and hurt someone. And my opinion was called for. I had to be honest."

Matt snorted. Sometimes Tallon could be so naive. "Richie was born when she was in college. She was only eighteen. Everybody wanted her to give him up, but she wouldn't. I remember her breast-feeding him in the canteen. His father wanted to marry her, but she wouldn't have him just for the sake of convention. She's been very successful as a single mother and, I'm happy to say, she is very successful as a business partner too."

"Well, obviously, I'm not talking about her, when I

refer to unmarried mothers – "

"That's what she is though, isn't it?"

"I'm sure she knew I wasn't talking about her," Sean protested. "She's an intelligent, rational and successful woman. Much too sensible to take offence at a passing little remark like that."

"True, Lit is quite sensible. But you did insult her son. Remember? A society made up of single mothers isn't a society at all!"

Seán froze and felt a horrible prickly feeling at the back of his neck. "Oh shit! Did I say that?"

"And you know what is really pissing me off, Tallon?"

"What?" Seán enquired.

"I always thought you and Lit – " He stopped abruptly.

Seán was looking at him vaguely. "Sorry – what?"

"Ah! Nothing. Goodnight, Tallon."

# CHAPTER 21

The next morning, Seán woke with something nastier than a thumping hangover, something that would take more than two Solpadeine to cure. An annoyingly persistent little voice somewhere in the middle of his head was repeating the words "smug, opinionated bastard" with alarming frequency. But he wasn't smug. He wasn't opinionated. He had realistic expectations about how society could function best. But that wasn't smug, was it? Matt called him smug, but that was Matt's way. He didn't really mean it as an insult, did he?

He showered under a cold stream of water and dressed in a light cotton T-shirt and shorts. He brewed up a pot of coffee and ate some hot buttered toast while he checked his e-mail and phone messages. His mother had seen in her own words "a beautiful stone-clad rectory in Wicklow" which he should seriously consider. A man on his income should be putting some of his money into bricks and mortar. She'd finished off her e-mail with a little dig – I mean it would be A GOOD ASSET. Love Mum. But he didn't need any assets. A roof over your head was just that – shelter and warmth. Assets were for other people. He replied to his mother's e-mail, promised her he would check out the house in Wicklow and said he would see her in the evening for dinner. Lara Naughton had left a message on his mobile, asking if he would like to join her at a dinner party in Donnybrook on Friday. Why did people have this urge to hold dinner parties? Dinner parties had tiresome rules – boy, girl, boy, girl – no religion, no money, no politics, no gossip, safe topics only like the weather, the next holiday, the admirable food, the palatable wine, the golf handicap, the state of Irish rugby, and then suddenly at around midnight when everyone was on their ear, girls massing in one corner feeding on fillet of absent friend, men huffing and puffing in another about their dazzling property portfolios.

He texted Lara to say he'd have to check his work diary first. He was aware that Lara was putting tremendous effort into playing exactly the right moves so that she wouldn't frighten him away with her eagerness or repel him with too much coolness. Every time they met, she seemed to be working to some plan that she'd come across in a book somewhere. He kept telling her he wasn't interested in settling down and that he didn't do seriously committed relationships, but she always smiled at him knowingly and deftly changed the subject. She was an expert at dismantling his barriers, skilled at anticipating how she might best put him at ease. In some respects, she was the perfect woman.

He stepped out from his apartment, which overlooked Sandymount Strand, into the warm sunshine. A light cooling breeze came in from the bay. He squinted up at the sun and briefly considered cycling to Harwood Park. But there was a lot of strange energy floating about in his system, and it needed to be worked off. He decided to jog.

He dreaded calling to Lit Doran's house, feared or rather knew quite well the frosty reception he would get. If he was lucky, she might not slam the door in his face at once. The most he could hope for was that she would stand icily in the hallway while he stammered through an apology about his indiscretion of the previous night. Would she call him a smug bastard too?

He jogged along Sydney Parade, crossing over the train line, lost in thought. He hated anything to do with women. It wasn't that he hated women. He quite liked them. It was just that he got it wrong so often. If he wasn't already in a sweat from running in the summer heat, the thought of being demolished by Lit Doran would certainly have brought him out in a lather of perspiration.

Why could he not get the hang of women? He never traded on his good looks but women flung themselves at him, which he could never understand. Why would any person fling themselves at any other person? People either connected or they didn't. There was no point in forcing the issue. If they weren't flinging themselves at him, they were either trying to mother him, ensnare him as Lara seemed to be doing, or to pretend he didn't exist.

Once, in the office, a very beautiful girl with auburn hair and green eyes spent a great deal of energy ignoring him and sometimes putting him down for no reason. "What have I ever done to her?" he asked Susan, the girl in accounts. "She fancies the pants off you," Susan said bluntly. "Then why doesn't she – ?" he began but never finished the question. He would never understand. One day the girl with auburn hair came into his office and confronted him. "You needn't think I fancy you because I don't. I have a boyfriend. You're not my type at all. You think you're great in your pin-striped suit and your big job. But you're not. You're just an arrogant, superior – " At that point, she choked up, burst into floods of tears and left. The following week, she changed jobs.

Lit stirred between the cool Egyptian cotton sheets which were a special shade of extra-white. She opened one slightly puffy eye and peered at the clock. Ten o'clock. Ten o'clock! That was the middle of the day! It was all right for Bonnie who could happily sleep on until mid-afternoon. But nowadays, even if Lit was tired as she was now and wanted to sleep in, her body wouldn't allow it. She got out of bed and slid her feet into cool cotton flip-flops. Then she padded across to the large bay window overlooking the road. For a few moments she reflected on her good fortune and good sense in buying a fine house in such a lovely road. Trees covered in blossom, wistaria clambering up decorative arched redbrick doorways, the lovely stained-glass windows of Mrs O'Greaney's house across the way, Edwardian houses lovingly and tastefully restored, and none more so than hers.

Someone had parked a battered old Renault outside

her house and the sight displeased her. It displeased her even more when she remembered that the car belonged to Seán Tallon and that he would be arriving at some point during the day to reclaim it. But she was planning on taking Dandy for a drive to the seaside and maybe if she got herself organised quickly enough she would be spared the awkwardness of his visit.

After showering, she sat at her dressing-table mirror and applied cream, then a lotion that promised to reduce her puffy eyes. It was Sunday so she didn't feel the need to put on any make-up, just lip-gloss. She hung a string of blue and green beads that Richie had given her around her neck, fastened her Rolex watch around her wrist and then surveyed herself briefly. She tried always to maintain a pleasant expression because Auntie Florence had told her once that a calm and pleasant expression did more to prevent the onset of wrinkles than the most expensive treatments in the world – that and genetics. She stood up, faced the mirror sideways, watching her figure, how she stood, shoulders back, tummy in, chin slightly raised but not haughty. She slipped into her denims, a plain white cotton shirt and brown leather loafers.

"You'll do. No beauty, but I've seen worse, a lot worse."

She splashed Thé Vert on her wrists and neck, ran a comb through her damp towel-dried hair. She briefly considered taking the hair-dryer to it. But that would be another twenty minutes of the day gone. Conscious of Bonnie's barb about not spending enough time with Richie, Lit decided that she would devote today to her son as well as her father. She planned ahead as she made the bed, folding down and smoothing the cotton sheets and cover. She would cook a big breakfast, whatever Dandy wanted and whatever Richie wanted. She would turn on the extractor-hood to banish the smell of frying from the kitchen. Over breakfast they would all plan a wonderful outing to the seaside. Brittas Bay was a little too far for Dandy to travel, but Greystones was only half an hour away and they could have afternoon tea in one of the nice old-fashioned hotels there. He'd like that.

She spread out the ivory linen and lace counterpane on the bed, plumped up the pillows and opened the window to get the best of the morning fresh air, then crossed the landing to Richie's room.

"How about a nice big breakfast, love?"

She thought she heard a low grunt.

"Bacon, sausages, fried eggs? Your favourite – fried potatoes and fried bread?"

"Grrrmmnn."

"OK. I'll keep some for you!"

Bonnie was asleep in the guest-room and Lit knew she might sleep on for another six hours. It was a shame because she was wasting the best part of the day, but that was her business. Bonnie had a very wasteful approach to time, took it for granted, let it slip and ride through her fingers, taking each day as it unfolded, never planning if at all possible, never fretting about being early or late. It was amazing really how she stuck to a school timetable at all.

Dandy was already ensconsed in his chair by the range and despite the promise of yet another boiling hot day, a bright blaze flickered in the grate.

"How about a nice fry?" she said cheerfully as she took a clean damp flannel to his face and hands.

He growled and rattled his paper, instantly covering his cleaned hands with newsprint. There was a good growth of bristle on his face, but the shave would have to wait until Richie decided to drag himself out of the bed.

"Did you sleep well?"

"I don't sleep any more. You know that. I never sleep except for a few minutes. I was awake all night."

"A nice fry will set you up for the day."

She heated a mix of oil and butter in a frying-pan and turned on the grill. She turned on the extractor-hood to deal with the cooking smells, hoping her father wouldn't notice.

"Turn that off. It's making me cold."

"But it's turned down low! You can't possibly feel it."

"I can feel it. There's a draught."

Suppressing a sigh of irritation, she turned off the extractor. She hummed to herself as she turned sausages under the grill and fried crispy aromatic bacon and mouth-watering black and white pudding on the pan. She set the table for three and brewed up a pot of strong tea for Dandy and a pot of fresh coffee for herself. She sat him down in the big old farmhouse chair and served him a Full Irish Breakfast.

"Any mushrooms?"

"Sorry. Didn't think."

She hollered up the stairs to Richie a few times and decided to give it up as a bad job. Just as she was helping herself to bacon and grilled tomato, the doorbell rang. She cursed and went to answer it.

Seán Tallon looked strangely incongruous in shorts and a T-shirt. He was studying the laces of his trainers very intently.

She eyed him steadily for a few moments, deliberately making him suffer an awkward silence before saying a perfunctory "Hello."

"Come to collect the car – oh, and thanks for last night."

"You're welcome."

He fished the keys out of his pocket, fidgeted with them and found the car key. He turned to go, but turned back again.

"What I mean is – can I come in for a moment?"

Lit gestured to the hallway.

Seán stepped in and tried to muster up a sheepish grin. He stood awkwardly, facing the seascape over the Georgian side table, staring intently at the way the sea met the shoreline in the painting.

She coolly observed his discomfort. She sensed he was about to apologise for his rash statements of the night before. If it had been anyone else, she might have invited him to join her for breakfast. But he was too awful for words – wooden, smug, opinionated, dull. What sane person would have breakfast with such a man? She would show him the bare minimum of courtesy.

"Coffee?"

"Thanks, I'd really love a coffee."

Dandy was halfway through his fry and helping himself to some more brown bread and butter.

"Good morning, Mr Doran."

"Morning."

Seán awkwardly resumed the examination of his shoes. Lit slid a mug of steaming coffee across the table to him and, ignoring him, tucked in to her own breakfast.

"May I?" he said as he lowered himself uneasily into a chair.

Lit watched him in sullen anticipation, just like she did when Richie was in trouble or trying to wriggle out of something. She'd let him say his piece and then she'd take aim and fire – with both barrels blazing. She'd blast him from here to kingdom come. Seán Tallon would leave this house a chastened man, a humble man, a man with his tail firmly between his legs. He would slink off home – vanquished, annihilated, obliterated, vaporised. It would be great fun altogether. And there was absolutely no question of him getting breakfast.

There was a thick oppressive silence. Lit was reflecting that it was unlikely Seán would speak up in front of her father when Dandy suddenly pushed himself to his feet, muttering something about not having seen the cat, and shambled off with surprising speed into the garden. Lit wondered if the old man had sensed the situation and was deliberately giving them space. But it would be unlike Dandy to be so subtle.

In any case, she was now alone with Tallon.

"Eh, last night . . . too much wine . . . shooting my mouth off like that. Of course I wasn't talking about you when I made that silly reference to single – I mean to – unmarried – I mean women who have children but don't have – I mean – " He shifted the mug around on the table. "I didn't know you weren't –" He drummed his fingers on his bare knees.

"Did Matt tell you to do this?"

"No! Just that I'd put my foot in it."

She cut gracefully through a slice of bacon. She was pleased to note that he was eyeing the bacon with some interest.

"It would take more than a few ill-informed comments to insult me."

"I was just using it as a random example. I –" He tapped his trainers nervously on the floor. "Look, I don't like going to parties. I'm no good at it. I always end up insulting someone."

"I wonder why?" Lit whispered into her uptilted mug.

She peered at him over the rim. He had left the steel-rimmed glasses at home and she noticed that he had blue-grey eyes. His sandy hair was cropped short and he had a fine jaw and a nice little dimple on his chin. He was broad-shouldered and lean and though he was an arrogant, lifeless cheesy prat, Lit had to admit that Bonnie was right: he was quite handsome. But not of course in the same league as Conrad.

The familiar wobbly feeling returned to her stomach when she thought of Conrad. And, as Seán sat silently before her, she mentally compared the two men. Conrad was polite, solicitous, tactful, good-humoured, friendly and sexy. Seán Tallon had all the sex appeal of a turnip. Conrad was an easy mixer, charming, level-headed and sexy again. Seán Tallon had as much social charm as Norman Bates. She shuddered when she remembered Bonnie kissing him the night before.

She didn't like to be down on Bonnie, but Lit wondered if her friend was becoming slightly, if not even very desperate – taking anyone she could get, even someone as pathetic as Seán Tallon. Auntie Florence used to say that picking a man was like picking wallpaper and curtains. A good contrast was better than a bad match. But Bonnie and Tallon were neither.

Dandy returned, eased himself into his chair and broke the uncomfortable silence.

"Give the man a bit of breakfast, can't you?"

"I don't think Mr Tallon is staying, Dad."

Dandy gave her the laser-beam look. He had never let anyone go hungry from his door. It was the old way. If someone arrived during a meal, a place was always made, a helping of food was always found. Common old-fashioned courtesy. He raised himself slowly from the big old farmhouse chair, embarrassed by his daughter's rudeness and began shuffling towards the cooker to get a plate of food for the guest. She opened her mouth to protest, but thought better of it.

"Sit down, Dad, and eat your food while it's hot. I'll put something on a plate for him."

Dandy returned to his chair and gave Seán a reassuring smile before tucking into his food once more.

Lit was furious with her father for making her look mean-spirited. She arranged the smallest rasher, an egg and a sausage on a plate and set it down in front of Tallon.

"Bon appetit," she said in a tone that would curdle milk.

Dandy played the genial host, chatting to the guest and generally putting him at his ease. "You didn't have much. Have another helping. Lit, put a bit more food on his plate."

"I'm afraid that's it. As it is, I'll have to cook up more for Richie."

Seán squirmed. He hadn't even wanted breakfast. He longed to escape.

"More coffee then," said Dandy, delighted to have someone new to talk to.

Seán was about to refuse, but before he could open his mouth the old man had refilled his cup.

"Thanks," said Seán.

"You're heartily welcome," said Dandy.

Lit could take no more of their instant camaraderie. If she didn't put a stop to it quickly, they'd soon be swapping golf yarns.

Disregarding Dandy's presence, she loaded up both barrels and took aim, firmly and steadily, at Seán Tallon.

"So you think single mothers are a curse to society? I

don't suppose you have any idea of all the great men down through the ages who were reared solely by their mothers because their overworked or vain or feckless or philandering or downright nasty fathers couldn't be bothered to involve themselves in the task?"

"I – " He stopped. He had no idea what to say. He glanced at Dandy who had suddenly disappeared behind the Sunday sports supplement.

"To my certain knowledge there is a lad living not more than a mile from here, who isn't yet twenty-one and has fathered ten different children by ten different mothers. Four of the babies were born in the same week in Holles Street. Is that what you call responsible male-hood – decent fatherhood? What sort of parenting skills will he impart to his ten scattered children – how to dodge the other girlfriends in the maternity ward?"

Dandy hauled himself back to the chair by the range, leaving Seán and Lit staring it out across the table – High Noon in Lit's Kitchen!

Seán put his mug to one side and leaned forward. "Come on! He's an exception. A guy like him should be castrated."

"And unmarried mothers stoned to death, I suppose?"

"Look, I don't – "

"In Richie's class of twenty, five fathers have run off with other women. Ten are away on business for weeks on end. One is in prison for fraud. Only three are from so-called happy well-balanced and well-adjusted homes."

"That's nineteen."

"What a truly amazing gift for an accountant! You can count! And Richie makes twenty. Which of those boys do you think likely to grow up the happiest, most well-adjusted, most ready to take on the future world?"

"The three with mothers and fathers, I would imagine."

"That's some percentage though, isn't it. Fifteen per cent. Eighty-five per cent of the class are without fathers. Are they all to be written off like Richie because they are without fathers? It proves my point."

"What point?"

"That men are no good at being fathers."

"You have a very low opinion of men."

"On the contrary, I am surrounded by men whom I love and admire deeply."

"Then you must have a very low opinion of me."

"I have no opinion of you, to be honest."

Yes! Yes! Scudmissile straight to the epicentre.

She hoped she didn't imagine the slight tic at the corner of his mouth. A slight tic was probably the full extent of his emotional range. He'd make a great James Bond, she thought. Roger Moore did the whole gamut of emotions with the eyebrows. Sean Connery could convey lust, bravery and admiration with only his chin. Tallon no doubt could do everything from ecstasy to despair with a simple tic at the corner of his mouth.

"Actually I feel sorry for men in the modern world. They are fast becoming surplus to requirements. Bonnie's kid brother has this summer job in an artificial insemination plant in Meath. They call it the Bulls' Hotel. There, the few chosen prize bulls of exceptional genetic standard are housed in splendid and angry isolation. Their prime sperm is taken and used to impregnate herds from all over Leinster."

"And?" he enquired coolly.

She was really enjoying herself now.

"All the dangerous and genetically low-class bulls

have been removed from the countryside. Country people no longer have to fear these angry, destructive creatures. The young are nurtured by their gentle and caring mothers, in rich, peaceful pastures. And the species continues to reproduce to the highest standards. A peaceful rural society and all thanks to the Bulls' Hotel. Perhaps we humans can learn something from that." She was talking bull and she knew it! But it was great fun.

He stood up. "I could answer that. But I won't. Sorry again for the silly blunder. Enjoy your paper, Mr Doran."

"Bye now," said Dandy. "Come again soon."

"It was a snivelling, grovelling apology," Lit boasted proudly to her son. "He was a quivering, cowering mass of cow's dung by the time I was finished with him. His legs were so shaky he could hardly make it out the front door. His hands trembled so much he couldn't put the key in the ignition. He'll need post-traumatic stress counselling – and probably long-term medication."

Richie was enthralled at the deadly cocktail of venomous sarcasm, withering looks and ballistic insults that his mother had served to Seán Tallon, as indeed she had served up to many other victims.

"I didn't notice much grovelling," said Dandy. "Anyway, what did the poor man do to have all this terror rained down on him?"

"He made a comment about single mothers. Nobody insults my son and gets away with it."

"Do you want to sleep with him? Is that it? I suppose he's married too – like that Menton bastard. Using you, driving you to a near nervous breakdown and you couldn't get enough of him. Someone else's husband, for Christ's sake!"

Dandy thought that every man who called to the house was "only trying to get into Lit's knickers" and she was unaccountably relieved that Seán Tallon had left before hearing this moral tirade. No doubt he felt that any woman who got involved with a married man should be shot at dawn without a blindfold. He would have strict moral views on that kind of thing – he would no doubt swing big moral words like deceit and promiscuity and bad parental example at her.

He probably never had a moral crisis in his life. It's easy to be a thoroughly moral man if you have no imagination or if you've never been tested. Lit figured that morality was a form of social tyranny designed by dull people who were so bored with their own lives that they just had to go out and run everybody else's life as well. Of course, she was a reasonably moral person. She just wasn't too keen on other people telling her how to live her life.

Dandy had taught her that people were complex and rarely what they seemed. He talked equally to tramps and bank managers. In one town, he made friends with a local eccentric – a hermit who lived half way up a mountain. Lit was horrified at the thought that her friends might catch sight of the dirty, unshaven, madlooking creature going into their house.

"Would you rather I entertained respectable people like Mr Brady the jeweller who puts his hands under little girls' skirts all the time? Or how about prosperous and handsome Mr Callaghan who has robbed his neighbours of their land? Or Mrs McIntyre with the venom of twenty puff-adders in her tongue?"

"Mrs McIntyre is lovely. She always gives us free sweets and asks how you are!"

"She does," said Dandy darkly, "and then she goes

prattling around the town about how Bernard Doran lets his children eat sweets from morning to night and other stuff you're too young to know about."

The thing which annoyed her most about Dandy was that he invariably turned out to be right about people.

One day she overheard Mrs McIntyre telling a neighbour that Bernard Doran's children would have to go into care because they were so neglected and badly treated by him and she whispered something else that Lit couldn't hear. Lit was horrified that anyone would lie about her father like that and terrified that she and her sister might really end up in care. She ran home crying to Dandy.

"There! I told you! The viper! Look at the way the witch has upset you."

And, infuriatingly, he turned out to be right about Harry Menton too.

Now he was going on with his lecture. "Menton treated you like shit and you kept going back for more."

"Richie, leave the room."

Richie dearly wanted to stay. This was shaping up to be a good battle. Dandy was hungover and lobbing lethal grenades of abuse. Lit was drawing herself up to take retaliatory action. Soon the shells and mortars of past conflicts would begin to fly again, old treaties reneged on, new more deadly weapons produced for effect. But he retreated.

Lit turned on her father when Richie was out of the room.

"How dare you speak to me like that in front of my son!"

"It's nothing he doesn't know already. He's not a child anymore. Why can't you get a decent man for yourself?"

"I might just do that!" she snapped haughtily and took

herself off into the garden.

She returned two minutes later. Seán Tallon's untimely visit had put her plan for a wonderful family outing clean out of her head. Richie was back, munching into his third bowl of Breakfast Crunchies, having missed out on the fry.

"It's a lovely day, Dad. How about a trip to the sea?"

"I'm tired. I don't think so."

"Richie? How about a lovely trip to the beach? We can pack a picnic – you remember, like we used to do when you were small – and put in loads of your favourite treats."

"Like where, Mum?"

"I don't know. Greystones maybe. We can bring a beach ball and a nice chair for Dandy to sit on. It would be nice to spend the day together. We can bring the camera – it's ages since we shot any film."

"I'd love to, Mum, but I promised Barney Ryan I'd call over to his place. Tell you what, why don't we do it in a couple of weeks? All my mates will be away then and Dandy won't be so tired." He put his plate in the sink and gave her a lazy bear-hug.

Lit tried hard to conceal her disappointment. So much for plans of quality time with the family. So much for golden moments to cherish forever. But maybe Richie was right. A couple of weeks one way or the other wouldn't make any difference.

Bonnie surfaced at two o'clock, made herself a cup of tea and joined Lit in the garden where she was trawling the Sunday papers.

"The love of your life was here earlier," Lit said casually.

"Who?"

"Darth Vader – His Intergalacticness – Mike Rowe Chip – who do you think?"

"Seán! Why didn't you wake me?"

"Didn't think there was much point. He looked like he needed rebooting or something."

Bonnie was tetchy. "Just lay off that robot stuff! OK?"

"Uuuhhh! Who's got a hangover? Can't I say what I think any more?"

"Lit – do you know something? Sometimes you can be a real pain."

"What's that supposed to mean?"

"It means Seán Tallon is a genuinely nice bloke."

"Do tell!" drawled Lit with undisguised disinterest.

"He's funny."

"He's all that!" retorted Lit acidly.

"He's nice-mannered. He's interesting. He doesn't talk about himself all the time. He is not obsessed with the three s's – sex, soccer and sex. He doesn't talk about his mum all the time. And he's considerate."

Bonnie glowed with pleasure when she talked about him. It was enough to make Lit want to throw up. She might rename them Miss Puke and Mr Vomit. When she heard the words 'interesting' and 'considerate' it was more than she could stomach.

"Interesting? Considerate? This is the smug bastard who thinks single mothers are a menace to society! This is the man who thinks I'm living beyond my means. This is the pathetic little shite who knows the London Underground off by heart! I thought you had more taste!"

"I know the single mother thing was silly – but he didn't know you weren't married."

Lit pulled a face. "So what? It's still his smug point of view!"

"Oh, come on, Lit! Like the super-smooth, icy-cool Lit Doran has never shot off her mouth in public and lived to regret it!"

"That's not fair!"

"Is so! Do you remember when you slagged off some singer at a party and discovered you were talking to his father? You had a reddener on you for weeks after that. Give the guy a break. It was his idea to drag Matt away last night. Why? Because he said that you looked tired and that you had been working very hard to make the night a success."

"So? That was just an excuse. He was probably bored out of his tree anyway."

"Well, thanks for that vote of confidence in the irresistible charms of Bonnie Ballantyne! Now who's insensitive?"

Lit was feeling quite annoyed with Bonnie. It was tactless of her to have had such a good time last night when she knew that at the very same time Lit was forcing herself to make the supreme sacrifice with Conrad. And Bonnie had enjoyed herself – openly, blatantly, flagrantly, with no thought for Lit's heroic struggle or the willpower involved in turning down hours of flattering attention and masses and masses of unbelievable sex with the man of her dreams.

In the few days since she had sex with Conrad, Lit realised how much she had missed the pleasure of it all. It wasn't so much the orgasms – but being with a man. She'd forgotten how smooth and hard men's bodies were. She'd forgotten the lovely musky smell, the feel of a strong hand on her back, the sensation of a man breathing on her skin. Bonnie had no right to be glowing and feeling happy when Lit was feeling gloomy and bad-tempered. It was time to burst her bubble.

"Anyway, Seán didn't come to see you, Miss Smug Smartypants. He came to see me!" Ha! That showed her. That wiped the silly grin off her face.

Bonnie shot her a sly glance, opened her mouth to speak, then stopped and smiled privately to herself. "There's no point in telling you," she said finally, mysteriously.

"No point in telling me what?" Lit did her best not to sound too interested.

"I've got a date."

"What with His – I mean, with Seán Tallon?"

"Tonight! He's picking me up at eight. We're going to a film."

"Let me guess! Last Tango in the Double Entry System? Accountants On the Verge of Being Human? Full Metal Calculator? Lord of The Ring Binders?"

Bonnie let her rant on.

"Then dinner in La Verona."

Lit narrowed her eyes. This was more than she could bear. La Verona was her favourite restaurant on the entire planet. It was fun and lively and the food was heavenly. And the waiters were friendly and didn't spend their time checking out if the customer wore a Rolex watch or not. Though it wasn't the most expensive eaterie in town, it was virtually impossible to get a table there without booking weeks in advance. If Lit really wanted to impress clients, she took them to La Verona. Sometimes she took Richie there for his birthday. It catered for everybody – families, business, birthdays, celebration parties.

"Don't be ridiculous," she said scornfully. "Seán Tallon wouldn't bring you to a place like that. How would he get a table?"

"We shall see. You know what? He's the first man I've

met in a long time whose mind is more interesting than his body."

Lit rolled her eyes to heaven. Bonnie was off again. Lit could nearly write the script: passionate union of two intellects, sex appeal of a brainy man, how they could see into one another's souls . . . "Remember to drink plenty of coffee."

"What for?" asked Bonnie.

"Because I guarantee you, after the first course, you'll be falling asleep."

"You're just jealous," said Bonnie blithely and picked up the property supplement.

Lit sighed and wished she had hidden it.

Bonnie lived in a rented flat in Ranelagh but she was constantly on the lookout for a place of her own. In fact, she had been trawling the property pages for six years now, waiting for the perfect house to come on the market. And in six years the price of houses had shot up about four hundred per cent. At first she couldn't find the right house. Now there were plenty of right houses – they were just too bloody expensive.

"Here's a nice one in Rathgar – well, it's Terenure really – but it could be Rathgar – "

Lit sighed and leafed through the business pages.

"Three-bedroom terraced, south-facing, circa 1850 – Jesus – they can't be serious!"

"Bonnie, you'll just have to take the plunge and buy something soon. It will mean giving up the expensive holidays and the Brown Thomas Fashion Floor for a few years – but it will be worth –"

Suddenly Lit sat bolt upright.

There on the third page of the *Sunday Independent* was a small article under the headline: Budd Builds Bedlam.

Bonnie continued reading out. "South Circular Road,

in walk-in condition, compact jewel – that means you can't swing a cat in it – "

"Bonnie, shut up! Listen to this – According to the Stoneyfield Residents Association, Conrad Budd has shown nothing but contempt for the residents and their concerns over his multibillion pound development in their area. Now, however, under the leadership of Gearóid Magill, the Association is hoping to once more bring their plight before the courts. Mr Magill had this to say: 'Justice will be done. This development will not be built. This historic site will be saved. We have right on our side.' When asked about this, Mr Budd dismissed the question with 'No Comment' and went on to make a remark of a critical and personal nature to the journalist in question – oh damn and fuck!"

"What's all that about?"

"Trouble. I have to call him – before he puts his foot in it again."

# CHAPTER 22

Gearóid Magill was pleased – jubilant even. In a matter of days he had succeeded where Pat Sullivan had failed miserably. Sullivan, he mused, couldn't organise the proverbial orgy in a harem. Now, under his personal direction, every single house in Stoneyfield had received a leaflet. Each house was canvassed for their support. A new picket-roster was drawn up with a minimum of twenty people to be on duty at any given time. A protest march was being organised. Gearóid felt he was coming into his own – that he was about to achieve greatness or have greatness thrust upon him. Perhaps he had even been born great. It didn't matter.

He sipped from a mug of hot espresso coffee and chewed contentedly on a warm apple Danish as he re-read the article in the *Sunday Independent*, particularly the bit which quoted himself. He liked the tone of his words. They had a touch of great oratory about them.

"What happens next?" Fidelma asked. She was curled up on the sofa next to him, her hair all tousled, wearing his dressing-gown, her arm draped around his shoulder.

He sat up straight and disengaged her arm. "I have to think about that. You'll have to go. I can't think when there's people about."

"Do I have to?" Fidelma was crestfallen. She was enjoying the cosy Sunday morning domestic side of being with him. She liked him. He was strong and out-spoken and nice-looking and despite the way friends slagged her about his culchie accent, she thought she might be falling in love with him.

He pulled her up from the settee and pointed her in the direction of the bedroom. "Home! I'll call you later. I promise."

When she had gone, he mulled over the envelope. What was the right thing to do? Should he consult with some of the others? Should he call Budd? Should he go straight to the press? He was clear in his mind about one thing. Whatever he did from this moment would be to save Stoneyfield. And if people didn't agree with his modus operandi now – then they would give him a hero's welcome when the hoardings came down and the cranes and diggers rolled off into the sunset without having turned one single sod.

Lit called Matt first to tell him about the newspaper article on Conrad.

Matt was laconic. "It could be worse."

"Yes, but if he gets bad press, we'll be held responsible somehow."

"You're overreacting. Chill out, babe. It's a hot Sunday in the middle of the silly season," he said, yawning. "All be blown over by tomorrow."

Lit didn't think so. She had a nose for trouble and she could feel trouble brewing, simmering, bubbling away quietly in some dark sinister corner of the city. "We have to do something."

"OK. I'll get onto my contacts in the papers. You deal with Conrad. He seems to prefer you for some reason!"

She swallowed. She wondered how Matt would react if he knew she had slept with a client. And not just any client – but their biggest, most important, most influential one. Conrad was renowned for being impetuous. Supposing he took a notion and decided to move on to one of their bigger rivals? Supposing he'd deliberately flirted with her to see was she professional enough to resist? Supposing he thought that she slept with all her clients? If she hadn't slept with him, her mind wouldn't be cluttered up now with all these silly thoughts. Instead of being clear-headed and ready to focus on the problem, her thoughts dashed about chaotically, like a class of unruly students. She had to play it cool with him, insist that from now on their relationship would be purely business. It would be tough to begin with. The business with the article in the newspaper was tricky enough without having to play all coy and distant as well. But she knew she could do it. She was a woman of iron will and self-discipline.

She made a mental note. Never, ever have sex with a

client again. Having sex with a client was like getting drunk with your dentist the night before he does root-canal work on you – likely to lead to very painful results.

"Maybe you should – " she said weakly to Matt.

"It's your gig – I won't hear of it. Keep me posted." He hung up.

Lit left Bonnie to her tea and property supplements and retreated to the study to call Conrad. She dialled the number of his penthouse. After the third ring a woman answered the phone. Lit guessed it was the elusive Angela.

"May I speak to Conrad?"

"Who is this?" She sounded – Lit struggled to describe the voice – not very interested. If the situation was reversed, Lit would be frosty to say the least.

"Lit Doran – PR company. It's an urgent business matter."

"One moment."

"Hi?" It was Conrad.

Did she detect the merest hint of surprise, of annoyance in his voice? So what? She had no right to feel sensitive about it. Most people didn't like to be disturbed with work-related matters on a Sunday afternoon. And he was with his fiancée. But all the same she felt like the mistress calling the married lover who had told her never to call him at this number.

"What can I do for you?"

"Business call," she clipped airily.

"Oh?"

"Have you seen the papers?"

"Nope. I never look at them until Sunday night in bed. What's the problem?"

"There's a story about you – we need to prepare a response."

"Now? Today? I'm going to the races."

"Conrad. In about two hours your phone is going to start ringing."

"I'm ex-directory."

"That doesn't mean anything. You want me to earn my money – that's what I'm doing now."

There was silence on the end of the line for a moment and then he said, "I'll send a taxi."

"No. Please – "

"I insist – we can cut through whatever this silly business is and then have a nice glass of wine – "

"But what about – " Lit didn't get to say Angela because he cut her short.

"Great. See you. Bye."

The maple-pannelled lift glided swiftly and silently up to Conrad's penthouse and when the doors slid open Lit found him waiting, arms folded, leaning against a pillar, a rueful smile on his face. Then he gave the little shrug of his shoulders that set her heart pounding at an appalling rate.

She felt her lips spreading into a warm friendly smile, but she bit the inside of her cheek and was able to halt the smile before it did any permanent damage.

"I'm really sorry about disturbing you on a Sunday. But we need to work through this."

"Of course." he led her through the double oak doors, across the marble-floored hall into a large room which looked out over the river.

Lit couldn't stop herself. She ran to the balcony like a little girl and began picking out places she recognised – the grand Old Gandon Custom House, in the distance through heat haze the cheerful little Ha'penny Bridge, in the other direction and barely visible – the big cranes on the site in Stoneyfield. There were all sorts of boats on the river – freighters, trawlers, barges, tugs. People sailing their yachts, windsurfers, solitary men sitting with packed lunches and fishing lines, lovers strolling along beneath the new young trees. A light breeze coming in from the bay felt deliciously cool on her skin. She longed to pull up a chair, put her feet up and just watch the world go by.

"Why don't we stay out here and chill for a while?" he said.

He had come up behind her and now he rested his hand lightly on her shoulder. She could feel his warm breath on the nape of her neck, and for a few seconds she closed her eyes to savour it. Then she turned and shattered the moment.

"I'm looking forward to meeting Angela."

"Ah!"

"Well, is she here?"

Conrad made a display of scratching his head and looking bewildered. "Sadly – she had to leave. You know – places to go, things to do, people to see. Busy woman, Angela."

Lit seized her opportunity. "Then we can get down to business right away. What I mean is that we can work on –"

"Don't you want to enjoy the view for a little while longer?"

"No, we need to work out a response to this article."

"Sure. Of course."

He didn't seem all that interested in working out a response to anything, but he led the way back into the large room.

It was safest to sit in the white leather armchair. Then he couldn't sit beside her and she wouldn't feel his breath or the warmth of his skin or the sensation of his thigh lightly brushing against hers.

She sat down. "Have you read the article?"

"It's nonsense. You know I didn't make a personal comment. They've just twisted my words. I don't intend to dignify it with a reply."

"All the same, we'd better not do anything in the future which could lead to more negative coverage like this."

It was the closest she could get to ticking him off about his comment to the journalist.

He smiled at her – a touch patronisingly, she felt, but she let it go. Instead, she led him deftly through the pitfalls of dealing with the media and how best to avoid them in future. She warned him against casual throwaway remarks, ironic quips and misplaced jokes which could be open to misinterpretation and blown out of all proportion.

He nodded impatiently. "Yes, all right, I get the picture and I'm suitably chastened. In future I will choose my words with much greater care when I'm dealing with those greasy little –"

Lit fixed her cornflower-blue eyes on him.

" – when I'm dealing with the media. Now I've given this business more than enough of my time."

He disappeared into what looked like a cavernous stainless-steel kitchen and reappeared with a bottle of chilled white wine and two glasses. He poured the wine and set a glass down in front of her. He hadn't even asked if she would like a drink. Then, quite casually, he rested himself on the arm of her chair, looked down at her and ran his finger lightly across her earlobe.

"Lit. I'm glad you're here – but not because of work. I want you. I want you now. I can't stop thinking about you. I lie awake at night thinking about you."

His fingers slid down her neck and ran lightly across her nipples. Lit cursed herself for not having worn a bra. Sunday was her bra-less day. Now her two nipples were behaving like two cheap slappers – sticking out and begging to be licked and sucked and generally played around with.

"Conrad! Please! No," she moaned breathlessly. "It's not fair."

Then he pulled her to him, grazing on her neck with his lips and his tongue. She knew she should slip from his arms, take up a formal position on an upright chair and start composing a considered response to the newspaper. She tried to summon up her iron willpower, tried to have a heart of stone, to reject him with steely determination.

"Not fair to whom?" he said as he chewed softly on her earlobe.

"To Angela. To me. We should keep this on a business footing." She hoped she sounded firm and in control, but it was as if he didn't hear her. And to be quite honest, she didn't really hear herself either. Maybe she could have just one brief and breathless embrace before putting things back firmly on the business footing. A few moments of physical contact was hardly going to change anything. He slid her T-shirt up and caressed her breasts with a gentleness that surprised her. A gentleness that paralysed her, that she never wanted to stop. The brief moment when she was still considering the business-footing option quietly slipped away beneath his light touch.

"Angela is not a problem. It's you I want," he whispered into her ear.

She knew she shouldn't listen to him. It was wrong.

Her brain screamed a sensible and finger-wagging 'No!' and her body screamed a hungry, irresponsible 'Yes!'. Then somehow the zip of her jeans was open and Conrad was stroking her softly with his fingers, making her wet. She tilted her face up to his and kissed him. Their tongues touched and flickered. Her body flooded with desire, hunger washing through her like warm fudge sauce. Never in her entire life had she wanted a man with such desperate, deep, animal longing.

Without saying a word he took her by the hand and led her into the bedroom. She unbuttoned his shirt, running her tongue across his nipples and biting them lightly. He pushed her firmly against the wall and bent his head to her breasts, cupping each one in turn in his hands and taking her nipples fully into his mouth. There was no resisting him now, no reassuring little stabs of conscience, no voice of reason to calm the torrent of pure lust that was coursing through her. She longed to feel him inside her, feel the weight of his muscle-hard body on hers.

Then they were naked on the bed. He slid, hot and hard into her, covering her face with sweet, gentle kisses, filling her ears with half-whispered words of desire. She felt tiny beneath him. Her whole body simmered and bubbled, deliriously abandoned, drenched in her longing for him. His body tensed and thrust one last time and she felt she would drown in the hot waves of pleasure that rippled through her.

They collapsed in each other's arms, sweat-drenched and sated. He held her close, cradling her head in the crook of his arm. They said nothing for a long time. Nothing needed to be said.

"Fancy an evening at the races?" Conrad asked at last.

"Maybe," she said and promptly fell into a contented sleep.

She was roused by the phone ringing and Conrad lifting her head from his arm so that he could answer it. She pulled herself up onto the pillows, momentarily confused in strange surroundings. Still only half-conscious, she tried to make sense of the phone call.

"Gearóid who?"

He listened intently, his dark eyes clouding over with growing annoyance.

Lit guessed it was something to do with the site, perhaps the article in the newspaper.

"I see. Goodbye," he said coldly at last.

He dressed hastily. Then he threw her clothes onto the bed.

"Fun's over."

Nasty little ripples of self-loathing were trying to make themselves heard in Lit's brain. But she would not entertain them. Self-loathing was for teenagers. Self-loathing was for lemming-like women who threw themselves at men in the sure and certain knowledge that they would be post-coitally spurned almost before the last pleasant little aftershocks had subsided. Sex with Conrad was entirely different – just a bit of fun between two consenting adults. No-one was spurning anyone. No-one had used anyone.

"Aren't you going to tell me what that call was about?" she asked, forcing herself to sound cool and professional.

"No. None of your business."

He might be right about it being none of her business. But why did he have to be so rude about it? Barely an hour ago he was whispering words of desire and devotion and admiration and a whole lot of other stuff into her ears. Now he was acting like a complete toe-rag. Perhaps he was simply reverting to type. Now that the sex was over, he was free to be the vain, self-obsessed, emotionally retarded man that he most likely was beneath the veneer anyway.

"Look. I shouldn't have snapped," he said his voice softening. "These days, I seem to lose my temper far too easily. I have trouble sleeping and you're not the only thing that's keeping me awake." He forced a small smile, the kind of small smile that would melt a polar icecap. "When the building is underway I can relax. It's the single, biggest undertaking of my life. Hundreds of millions of pounds are at stake. Hundreds of jobs are involved, people's lives, their families – all depend on me. It's plain terrifying."

She'd never thought of it in those terms. She had trouble imagining Conrad being terrified about anything. And in spite of his recent rudeness, her heart went out to him and she was overwhelmed with a dangerous urge to comfort him.

"Anyway, I'm sorry – I'm not normally like this." He leaned forward and kissed her lightly on the cheek.

It was the last straw really. Impossible now to remain hurt and indignant. She squeezed his hand and ruffled his hair and told him it was OK and that she understood completely.

"And the phone call? Can't you talk about it?"

"It's tricky. And maybe you'd be better off not knowing."

"Maybe I could help."

"Doubtful. But you're probably going to find out anyway now. May as well hear it from the horse's mouth. Just give me a few minutes alone. I need to think this out."

She slid as languidly as she could from the bed and went to take a shower. In the luxurious marble and granite bathroom, she showered and dried herself. She noticed some Van Cleef & Arpels body lotion in the cabinet. It wasn't the kind of scent she would have associated with Angela for some reason. But perhaps it had been a gift. Maybe it was Conrad's preferred perfume. She wondered what Angela looked like. She imagined a petite woman with short ash-blonde hair and a pretty heart-shaped face. She hadn't noticed any photo of the happy engaged couple in the apartment. Perhaps he'd hidden them from view. Her heart sank again. She'd just done a horrible, nasty thing. Angela with her ash-blonde hair and her Van Cleef perfume was probably deeply and profoundly in love with her fiancée and that alone made Lit's involvement with Conrad unforgivable. She could convince herself that the night in the Shelbourne was just a one-night stand to be filed under 'fabulous but forget'. But there was no excuse for letting it happen a second time. Of course it didn't say much for Conrad either, that he would actively seek to be unfaithful to his fiancée again, without so much as a flicker of guilt. So now she was awash with his guilt as well as her own. It couldn't go on. She would tell him exactly how she felt and that would be the end of it. But first she had to find out about the phone call.

After ten minutes she reappeared in the vast open space that was his lounge area, to find him sitting on the couch, deeply preoccupied and staring into space.

"Conrad?" she said finally.

There was no response. She considered raising the Angela and guilt issue, but quickly realised this was not the right moment. She even considered asking about the phone-call again. But something about his demeanour made her hold her tongue. She gathered up her things. She took one last lingering look across the river from the balcony. What was the point in staying if he wasn't going to talk to her?

"I'll call you in the morning," she said and made for the door.

"Wait. Do you want me to tell you about the phone call or not?"

"Is it something I should know? I mean if it's private – it's none of my business really."

"It was a man called Gearóid."

"Who's he?"

"I haven't the faintest fucking idea. But it seems he's top dog in the Stoneyfield Residents Association now."

"What did he want?"

Conrad stood up abruptly and walked over to a fax machine. "It's just coming through now."

He held his hand over the machine as a sheet of paper printed out.

"Have a look."

To begin with she couldn't make any sense of a photo-copy of two banking slips. One was a withdrawal from Conrad's account for a hundred thousand euros, and the other a deposit to the account of Brendan Browne for the same amount on the same day.

"Is this what I think it is?"

He nodded.

"Why?" she asked.

The idea of Conrad dealing in grubby little brown envelopes and paying bribes was a hard one to recon-cile. Somehow, she had imagined him immaculately above and beyond such sordid little tactics. And seeing the proof here in front of her eyes made her feel implicated too. That was certainly something she didn't want either personally or professionally. Lie down with a dog and you'll get up with fleas, Laetitia dear, was yet another of Auntie Shiela's pearls of wisdom. And she might just be right on this occasion.

He shrugged. Like it was a perfectly moral thing to do to bribe a politician.

"But that's appalling," said Lit. "It's wrong."

Yet another rueful 'I know I've been a bad little boy – but I know you'll forgive me' look. But the thing was she couldn't forgive it. It was Sleazy! Slimey! Slick! Greasy! Grubby! It was common, beneath contempt. Even if he was the most handsome, most eligible, most successful, most charming man she'd ever met, she couldn't condone it.

"It's only a matter of time before this hits the newspapers. There's nothing I can do to stop it."

He cursed and glowered and generally expressed his bad temper about the whole thing. Lit wasn't inclined to be overly sympathetic. She didn't particularly want the job of putting a nice, acceptable spin on what was clearly a bribe. Not even for Conrad.

"How will we handle this?" he asked.

"A bribe is a bribe. That's corruption. You could go to jail."

"Thanks! That's really helpful!"

"It's the truth."

"The truth? You haven't even asked me for the truth! You jumped straight in and assumed the worst. Don't you even want to hear my side of the story?"

She picked up the fax and examined it once more. There was no denying the truth of what she saw with her own two eyes. There was also no denying the fact that neither she nor Matt could afford to drop Conrad as a client. Yet another fact which couldn't be denied was that she'd allowed herself to become involved with a man who had most probably bribed his way merrily through every stage of the planning process. All in all – a load of facts which couldn't be denied – a classic moral dilemma. Her head thumped from the strain of it. She needed to get away to think it all out. She needed to talk to Matt.

"I have to go."

"I wish you wouldn't."

"Call me later."

She bolted for the door before he could make any attempt to stop her.

Later, in the comfort of her own kitchen, she made a big show of peeling carrots and washing cabbage for Dandy. Cabbage left an awful smell. But she had decided that from now on she would give him as many of the things he really liked as she possibly could. And she would bite her lip if he complained. And she would try to be less fussy about his clothes. And she wouldn't get cross when he drank his tea from a saucer or slurped his porridge.

She roasted a fine leg of lamb and set the kitchen table with all Dandy's favourites – mustard, brown sauce and mint jelly. She opened an expensive bottle of red burgundy that she had been saving for a special occasion. But Dandy liked a good wine and there was no time like the present. Then she baked the only pudding she knew how to make – bread-and-butter pudding – his favourite. She gave it the full cholesterol treatment with free-range eggs, rich dairy cream, little triangles of bread liberally spread with butter, then vanilla, a dash of brandy and juicy sultanas and sugar. Richie liked her bread-and-butter pudding too and sometimes he would put a cold slice of it in his lunch box. She wasn't much in the mood for idle banter at the dinner table. Dandy made a couple of half-hearted attempts to knock a rise out of her but gave up when she didn't even respond. Richie had even less success.

"I'm going over to Barney's house, Mum."

"Fine."

"Yeah, a party for his older brother. His dad's organised a pole-dancer and a stripogram."

"That's nice," she said, absently stacking the dishes in the dishwasher, while her head spun with the problem of what to do about Conrad.

"There's kegs of beer and his mum's rolling a few joints for us."

"Mm!"

"And after that we're all going skinny-dipping in the Forty Foot."

"Don't forget to bring a towel, love."

"What's a pole-dancer?" enquired Dandy. "Do you think Barney's mum would roll a joint for me?"

Lit sighed and smiled absently, so absently that Richie came and wrapped his long arms around her and gave her one of his languid hugs.

"Something up?"

"No. I'm just tired."

"We're only kidding. You know that, don't you? Barney's parents don't even drink."

"Yes, I know," she said, not wanting him to know she hadn't heard a single thing he'd said.

She was always thrilled when Richie gave her a hug. It didn't happen so often these days, a far cry from the five-year-old who would fling himself into her arms and tell her "Mum, I'm just crazy about you!". Now he seemed to be developing Dandy's gruff ways. Some day he would probably also be a father, pouring all his affection into some simple little gesture like patting his son's head or showing him how to swing a golf club. Relationships with men could be complicated and unsettling and emotionally draining. But she felt safe and secure with these two gruff males and their reserved, uncomplicated affection for her.

On the flood-lit patio, listening to the fading sounds of the birds as they settled for the night and the water fountains splashing, she sipped a mineral water and tried to think of what to do about Conrad. She'd called Matt and, without mentioning specifics, told him that they needed to talk fairly urgently. He was in a bar somewhere, knee-deep – well, probably elbow-deep in craic, and said that whatever it was would wait until the morning.

So here she was alone on the patio, with no-one to confide in, grappling with her father's illness, her involvement with a practically married man, bribery and corruption amongst the highest in the land, and her own lack of professionalism in getting involved with a client. She could do nothing about her father's illness only accept it and come to terms with it. But being party to Conrad's infidelity made her blush for shame. It was all very well for Bonnie to go on with all that 'fuck 'em and chuck 'em' stuff. Lit had tried to be like that with Conrad, but it just didn't work for her. She could put herself far too easily into Angela's shoes, could imagine how desolate and hurt she would feel if Conrad cheated on her. Even now, imagining him in the arms of some other woman made her feel a bit fretful – even though she had no right to feel that way.

But she forced all of that out of her mind. There was only one problem that she absolutely had to address now – and that was the bribe. She turned it over in her mind, time and time again, thinking so hard that she got thinker's block and nodded off, to be woken a good hour later by Richie.

"Mum – what are you like – dozing on the patio in the dark?"

She grinned up at him sheepishly. "I thought you were going over to Barney's for some kind of teenage orgy."

"Nah! Decided to stay home. I don't really like his brother anyway."

"Why?"

"Dunno!" Said with a shrug and amiable grin and absentminded scratch of the head. He pulled up a lounger beside her and flung himself into it.

"So, Mam – what's the story? What's the craic? What's bugging you? You hanging out with the wrong kind of people, doll? Someone messing with your mojo? What?"

He did a bit of 'umphs-umphs' techno-rapping with the palms of his hands on his knees while he waited for a reply. Lit was a bit gobsmacked that he'd even noticed how out of sorts she was. Sometimes she confided in him with little worries, mostly things about the house – like should she get better locks put on the doors, or should she get someone in to clean out the storage tank. She was very tempted to confide in him now, even talking through the problem with a third party might make it clearer in her head.

"I've a load of stuff on my mind. That's all."

"Work?"

"Yeah, work," she lied. Above all she wanted to tell him about Dandy, soften the blow for him, break it gently in stages. She knew he would be devastated when the time came. But she was sworn to secrecy. "I'm sorry.

I'm not the best mother in the world, am I?"

"Well, I'm stuck with you – so there's no sense in complaining. It's not like you're going to change."

"Would you like me to?"

He shrugged and resumed techno-rapping his knees. "Anyway it's two of us against one of you."

"How do you mean?"

"Me and Dandy," he said finishing off his rap and slouching off to bed.

# CHAPTER 23

Lit was awake all night fretting and sweating about her father and Conrad. Finally, when that irritating little twat of a bird who always seemed to want to be the loudest bird in his particular oak tree, who would never rest until he had got all the other birds in all the other trees twittering, when he began the first sharp notes of his morning twitter to the nation she realised that sleep would not come. She got up at five, dressed in shorts, T-shirt and trainers and went for a run in the park. Ordinarily she would have savoured the cool early morning mist on her skin, relished the solitude, delighted in the pure eloquence of the birdsong, smiled benignly at the ducks in the pond still in a drowsy early morning pre-quacking state. But today she was just too tired. One lap of the park and she felt like she'd run the marathon.

Back at home, she made porridge for Dandy followed by a creamy, grainy scrambled egg on crisp buttered toast. Then she did the five stages of the 'Wake Up Richie' process before driving to work. She was at her desk by eight o'clock.

When Maura arrived and saw the gaunt and drawn form of Lit huddled over some papers, she was less than sympathetic.

"Hey, look! The zombies have moved in overnight!"

"There's a pile of post on your desk," Lit snapped.

"Do you have to be so rude? No sense in coming to work at this hour if you're going to be so grumpy!"

"Lay off, Maura. I've a lot on my mind." Lit disappeared into her office and closed the door. She knew Maura would be offended by the closed door – but she couldn't help it. She desperately needed to be completely alone.

Now even the simplest chores exhausted her. She tried to do the less challenging stuff first, like checking the e-mail and prioritising her to-do list for the day. But phone-calls had to be answered and it wasn't easy being all chirpy and proactive over the phone when she hadn't slept a wink. Dara Cornwell called to query her choice of the Martello Tower as the venue for launching a new range of organic seafood paté. He'd hoped he could sort out the matter with Matt and was less than charming when Lit told him that Matt was at a very important meeting with their newest client – Super Duper Fast Foods – the supreme satanic force of junk-food evil.

"Can I help at all?"

He sighed and supposed that she would have to do. Then he had a little rant about the Martello Tower.

"I thought you'd like it. It's by the sea. Seafood and all that. Did you have somewhere else in mind?" She could barely keep the tetchiness from her voice.

"Not a clue. That's your job surely? What you're paid all that ridiculous money for."

"Right, Mr Cornwell, I'll have a chat with Matt about

it. How's Poppy by the way?"

"Couldn't be better. She's giving tai chi classes to some inner-city kids. She loves that sort of thing. I was fortunate to be able to set it up for her."

Lit bit her lip. Somewhere deep inside Poppy Cornwell was a magnificent woman, someone who didn't think the solution to the needs of inner-city kids was to give them tai chi classes, someone who didn't believe that the rest of mankind was in dire need of being rescued from their own lack of willpower, bad diet, vanity, laziness and their quietly contented lives in the suburbs. Poppy was struggling to break free of her mealy-minded husband. She felt sure of it. If Poppy held the reins of Wholesome Foods things would be very different.

She struggled on until lunch-time, scouring the papers for any reference to Conrad. Mercifully there was none. She sent out for a wholemeal salad sandwich, nibbled half-heartedly on it, threw most of it in the bin and tried to keep herself going with black coffee.

Matt was due back in the afternoon and she dreaded telling him about Conrad. They'd made many pacts when they first went into partnership, about all sorts of things, but Lit had been the most vehement on the subject of getting emotionally or sexually involved with clients. Matt didn't see what the big deal was and had told her she was just being prissy and prim. But she'd insisted, made him promise and vowed herself never to date clients. It had all worked perfectly until Conrad came along and tempted her into breaking her own rule.

What would she say? Hi, Matt – did you know that our biggest client, the jewel in our crown, is up to his eyes in blackmail and corruption? Then Matt would reassure her and say – that's not our problem. We just do our job. We can't be responsible for what he did before he employed us. And then she would say – but what if he tried to blackmail us? Then Matt would reply that there was nothing Conrad could blackmail them about and then she would have to own up about having sex with him and then it would get around and people would think she was a slut and Richie would probably get wind of it. Barney Ryan's mother, for all her generous home-baked apple-pie and steak-sandwiches-on-demand hospitality, was a notorious gossip.

Lit told Matt about the bribe first over coffee in his office.

His reaction was typically laid-back.

"I don't see that it's our problem really. We're his PR company – not his legal team."

"But he's corrupt. It's unethical. We have standards to uphold."

"And we do – uphold them. But nobody's proved yet that he's bribed anyone."

"I saw the cheques. He didn't deny it."

"Anyway, there's not much we can do for now."

"I feel so guilty."

"Why? It's not your fault."

There was no point in putting off the moment any longer.

"I've – well, I've – " She was blushing. Something she hadn't done since the Harry Menton days.

"What?"

"Well, you know that he's – that people say he's sex on legs."

Matt gave her a knowing, disapproving look. "Sleeping with a client – bad idea! Don't do it again! Naughty girl! It complicates things. And he's practically married. And it goes against your own rules. There! Is that what you wanted to hear?"

"You knew?"

"You were a dead giveaway at the party, to be honest. Forget about it. It's no big deal. But in this case, I would seriously advise that you don't let it happen again."

She could have hugged Matt only she was too exhausted even for that. But she certainly wouldn't let it happen again. Ever. There was no denying she liked Conrad, enjoyed his company, fancied the pants off him, lusted after him in the most disconcerting way. But his image was slightly tarnished now. So with a gargantuan effort, she put all thoughts of him aside and carried on with her work.

She went to a meeting on the other side of town with the advertising agency about a poster campaign for Super Duper Fast Foods. When she returned in the late afternoon, she locked herself in the office, diverted her phone lines and drafted a set of proposals for a small sports clothing manufacturer who were preparing to break into the European market. She costed everything and drew up a realistic timeframe for the project. The lack of sleep played hell with her concentration. But she forced herself to continue working, until she was satisfied with the end product. Everyone had gone home, including Matt and Maura, by the time she closed up her laptop for the night.

It was eight o'clock. She drove home along the canal in the golden evening light, too tired even to listen to music.

Richie quite liked his family, but he generally kept quiet about that. When his father was in Ireland, Richie saw him constantly – otherwise they kept in touch through daily e-mailing and phone calls. At present his father was working in Berlin and Richie was planning to join him there for three weeks in August. They were planning to drive down to Italy and stay with some of his father's friends in Umbria. It was one of the pleasures of being a member of a dysfunctional family – extra holidays and a wider circle of friends and acquaintances. He enjoyed the things they did together – football, films, the odd play. His dad was kind in an offhand way and Richie liked the way he teased him, just enough to make him squirm slightly, not enough to damage his fragile self-esteem.

Self-esteem was an important part of being a teenager apparently. The very earnest careers guidance teacher at school was always on about it and her shelves were crammed with big thick books like Building Self-Esteem and I'm OK – You're Not So Bad Yourself. After four years in secondary school, endless sessions of sitting in circles and getting in touch with his inner self and the inner selves of his mates, meditating and finding his special place, mountains of handouts where he had to answer questions about what made him angry or happy or uncomfortable, Richie was not much wiser on the self-esteem issue.

Did he like himself? He lay in the bath and said it out loud as though he were interviewing himself for prime-time television.

"Richie Doran, do you like yourself?"

Well, it was a stupid question really because even if you didn't like yourself, you were stuck with yourself forever anyway. It wasn't like sitting next to Brendan Cullen, a slimey greaseball that he could move away from. So if you didn't like yourself you just had to grin and bear it. No other solution suggested itself to Richie's simple mind. He wasn't the kind to have suicidal thoughts which would involve too much conscious mental and logistical effort. That was all 'academic' anyway (as Miss Cass the English teacher would say) because when he thought about it, he did. Like himself. He wasn't a bad auld skin. Reasonably good-looking – even Bonnie of the beautiful legs said so! Thick, softly curling dark brown hair, well-built with a decent bit of muscle on his arms and a reasonable six-pack. Average intelligence – just enough to get by – not enough to set him apart from his mates. A few sports trophies to his name – but not enough to make him a beefcake like Barney Ryan, who was a prop for the school rugby team and reported to be on a diet of raw meat and creotine. He was well-liked in school and his PE teacher said that he always had a smile on his face – though he tended not to smile as much at home. It just wasn't the done thing.

His main ambition in common with most of his classmates was to get laid. He would put it down as one of his basic psychological needs. Getting laid would definitely take care of security, belonging, self-esteem and all that other stuff. Plus he could really do with it now. To be a virgin at sixteen and a half wasn't catastrophic, but it was a nuisance when certain topics came up for conversation and he had to wear his 'Yeah, I know what you guys are on about – been there, done that' expression. There was only so much a bloke could do on his own. All the real sex stuff came when you did it with someone else.

For nights on end he would lie in bed thinking about how it would be, fantasising about who it would be with. In his dreams, she, whoever she was, but mostly Bonnie, would come to his room and beckon to him. Then she would slip out of her gown and stand naked before him, gently kissing him all over and undressing him at the same time. Her hands would roam softly over his skin and Richie would give himself up to her, drowning in her caresses.

The embarassing encounter with Janet Byrne temporarily put him off the entire idea of sex and he hadn't fantasised about getting laid for almost an entire week. But then Bonnie stayed over the night of the party and once again he gave himself up to lovely soft-focus dreams about how she would stay overnight with them and how she would have to come to his room for something important and she would be wearing only a towel, because she would be just out of the shower and then the towel would fall away . . .

"Richie – are you going to stay up there all day? I want you to do a job for me!"

Richie cursed and climbed out of the bath. He had wanted to give some quality time to thinking about his other pressing ambition. He was not a daredevil in any sense of the word and even when his mates did daft things on bikes or 'borrowed' their mother's cars to go speeding, Richie always held himself aloof. He couldn't see the sense in risking his life.

"You're soft, Doran," someone said to him once when he wouldn't go speeding down Dun Laoghaire pier on his bike.

He wriggled out of it by offering to be the timekeeper. He remembered the day vividly because Barney Ryan, never an elegant sight on a bicycle, had pedalled down the pier jerkily at breakneck speed and hurtled straight into the murky waters at the other end. Luckily for Barney, he was a strong swimmer and he lumbered philosophically up the steps of the pier in his dripping wet track suit and soggy trainers.

Barney's subsequent dose of pneumonia had left Richie in no doubt that the daredevil antics of his friends were foolish and didn't prove anything much. Though his own ambition was potentially much more dangerous than any of their little escapades. For that reason he never talked about it to them in case they dared him into doing it.

In his bedroom he looked at the model tower crane, the single remaining toy of his childhood which still held pride of place on the minimalist, Japanese-style cherry-wood shelving system that his mother said was perfect for a young man's room. Every so often he took the crane down and gave it a wipe with a lightly oiled cloth and fiddled around with the simple toy-like mechanisms. It was a well-proportioned and lifelike model, standing four feet in height. The hoist drum was balanced against the weight of the jib to stop the crane with its load from toppling over. The trolley moved realistically along the jib, pulled backwards and forwards by strong cables wound around the trolley drum. The operator's cab and the jib could swing around just like the real thing.

He remembered vividly the Christmas when he woke at dawn to find an enormous box at the foot of his bed. Tearing away the paper in a rush of excitement, he had found the box to contain hundreds of bits of yellow metal, wire and screws, together with very complicated assembly instructions.

That day he and his dad had worked for four hours, arguing and squabbling, rummaging for tiny but crucial screws or bolts, until slowly but surely the crane was assembled. Together they sat back on the bed, surveying their handiwork.

"Do me a favour, Richie. Next Christmas – maybe ask

for a football or a Playstation game."

He could still feel the bond of contentment and satisfaction which suffused that moment with his dad and
each time he looked at the crane now at this more ana-
lytical phase of his life, he thought it symbolised something important between them.

Now in the kitchen, while Dandy chewed diligently
on his lamb chop, Richie did some multi-tasking – eating, drinking, smoothing gel through his hair and shov-
ing his size-ten feet into laced-up trainers.

"Why can't you just eat sitting down like a normal
person?" said Lit. She trudged wearily around the
kitchen, clearing up the debris of the men in her life.
She was too tired to complain about it. The cleaning
lady wouldn't be round for another two days and she
couldn't endure the mess until then.

"Going out. Meeting Barney and Neil in The
Catacombs. Can't stop." He finished gulping down his
food and put the finishing touches to his hair.

Lit was not too keen on The Catacombs. It wasn't
exactly a bar, but it did serve some alcohol and she
didn't want Richie hanging out with the weird
crowd who met there. There was so much danger and
temptation now. Having a few beers or self-consciously
smoking a furtive joint in someone's garden shed were
tame and innocent pleasures in comparison.

"Be good and careful and behave and don't take any
drinks from strangers and don't hang about anywhere
alone. Remember to leave your mobile switched on and
call me if you have any problem."

"OK, Mum." He bent down and gave her a peck on
the cheek.

"Keep enough money for a taxi home. If you can't get
a taxi – call me."

"Mum. I'm going down the road to The Catacombs. I'm only sixteen. I won't get in anywhere else. I'll be home at eleven."

"Be nice and respectful to the girls. I know the way Barney Ryan goes on. But you don't have to be like that."

"Mum – shut up – night."

Lit curled up on the sofa to watch the hurling match with Dandy, who was propped up in the armchair with the Foxford rug draped across his knees. He hurled abuse and compliments and indignant queries at the teams and the referee. Occasionally he would nod off with his glass of red wine hanging ominously over a prized Persian rug. She daren't remove it.

Then he would wake with a jolt, swear gratuitously at the referee and mumble nostalgically about Jack Lynch in his heyday.

Wine always made her sleepy and now she dozed fitfully on the sofa. Besides, she wasn't that interested in sport. When she wasn't fretting about Conrad, she was speculating enviously about Bonnie and Tallon in La Verona. How was it that Bonnie, who had such a complicated sex life, always seemed to have such an uncomplicated way of enjoying it? She thought of calling Bonnie on her mobile and wishing her a pleasant night – but decided against the idea. The last thing a basking girl having a good night needed was a call from her friend telling her to have a good night. Anyway, Bonnie hadn't texted with a progress report which probably meant that as predicted, Seán Tallon's microchip had dislodged or disconnected.

She was just on her way to bed when the door bell rang. It was too early for Richie to be home and besides he had a key. She cursed softly and went to open the door.

It was Conrad, clutching a simple bunch of freesias and a bottle of something bubbly with a very expensive label. She wasn't exactly dressed in old jog pants and battered trainers, but she felt grey-looking and puffy, like she did before a period. She wished he hadn't come. But she daren't risk getting on his bad side.

"I wasn't expecting you," she said, the closest she could come to a scolding.

"Yes. I'm sorry about that." He dipped his head and did the apologetic ice-cap-melting smile. "Would it be OK if I came in?"

No, it wouldn't be OK. She was tired from lack of sleep. Even more tired from all the effort of psyching herself up to having no further sexual encounters with him. She'd planned a long bath with a de-stressing face pack and something gooey and expensive made by someone in Bavaria to put in the water for restoring something or other. Then the plan was bed with a page-turning novel that she had been reading for about six months now. The story was good, but it was a miracle if she managed to turn one page a night.

Lit had tremendous willpower about most things. She'd gone on a strict diet after Richie was born to regain her figure. She'd given up cigarettes, biting her nails and Walnut Whirls. She'd even stopped watching *EastEnders* when she found it becoming addictive. But she realised that Conrad would be a far harder habit to break, especially if he got into the habit of landing on her doorstep at the witching hour when her thoughts were naturally turned towards bed anyway.

"The thing is, Conrad, I'm really tired," she said at last.

"I understand." He handed her the bunch of freesias and the bottle of bubbly and did that little-boy-lost routine of looking sadly at his shoes. It was too much.

"But not too tired for a nightcap," she said, giving in.

Her preferred venue for the nightcap was the kitchen where she knew her resolve would hold, seeing as Dandy was barely a few feet away in his bedroom. But as soon as she had the idea, she remembered that the kitchen was in its usual mess. She had tidied up, but it was cluttered and smelt of cooking and Dandy's infernal fire in the range. Instead she led Conrad out onto the patio and turned on the floodlights.

"It's a nice garden. I didn't really get a good look at it the other night."

"Thanks. I can't take all the credit, except for the borders round the patio. The rest came courtesy of Aisling Garden Design."

They sipped champagne and chatted about gardens for a while. Conrad told her about the old Georgian mansion he'd bought in Waterford which was being completely restored and refurbished. It had a garden which once featured in *House & Garden* magazine. It also had a walled garden.

"Sounds lovely."

"Yeah. I don't know anything about gardens to be honest."

It was on the tip of her tongue to say something about Angela, but she was determined to keep the conversation bright and breezy and non-controversial if possible.

"So – " She hadn't a clue what she was going to say next. "So – all this property and building – does it run in the family?"

"No. My dad ran a little hardware store on the main street of a tiny village called Hollymaine. Wanted me to go into the business and expand it. I went to college and got into bricks and mortar instead."

Lit smiled to herself. It would be impossible to imagine Conrad Budd in a brown overall, leaning on the counter of a village hardware store, doing up bags of six-inch nails and getting excited about junction boxes and s-bend pipes and salmon-pink bathroom suites. Snatching the odd glance at him in soft patio light, she reckoned he really was in a much grander league than most other people she knew. It wasn't just his good looks or his money. He had charisma. He was an enigma. But there was the bribe, the grubby brown-envelope business. What was charismatic or enigmatic about that?

"Do you want to know why I called to your house?"

She knew exactly why. To get into her knickers. That was why. And possibly to talk his way out of the business of the bribe. Either way, the champagne had cleared her head remarkably and she was determined not to be sucked in again to the dreadful lusting and drooling which had inflicted her for the past few weeks.

"If it's about Sunday – "

"First of all – Brendan Browne – "

"Please, I don't really – "

"You have to listen to my side of the story."

She didn't really have to listen to anything. It was late. She was tired. He needn't think a few measly freesias and a couple of glasses of champagne would soften her up. She would tell him that right now. She began dead-heading a pot of delicate white asters. "Listen, you needn't think that a few flowers – "

"No! You listen!"

She didn't like his tone at all. Don't you speak to me in that tone of voice, she wanted to say, like she would say to Richie. But she didn't get a chance.

"If I was trying to impress you, do you think I would turn up on your doorstep with a bunch of flowers I picked up in the local florist, a bottle of champagne I grabbed in the off-licence? I mean, think about it! I could fly you to the freesia capital of the world and buy the shagging place for you – if it took your fancy. In ten minutes, I can have my own chartered jet on standby at the airport, to fly you to the Champagne region and buy you the whole bloody vineyard."

She sniffed scornfully and tossed dead heads into the back of the border. "Well, why didn't you?"

"Because it would be a waste of time and it wouldn't impress you. Look, I didn't bribe anyone. That's all I came here to say."

Well, he would say that. He had to say that. What else could a rich, handsome, enigmatically charismatic – or was it charismatically enigmatic man – say?

"Brendan Browne was a neighbour of ours when I was growing up. The family bought all their farm machinery from my father's shop."

Oh, here we go, she thought – a sordid little tale of hardware and territory folks sticking together and always being friends.

"But you don't want to hear all that really, do you? You've made up your mind that I'm guilty already!"

There was no denying that.

"Browne has family problems. His wife left him. He's penniless, barely owns the shirt on his back. He came to me and asked me for help – money to buy a little apartment somewhere. What's a hundred grand to me? I gave it to him for old time's sake."

"But he's a politician in Stoneyfield. Please tell me you see the problem."

He shrugged and shoved his hands in his pockets and

paced around. He seemed genuinely flummoxed that his good deed to Brendan Browne could be twisted and used against him.

And of course the essentially sweet nature of ice-cool and occasionally morally superior Lit Doran rose to the surface.

"I believe you."

"You do?"

"I do. And what's more we can handle your side of the story easily when it gets to the media."

"You're a treasure." He pulled her gently towards him and hugged her. Oh, the shy huskiness of his voice, the little hesitant catch in his throat which made the words sound suffused with deep emotion and desire. It was enough to tempt the purest of saints.

She pulled away abruptly. It wasn't easy. The musky scent of him, the smooth curve of his lightly tanned and most perfect chest that she longed to rest her head on, his warm breath on her face – was there a woman born who could fully resist such exquisite temptation?

"The thing is, I've made up my mind, and the other day – and of course the other night – you and me – the wine and the hot weather which has a really bad effect on me – of course it was wonderful – I mean I really enjoyed it – but –"

She couldn't stop herself babbling.

"I've never met a woman like you before."

Well, that was a bit clichéd! Somehow she figured he'd have something more original to say. She was grateful though because it stemmed the flow of her babbling.

"Let's just stop it there." The words came freely now. "You're engaged to Angela. You are also a client of mine. I feel a complete bitch for having been weak enough to have sex with you – and not once but twice. And I can't do my best work for you, if my mind is clouded by other emotions."

"There's something you should know about Angela."

And now, she thought, they'd reached the 'there's something you should know' stage. But to quote the obnoxious Barry Owens, she'd been there, done that and got the T-shirt – with Harry Menton. How would Conrad put it? That he and Angela had an understanding – the 'what goes on tour, stays on tour' kind of understanding? That Angela didn't love him? That he was no longer engaged to Angela? That he felt obliged to marry her because she was the mother of his child? That Angela was suffering from a nervous breakdown/ sexuality crisis/panic attacks/cold feet or all of the above? Well, it wouldn't wash.

Steeled with the strength of her own resolve she observed coolly, "There's nothing I need to know about Angela. She's your fiancée – the woman you are going to spend your life with, have children with, grow old with. You have made a commitment to each other. Maybe I'd prefer it to be otherwise – but I wish you both a long and happy life together."

"Don't you even want to know? It's not what you might think. In fact, it might surprise you."

If he was trying to arouse her curiosity, he'd succeeded. She was just on the point of telling him so when she heard Richie's heavy step in the hall.

## CHAPTER 24

She slept well on a clean conscience. Temptation had come and danced around her seductively, but she had resisted. She was after all a good person, not the nasty sort who would steal another woman's man. The next time it would be easier to resist him, and each time it would just get easier and easier until she would eventually reach that most perfect state of emotional wellbeing – the 'what did I ever see in him' state. Of course, the arrival of Richie on the patio had helped to stiffen her resolve – and the fact that he wouldn't take the hint and leave. Instead, he chatted animatedly about cranes until Conrad suppressed a yawn and announced that he had a tough board meeting in the morning and was going home to bed.

She slept until seven, woke in good humour and chatted cheerfully to Dandy as she made his breakfast. This morning he got up later than usual. There was nothing remarkable in that. He was probably not sleeping so well with the clammy night heat. But otherwise he looked fine. She could see no difference in him.

"I think I'll go to Croke Park for the football final this year."

"Why not? We'll all go. I have good contacts in the GAA. I can get us tickets for a box. We can have lunch and make a day of it."

"I was thinking more of a flask of tea and a few sandwiches in the terraces."

That of course was said to rise her, but she ignored it and set a plate of scrambled egg in front of him. If he announced that he planned to go bungee-jumping off the Cliffs of Moher with members of the meths-drinking club, she wouldn't argue.

The day flew by in a flurry of meetings, conference calls and paperwork. With a good night's sleep and a clean conscience, she worked quickly and efficiently, barely recognisable as the zombie of yesterday. When she got home, there was even time to cook a real dinner for Dandy and to sit and talk to him about the old times and growing up in the West of Ireland. As usual he talked for almost an hour, answering the questions that she knew he wanted her to ask. She didn't know where he got the energy to talk so much.

"And tell me again about that job that you do?" he asked at last, as he periodically did.

"It's called Public Relations and Image Consultancy," she answered, as she had answered so many times.

"People need advice and direction and contacts in advertising and marketing when it comes to presenting themselves to the world at large. We provide that service."

Why did it sound so thin and tacky when she explained it to him?

"And people pay money for that, do they?"

"Yes. They pay a lot of money to get it right."

He guffawed loudly. His scornful disregard for her chosen career was stinging, but she said nothing. He would never understand. In the past ten years his clock seemed to have turned back to some rare and rose-tinted old time in the 1950s when everyone drove on quiet country roads at thirty miles an hour in Ford Prefects, from homely white-washed cottages to County Finals in warm September sunshine, and ate ham sandwiches and drank cold bottled tea. What would he think if she took him to Conrad's penthouse or showed him Conrad's plans for Stoneyfield? How could he understand that the shared recreational substance of choice was no longer cold bottled tea but neat lines of readily available coke?

Her mobile buzzed and bleeped that she had a text message. It took her a while to find her phone, on the counter somewhere hidden in the middle of all the clutter. She thought the message might be from Richie, but it was from Conrad, which surprised her. She didn't think that Conrad was a text-message type of person. Perhaps it was something to do with the television program or the rugby sponsorship. She pressed 'read' and his message came up. But the topic was not television, nor rugby, nothing at all to do with work in fact. Thinking she had misread the words, she set the phone down very carefully on the counter and finished stacking the dishes in the dishwasher. She looked at the message again. There was no mistake. She hadn't misread the words. The message said simply: "I love you and you have to let me tell you about Angela. Yours always, Conrad."

She was so shocked that she didn't even think of texting him back. Could it be true? Could he really be in love with her? Could he be hers always? If he loved her and not Angela then it would be wrong of him to go ahead and marry a woman he didn't love. Then it wouldn't be so bad for Lit to love him back. The calm contentment of the day evaporated and once again she found herself hurtling into a tornado of high emotions. Her father dozed in his chair, oblivious to the tornado.

She picked up the phone and went out onto the patio. This was definitely a moment for calling Bonnie, even though she knew Bonnie was on yet another date with Seán Tallon. A declaration of love from Conrad Budd – it was almost too good to be true. She desperately needed to talk to Bonnie, couldn't wait to tell her. She would be so happy for her, so envious in a nice, best-friend sort of way. Bonnie would know what to do. Of course, she knew quite well what to do herself – but Bonnie had a good nose for these kinds of situations.

It was very bad form to call a friend on a date – but

this was an emergency. She punched in Bonnie's number and waited. After about the sixth ring Bonnie answered.

"Lit! What the hell do you want? I'm – we're – well, you could have picked a better time."

"Sorry, Bonnie – but this is an emergency."

"It's not Dandy, is it?"

"No. It's Conrad."

"Conrad? What's he done now?"

Lit could hardly contain herself. She felt as though she might very well burst in an instant.

"He loves me!"

"Of course he does. Is that all?" Bonnie sounded distinctly unimpressed.

"Well, I don't know what to do? I mean there's Angela and it's terrible to take another woman's man – but on the other hand, Conrad Budd loves me and it's more than I ever could have dreamed of!"

Lit could hear some muttered conversation in the background. She briefly wondered what Seán Tallon would think of her winning the heart of one of Ireland's most eligible bachelors. Even he would have to agree that it was a sound financial investment.

"And do you love him?" Bonnie enquired with clinical detachment.

"Love him? Love Conrad Budd? Bonnie, how can you even ask such a question? How could anybody not love him? There is nothing to not love about him!"

"Well, if you love him and he loves you – then there's no more to be said. Now if you'll excuse me – I'm having my navel licked here. Talk to you tomorrow." And she hung up.

Yuck! How disgusting! Having Seán Tallon licking your navel!

Lit slumped back in the garden chair, feeling oddly dissatisfied with the conversation. Bonnie was supposed to go all jealous, and then all tearful and happy and sad at the same time. And then she should have immediately suggested summit meetings to discuss the best way of getting him to propose, then keep him waiting for an answer, then wedding dresses and bridesmaids and honeymoon destinations. Instead, she had been all cool and sensible.

Lit paced up and down the floodlit garden, tugging absentmindedly at tall white delphiniums and deadheading rose bushes. There was too much to think about – her father, Richie, work, the business about the bribery and now this – a declaration of love. Her head was spinning from it all. Thoughts banged and slammed about chaotically like deranged molecules.

Ordinarily Lit prided herself on being able to see things coming – but this was truly a bolt from the blue. Could she have made a mistake? She checked the message again just to be sure. Was he joking? That was unthinkable. Some men had a cruel nasty streak in them and they enjoyed building women up just so they could have the dubious pleasure of watching them fall flat on their faces. But Conrad couldn't possibly do a thing like that. Perhaps he was one of those love addicts who thought they were in love with every woman they made love to. But Conrad was too cool, too suave for that.

Then where did Angela fit into the picture? What sort of man would declare his love to one woman while he was still engaged to someone else? The worst sort – the love rat, the cheating heart, the sex fiend, the traitorous cad, the unfaithful bounder. But none of those descriptions seemed to fit him.

She looked about her in the floodlit darkness, desperate for some physical activity to settle her mind. A favourite night task was the extermination of slugs – sprinkling salt on them and watching them shrivel up, or catching them in beer traps or watching them nibble at blue pellets and gasp their last. Sadly though, the hot, dry summer had put paid to this particular ghastly morbid pleasure. All the slugs must have packed their bags and headed off to somewhere wet and damp in Norway. For there were none in her garden.

She went into the kitchen and cleared out Richie's food cupboard. When all else fails, when tragedy looms or when momentous events threaten to overpower you – clear out a cupboard. That was Auntie Florence's advice. Lit remembered sneering heartily at it when she was all of seventeen. What a sad reflection on the warped mentality of adults, to think they could cope with some of life's most exhilarating and terrifying events by simply clearing out a cupboard! At seventeen there were far more exciting alternatives to help her cope with upheaval – like going for a midnight swim with no clothes on or staying up all night to watch the dawn, or writing epic poems exploring the endless tortures of unrequited love and not being allowed to stay out after midnight.

But Auntie Florence, as ever, turned out to be quite right. Midnight swims and staying up all night were indeed dramatic gestures – but they invariably left you with chills and horrible bags under your eyes. Clearing out a cupboard, on the other hand, was a small, manageable task which offered an instant sense of achievement.

Richie's cupboard was a cornucopia of prawn-flavoured noodles, boil-in-the-bag pasta carbonara, tinned beans, tinned spagetti hoops, tinned chocolate pudding, microwave popcorn, peanut butter, Nutella, maple syrup – his own little culinary empire. First she turned everything out, then she discarded anything past its sell-by date. Then she washed the shelves down and replaced the tins and packets neatly like a display in a shop.

"There!" she said proudly. "I haven't thought of Conrad Budd for fifteen minutes. If I go through another four cupboards, that will take me well past midnight and then it will be time for bed."

Then she looked at her watch and remembered Richie. Where was he? It wasn't like him to be late. She didn't want to be one of those awful fussy mothers who insisted on knowing where their children were at all times, but he was late and he said he'd be home before eleven. She rang his mobile and he answered almost immediately.

"Mummmm – gooood of you to call."

"Richie, have you been drinking?" she asked sharply.

"Nnnoooo!"

"Why don't I believe you?"

"I swear, Mummm – no drinking – I swear . . ."

"Where are you?"

"I'm with Barney and his big brother Jamie and Neil and Lara and Zzzzoooooeeee."

"I thought you didn't like Zoe."

"Yeah. Hommme in five minutes. Prommmise."

It was all she needed. When she heard his key in the door she positioned herself in the hall with her arms folded. Oh God, she thought, I feel just like Auntie Sheila and I know exactly what I'm going to say next.

"What time do you call this?" Lit couldn't believe she'd said it. She'd promised herself long ago that she would surely come up with something more inventive if

Richie ever rolled in late.

Richie stopped in his tracks, shoved his key in his pocket, ran his hand through his dark hair and put a finger up to his lip.

"Ssshh, Mummm. Barney's with me."

"I don't give a f– a hoot about Barney. Where were you?"

"In the park."

She nodded scornfully and pulled her chin in so that it must have wrinkled just like Auntie Sheila's. Then Barney Ryan lumbered through the door with a big idiotic grin on his face.

"Mrs Doran. And don't you look fetching this fine summer night. A proper yummy mummy!" He grinned at her inanely.

"Go home, Barney, or I'll tell your mammy on you." She knew the word 'mammy' would deflate him.

And so it did. He smiled sheepishly this time, said goodnight and shuffled out the front door.

Arms on her hips now, she turned to confront Richie.

"Don't lie to me. You have been drinking."

"No, Mumm." He was trying not to grin.

"You haven't – " But of course! Why hadn't she spotted it straight away? After all, she and Bonnie had rolled home more than once, high on dope kindly provided by Bonnie's older brother. "Go to your room. You're grounded."

"Yes, sir, ma'am. Anything you say. Night. I love you." He pecked her on the cheek. Then he shuffled off up the stairs, giggling to himself.

# CHAPTER 25

In the office next morning, Maura was having a Fatal Attraction moment. She narrowed her eyes just like Glen Close, picked up the phone and dialled a number.

"Hello? Mrs Owens? How are you? Good. It seems like ages since I was over to see you and I was thinking – would you be at home this evening?"

Lit was still grappling with the horrible worry that her son might turn into a worthless drug-addict, but she couldn't help hearing Maura's conversation and she was curious. What was she up to?

"Well, you know things haven't been so good between Barry and myself this last few weeks – that's why I wanted to talk to you. Yes. Yes – I still have the lovely Kaffe Fassett sleeveless polo-neck you knitted. Wear it all the time. Yes it probably is a collector's item now. I think we need to talk, Mrs Owens. What's that? Barry's moved back into his old room! Well, isn't that nice! I suppose he has all his treasured possessions there around him. And his pet dog as well. You know, Mrs Owens – I'd love to see the room and the dog – bring back memories of happier times. See you this evening then."

"What are you up to?" Lit asked her.

"What do you think? I'm going to make that bastard Barry Owens sorry he ever laid eyes on me. And as for his stupid, interfering mother who thinks she's 'with it' in her designer track suits and trainers – I'll sort her out as well. If it wasn't for her, he wouldn't be such a bastard."

Since becoming the mother of a son, Lit always felt obliged to leap to the defence of men's mothers. It horrified her to think that out there somewhere in the city was a young girl she didn't yet know, who was genetically programmed to meet her at some point in the future and socially conditioned to regard her, the mother of the boyfriend, as the bitch from hell. And there wasn't a damn thing she could do about it. Perhaps that was why mother-in-laws could be such bitches. They were simply playing the role that the sons' girlfriends allotted them.

"You can't blame his mother. He's a bastard in his own right."

Maura narrowed her eyes again and her mouth twisted up into a nasty grimace.

"I'm taking a long lunch-break. I have to go to the hardware store. And don't ask. Some things you're better off not knowing." She intoned the last bit with morbid finality.

Lit thought about pursuing the matter for a moment and then she realised that she didn't have the energy. She had enough of her own problems to deal with. If Maura was going to slaughter the entire Owens family with an axe and a pitchfork, that was her business. Lit really didn't have the time to worry about it. The discovery that Richie was dabbling in soft drugs was an added concern she didn't need right now. How should she tackle it? It would be foolish to overreact, but she was his mother. It was her responsibility to show him the dangers, warn him off.

"By the way – I almost forgot," said Maura. "Matt's on the golf course with Seán Tallon. Talking business."

"That I would like to see. Matt thinks backswing is something you do to a pint."

And then for some unaccountable reason she felt slightly annoyed. Seán Tallon had waltzed into their lives a few weeks ago and now he was dating Bonnie and playing golf with Matt. Not that she wanted to either date him or play golf with him but, still, in spite of their obvious mutual dislike for each other, she felt oddly excluded.

The news reporter called and she arranged for Conrad to be interviewed at three o'clock, in and around the site. If there wasn't a surprise international crisis, the piece would go out in the features section after the evening news. She set up the board-room and readied herself. It promised to be an interesting day.

Matt shuffled to the tee of the ninth hole in Glencastle Golf Club. His heart wasn't in it. All this walking through damp grass made him uneasy, and as for swinging a club – well, the human body was never meant to be twisted around like that. He eyed Seán Tallon with a mixture of friendly contempt and half-hearted anticipation. Golf was one of the things people in business did these days. If you didn't play golf, you were regarded as some sort of psychological misfit, incapable of reaching the real heights of human endeavour and communication i.e. how to negotiate a subtle game of eye contact, body language, minimalist-style dialogue and a treacherous dress code with the purpose of clinching tricky deals, forming delicately balanced partnerships, wooing new clients, dismissing unsatisfactory ones.

As Seán effortlessly sent a ball flying off into the far distance and on target, Matt wondered what he was doing there. Everybody knew that he was allergic to participating in any form of sporting activity. As far as he was concerned, there was something almost alien about sporty people. It was as if they couldn't get their heads around language and normal social interaction and had opted instead for a life of endlessly pursuing the same ball around the same pitch, course or court. Their communication was with the ball. Their relationship was with the ball. They talked endlessly about the ball and where it lay and how they could get the better of it. They spent thousands of euros on equipment to help them get the better of the ball and at the end of the day when the ball had been dispatched, they talked the night away planning how they would out-manouevre the ball and vanquish it altogether on future occasions.

"Nice shot, Tallon." He knew that an important element of good sportsmanship was to admire the skill of the opponent.

"Not bad. My swing is improving. Your shot."

It was Matt's ninth tee shot and each time he felt as though he was stepping up onto a little stage in a field. He bent and placed the tee in the ground close to the spot where Tallon's tee had been until it shot backward when he hit the ball. As he put the bright orange ball in position, he ruefully reflected on the absurdity of what he was doing – the sheer silliness of taking a long thin stick and whacking a ball towards a hole that was miles away. The world and its mother played golf. Even Lit occasionally swung a club. Ireland was turning into one big golf course and he, Matt, was an outsider, alienated by his outlook, doomed forever to view the world of sport as an alien planet, with an alien tongue and alien rules.

"This is absurd," he couldn't help muttering as he straightened up to take his shot.

Tallon was in relaxed mood and smiled tolerantly. "Now remember what I told you about the grip. Place the thumb of your left hand . . ."

Matt didn't listen to the rest. "Right – watch out anyone in New York!" he cried with a feeble attempt at humour. He raised the club behind him, swinging it back awkwardly like a man attacking a tree with an axe. The ball launched into the air and travelled off left into the rough.

"You just need to work on your back-swing a little," said Seán mildly.

"It's not my fault the fairway's crooked," Matt replied in his own defence.

"How's work?" asked Seán.

"Fine. Now we have this Budd contract in the bag. We've hit the big-time, Tallon. I wouldn't be surprised if some big multinational comes to buy us out pretty soon. Of course, I wouldn't say yes straight away. But hey, if they said ten million, I don't think I'd have to think about it for long. Why do you ask?"

"Oh, you know me. Belt and braces."

They continued walking through the damp grass in silence. Their shoes made a light swishing sound and their carts trundled behind them like very quiet, very obedient dogs.

"The Cornwells?" said Tallon tentatively after a long silence.

"Sound as a pound. I know they're unconventional, eccentric even. But they trade worldwide. They have fended off several takeover bids."

"There's something unsettling about them all the same."

Matt was in the rough now and swiping angrily at the bright orange thing. "Don't see what you're worried about. They have over a million customers who claim to derive clear health benefits from saturating their backsides in carrageen moss or who stave off the menopause by ingesting the boiled stings of bees from the shores of

Lough Ree. Who gives a fuck? They're a good contract."

The ball rolled jerkily forward about thirty feet.

"Have you seen any money?"

Matt sighed and turned to his friend. "We operate on a trust basis. We have to. With a big company like that you have to take them on trust."

"What if they don't pay up?"

"Of course they'll pay up. Besides, I'm not a cretin. I have checked out their credit rating. They're OK."

"But how do you know?" Tallon was on the green, effortlessly putting towards the hole. The ball stopped short by an inch. "Are you going to give me that?"

Matt was aggrieved. He had started the game sluggish and half-asleep, dragging his feet after his friend. Now he was wide awake and angry. "No, I'm not going to give you that!"

"But I let you take a second shot off the fifth tee!"

"That's different. I'm golfically challenged. Besides, you should have been able to sink that putt."

Now they stood, glaring each other down, hands on hips, legs akimbo, like they had stood twenty years ago in childish games of cowboys and Indians, earthlings and aliens. Both their faces were clouded with anger, each trying to suppress it.

Matt broke first.

"I'm not a fool. Sometimes you treat me like a fool even now, after all these years. You were the athletic one. I was the podgy one. You were the mathematical genius. I was only good at art and English. I'm pretty good at what I do and I never question your business."

"Sorry," said Seán almost immediately and poked his friend in the shoulder with his fist, a man's gesture full of affection and contrition. A woman could say it all with a torrent of words and facial expressions and extravagant hugs and kisses, but a man was condemned to the stock gestures of back-slapping and shoulder-punching and head-shaking.

Seán turned to the fairway to play his ball, then looked back at Matt with a rueful half-smile. "I don't think you're stupid. You're rich and successful. You have a far better social life than I do and a gift for making and keeping friends. Now don't jump down my throat when I say the next thing. OK?" His hand was raised in a placatory gesture.

Matt frowned. He knew his friend was building up to something. Now that he thought of it, this must be agony for Tallon – playing golf with probably the worst sportsman in the world. There would have to be a very good reason for him to take Matt on a golf course.

He was finally on the green. He reached into his bag and withdrew the putter. "Well, go ahead! Say whatever it is."

"Wait – study the line between the ball and the hole. And there's a slope so curve the ball slightly away from the hole."

Seán held the flag for his partner.

Matt made a show of studying the line. He crouched on his hunkers like he had seen them do on TV. He closed one eye and opened it almost immediately because he felt stupid – like John Wayne looking down the barrel of a shotgun. Finally he putted without having the faintest idea what he was doing and the ball rolled to within an inch of the hole.

"I've heard talk about the Cornwells."

"Will you give me that shot? What kind of talk?"

"Why should I give it to you? Oh, you know – rumours mostly. Nothing specific. But I tend to take rumours seriously, especially if they're coming from disinterested parties."

The two men stood facing each other at the ninth hole.

"Can't you be more specific?" Matt was uneasy. His accounting, banking friend had an uncanny knack of nosing out bad customers. It was said in some circles that Seán Tallon could assess your financial situation simply by looking at you. If he spoke to a person for longer than ten minutes he could make an accurate guess at their assets, their liabilities and above all their future progress. It was Seán who had picked up the first hint that Brian Pinto the selfmade Irish software giant was about to fold. So something about the Cornwells must have unsettled him.

"Not really."

"The Cornwells are very strange people and the establishment likes nothing better than to spread nasty rumours about strange people. Maybe that's all it is."

"Maybe," replied Seán doubtfully.


When Conrad arrived at the office of Shiels Doran for what he insisted on calling make-up lessons, Lit forced thoughts of his text declaration of love out of her mind.

"You never answered my text," he said, pretty soon after he arrived.

"I've been up to my eyes. Sorry." She was trying to sound cool and not bothered, while the mere sight of his tanned physique barely contained in a short-sleeved navy polo and taupe cotton drills was putting the region below her belly-button onto standby red-alert mode.

But she resisted, spending two hours in the board-room, coaching Conrad on his body language, his choice of words, his tone of voice. She told him to listen actively, not to call the reporter by his first name, to dress smartly as befitted his position, to hold something like a map in his hand, to keep his answers short and clear. She explained how to sidestep an awkward question, how to say 'I'm glad you asked me that' and sound as though he meant it, how to answer a question that he wanted to be asked but wasn't: "The important thing to remember is . . . let me just say . . . let me put your question in context . . . "

Together they ran through the points he needed to get across – his own private investment, creating wealth and employment, long-term benefits to the community. They tried to anticipate what questions might be asked, what angle the interviewer might take.

They sat on either side of the large boardroom table. Lit had engineered it that way so that there would be no distractions. Conrad was quick on the uptake as she would have expected, though he had difficulty accepting that some of his views might be considered arrogant.

Then she tried him with the sort of questions the reporter might ask, first some easy ones and then a stinker.

"Mr Budd. A document has come into my possession which seems to suggest some sort of financial transaction between yourself and Brendan Browne TD. Would you care to comment?"

"It's my word against his. No further comment."

"No. That sounds arrogant and it's too late for no comment. You'll have to say something like . . . your lawyers are looking into it though you yourself have no recollection of any unethical financial dealings with Browne."

He nodded at her dubiously.

"Next question. Mr Budd – did you in fact bribe Mr Browne so that he would not block planning permission for the Stoneyfield site?"

"That's a libellous statement."

"No. Never attack a reporter. It only gets his back up. You have to listen carefully, be sincere, respectful and anxious to help."

"Respectful? To grubby little hacks?"

"They're not all grubby little hacks as you call them. And like them or not, they're what keep the people who run this country on their toes."

"Spare me the sermon, Lit. They destroy. I create. That's the basic difference. They can write volumes about integrity, from their little moral high grounds. But what do they really know about integrity? And by the way it's a much over-valued commodity. Do they really think the world advances on the backs of people who are always upright, honest and pure? The world progresses because of people like me – arrogant, vain, ambitious, self-seeking, greedy bastards!"

Lit bit her lip. It was not a time for arguing about the big moral questions.

"Study the history books – if you don't believe me," he added.

"I'm not going to argue or talk morals or philosophy with you. It's not what I'm here for. Just show them respect. It's basic courtesy – and it looks good."

He bent forward and planted a light kiss on her lips. "I meant what I said in the text, you know."

Her heart thudded, but she glanced at her watch and realised they were running late.

"Can we talk about it later? I mean, really talk."

"Of course."

Maura had arrived back from her mysterious trip to the hardware store and they all set off for Stoneyfield in Conrad's Mercedes. As the driver turned the final corner before the site entrance, Miss Dillon seemed to appear out of nowhere, clad as usual in her warm Kangol beret and heavy wool cardigan. She stood out in front of the car so that the driver had to stop. Then she sidled genteely up to Conrad's window and tapped lightly on it.

The window slid down and Conrad smiled pleasantly at her.

"Miss Dillon! Good day to you. Do you have a death wish?"

"Don't go down there, Mr Budd," she said ominously.

"And why not?"

"They're baying for blood. They're real angry. Gearóid Magill has them all wound up. I'm telling you – don't go."

"Beware the Ides of March – eh, Miss Dillon? Don't you fret about me. Take care of yourself now."

They drove on past the blue and gold hoarding with Budd Construction emblazoned all over it. In a few places someone had painted out the 'Con' and daubed in 'De' so that it read Budd Destruction. As they neared the site entrance, they could see a large crowd, chanting with fists in the air. The crowd was much larger today – about a hundred or so and all eyes were on a tall, well-built man who was addressing them from a hastily erected platform.

"So this is the great Gearóid Magill – champion of the oppressed, friend to the working man," Conrad said contemptuously.

Lit said nothing. Least said, soonest mended.

The car moved slowly through the crowd as guards and the residents' own stewards tried to keep them in order. All the same it was quite intimidating and occasionally Conrad's driver had to halt the car altogether as the crowd bore down on them. When Lit looked out at their faces they were scowling and shouting abuse and some of them threw eggs or spat at the car.

When Matt had pitched for the Budd contract and given her the running of it, she never imagined this kind of trouble. Up to now the most frightening thing that had happened to her in the line of work was when a fight broke out at a sporting awards ceremony between two members of rival hurling teams. She tried to look as if this sort of thing happened all the time and didn't bother her, but she suspected she was failing miserably. In spite of herself, her brow kept furrowing and her fists kept clenching. Though the car was comfortably air-conditioned, she could feel patches of cold sweat breaking out all over her body and a nasty tingling sensation at the back of her neck. Someone came right up to her window, gave her the two fingers sign and shouted "Slapper!" at her.

Maura was made of sterner, though far from diplomatic stuff. She was on the point of rolling down her window and telling them they were all a bunch of whinging wasters when Lit stopped her. Then in the crowd, Maura recognised someone.

"Jesus! Would you look at him? Gorgeouser than ever. What's he doing here?"

"Who?" Lit hoped that Maura wasn't referring to Gearóid. It was as well to keep the lines of battle firmly drawn. It wouldn't do for Maura to be fraternising with the enemy.

"Pat Sullivan!" And before Lit could stop her, Maura had rolled down the window and yelled over at Pat. "Hey – Patsy Sullivan! Aren't you going to say hello?"

"Maura, I don't think this is the time," Lit said hastily but it was too late. Pat Sullivan smiled and gave Maura a big wave and bounded over to Conrad's Mercedes.

"Maura – working with the enemy!" he said without a trace of hostility.

"Never mind that. Can you use your charm and get some of your friends to back off here."

Pat looked balefully about him at the angry seething swarm of people and then back at Maura. "Like how?"

"I don't know. You'll think of something," she said.

She beamed encouragingly at him.

She turned back to Conrad and Lit who rewarded her with glum expressions and a stony silence. Pat shook his head in disbelief and rambled off, scratching his head. Then he began to move through the crowd, picking out individuals here and there and whispering quietly in their ears.

"I wonder what he's telling them," Maura said, tracking his movements closely.

"This is hopeless," said Conrad. "How will he possibly get through to that lot?"

But gradually the chanting of the crowd died down and instead of brandishing their fists and throwing little missiles, they stared with subdued hostility at the car and its occupants. They edged slowly to either side so that it was now possible for the car to proceed through the entrance.

"See I told you he'd do it. Wonder what he told them?" said Maura.

She mouthed a discreet 'thank you' at him and was rewarded with an even more discreet wink.

Past the huge iron gates, a posse of security men who looked as though they'd seen action in the Marines appeared and forced the gates shut.

In the large Portakabin site office, Lit heaved a sigh of relief. She was only the PR consultant after all. Conrad was a corporation with lawyers and accountants and bankers and engineers and architects and surveyors to support and advise him and guide him through the fracas with the residents. At this moment, he was deep in conversation with his solicitor, Fergus Cunningham, and Jack Kennedy. They were the main men. Her role in events was merely cosmetic. Once the interview was over, and the sponsorship deal with the IRFU was up and running, and the razzmatazz of the official opening day was over, the toughest part of her job would be done.

She walked up to the reporter who was doing a microphone test, introduced herself and smiled her most charming smile.

"Mr Budd will be ready in a few moments. He's looking forward to the opportunity of putting the record straight."

## CHAPTER 26

Conrad was charming, respectful, listened carefully and answered the reporters' barrage of questions simply and without the slightest hint of arrogance. He walked about the site with boyish enthusiasm, his hair ruffling slightly in the warm breeze, map in hand. He spoke about his vision of the future and related with obvious humility his significant contributions to various projects in the area. He understood the concerns of the residents and, even at this eleventh hour, he was prepared to do everything in his power to address those concerns. He was one with them – offering them work, giving them the certainty of individual and communal wealth – and they wouldn't have to put up one penny. The risk was all his.

"Surely this man must be the son of God!" quipped one of the cameramen sardonically.

Shots were taken of the massive Lampson crane, the teams of strong contented working men clambering busily over the site, the engineers and the architects studying maps and plans, the scaled model of the completed development. If he was putting the feature together, Conrad could hardly have done a better job himself.

Back in the Portakabin, the reporters had a few final questions.

"Mr Budd – these allegations – these receipts for money – have you any comment?" It was the same reporter who'd questioned him on the day he'd wanted to show Lit around the site.

Conrad considered the question carefully and looked the reporter candidly in the eye.

"These are serious allegations and my lawyers are looking into them."

"Do you deny that you bribed or indeed blackmailed Brendan Browne into letting the planning permission through?"

"I have no recollection of any irregular financial dealings with Mr Browne."

"Did you in fact bribe Mr Browne?"

"I have answered your questions truthfully and have no further comment. Thank you."

He gave an earnest and sincere nod to the reporter and turned away with what seemed like great reluctance.

And that was how it all appeared that evening on the news features programme. In the TV room in Harwood Park, Lit and Matt watched the screen in amazement as Conrad metamorphosed into a caring visionary man of the people, a man who wanted to share his success with the people of Stoneyfield. Every shot and every clip and every word that Lit could have wished for was included in the feature.

"Jesus, what did you do to him? He's perfect."

"I know!" Lit said, bursting with pride. Conrad, her client, her lover, her student, had blossomed into perfection in front of her very eyes.

But she should have known that it was all too good to be true.

Almost immediately Brendan Browne's bloated pasty face loomed up on the screen and he spoke of the pain of his broken marriage, the agony of accepting a bribe just to keep a roof over his head, the despair of acting against his conscience and allowing the development to go ahead.

"Why are you going public on this now, Mr Browne? Surely this is political suicide."

"Conscience, Jim. It's time for me to atone. It's not too late for the people of Stoneyfield and it's not too late for me. There is more joy in heaven over one sinner repenting than – "

"But these are still only allegations. The documents in question prove nothing. It's your word against his."

"The truth will out, Jim," Brendan wheezed breathlessly. "Conrad Budd knows the truth. I know the truth."

"But is there any other proof?"

Browne smiled mysteriously. "The truth will out."

The journalist thanked him and rounded up his report.

"And in a surprise announcement, the government is to set up an immediate enquiry into these latest allegations of corruption – it is likely that both Mr Budd and Mr Browne will be called to give evidence – "

Lit pressed the mute button and an eerie silence

descended on the room.

"What next?" asked Matt.

"We have to run with it, whatever happens next." She shrugged. "Anyway, there's nothing to it. He told me so himself. He did help Browne out a bit financially – but that's all. It's not a crime to help someone who's a bit strapped for cash."

"I sure hope the enquiry sees it that way."

Matt stayed for dinner.

Richie spent much of the meal scowling at his mother and doing things just to annoy her like putting his elbows on the table and chewing with his mouth open and belching loudly.

Lit glared at him across the table.

"What?" he exclaimed with false innocence. "It's an ancient Arab custom – shows appreciation for the food."

She could feel an uncontrollable rage bubbling up inside her and she had a violent urge to slap him roundly in the face. "If you want to be grounded for another week, keep that up!"

"What's this about being grounded?" Matt asked innocently.

"I had a couple of spliffs with Barney Ryan and his brother in the park. Big deal!"

"Spliff?" enquired Dandy.

"You don't need to know, Grandad."

"Ah!" said Dandy. "It's serious big trouble then."

Richie nodded despondently and poked half-heartedly at the food on his plate.

"Take it on the chin, lad. Your mother knows best."

Lit almost fell off the chair. She stopped chewing and looked her father in the eyes. But she could read nothing. Inscrutable grey eyes held hers for a second and then lowered to his food.

"What's this green stuff?"

"Broccoli."

"Never heard of it."

"I'm always telling you! And you've had it every week for years!"

"It's horrible. Don't give it to me again."

And so the evening passed. The man she had worked so diligently with all afternoon, the man who said he loved her, didn't call. Perhaps she should call him – but on what pretext? But she didn't need a pretext. After all, they were in love. She had every right to call him. But suppose he was with Angela, telling her the news, trying to finish the engagement with her? Then the last thing he would need was a call from Lit. So though she desperately wanted to call him, to talk about the report, to talk about the enquiry, to discuss the opening of the site, to tell him the IRFU were delighted to take up his offer of sponsorship of promising new players, to find out once and for all about Angela, she couldn't – because that wouldn't be playing the love game.

Now she remembered the tedious pretence and the whole falseness of 'falling in love'. She had to pretend not to be interested. She had to 'treat him mean and keep him keen'. If she treated Richie or Bonnie or any of her other friends like that, they'd be gone in a flash. In spite of sexual liberation and equality, one fact would remain utterly unchanged until the end of time – women still had to play hard to get.

So she called Bonnie instead.

"Fancy a drink?" she asked in a jaded monotone.

That was another good thing about friends. You could be as dull as you liked. You didn't have to sparkle at all. You could be a couch potato, a bag of shit, a zombie and it wouldn't make any difference to the friendship because your friends could be like that too.

"Lit Doran wants to go out for a drink in the middle of the week? You must have had a tough day."

"Did you see Conrad on the news?"

"Yeah. Seems like he's in a spot of bother."

"Of course, he's done nothing wrong," Lit was quick to point out.

"What? The whole world knows Conrad Budd is a crook. You may be sure this is only the tip of the iceberg. Nice guys finish last remember? You know that surely? Lit, tell me you knew!"

"Bonnie – that's a terrible thing to say! Where did you ever hear such a thing?"

"I just know," said Bonnie. "See you in the Cartagena Club."

Lit issued strict instructions to Richie about what he could and couldn't do for the evening. There was to be a total ban on friends in the house for a week and he was not to go out anywhere in the evenings until the problem of his drug incident was addressed. He scowled and glowered and sulked and informed her that she was being totally unreasonable.

"It's lucky I caught you. You've probably been at this all summer. Next, I suppose, you'll be snorting cocaine or worse."

"Mum – I smoked a third of one joint!"

"You think I'm a fool? I know where this type of thing ends. I've seen it happen."

She was in full flight and Richie knew there was little point in reasoning with her.

"When you were small and I worked in Devlin Satchwell, one of the most talented guys in the company was Karl Gibson."

Richie rolled his eyes to heaven. He'd heard the cautionary tale of Karl Gibson more times than he cared to remember.

"You may well roll your eyes to heaven, but Karl Gibson was top of his class, won awards, was the toast of the advertising world until he discovered cocaine which made him feel good for a while before it made him feel paranoid and delusional. He became careless and irresponsible and in the space of a couple of years no-one wanted to do business with him. He'd disappear for weeks on end, make appointments and not keep them, make up grandiose schemes which he never followed through on and then he began to get violent and aggressive. Where is he now?"

"Living in a mansion in Killiney?"

She ignored the flippancy, that indispensable building-block of teenage conversation.

"He's living rough. Handsome Karl Gibson who had the world at his feet, is living out of a plastic bag and sleeping in shop doorways. Is that how you want to end up?"

"I guess it depends on the shop. I mean a nice slot outside the Formula One shop in Milan in summer mightn't be so bad."

No-one in the world had the power to enrage her like her own son. She wanted to take him by the shoulders and give him a good shaking and shout at him to grow up and start acting his age, that she loved him more fiercely than any mother alive and that she was telling him these things for his own good!

"One day you'll understand why I'm so concerned," she said instead and went upstairs to take a shower before meeting Bonnie. She took a taxi to the Cartagena Club off Leeson Street, another one of Bonnie's favourite haunts. She sat at the bar sipping a wine spritzer, and looked about wearily at the old oak floors, the smoky cerise-coloured walls, the bordello-like furnishings. This was one of the places where you went if you were on the pull. She drummed her fingers on the counter and checked her text messages, trying desperately not to look as though she was on the pull, trying not to catch the eye of a lean and hungry-looking young fella who was leering at her as though she was his dish of the day. After a few minutes, he sidled along the bar, pint in hand, and stood right beside her. He released his pint for a few moments and spread out two slender hands before her. He had bad breath.

"Will you be my Mrs Robinson?"

Seeing him close up, Lit realised he couldn't have been more than twenty-one. Still, that was no excuse for putting her in the Mrs Robinson category. She wasn't quite ready for the 'mysterious mid-life woman of a certain age' image just yet. Of course, she would embrace that stage of her life when it came – but it wasn't for a while yet. The best ploy was to ignore him. She turned away, willing Bonnie to appear. But he persisted.

"How old are you? I've always wanted to have sex with an older woman. I'm told it's electric – and you're OK-looking for an older woman."

"I didn't know they had reduced the age limit here," she responded. "Tell you what – there's a good teenie bar down the street – all Britney Spears and West Life – you'll feel right at home. There's nobody there over eighteen."

"That's mean. You've missed your big chance now. Women go wild for me. Can't get enough of me. I'm a sexual Tyrannosaurus."

"And you do know that dinosaurs are extinct?"

Bonnie appeared just in time, for Lit was seriously

considering swatting him with her handbag.

Bonnie looked him up and down briefly. He didn't interest her.

"Go on! Hop it!," she said, grinning broadly at him. "The big girls want to talk in private."

He sidled away, and when they were alone, Bonnie flashed a smile at the barman and ordered a Cosmopolitan.

"And easy on the cranberry juice," she warned him. "Want one, Lit?"

"No, thanks. What's all this about Conrad being a crook?"

"You seem surprised that he's being accused of corruption."

"That's putting it mildly. Though I'm beginning to think he's the victim in all of this."

Bonnie threw her head back and laughed. "Conrad! A victim! Never! He's always been master of his own destiny."

"That doesn't mean he's a crook."

The barman returned with the Cosmopolitan. Bonnie took a sip and smiled at him approvingly. "Mmmm! This is good. You sure you don't want one, Lit?"

"No. I don't."

"Conrad's just a hard-ball player. Likes to get his own way."

"And . . ."

"And he's not all that patient with bureaucracy. So he likes to speed things up - with sponsorship and gifts and donations to various causes. It's a grey area. Like that time he made a massive donation to the Stoneyfield Addiction Treatment Centre."

"Well, what's wrong with that?"

"Exactly! Nothing! The Addiction Centre could afford

to move to wonderful new premises in the suburbs and Conrad acquired another ten acres for the development site. I only know this because Joe that teaches with me helps out in the Treatment Centre."

Lit nursed her drink thoughtfully. "So do you think I'm wrong to get involved with him?"

Bonnie shrugged. "It's none of my business. Conrad has told you he loves you and I asked you if you love him and you spouted a whole lot of drivel about the perfect man, and gushed about the dream lover."

"Are you jealous?"

Bonnie was horrified. "Of what?"

"You've always had a thing about him."

"All's fair in love and war! If Conrad has the hots for you – well, that's the type of guy he is."

"What's that supposed to mean? 'That's the type of guy he is'? I think you are jealous."

Bonnie shrugged and polished off her drink and the pair of them sat in uneasy silence for a few minutes.

Then Bonnie said, "Conrad is – well – you have to understand him. Like I said earlier, he's the sort of guy who gets what he wants."

"And he wants me."

Bonnie nodded in half-hearted agreement. "True. But he might want something else next week. And it's a bit sudden, isn't it?"

"So? You're the one who always says 'follow your heart'. You're the one who's always on about love at first sight and all that sort of crap. Now you're telling me to be sensible and I think it's because you're jealous! After all these years, I was the one to get to Conrad first. What's the matter? Did Obi Wan Kenobi let you down?"

Bonnie closed her eyes for a few moments, blissfully

recapturing the hours of pleasure she had spent with Seán Tallon.

"Category 4," she purred in remembrance of things past.

"What?" Lit practically screeched. She was aghast at the very idea that Bonnie would put Tallon in the same list as Conrad, let alone the same category. There had only ever been one man in Category 4 and that was Conrad.

"I said: Category 4!"

"So when are you seeing him again?" Lit asked pointedly.

"I'm not."

"Why?"

"He's not interested in getting involved."

"But you slept with him, stayed over in his place, had steamy sex with him!"

"So! We were both as horny as hell. Why not?"

Lit thought she detected a note of bravado in her friend's answer and then she felt sorry for being so mean. "Good for you!" She grinned encouragingly at Bonnie. "Life's too short for the agony of romance."

"Right!" said Bonnie with grim determination. "Romance – I hate it. You feel all gooey and you start liking awful music."

Lit continued in encouraging tones. "Was he really Category 4?"

Bonnie sighed involuntarily, then grinned to herself. "You have no idea – and so considerate – some woman trained him in real good – "

Lit could feel her jaw dropping in spite of herself so she changed the subject. "What did you talk about in the restaurant?"

"Stuff. His time abroad. The woman he used to live

with. Family. He asked quite a bit about you?"

"What does he want to know about me for?"

"I think he felt really bad about his blunder at the party. And we met at your party – so I suppose you're a mutual connection."

"Oh really!" said Lit scornfully. But then plain old curiosity got the better of her. "What else did he say?"

"He said he knows you don't like him very much."

"Top marks for perception."

"And that he's not that keen on you either."

"Huh! As if I care."

"Yes. Now let me remember what he said – he said that you were cold, superior, sarcastic, that you always deliberately took him up the wrong way and that you had a cruel streak. He called you 'The Frosty'."

It's a painful thing to see ourselves as others see us. Listening to the litany of faults Seán Tallon had attributed to her, and which Bonnie had so gleefully related, Lit couldn't deny one single word. She was guilty as charged. Of course it didn't matter a bit what he thought of her.

"He did say one good thing about you."

"What's that?" she said, trying to sound totally disinterested. Because she was. Totally disinterested.

"He said that you are a very capable businesswoman and that Matt is lucky to have you as his partner."

She racked her brains to muster up the nastiest, most sarcastic, most scathing response imaginable, but nothing came to mind and she was relieved when the little green light on her mobile flickered to tell her that someone was calling her. In a split second her mind shot from the ludicrous insults of Tallon to Conrad. It must be him calling her. Perhaps he wanted to call over and talk about Angela. Who else could it be at eleven o'clock at night? She sucked in her breath, let it ring four times and then answered.

"Hello?" she said, trying not to sound breathless and excited.

"Oh thank God, Mum!"

"Richie – what are you up to? I thought I told you to – "

"It's Dandy. There's something wrong with him. I think I should call an ambulance."

# CHAPTER 27

When Lit and Bonnie arrived at the hospital they were told that Dandy was undergoing tests and that Lit wouldn't be able to see him just yet.

They found Richie sitting on a red plastic chair next to a big plant, miserably staring at the floor. Haltingly, making no eye contact, he told them what had happened. He'd been sitting with his grandfather, watching Russell Crowe in *Gladiator*. Dandy had a glass of wine and was thoroughly immersed in the story. Then suddenly he'd groaned softly, doubled over and clutched his stomach. Richie insisted that he was going to phone a doctor and Dandy said he didn't want any doctors in the house. But then the pain seemed to get hold of him again and at that point Richie called, first his mother, then an ambulance. He was now clearly in a state of shock and deep distress, hardly even noticing that Bonnie was sitting beside him, holding his hand tightly in hers.

"I'm going to see if I can talk to a doctor," Lit said.

She wandered up and down the corridor, trying to

attract someone's attention. Nurses dashed about, pushing trolleys, administering to patients. Doctors moved hurriedly through the wards.

"Excuse me . . . please could you tell me . . . could someone tell me . . ."

Each one referred her to someone else. At last she got hold of the doctor who was looking after Dandy. He took her aside into a little office.

"Doctor Barnes," he introduced himself.

"I don't understand," she said. "He hasn't been in any discomfort. In fact, he's been so well it was hard to believe there was anything wrong with him. Doctor O'Connor told me that it would probably be months yet. Then all of a sudden – this happens."

Doctor Barnes nodded. "Your father is lucky."

"Lucky?"

"He will be spared the worst of the pain. He's very old. His body will give up before the cancer does its worst."

She felt a horrible clammy shiver run through her.

"I wouldn't go too far from the hospital if I was you," he said sympathetically. "It could be a matter of just hours." Then he gently excused himself.

She walked back to Richie, bracing herself to tell him the news. He didn't even acknowledge her arrival and she was suddenly convinced he already knew. His head was bent and he was scowling at some spot on the polished lino floor. He picked at a thread in his black jeans, doggedly refusing to look up at her.

"I'll go and get us some coffees," Bonnie said and left Lit alone with Richie.

"Richie," she said.

No response.

"Please. Don't be like that with me. Don't shut me out.

354

We need to talk now . . . there are things I have to tell you, that maybe I should have told you before. And I'm sorry I didn't."

She tried to put her arm about him, but he pushed her away.

A pout of the lips brought the "psssh" sound almost involuntarily and he shook his head.

She forced herself to continue. "Dandy is . . . that is . . . he's very ill . . . the doctor told him last time when he went for his check-up . . . and now . . ."

Lit could feel the tears coming. She'd read all the coping-with-adolescence books and knew about keeping the channels open. But that wasn't so easy now. What she wanted to do was to throw her arms around her son, hold him and tell him everything would be all right. But that was not what Richie wanted her to do – or was it? If she held him, he might thrust her away but, if she didn't make the effort to comfort him, he might become more resentful.

She tried again. She put her hand on his shoulder once more and squeezed gently. He twitched away like a horse twitching a fly from his shoulder.

"I should have told you."

Grunt.

"But I was trying to spare you."

Sigh.

"Richie, I love you more than anything and – "

"Pssshhaw!"

"Please talk to me. Look at me even."

Shrug.

"Richie, we need to talk about this."

Richie had now turned his undivided attention to the large plant.

"I was wrong," she said. "I didn't want to hurt you.

And Dandy didn't want you worrying. He wanted your last times with him to be happy ones. He made me promise not to tell you. I was going to tell you, but I didn't think there'd be any harm in waiting a few weeks. And now . . ." She stopped, hoping he might say something. "It's not so bloody easy for me, you know. He's my father. I know he's a father figure to you, but I've known him longer. So please try to imagine what I'm feeling. Just put yourself in my shoes if you can."

He slapped his knees with the palms of his hands and leapt to his feet. "Well, that's just typical of you, isn't it? You figure you can arrange all our lives into some harmoniously, whitewashed public relations spin! What did you have in mind? Richie, I have something to tell you –" His voice cracked with emotion. "Dandy has been dying for six months. The doctors think that he might die today so it's time you knew. I didn't want you getting upset about it before now because really I haven't had time to sit down and deal with your emotions. Now be a good little boy and grieve for a few days. I'm good for a chat until the weekend. Oh and by the way, here's something really important you should know – Karl Gibson the cocaine addict is sleeping rough!"

He stormed off down the corridor, before she could reply.

"But it's not like that at all," she said to his back as he went.

She turned to see Bonnie standing there with the coffee.

"Should I go after him?" asked Bonnie.

"I don't think it would do any good," said Lit. "He's too angry."

They sat down silently and began to sip the bitter hospital brew.

"God, you look a fright," said Bonnie.

"Thanks."

"What did the doctor say?"

"Not to go far from the hospital."

"Oh Lit – I'm so sorry!" said Bonnie and tears began to spill down her face.

The darkness of the night passed and grizzly morning light drenched the grey corridor. Lit and Bonnie slumped semiconscious in the uncomfortable red plastic chairs. She'd made all the phone calls – to Azelia in Argentina who had gone into hysterics on the phone and wailed for ages about how desperately she would miss her father, how empty life would be without him. How it was all right for Lit she'd had so much time with him but how it was so much harder to be living far away on another continent. Lit bit her tongue and tried to sound sympathetic. This was not a time for family conflicts. Azelia intended to come home at once. She only hoped she'd make it in time. Auntie Sheila began to cry, genuinely distressed, so distressed she forgot to even offer Lit any advice or tell any horror stories. She would be there as soon as possible.

At last a nurse came and said Lit could see Dandy now.

"How is he?" Lit asked.

"He's conscious – but still heavily sedated."

She sat by her father's bed and looked down at him, his grey head resting on the pillow, his jaw slightly open. He had been washed and shaved and his white fluffy hair was trimmed and combed neatly into place. She marvelled at the mysterious powers of nurses. He looked calm and peaceful, like he was just having a snooze.

Dandy stirred on the pillow. He returned to consciousness slowly and looked about him until his eyes came to rest on Lit.

"Can I not get a decent night's sleep now without you spying on me?" he grumbled weakly. His eyes strayed around the room. "How did I end up here?"

"You took a little turn. But you're fine now." She patted his hand lightly.

"Where's my breakfast?"

"I'll get some for you now."

"Just tea and toast. I'm not that hungry."

"OK"

"Right. Well, as soon as I've had breakfast, I'll get my things and we'll be off. I thought I might get home in time to watch the match this afternoon."

Lit didn't know what to say or think. Doctor Barnes had said that she shouldn't leave the hospital, that Dandy might be gone in a matter of hours. And here he was wanting breakfast and looking forward to going home.

"Why don't you watch the match here? They did tests. You're supposed to rest after tests. It's nice and comfortable here."

"Tests? What are they trying to find out now? Why can't they just let a man meet his death in peace instead of poking and prodding at him? There must be something in the doctor's manual about tests – 'First find your patient and do some tests'. Something like that. I don't want to watch the match here. I can't see the trees. And there's only one blanket on the bed. What sort of service is that? I hope this isn't a private room. One blanket on the bed – "

He grumbled and rambled to himself for a while and then, forgetting entirely about the breakfast, drifted off into sleep. Lit sat watching over him. Odd disconnected thoughts raced through her head. She found herself thinking about silly things – like how the patio tubs needed watering, how there was none of her favourite brand of coffee in the pantry. She wondered if Barney Ryan had got into trouble with his mother. A picture of Matt and Tallon playing golf kept springing into her mind. She wondered if Harry Menton was now completely bald. She tried to think about Conrad, but somehow her mind wouldn't focus on him. Instead she kept thinking about Barry Owens whom she didn't even like and how he had done the dirt on Maura. Had Maura gone to his mother's house and exacted some horrible revenge? Perhaps she should call and find out. She nodded off in the chair for a while and dreamed about being a little girl on the beach with her sister and Dandy. They were all happy and playing in the sand. Then the dream became a nightmare and Conrad was building a skyscraper which was going to block out all the light from the city. In the dream he smiled charmingly at her, took her hand and led her to the top of the building. She screamed and said that she didn't want to go, but he just smiled and told her she had no choice. Then the dream changed and Seán Tallon was telling her that she was a nasty, cold woman with no heart. She began screaming at him and beating him in the chest and he held her by the wrists to stop her.

She woke suddenly when the door opened. It was Richie. He tiptoed in and sat beside her. For a while they just sat in silence, looking down at Dandy, who was in a deep slumber.

"Sorry, Ma. I've been a bit of a dickhead," Richie whispered.

"Me too, Richie. I wasn't thinking straight."

He shrugged – a gesture of forgiveness and reconciliation.

She took his hand in hers, rubbing absentmindedly at the face of his Swatch watch.

"What's the news?" he asked softly.

"I don't know, love. He was talking to me earlier. But the doctor said it could be – it could be – a matter of hours." Tears channelled down her cheeks.

Richie wrapped his big lumbering arms around her, and hugged her tight. "That's it. Have a good cry, Ma," he said, patting the back of her head softly.

"I should have told you – in spite of what Dandy said. And it was horrible for you to find out the way you did. I've not been a good mother lately – getting bogged down in the wrong things, I suppose." She sobbed quietly on his shoulder. "Sometimes it's not easy having the responsibility of you all on my own. I love you so much and want everything in life to be perfect for you."

"Hey, steady on! Don't go getting all soppy with me. It's not cool. What would the guys say? There you are, see – you're smiling again."

She went to the sink and splashed some water on her face.

"And I know this is not really the time to bring it up, but I'm sorry about the spliff," he said.

"Maybe I overreacted," she said, "so let's forget about it."

Dandy was sinking fast. His conscious moments were like the last flickers of a dying fire, with occasional bursts of flame. Through it all, Lit held his hand, with Richie by her side.

"I hope you're not expecting any last-minute speeches!" Dandy snapped in one of his lucid moments.

"What do you mean?"

"I mean all those disgusting American films where the designated dying person has to say he loves a designated living person and then there's a lot of weeping and gnashing of teeth."

"Well, is there anything that you'd like to say?"

"No!"

"To ask?"

He stared into space for a moment. "What do you call that green stuff again?"

"Broccoli."

"That's it. Don't give it to me again."

"OK. If that's what you want. Would you like to see anybody?"

"Audrey Hepburn. I'd like to see her."

"She's dead."

"Then there's nobody else."

"Oh, by the way, the priest was by a while ago, he said if you wanted – if you – he's a nice guy."

"Wants to come and do the mumbo-jumbo, does he?"

Lit nodded. She wasn't in any great sense religious, but the sacraments were as good a way as any for marking the big transitions in life. The last rites were sweet and comforting and besides Auntie Sheila's atoms would probably split spontaneously and cause a minor nuclear explosion if she found out her brother hadn't been anointed.

"Tell him to wait until I'm unconscious. How's that for shuttle diplomacy?"

"Not bad." She smiled fondly at him. "And for the record, I love you – you cranky old man."

He chortled weakly. "Humph! More fool you! Find a good man and love him instead."

"I'm working on it. OK?"

361

"And Richie," he said, his voice growing weaker now. "Be nice to the chicklet babes and try not to snog them all in one go . . ."

"I won't, Dandy."

"Did I ever tell you about the time I was chased by the Black and Tans?"

"No, Grandad. Tell me."

"I was carrying a can of buttermilk to my grand-mother's house . . . I took the shortcut . . ." His voice was almost a whisper now. "Across the fields . . ."

The nurse came and felt his pulse and said, "Another little while."


# CHAPTER 28

Sometimes in the moments before old people die, they detach, like they're setting out on a journey. Men harness up horses and drive them desperately onwards through the storm, becoming little boys again on their last big adventure, riding nursery horses, or driving fast cars. They shout "It's not far now!" and "We'll soon be there!", their bodies arching and twisting with the sudden urgency of the journey.

Though Dandy didn't go on horseback or comman-deer a Ferrari, he did become a boy once more, shouting encouragement at his team-mates, weakly brandishing an imaginary hurley in the air.

"Come on, Byrne! Keep your eye on the ball – that's it – only ten minutes to go – we have them – pass it – pass it!"

Lit watched over him like a mother keeping vigil over a delirious son, helpless, confused and dreading the moment when he would finally let go. She held his hand for hours on end, noticing every squeeze and every little twitch of the fingers. Occasionally she felt for an increasingly faint pulse.

Richie sat with her. He had no experience of death before and it frightened and awed him. It was the scariest thing in the world and it was the most fascinating. He hated the idea of losing his grandfather, could not even bear to think of what life would be like without him, but he was mesmerised by the awesome inevitability of what was going on before him.

Finally Dandy pushed Lit's hand away with every last bit of strength.

"I'm finishing it now," he whispered and then struggled restlessly in the bed. "We've got the bastards – they're beat!"

He tossed and turned until Lit was afraid he might fall out of the bed and hurt himself. She realised this was a perfectly silly worry but she wanted him to go peacefully, not from a sudden collision with the floor.

After a few minutes his breathing lightened so that he was hardly breathing at all and his face calmed and softened. Then there a little catching sound in his throat and he was gone.

Lit held onto his hand for several minutes, hoping she might feel the faint pulse again. But at last Richie went out into the corridor and called for the nurse who came and checked his grandfather's pulse and closed his eyes.

Lit clung to Richie, both of them sobbing inconsolably. Home would never be the same again for either of them. Life would never be the same again.

Much later, having said their goodbyes, the nurse led Lit and Richie away. Lit barely noticed the doctor slip into her father's room and sign the death certificate. Outside in the corridor, Matt had turned up with Seán Tallon in tow. Matt hugged her and promised to do anything he could to help.

"And you're not to worry about anything at work. We'll manage."

"What about Conrad – somebody should call – there's all the stuff for the IRFU – the opening of the site – "

Matt cut in. "Stop! Put it all out of your mind. The men are here! This is what's going to happen. Richie, you and I are going to do the stuff that needs to be done here, then we're going back to the office to make the phone calls. Lit, Tallon has offered to take you home and help with the arrangements."

Though the prospect of arranging her father's funeral with Seán Tallon was not one she looked forward to, she didn't have the strength to argue. And so, though he'd probably start haggling with the undertakers, she nodded her assent.

When Lit had dealt with the inevitable hospital paperwork, she trudged meekly and apathetically down the corridor to join Tallon.

They travelled down the five floors in the lift in silence, then he held the door for her and they walked to the carpark.

"I think we should use my car," he said.

"I'm perfectly capable of driving!" she snapped.

"All the same – " he persisted as they walked past the rows of cars.

"All the same – it's my father that's dead and I will do what I like. Besides, think of the petrol you'll save."

He stopped suddenly and turned to her. If it wasn't for the fact that she knew Seán Tallon was incapable of anything so emotional, she could have sworn that he looked angry. But it probably wasn't allowed in the Seven Habits of Deadly Boring and Effective People.

"What? Why are you looking at me like that?" she said at last, disconcerted.

"I'm trying to help. OK?" He spoke quietly, but there was no mistaking the challenge in his voice.

His eyes held hers angrily for a split second until she turned away and threw up her arms in an exaggerated gesture of helplessness. Then she followed him sullenly to his car.

*I am to be dressed in my grey suit, with a hurley and sliotar in my hands. There are to be no rosary beads, no prayer books or any of that rubbish. I am to be brought to my daughter's house in Harwood Park and laid out there overnight, during which time my daughter is to wake me with relatives, friends and neighbours. I have put aside one thousand euros to provide food and drink for the occasion. The doors and windows are to be left open to allow my soul to pass out.*

*I consent to a funeral mass. But no jumped-up little Johnny from Maynooth (or wherever they come from these days) is going to use the occasion of my death to practice his sacred eloquence or speak words in praise of the late me. Instead, I would like my daughter to say a few words and my grandson also. The church music should be joyful – not sad – Mozart's 'Laudate Dominum' will do fine and I suppose an Ave Maria will be acceptable. 'We Are the Champions' by Queen is to be played as people are entering the church to get them in the proper mood. I also wouldn't mind Louis Armstrong singing 'Making Whoopee'.*

*I leave my house in Templeogue and my savings of twenty thousand pounds in trust to my grandson Richie. To my daughter, I have already given encouragement, love*

*and shelter. Whatever else she needs cannot be provided
in a will.*

Lit sat in Dandy's armchair by the range reading and
re-reading his will. She had never seen anything like it
and didn't know quite how to proceed without offending somebody.

"I don't know what you're getting so worked up
about," said Bonnie who had instantly taken on the role
of general do-it-all and was moving about the kitchen
sorting and tidying the clutter on the counter.

"But the aunts – the old neighbours from Galway – the
priests – why couldn't he just have asked for a normal
funeral like everyone else? And a wake in my house –
the neighbours round here aren't used to that kind of
thing. You have ancient relatives living down the country – you know how they go on at wakes – drinking and
singing for hours on end. It's fine in the country – but I
can't see it going down well here. What will people
think?"

"Who cares what anybody thinks? Even in Harwood
Park, people must die from time to time."

"My neighbour, Miss Lonergan, died a few weeks ago
in the heatwave."

"There you are."

"She was removed discreetly from the house at seven
thirty in the evening accompanied by her nieces and
nephews. The rest of the people on the road, myself
included, stayed tactfully out of the way until the hearse
had been and gone and taken her to a nice little funeral
parlour in town. The following day, we attended her
mass, extended our sympathies and went off home.
Nothing happened in her house. Nobody was invited to
her house. Nobody was expected to want to see her
body."

"That's a shame."

"You have to give him a wake. It was his dying wish," Seán Tallon chipped in, between phone calls.

And who the hell asked you, Lit wanted to say, but of course she couldn't because he had spent the past half hour on the phone, calling undertakers and caterers and priests. Instead she bit her tongue and changed the subject.

"What time do you have to go to the mortuary?" asked Bonnie.

"Five o'clock."

"Right. I'm going home to shower and change. I'll be back at four."

"Bonnie?"

"What?"

"Thanks."

"For what?"

"Stuff. Whenever anything big happens to me – you're always here."

"That's me – love a bit of drama. See ya." Bonnie smiled and breezed out, leaving Lit alone with Seán Tallon.

It was the strange interim period between death in the hospital and the removal to the home and there was nothing for Lit to do so she stayed sitting in Dandy's armchair and cried some more. The house felt cold and empty. An impeccably tasteful statement, an elegantly restrained shell. Only the kitchen offered any feeling of comfort: the big old painted dresser, his stack of dusty books in a basket by the window, the range which Bonnie had insisted on lighting in his memory, the tabby cat curled up for once in her basket, confused by the absence of the person she'd relied on for scraps. They were all part of her father's presence in the house.

She thought he might emerge from his room at any moment and start grumbling about broccoli or what she'd done with his old shirts.

Tallon stayed out of her way for a while and continued with the phone calls and arrangements. Then he made coffee for both of them, pulled up a chair and cleared his throat.

"I – eh – I remember when my father died."

She looked up at him in confusion. "How old were you?"

"Sixteen. I couldn't talk to anybody. I kept pretending it didn't matter and that I was over it."

"Sixteen. That's sad."

"I had to grow up real quick. My mother made sure of that. I went straight from sixteen to thirty in the space of a week. Anyway. I know a bit of what you're going through."

Through the tears and from behind her crumpled tissue, she studied him for a moment and felt an irritating wave of sympathy for him – no, it was worse than sympathy – it was understanding. But she would put a stop to that. He needn't think that he would wheedle his way into her good books that easily.

"We all have to go through it, I suppose," she said coolly

He smiled wryly to himself. "My mother used to say stuff like 'You're the man of the house now, Seán' and of course on one level I was as proud as anything to be the man of the house. But it was a huge burden and I missed out on all the daft stuff that people do. Matt was my only link with the wild life."

Why was he telling her all this? She wasn't interested, though it did explain why he was so sensible and straight and it was plain to see that he was trying to be nice – well, as nice as a person like him could be.

"Would you like a drink?" she asked finally.

"Scotch, please."

She poured two large Scotches.

"Sorry," he said. "I'm babbling."

"It's OK. Is your mother alive?"

He nodded and held up his glass. "To your father!"

"Yes. To him."

They sipped in silence and, for some unaccountable reason, she began to feel very uncomfortable. It was very easy to be nasty to Seán Tallon, very comfortable in fact. But now, here they were, exchanging confidences over a drink. It was spoiling the entire balance of a relationship built on mutual dislike and scorn. She tried to remember all the nasty things he had said to Bonnie about her. Cold – huh! Ice-queen – huh! Sarcastic – huh! Then a cold prickly feeling ran down the back of her neck. What if he knew that she called him R2D2, His Robotship, His Intergalacticness, Mike Rowe Chip? Maybe Bonnie had told him. Suddenly she was ashamed of herself and fought to stop her face reddening. She lowered her eyes and ran her finger thoughtfully around the rim of her glass.

He sat forward in his chair, leaning his elbows on his knees.

"Lit?" he said a bit hoarsely.

"What?"

"There's something I've been meaning to say. Only there never seems to be a right moment."

Lit felt odd, in a pleasant, cosy sort of way. Perhaps it was the Scotch? Whatever it was, she would have to put a stop to it this very second.

"Look . . ."

She waited.

"If you're wondering about medical insurance – don't worry. And I know I can offset some of the funeral expenses for tax."

She stood up abruptly, careful to avoid eye contact. "Excuse me. I need to change."

Then he stood up too and faced her down. "It was something else completely I wanted to say. But forget it."

She glared back at him, willing her withering eyebrow to curl up and incinerate him. But it wouldn't, so she quickly turned on her heel and left.

# CHAPTER 29

Lit's house and garden were packed to capacity with mourners. A bus had been hired from Dandy's home village in the west to bring friends and neighbours to his wake. Now the motley crew of old farmers in stiff suits and cloth caps, and country ladies in fine woollen costumes gathered in little groups about the house, mingling with city folk – the people from the American bank, the hotelier, the directors of sporting organisations, one or two politicians, pretty young girls from the advertising agency, Cal with streaked blond hair from Northern Lads, Dee Dee Caulfield the celebrity (most famous for having presented a game show for two months sometime in the 1980s). Azelia was even homeward bound on a late flight.

What most surprised Lit was that almost every neighbour in the road was there: Mr Redmond from next door, old Mrs O'Greaney over the road and Eamonn and Anna, a young couple who arrived complete with their three-month-old baby. They all told her what a wonderful man her father was and how much they would miss him.

Miss him? How could they miss him? This was Harwood Park where neighbours didn't socialise together. But over the afternoon, she discovered that Dandy had been invited into almost every house in the road and that sometimes while she was out working, neighbours would drop by to keep him company. Anna was especially upset because she used to visit him with her new baby. And she loved listening to his old stories.

"We all loved him," she said simply.

Out of the corner of her eye, Lit saw Auntie Sheila cutting a swathe through the crowd and heading inexorably in her direction. She quickly took herself into the garden, hid on the little seat behind the oak tree, and for a while watched a bright red sun setting low on a purplish horizon. Dandy was a great weather-watcher. A low bank of clouds meant rain. A bright yellow sky at sunset meant wind. A pale yellow sky or pale setting sun meant certain rain. "When the sun sets sadly, the morning will be angry," he used to say. But on the evening of his wake, the sun set happily. He would have been pleased with that.

She stood up, braced herself and made her way back into the fray.

Richie sat in a corner of the garden with Barney Ryan and Simon who were busy taking the opportunity to get drunk.

"Get's another Bud there, Doran," demanded Barney Ryan.

"You've already had three."

"So? Who's counting? No-one notices how much you

371

drink at funerals. They're all too upset or pissed themselves."

"I suppose," Richie admitted reluctantly, "it's a teenage rite of passage – getting drunk in front of the adults."

He stood up unsteadily and made his way up the garden to the makeshift bar in the kitchen where he was intercepted by Auntie Sheila.

"Terrible about your poor grandfather, Richie. The poor man!"

"Yes."

"I believe you were with him at the end?" she intoned sorrowfully.

Richie nodded gravely.

"Death the Leveller, Richie – sceptre and crown will tumble down – ashes to ashes – I hope you weren't too traumatised. Death can be very traumatising for a young person, especially if – well, of course you're too young to understand. Death isn't easy, Richie."

"He just stopped breathing," Richie said a bit queasily and turned on his heel.

When Auntie Sheila caught sight of her niece, she pounced on her with dollops of treacly sympathy.

"Ah, there you are, Laetitia dear – I'm so sorry about your father that I didn't get here in time to say goodbye."

"Thanks, Auntie Sheila."

"Poor Bernard. May I see him?"

"Of course." Lit led the way into the dining-room where her father's body was laid out.

At the sight of the hurley and no rosary beads, her aunt exclaimed and her hand rushed to her mouth to restrain the gasps of dismay.

"Had you no rosary beads in the house? No crucifix?"

She rummaged frantically in her bag, turning the contents out on the sideboard – lipstick, purse, address book, a small prayer book, perfume, a plastic rainhat, a scratch bingo card, a small statue of St Martin de Porres, *The Little Book of Calm*, a leaflet on Maslow's Hierarchy of Needs, a bottle of Rescue Remedy, a set of worry beads.

"No, dear. I can't find them."

She cast a more critical look over the mortal remains of her oldest brother.

"Ridiculous – got up like that with a hurley! Always looking for notice, your father – even in his coffin! Never ask for whom the bell tolls – it tolls for thee!"

Lit listened in silence. There was no sense in trying to stem the flow of Auntie Sheila's reflections on mortality. Like the flaccid air in a badly repaired bicycle tyre, they would seep out in the end anyway.

"Still, I suppose it's a relief to you – now that he's gone. If he'd gone on much longer, you'd have had to take him out and shoot him – ha – ha!" She clucked hen-like at her own grim little joke.

Lit consoled herself by imagining her father was listening, chuckling as his sister inspected the quality of the coffin and the cloth in his grey suit.

"The Last Sacraments?" she enquired pointedly.

Lit nodded gravely. Perhaps if she passed her aunt the holy water from the sideboard to sprinkle on him, she could be sidetracked from her investigations. She found the little plastic bottle in the shape of the Virgin Mary which Auntie Sheila had sent from Knock years ago, and placed it gently in her hands. Sheila unscrewed the top which was in the shape of a gold crown of stars and sprinkled the water with exaggerated reverence on his hands, inadvertently blessing the hurley and sliotar at the same time.

It was too much. Lit turned away hastily and bolted from the room, trying to suppress a spasm of hysterical laughter. She darted across the corridor into the study where nobody could see her and she gave vent to it – heaving, gasping uncontrollable whoops of laughter. She bent over double, clutched her stomach, banged her fists on the desk, stamped her feet on the floor, but nothing would stem the distressing tide of laughter until the door opened and Seán Tallon stood in the doorway. He watched her for a few moments, then stepped forward and closed the door quietly behind him.

"Is everything OK?"

Lit was incoherent. Tears of laughter streamed down her contorted face. Suddenly he was right in front of her, shaking her by the shoulders. He seemed to raise a hand to her. Then, appearing to change his mind, he took one of her hands in his, lifted it up swiftly, and holding it firmly by the wrist, he administered a sharp and painful slap to her face by her own hand.

"Ouch!"

"Sorry! It's all I could think of doing."

"Why did you do that?"

"You were hysterical. You might have hurt yourself. I've seen it happen. I'll get some ice if you like."

Why did he of all people have to find her in such an embarrassing state? Now he probably thought she had flipped completely. Single Harassed Mother Rounds The Final Bend – Unmarried Mother Descends Into Madness – Single Parent In Bizzare Paranoid Schizophrenic Outburst. And though she hated to admit it, the slap had worked. Whatever insane demon had possessed her and sent her whirling around the study, like a hyena on cocaine, was now well and truly banished. She flopped backwards against the edge of the desk, feeling drained, and horribly empty and sad.

"Are you feeling better now?" he asked her softly, his head tilted down, trying to catch her eyes.

Afterwards Lit put the incident down to exhaustion, because even though it was the worst moment possible, even though she was in the presence of an alien life form, the tears burst out of her and rolled down her creased-up face. She gasped and sobbed uncontrollably as she began to speak.

"I feel so lonely . . . I don't know what to do . . . I know he was very old . . . but that doesn't make any difference . . . in a way, it makes it harder because we were more like devoted bickering friends than father and daughter . . . I just can't picture life without him."

Then, in a split second, both his arms were firmly about her, holding her head gently against his chest and lightly stroking her hair. A damp patch of tears was forming across the front of his crisp white shirt, making the material temporarily see-through. She was mortified to discover that she was rubbing her cheek lightly against his chest and nestling her head in the crook of his neck and shoulder.

He didn't say anything at all.

By and by her sobbing subsided and it was time to pull away and blow her nose.

"You must think I'm crazy," she said, blowing heartily into a tissue.

"Grief comes out in different ways."

He pulled a large white hanky from his pocket and folded it up into the shape of a little round pad. "Here," he said and began dabbing lightly under her eyes. "The black stuff – it's run a bit. There now. That's better. You look – you look – you don't even look as if you've been crying."

"I feel a lot better," she said briskly and straightened up her shoulders. Then she added as clinically as she could, "The cry helped."

It was as near as she could bring herself to saying thank you.

There was an awkward silence for a few seconds. Lit might even have been shamed into saying thank you if it wasn't for the fact that, at the very moment she was about to open her mouth and force out two of the hardest words in the English language, the door opened suddenly once more and Conrad was standing there with a massive bouquet of crimson roses.

She ran to his arms, forgetting completely about Seán.

"It's so good of you to come. I didn't expect it. It's been awful."

"I really am sorry. I was in Berlin at a meeting. I only found out a couple of hours ago." He held her closely for a few moments before breaking away and presenting her with the flowers. "These are for you."

"They're beautiful! Don't worry about me, I mean, work – don't worry about work – I'm still on the case – the IRFU – Brendan Browne – "

He took her chin lightly between his thumb and forefinger and smiled easily into her eyes. "Whenever," he said and planted a moist kiss firmly on her cheek.

Seán coughed. He needed to get out – but Romeo and Juliet were blocking the doorway.

"Tallon, how's it going?" Conrad flashed him a brief smile of recognition.

"Fine, thanks – excuse me," he replied dismissively, showing scant regard for one of Ireland's finest gentlemen.

In the garden, Auntie Sheila had commandeered Bonnie and was speaking very earnestly about her concerns for Lit and Richie.

"The boy needs a role model."

Bonnie, distracted by the sight of Seán Tallon making an oddly hasty exit through the patio-doors, was only half-listening. "Role model?" Seán had just deliberately kicked the oak tree and sworn aloud. Now what was that all about?

"Yes, dear. Did I tell you I'm reading psychology in the Open University?"

"That must be interesting," said Bonnie. Matt was now shambling across the lawn to join Seán under the oak tree.

"Yes, dear, it is. I download the material from the Internet. Last week I did role models. The week before I did 'The Making and Breaking of Attachment Bonds'. Anyway, as I say, the boy needs a role model. It's a disgrace. It's a dysfunctional family."

"Dysfunctional family?"

"You see, it doesn't function properly. His mother is projecting the role of husband onto him. He needs a father to slay and dethrone from a godlike position. Otherwise he will fail to break his attachment bonds and he will suffer from self-esteem and autonomy. Well, I ask you? Where is he going to get a proper persona? The end result will be homosexuality – you mark my words. I've done my research."

"Richie – gay?"

Auntie Sheila nodded insistently. "All the studies prove it. He has to establish a new architrave of his own because the parental architrave lost its ascendency by the time he reached thirteen – but he doesn't have one because – well, you mightn't understand, dear. It's a whole Oedipal thing."

Meanwhile the subject of their discussion was getting pissed off with Barney Ryan who was still downing beer and making comments about all the women.

"My auld one's mates are all drawing the pension, but your old lady seems to know plenty of cool older babes. That Bonnie's a ride – she can teach me any time. I caught her looking at me. Reckon she likes the younger man – I'll give her one no bother!"

"Shut up, Barney. It's my grandfather's funeral. Can't you talk about something else?"

"It's just all the older babes around — Dee Dee Caulfield is a bit of a dog, but the rest – phoargh!"

"Babes . . ." nodded Simon blearily.

"Will you guys shut up?" Richie hissed. "My grandfather –"

"Sorry, Richie – we couldn't help it."

Ordinarily Richie was amused by their banter. He knew that neither of them were technically virgins any more. But at the same time they were hardly in any sense of the word experienced sexual activists. Simon had slept with Laura who was his sister's friend in sixth year. She had gone to bed with Simon for a bet. It had lasted fifteen minutes, and when he was finished Laura jumped out of her parent's bed and shouted downstairs: "Ohmygod, Julie, you so owe me fifty pounds and I so deserve it!"

Barney Ryan on the other hand was slightly more experienced and loved to brag about it. He had been seeing a girl for about six months until he realised that he didn't want to be tied down (neither by leather thongs nor emotionally). One weekend when her parents were away he stayed with her and they had sex about six times. He was so proud of his experience that he told Miss Cass the English teacher about it the next day.

"OK, class, we're going to do a descriptive passage about some little experience we had over the weekend – some simple little event – breakfast, training, going to visit your granny in hospital – "

"Miss?"

Barney's hand was up eager to impress.

"Yes, Barney?"

"I've just spent the weekend having sex with my girl-friend for the first time. Can I write about that?"

"How do you think your girlfriend will feel about you broadcasting that kind of thing to the class? A gentle-man doesn't brag about his sexual exploits."

Barney had the good grace to blush and Richie remembered the whole class sniggering with a mixture of envy and delight at seeing Barney Ryan put in his place.

But now Richie couldn't stick the sexual banter a moment longer. He stood up abruptly and went to talk to Seán Tallon and Matt who were standing beneath the oak tree.

"Well, I guess I'm the man of the house now – so either of you want another drink?"

"I'll get it," said Matt and he loped off into the house.

"Man of the house, eh?" said Seán.

"Yep!" replied Richie with all the untested certainty and assurance of the sixteen-year-old.

"I wouldn't race to be the man of the house if I were you."

"My mother expects it."

"Has she said so?"

"Not in so many words." Richie shrugged.

"I'd say it's the last thing she wants."

"How would you know?"

"Call it an educated guess. My mother wanted me to be the man of the house."

"And were you?"

"Sadly, yes, and I don't think I've ever forgiven her."

"First you love your parents – then you blame them – sometimes you forgive them. Lit has that on a fridge magnet." Richie drawled it as though he was reciting a particularly boring French irregular verb. "All adults are mad," he added with vehement conviction.

"Me?"

"You're a sap, a bore, a psycho, a maniac –"

Tallon chuckled wryly.

"What's so funny?"

"At least your opinion of me is better than your mother's." Seán placed his empty can on the wrought-iron table and turned to leave. He rested his hand lightly on Richie's shoulder. "Take care. Remember what I said about not being the man of the house."

# CHAPTER 30

By country standards the wake finished early and at midnight only Bonnie and Lit and Richie remained, all slouched around the kitchen in various stages of hazy inebriation, and all very melancholy. Bonnie made some half-hearted attempts to stack dirty glasses and plates in the dishwasher, but Lit told her to leave it until the morning. It would be something to do, something to take her mind off the fact that there would be no-one to make porridge for any more, no-one to scold about changing his shirts, no-one to tease her about the ridiculous way she made her money. Richie had drunk quite a few bottles of beer, the most he'd ever consumed and he kept nodding off in the chair, snoring lightly until his head lobbed to one side and jerked him back to consciousness. At last he couldn't fight the sleep any longer. He kissed Lit and gave Bonnie a sweet, affectionate peck on the cheek before shuffling off to bed.

"Come on, Doran! Where's your stamina? One for the road," said Bonnie, producing another bottle of chilled white wine.

"Not for me, thanks. Any more wine and I'll fall asleep in the chair."

Bonnie ignored her, uncorked the wine and poured two healthy glasses.

"Get that down you. It will do you good. Besides Dandy wouldn't want his wake finishing at midnight."

"I suppose not." Lit was tired and emotionally drained. But instead of sending her to sleep the wine perked her up. "Did Auntie Sheila give you the 'psychological tasks of adolescence'?"

"Just the edited highlights."

"I suppose she means well. And she's quite funny in small doses."

"She's not so bad. You should meet my Aunt Cora. Even her own kids can't stand her. One Christmas she walked out on her entire family and they wrote and begged her not to come back. Of course she came back – just to spite them."

"Conrad was here," Lit said a trifle breathlessly.

"Yes, I know. I spoke to him in the garden."

"And?"

"Nothing. Just chit-chat. Talk about the old days."

"He had to leave early – he was expecting some calls to do with the enquiry. He brought the most beautiful bouquet of roses!"

"Never trust a man who makes extravagant gestures. You know, the sort who sweeps you off your feet, with flowers and diamonds and champagne and Chablis Grand Cru – "

"Why ever not?"

Bonnie gave her the Bonnie 'do you even have to ask that question' look, and promptly changed the subject. "Anyway, tell me what I really want to know."

"What?"

"Well, I'm listening to Auntie Sheila's psycho-babble, when Seán Tallon comes charging out through the patio doors, stalks down the garden, kicks the trunk of the oak tree and says 'Bollox!' quietly to himself."

There was silence for a brief moment, then Lit sniggered derisively. "He probably thinks 'Bollox' is a type of tracker bond."

"Well, he looked pretty pissed off to me."

"Maybe he's mad for love of you."

"I don't think so. Told me he took an instant liking to me and he enjoyed my company, but that I wasn't really his type."

"God! Typical! You must have felt like hitting him!"

"No. I like that kind of directness. That way there are no misunderstandings – no will he, won't he's – no does he, doesn't he's. He won't and he doesn't. And that's disappointing – but at least I don't have to waste any emotional energy on him."

"It's a bit clinical though, isn't it? Now Conrad is different. He's so – "

"Have you met Angela yet?"

"No. I suppose he's not that keen on us meeting."

Bonnie swivelled her head around to look straight into Lit's face. "Do you love Conrad?"

"We've been over this. What's not to love?"

"That won't do."

Lit sat up straight and began counting on her fingers. "OK then – his looks, his charm, his body, his personality, his good manners, the way he sits awkwardly in a chair, his shoulders, the way his jaw juts out sometimes, his intelligence – is that enough?"

Bonnie eyed her dubiously. "Do you think that he loves you?"

"He's told me so."

"Oh, right! The Declaration Of Love. Now tell me again, how did that happen?"

"He sent me a text message."

"A text message! Has he mentioned it since?"

"Yes, of course! But, with my father and everything, we haven't had time to discuss it."

Lit was beginning to feel uncomfortable for some reason and was glad when the phone at her feet began flashing in the darkness.

"Hello?"

"Lit?" It was Conrad, sounding hesitant and concerned. "I'm sorry if I'm disturbing you – I didn't know if it was too late to call –"

"No! Not at all!"

"I meant to do it earlier, but those calls went on and on – I just wanted to see if you're OK . . . "

It was so wonderful and thoughtful of him. It almost made her cry to think that he had time to worry about her in the midst of scurrilous media attacks and vindictive slanders and billions of euros and government bodies and judicial inquiries. "Of course I am. But what about you? How did the calls go? Is everything all right?"

"Now, don't you worry your beautiful head about me.

I'll be fine. Is there anybody with you? I mean, a friend to keep you company. You shouldn't be alone."

"Bonnie's here."

"Bad Bonnie Ballantyne . . . Then you're in good hands. I just wanted to say goodnight and that I'm really thinking about you right now."

"Me too, Conrad," she whispered, her voice full of affection and longing.

Her heart fluttered and jumped, pirouetted and somersaulted and this time she made no attempt to stop it. It was all right now to let it flutter and jump because his heart was most probably fluttering and jumping too. He loved her and so the barriers that she had built around her heart began tumbling suddenly and inexorably – like the Berlin Wall. She no longer had the will to keep them there.

"And I wanted to tell you about – but, what an idiot I am – no, I'll handle this myself – "

"What? What will you handle yourself?"

"Nothing! I won't say another word."

"Conrad, please!"

She could hear him sigh, apparently wrestling with his conscience.

Then, after a lengthy pause, he continued with a new note of urgency in his voice, "Well, the inquiry is this day week at four in the afternoon. But I'll be fine. I've been over the legal stuff with the lawyers and Jack has the financial end of things sorted."

She couldn't bear to think of the trouble that was ahead of him. And where was Angela? Shouldn't she be at his side? Perhaps, after all, she just didn't deserve him anyway.

Now Lit was the one who was adamant. "You have to let me help you. I just need a few days to sort things out here. It doesn't give us much time – but it's just how you present yourself. You've done nothing wrong. You have the answers. I'll help you to deliver them properly."

"But your father – it's too soon. You need time – it's not fair –"

She cut in quickly. "Conrad, how could I bear not to help you?"

He sighed again. "Right then! I accept . . . but very reluctantly. I really don't deserve you. If I were with you, I could pay you in kind . . ."

"Well, you can't! Not tonight at any rate. Anyway, it's all part of the service – em, my helping you with the case, I mean!"

He chuckled. "Goodnight, Lit."

She replaced the phone and gave it a lingering, affectionate smile.

Bonnie watched her sceptically.

"How could I bear not to help you?" she mimicked Lit's voice. Then, she added with a motherly rueful smile, "You don't know your arse from your elbow, do you!"

"What do you mean?" asked Lit.

"I mean about Conrad. I mean about love. You don't know a damn thing about love."

Lit tossed her head dismissively.

Bonnie rolled her eyes to heaven, pursed her lips and then gave her an affectionate and resigned hug. "Sorry. Was what I said out of order?"

"What are friends for? You're only watching out for me. Right?"

"Right!" agreed Bonnie.

# CHAPTER 31

So Dandy was laid to rest and the priest wasn't too cheesy or sanctimonious and the relatives didn't walk out when 'We Are the Champions' was blasted out on the church PA system. When Louis Armstrong sang 'Making Whoopee' the congregation smiled fondly, remembering a mischievous and steadfast old man from another age. Loads of people wore sunglasses because the day was so bright and hot and Bonnie remarked that it was more like a Mafia funeral than anything else.

Azelia turned up at the church and made a late and rather rushed, but terribly grand, entrance, turning plenty of heads as she sailed down the aisle, dressed in a broad sweep of black hat and a white silk dress with crimson splashes.

At the graveside, Richie was flanked by his mother and Bonnie. At the precise moment when the priest said "ashes to ashes" as unsanctimoniously as he could, Bonnie squeezed Richie's hand and gave him a motherly peck on the cheek. He thought Dandy would have approved of the kiss and the squeezed hand and he was quite amused to see Barney Ryan eyeing him enviously from the other side of the grave.

In the end, in a funny way that Lit couldn't quite explain, Dandy's funeral was a happy, joyful occasion but she felt lonely and sad when people began to say their goodbyes and leave.

A small number of close friends and relatives returned to the house with Lit, but Azelia, to no-one's surprise, had to leave immediately. She was devastated, she said, to have to go so soon – but she would always keep her father in her heart.

"Hypocrite!" murmured Auntie Sheila, in a rare

moment of stinging criticism.

Later, Lit found she was even sad saying goodbye to Auntie Sheila – who had very thoughtfully written out the names of a few bereavement counsellors.

"Denial, anger, despair, acceptance – you'll have to work through all the stages, dear – or is it anger, denial? Anyway, keep in touch."

Lit hugged her fondly and promised to visit her very soon.

"Mind yourself, Lit dear," she said before her small slender frame disappeared into the back of a taxi to take her to the station.

Matt warned her against coming back to work too soon.

"You need time to yourself. Go away with Richie for a few days. Maura has everything under control. Don't worry – we'll call you if anything urgent crops up."

She protested, but Matt was adamant and since there was nothing else for it, she booked herself and Bonnie into a quiet little seaside hotel in West Cork and was surprised and pleased when Richie agreed to go with them.

"Someone has to keep an eye on you two," he said by way of explanation. "Who knows what mischief you'll get up to otherwise?"

The hotel was an old rambling Georgian house, with creaking polished oak floors and slightly faded chintz curtains. The plumbing was old-fashioned and noisy, the decor cosy with lots of brocade and tapestry. Lit could see the beach from her window and in bed at night she could hear the waves breaking gently on the shore. For five days they slept too much, ate too much, drank too much, strolled on the long beach in the morning and rambled along windy hawthorned country lanes in the evening. They had planned to play golf and to swim in the sea and to hire bicycles. But somehow they never got round to it. Time filled up easily and passed pleasantly. Richie was great company, keeping them amused with his endless stock of jokes and arguing with Bonnie about everything from the music of Bob Dylan (his latest discovery) to where to get the best bag of chips in Dublin.

"He's just amazing," Bonnie said to her one night when they were on their own.

Lit beamed proudly and then felt a stab of guilt that she didn't spend more of this kind of easy, relaxing time with her son. Forced for once to tear herself away from work, she realised with a shock that she'd hardly spent longer than one consecutive hour with him in the past six months. Some of it was the normal cut and thrust of teenage life – when to be seen out in public with one's mother was to commit social suicide. He wouldn't go to the pictures with her any more. He wouldn't go shopping with her. It was all she could do to coax him and his friends into having a meal with her occasionally. But it was mostly that she didn't have the time to be with him. It was all very well to talk of bringing up children in a spirit of benevolent neglect, but rambling around the back lanes of West Cork with him, she was forced to admit that she had lost out on great slices of his life in the past few years and that she really missed it. And then she remembered the stinging criticism of Seán Tallon about single mothers. Perhaps, after all, he had hit a raw nerve, in his tactless way. Was that why she hated him so much?

Back in Dublin, a pile of letters of sympathy and legal correspondence awaited her and she sat in the study for several hours wading through it. Richie, starved of the company of his peers for the past few days, went to see yet another campus horror movie with a gang of his classmates. She fretted about drugs and drink and unprotected sex, issued a few dire warnings and let him go. He had to find his own way to adulthood. But she didn't sleep until she heard his key in the door and his steady step on the stairs. He tiptoed into her room and kissed her goodnight.

"See, Mam. Sober and not under any influence. Night."

In the morning just to keep herself occupied, she planned to clear out some of Dandy's things. But when she went into his room, it all proved too much. She sat down on the bed and cried herself into a stupor.

The sound of the doorbell ringing brought her back to reality. She realised she was desperate for company, anyone to fill the emptiness, found herself wishing it would be someone calling to visit her, and not for instance the milkman. She'd taken for granted the constant presence of the old man in the corner and the fact that, through thick and thin, he'd always been there. Now she missed him terribly. She splashed some water on her face and went to answer the door.

When she'd said she was desperate for company, any company, of course she didn't mean that to include Seán Tallon. And his arrival on her doorstep was sure proof of the old saying: be careful what you wish for.

"I was just in the neighbourhood." He held out a large brown-paper bag with something squishy inside. "Croissants and pastries. Wasn't sure which you might like so I got some of each."

She eyed him and his large paper bag with suspicion.

"I owe you breakfast," he said. "Remember?"

Lit racked her brains. When had she ever eaten as

much as a biscuit in his company? Then she remembered the morning after the party and her Bulls' Hotel tirade. She was about to tell him to keep his croissants, but realised she couldn't. He'd done so much to lighten the burden of organising the funeral for her that she no longer had a decent reason to be downright rude to him.

"Come in." She forced a smile.

"Thanks," he said and held out the bag once more. This time she relieved him of it and led him towards the kitchen. But he stopped short in the hall.

"I knew it! That painting. It's Chatham Harbour in Cape Cod."

"It is?"

"Yes. I worked there one summer when I was a student."

What as, she wondered – a halibut?

Lit hadn't looked at the painting since the interior designer decided that the best place to hang it was in the hall to catch or not to catch some light or other. She'd never even been to Cape Cod. The picture had been bought in a little gallery in New York on one of her business trips there.

"Coffee?" she offered, hoping to prise him away from the painting, and from this embarrassingly artistic side of his character.

Paintings, after all, are a good financial investment, she wanted to remind him. You don't actually have to like them.

"Great light in Cape Cod for painting," she heard him say as she strode on to the kitchen. "I have something similar to this."

There was really no point in pursuing that avenue of conversation.

He was wearing a plain navy T-shirt in light cotton

material and she couldn't help but notice his broad chest, the one she'd cried on, and a smooth stomach. In the kitchen, he ambled about, examining of all things her collection of fridge magnets – Kitsch Corner, Bonnie called them. She hardly noticed most of them now – but over the years they'd built up, brought back from trips abroad: jokes about mothers, jokes about sons and teenagers, jokes about grandfathers, a picture of Elvis that lit up and sang 'Jailhouse Rock' when you pressed it, and her favourite – a little martial arts hamster that sang 'Kung Foo Fighting'.

"So," she said when she set the coffee and pastries down in front of him. "What can I do for you?"

"Is it that difficult?" he asked, looking across the table at her steadily with his blue grey eyes.

"What? Is what difficult? If you mean – "

"I mean is it that difficult for someone like you to face the fact that someone like me might just call in to see how you are?"

"I'm sorry." She needed to change the subject. "Tell me about Cape Cod."

"Good times," he said, tucking into his croissant. "I worked in the port – in a boat-hire shop during the day and in a bar at night. There was a gang of us – all over from Ireland and – well, as I said, good times."

"I never got to do anything like that. Oh – of course I had plans. But then – "

Now that was a conversation cul-de-sac she should have been able to avoid. She finished the sentence in her head: but then of course I had rampant depraved sex with an entire rugby team in one evening and conceived Richie and subsequently became responsible for all the appalling social problems that plague society today.

"In a way you're lucky," he said.

"Lucky?" She was expecting yet another sermon from the Mount of Self-righteousness.

"Yes, because you can start to do all those things now and really enjoy them. Richie is nearly grown up and you have the best years of your life ahead of you."

"Maybe."

"I'd like to say again how ashamed I am of what I said to you about single mothers. I wish there was some way I could take it back."

He looked genuinely remorseful, truly ashamed. She ought to put him out of his misery. But she couldn't just say 'apology accepted', could she?

"Forget it."

"No! Let me finish. It was arrogant, condescending, ill-informed and stupid."

"Yes, well, I suppose we all put our foot in it sometimes," she said quickly. It was as much as she could manage.

They munched awkwardly on croissants for a while until he broke the silence once more.

"There is something you could do for me as a matter of fact. A sort of favour."

Of course! She knew it! A man like him was never off-duty. Of course he hadn't just called to see how she was feeling! He had no concept of feelings. There had to be something in it for him. She began clearing the table and stacking things in the dishwasher with staccato efficiency.

"The thing is," he went on, "my mother has this bee in her bonnet about me buying a house. And she's seen this place down in Wicklow – a rectory or something. To be honest I couldn't care less about houses, but she seems to think I should buy a house now."

"Sound financial investment!" she sniped.

He ignored her and continued. "Anyway, they've arranged for me to look over the house today and I'd really like a woman's opinion."

She was astonished. "Mine?"

He nodded.

"Is there nobody else?"

"Bonnie's having lunch with her parents. My sister lives in Sligo. There is one girl, but I'm afraid that if I ask her along to view a house, she'll think it's my subtle way of asking her to marry me." He smiled sheepishly.

Lit couldn't help it. She threw her head back and laughed in his face. "What's so funny?"

"You. You're funny. Vain in a fiendishly modest kind of a way."

He smiled warmly at her, teeth and everything. White, regular teeth. "Is that a yes or no?"

"It's a yes, but only because I have nothing better to do today."

There's nothing like the close intimacy of sitting in an hour-long traffic jam, heading out of the city in blazing summer heat, to break the ice – more lethal than ten vodka martinis, more potent than all the moonlight and soft music in the world.

He'd insisted on taking his old banger of a Renault, even though she had offered her shiny red BMW. Of course, it was a big Renault – and by most standards it wasn't a banger at all – but a respectable three-year-old.

"Why don't you change it?" she asked in a spirit of casual condescension. "It's just as cheap to buy a new one."

"Can't be bothered. I mostly only use it around the city. I'm not bothered much with things."

"People always say that until they have money and

then they're just as greedy and materialistic as the rest of mankind. So what would you do if you had a million euros? Give it all away to charity? I doubt it."

He grinned broadly at her.

"Who knows! I don't give it much thought to be honest," he replied.

The sun beat down relentlessly on the car and the air-conditioning didn't work too well. The snarling and hissing traffic inched forward very slowly. The heat and the silence were oppressive. He didn't seem to notice, sitting patiently, tapping his fingers lightly to the low music in the background. But Lit was getting quite edgy, anxious to fill up the silence.

"So about this house . . ."

"I'm looking at the house with a view to buying it and you've obviously got a knack for picking a good house, so what's your advice? What should I be looking for?"

"Location, location, location?"

"No! I mean what should I really be looking for? What made you decide that house was the one? Don't tell me the location clinched it. It must have been something else – something not so easy to define."

At last the traffic loosened out and began to flow. Lit opened her window and savoured the cool breeze on her skin. Picking up speed, they drove away from the thinning suburbs, passing the Sugarloaf Mountain and on into the lush wooded landscape of Wicklow. She tried to think what it was about the house which made it special in her eyes. The elegant bay-windowed rooms, the lovely carved oak banister, the garden, the pannelling, the plaster coving, the redbrick arched doorway – it wasn't any of those things.

"I don't know," she said at last, flummoxed by his question.

"Maybe it was the kitchen?"

"No! Definitely not. That was my father's idea. I was all for gutting it and doing it in stainless steel and slate. But he refused to live in a kitchen which he said would be like a hospital sluicing room."

Seán laughed at the description. "Quite a man, your father. And maybe he was right about the kitchen."

And who asked you, she thought, and returned to wondering why she had fallen in love with the house in Harwood Park.

They drove about thirty miles on the main road. Then he indicated to the left and turned down a narrow road. Winding and overhung with oaks and beeches and chestnuts in full bloom, there was barely enough room for two cars to pass. They drove for a few miles, then crossed over a little humpback bridge and came to a cluster of old rose-washed houses on a crossroads. An elderly man sitting on a wooden porch taking the sun reminded her of Dandy, who used to love to sit in the sun. An indolent dog lay along a stone wall and eyed them with mild curiosity. There was a small shop with the name painted on a wooden panel over the door and an ice cream sign outside. She was hot and sticky and thirsty and the ice cream sign set her mouth watering. A little patch of sea, just visible over the brow of a hill, glinted enticingly. She imagined diving into it, the cool salt water breaking and splashing on her skin.

"I have to collect the key here," he said, pulling up outside the shop.

She considered asking him to get her an ice cream, but he was most probably one of those intolerable men whose cars were food-free and litter-free zones. She'd long ago given up the ghost on the whole food-and-litter-free car issue. The back seat of her lovely new car was already submerged under a mishmash of sports and Playstation magazines, sweet wrappers, empty mineral bottles, several CDs and a couple of T-shirts. Every so often she would let a few fishwife roars at Richie about not being his personal servant and threaten him with dire consequences if he didn't clean out the back seat of the car this very instant. Finally, simmering with resentment, she would gather up all the rubbish and sling it petulantly in the bin. So much for consistent parenting.

While she waited, she checked out the rose-washed houses. They were nicely proportioned, probably a few hundred years old. Pretty mullioned windows framed rippling panes of glass, and flower-boxes of colour cascaded everywhere. A simple painted sign on the side of the road said: Please do not leave your litter in Laraville. It was a pretty name for a village, though it was hardly a village really.

Tallon re-appeared, clutching two of the biggest ninety-nines she'd ever seen in her life, the rich creamy spirals of ice cream threatening to capsize in his hands.

"She was over-generous – so better tuck in quickly."

Lit sank her lips eagerly into the cool creamy mixture, her tongue grazing and lingering on the crumbly chocolate flake.

"That is delicious. Thanks."

"We'll have something decent to eat later."

Later? What later? He hadn't mentioned 'later' before. She was doing him a favour, giving freely of her hard-earned time, just so that he could have a second opinion on a house. A house that might turn out to be one of those dreary castellated Victorian Gothic horrors. Talk about taking advantage!

"I really don't think – "

"It's the least I can do. After all, you're doing me a big favour."

Did she detect the merest hint of irony in his voice? As if he was reading her mind? She decided not to argue, to maintain the relatively civilised atmosphere which had sprung up between them.

"I'm in your hands," she said. He wasn't the only one that could do irony.

"It's not far now. The man in the shop said it was a gate on the left-hand side."

Lit was expecting any one of a number of types of gates – big Victorian wrought-iron things, or some fancy ranchy wooden structure or even plain old working farm gates with cattle grids beneath. But the entrance to Sweetbriar House was different and, in its quiet country way, it rendered her temporarily speechless.

"Look at the little churchyard! And that tiny chapel!" she said at last.

The entrance was wide and semicircular, flanked on one side by the aforementioned little churchyard and by a row of oak trees on the other. There were no gates at all, just the solid stone pillars which once supported them, and ahead a long curving driveway. In spite of her determination not to be impressed, she couldn't wait to get to the end of the drive to see what awaited them. It didn't take long. The driveway curved to the right past a mini-forest of trees and across a couple of acres of plain mowed lawn was the prettiest house she'd ever seen.

Long, stone-clad, with a low-pitched slated roof – and in front a few stone steps up to a perfect little fan-lighted door. The lawns were edged with generous borders, brimming with flowers and shrubs, planted and tended by some devoted gardener.

"Well, what do you think of it so far?"

She wanted to say something dismissive, something which would show she wasn't the least bit impressed. She longed to mention the much bigger, much grander stately aristocratic pile that Conrad was currently restoring, with its walled garden and its balustraded roof and its Italian fountains. But she could find nothing dismissive to say about Sweetbriar House with its warm and friendly charm.

"It's just beautiful. Your mother must have very good taste."

"Come on. Let's have a look around. The owners are away for the weekend."

Inside the house smelt of polish and fresh flowers and baking. The walls were brimming with paintings and family photos. A big old dresser in the large, low-ceilinged dining-room displayed sporting trophies and certificate awards for music and dancing and even one for life-saving. The people in the photos looked like a very nice family – happy and close – and normal. In amongst the normal smiling pictures of the family, one photo showed the father and one of the sons having a mock showdown over a dinge in a car. Another showed the brother and sister fighting over the last sausage from a barbecue. She sat for a while at a low panelled window which looked out across the lawn. It was the sort of place she'd always imagined when she was a girl – a window to sit in – a good book – and a pretty view.

She followed him up the polished wooden staircase to a long narrow landing and they inspected each of the rooms. The master bedroom also looked out over the lawn and the sea was visible through gaps in the trees. She sat on the bed and drank in the view and the peaceful silence. She was disappointed when it was time to leave.

"I've decided. I'm going to buy it," he said finally, locking the front door behind them.

"But you should look at other houses. You should get a surveyor's report. This place might be riddled with dry rot – for all you know."

"Doesn't matter. I've made up my mind. I like it."

They drove back down the driveway in the evening sunlight and returned the key to the village shop. Lit glanced at her watch. She was hungry and she had to admit she'd had a nice day – even if she was only doing him a favour.

"Hungry?" he asked.

"I should really be getting back."

"I won't hear of it. There's a lovely little pub over-looking a beach only a short drive away."

A pub! He was taking her to a pub! A country pub, that smelt of beer and tobacco where they might get a stale ham sandwich if they were lucky, where the words 'vodka martini' would send shivers of panic through the barman.

The pub was called The Sailor's Cabin and it consist-ed of a series of interconnecting timber-panelled rooms, each one packed to the gills with lively groups of young people and families, tucking into food which didn't look remotely like stale ham sandwiches. And the barmen looked sparky enough to give the smarmiest cocktail waiters in Manhattan a good run for their money. Seán led her through the warren of rooms and out to a terrace at the back which faced directly onto the beach. He beck-oned to a waiter.

"I've reserved the pergola."

The waiter led them to a wooden pergola, with

scented jasmine clambering through the framework. Inside was a table set out for two diners. It was the best position on the terrace. There was a perfect view of the beach and a little further down she could see the trawlers coming and going at the busy little harbour.

"Like it?" he asked.

"It's OK."

The menu set her mouth watering at a ferocious rate – every kind of fish – cooked in every kind of way – from the simplicity of grilled sole to rich lobster thermidor.

"If you're stuck for choice – I'd recommend the deep-fried scallops."

Lit examined the menu once more. Deep-fried scallops was a new one on her. Who, in their right mind would deep-fry something as tender and succulent as a scallop? Whatever next? Crispy roast oysters? A scallop was something to be treated with gentle respect – not tossed violently in batter and plunged ruthlessly into a deep-fat fryer. She decided on the baked monkfish in a chilli dip instead.

They drank wine while they waited for the food to come and the combination of hunger, warm evening sunshine and crisp Sancerre brought a sparkle to her eyes and made her feel quite light-headed, quite rash in fact.

"So tell me about this girl who wants to marry you? Maybe she doesn't want to marry you at all. Maybe you're just a vain man who's imagining it all."

"That's possible and I won't deny that I'm a bit vain. But I blame my mother. She thinks I'm perfect – poor dear. As for Lara Naughton – she's conducting her campaign with relentless military precision."

"How do you mean?" Lit was fascinated. She couldn't imagine any woman getting obsessed enough with Seán

Tallon to actually devote all her energies to marching him up the aisle.

He laughed and smiled warmly at her. "Ah, you know, all those books telling a woman how to get her man – I've seen my little sister reading them. Play it cool, never call him unless you have a cast-iron excuse, never be available for a date less than three days in advance – flatter him subtly – let him think he's in control – and those books are usually written by women whose husbands divorce them. Anyway – that's how Lara goes on. And I have to admit she's bloody good at it. She won't snare me though – but by God she'll nab some other poor bloke when she realises the game is up with me."

"Not interested then?" enquired Lit coolly – well, not all that coolly. Unaccountably, she was quite interested in his love life.

"Definitely not. I believe in old-fashioned stuff – like love and desire and respect and companionship. I'm not planning on being Lara Naughton's trophy and I don't plan on picking up any trophy wife for myself either."

"What about Bonnie?" Sickening – but she had to ask. The wine was flowing freely and the seafood cooked to order hadn't arrived yet. She was so hungry she was considering plucking at some of the scented jasmine leaves.

"Bonnie's great. But that's just a bit of fun for both of us. How about you?"

"Me? What about me?"

"Is there someone? Conrad Budd or someone?"

"It's complicated," she said, and wondered how to change the subject. Even if she wanted to tell him about Conrad, how could she explain about Angela? How could she tell all that to Seán without sounding mean, opportunistic or plain foolish?

"None of my business," he said. "Shouldn't have asked."

Luckily the food arrived just then and saved the moment.

Lit's monkfish was a bit too chewy and the chilli sauce spicier than she would have liked. In contrast, the deep-fried scallops on her companions plate looked annoyingly mouth-watering. They were lightly dipped in seasoned flour and fried to a pale golden colour. She watched enviously as he bit into each succulent piece of fish.

"How's the monkfish?"

"Absolutely delicious."

"Want to try a scallop?"

"No, thanks. I'm fine."

His mobile rang. It was his mother.

"Excuse me while I talk to her," he said and took himself off to a quiet corner. In his absence, Lit couldn't resist helping herself to a scallop. It was melt-in-the-mouth divine. She had another, then another. She stopped when she realised there were very few left on his plate.

When he returned, she was chewing industriously on a piece of monkfish.

"She called to know if I liked the house."

"Does she think you should buy it?"

"She's like you – thinks I should get the surveys done first. Anyway, the main thing is that she's happy now I've actually gone and looked at it." He looked at his plate in some surprise. "That's funny. I thought – "

She gazed at him with innocent cornflower-blue eyes.

They followed the main course with two whopping portions of wild strawberries and cream, followed by two large frothy coffees. When he'd paid the bill, they walked back to the car. The sea was now a golden bronze colour beneath the setting sun and the beach was almost deserted, except for a couple of seagulls and an elderly couple walking their dog.

Seán looked longingly at the beach. "I shouldn't have had the second glass of wine. I need to clear my head and that beach is just way too inviting."

Before she could protest that they should be getting back, he strode off down the little boardwalk and kicked off his shoes and socks, urging her to do the same. She hesitated for a moment, but she couldn't resist the temptation to walk barefooted for a while. The sand felt warm and soft under her feet and they walked along the shoreline, splashing through the cool shallow water, saying nothing in particular, until they came to a rocky outcrop. He sat down, leaving the smoothest rock for her. She listened for a while to the water gently rippling and the seagulls calling until a long-forgotten feeling washed gently over her. She couldn't even put a name on this odd forgotten feeling at first. And then she realised what it was.

For the first time in a very long time, Lit was relaxed, at ease with the world. It was unthinkable that she should reach such a nirvana-like state with someone like Seán Tallon, but there was no denying the easy contentment of sitting on a rock and having nothing at all to do except look at the sea.

She thought he might be one of those awful people who said things like "Isn't this nice?". But he didn't. Occasionally he tossed or skimmed a pebble into the water – and she found that oddly absorbing.

At last, the sun which had been hovering on the deep crimson horizon, dipped and bowed out for the night.

The evening darkened and there was a sudden chill in the air.

"Time to go, I guess," she said, standing up and dusting the sand from her jeans.

"I suppose so." He showed no inclination to move. Instead, he reached out and took her hands in his. "You are a very pretty lady, Miss Lit Doran."

Perhaps it would be rude to pull away from him too suddenly.

"Pretty and smart and kind." A smile hovered at the corners of his mouth.

What was he thinking? Had the wine gone completely to his head. She had no option now but to look deep into his eyes. But he wasn't drunk. Far from it. Without batting an eyelid, he was coolly and shamelessly flirting with her. And she didn't know if it was just the effects of the wine, but there was a battle royal going on in the pit of her stomach. She hoped the pangs were little darts of revulsion at the very idea of kissing Seán Tallon. But she was horrified to discover that what she was feeling were the warm, first flutters of desire. And more than that – she found herself unable to dislike him any more.

He pulled her gently towards him and despite severe warnings to her body to resist and retreat, Lit found herself yielding very disobediently and drawing near to him. Then – who knows how these things happen – his lips were on hers, planting a sweet and firm kiss on her lips. It was a fleeting moment of a kiss and she wanted more. She leaned forward to respond but he pulled away suddenly.

"Sorry," he said, straightening up. "Shouldn't have done that. Out of order."

So that was it. Just like any other man, he couldn't be alone with a woman without trying it on, the old "I could have her if I wanted" routine. Her stomach churned now in revulsion at how she'd almost decided he was a nice guy, nearly wanted to kiss him back. Drinking wine in the sunshine was silly and two glasses in the sunshine was bound to be the equivalent of four glasses after dark. She stood back, hands on hips, and cleared her throat. Then she gave him the benefit of a deeply patronising smile – the sort she'd give to Barney Ryan when he called her a yummy-mummy.

"I hope you didn't think I was flirting with you," she said at last. "It's just the wine. It goes completely to my head."

He didn't say anything, just shoved his hands in his pockets and turned to walk back to the car.

# CHAPTER 32

A few days later, Conrad was back in town and psyching himself up for battle in his suite of the Shelbourne. While Lit fielded calls from the press, he armed himself with facts and figures and spent a long time pondering on who his real enemy was. Fergus Cunningham the solicitor thought it was certainly Brendan Browne, who himself had dabbled disastrously in property development and was probably settling an old business score. Browne simply wanted to see Conrad fry.

Jack Kennedy thought Browne was just a puppet for someone else.

"That's all a bit – John Grisham, isn't it?" said Conrad.

"Think about it. What's in this for Browne? He's destroyed as well – his reputation, his family. He's ruined. Unless – "

"Unless what?"

"Unless – he's in with someone who wants the site for themselves . . ."

"Does it matter who it is?" asked Lit innocently.

"It matters who the real enemy is."

"Why?"

"Because there's no point in nailing the wrong man."

"Nailing?"

Jack Kennedy rested his hand on Lit's shoulder. He would like to have left it there for a while, but she flicked it off like a nasty little horsefly. Nevertheless, he was determined to put her straight.

"Why don't you leave the strategy to the big boys, Lit?" he said smarmily.

She couldn't stop herself. She looked down haughtily at him. "Big boys? That's you out then!"

She knew she shouldn't have said it. It was a very mean thing to attack someone on the basis of their personal appearance. He couldn't help it if he was five foot nothing. On the other hand, he had asked for it with his slimy little pre-historic remark. In other circumstances, she might have given him the benefit of her devastating stare for a few moments longer. But there was no time. She was here to help Conrad.

She didn't like all the stuff about nailing and enemies. It was as if she had suddenly found herself representing a criminal gang, not a highly respected property consortium. But here she was and here she would have to stay – for love and for money.

She put her personal dislike of Kennedy aside and quickly seized the initiative.

"Conrad, it's important that you spend half an hour on presentation. As your PR, I insist on it. Otherwise, I will not be held responsible."

He looked straight into her eyes, his handsome brow slightly wrinkled with the concerns of the day, determination evident in his jutting jaw. She wanted to run her hand along that jaw and tell him everything would be all right. She wanted to kiss his forehead and soothe him and let him know that together they could overcome any obstacles. But she would have to wait until they were alone. Their relationship was still technically a secret. Conrad was still technically engaged to Angela – Angela whose devotion to her fiancée didn't apparently stretch to being at his side in his hour of greatest need.

"I'll wait in the foyer. Excuse me, gentlemen," she said coolly.

The next day, she waited anxiously for Conrad outside Dublin Castle. Nobody had been allowed in except his legal team and she had said goodbye and wished him luck, like a mother anxiously watching her son go off to war. Jack Kennedy asked her to join him for coffee, but she wouldn't. Instead, she alternated between sitting on a bench and walking around the empty cobbled square in bursts of nervous energy. Her mind swung back to Dandy and then inevitably to Richie. It was hard to believe that Dandy was gone and she knew she should be spending more time with Richie now because of this big new gap in his life. She'd promised herself she would. But Conrad was fighting for his business life. There would be time for Richie later.

Outside the gates of the castle, the residents had mounted a picket. This time, though, they were quiet and orderly and Pat Sullivan even came over to talk to her. He was licking happily on a ninety-nine, licking in circles and taking occasional bites from the flake.

He grinned a bright, uncomplicated smile at her.

"Where's Maura today?"

"Office. Catching up. My father died a couple of weeks ago and I had to take some time off. So there's a lot of catching up to be done."

"Sorry. I'm really sorry. Tell you what? How about a ninety-nine? I'll send one of the lads. Hey, Nick – get's another ninety-nine, will you?"

Lit didn't have the strength to refuse. She couldn't help remembering having the ice cream with Seán Tallon a few days earlier and, when she thought about it, a big ninety-nine with a nice bit of crumbly flake really appealed to her. The day was hot and she was tired, emotionally drained, sad, anxious, confused.

Pat sat beside her on the bench.

"How did you get into this game?" he asked.

"By accident in a way. I enjoy it and the money's good."

"Ah – money – see, that doesn't interest me much at all."

"No?"

The concept of someone not being interested in money was almost alien to Lit.

"No – see Conrad there – all that money, all that power – I wonder when was the last time he sat back and read a good book, just for the pleasure of it? Do you think he notices when the seasons change – do you think he ever just takes the time to watch the world go by?"

Lit smiled at the thought of Conrad sitting for longer than five minutes. He couldn't. It wasn't in his nature. "But he's doing what he likes. He's a player not a spectator. I'm sorry – that sounded condescending."

"No offence taken. But I'm a player too. I just like to play at more important things."

The end of the cone disappeared into Pat's mouth and he sat back contentedly on the bench.

"I suppose you're hoping the enquiry will dish the dirt on Conrad," she said. "You must hate him."

"He's not my favourite person and I don't imagine Conrad and I have anything in common. But I don't hate him."

"But you want him to fail. You want to stop the development."

"True – but not from a grubby little tribunal – not from brown envelopes. Not from stabbing a man in the back."

"How then?"

"This development is just not right for the people of Stoneyfield. That should be enough to stop it."

Lit looked at him sideways. He was nice-looking in a slightly dishevelled way. And he was intelligent, good-mannered, strong, quiet and unassuming. So could he possibly be so naive as to think that Conrad would stop a development simply because it wasn't 'right for the people'? Conrad was a towering man of steel – power-ful, unstoppable, a little ruthless perhaps – but well-intentioned. Pat Sullivan was decent but insignificant, a mouse up against a lion.

"Here's Nick with your ice cream." He fished in his pocket and handed Nick a pound.

"Thanks."

She sank her perfectly outlined, frosted-pink lips deep into the cold whipped ice cream, forcing memories of Seán Tallon and his presumptuous kiss out of her mind.

"This reminds me of when I was a little girl. Sunday afternoon on the beach, a ninety-nine in the back of the car on the way home and my father warning us not to get sick in the Ford Cortina."

"We only had banana wafers."

She slurped and licked and munched contentedly, savouring the hedonistic pleasure of the simple ice cream cone.

"So how well do you know Maura?" she asked, licking at the corners of her mouth with her tongue.

"A few years. We lived in the same road for a while. We used to do daft stuff together."

"Like what?"

"The usual – mostly it involved getting very drunk and disturbing the neighbours. But I'm an older, wiser man now."

"So you must know Barry Owens?"

Pat grimaced. "Prick. Sorry – excuse the language. Never did a decent day's work in his life. Don't know what she sees in him."

"Not a lot now, I should imagine."

"Why?"

"She's ditched him."

Suddenly there was movement at the main entrance and a flurry of clerks and busy, preoccupied-looking people spewed out through the doors.

"Here comes Conrad," Jack Kennedy said, darting forward quickly.

Lit jumped to her feet and for some silly reason tried to hide the remnants of the ice cream cone behind her back. Conrad passed out magisterially beneath the pillars, surrounded by Fergus Cunningham's legal team. Kennedy was instantly at his side. Reporters swarmed about him, pushing large microphones into his face, jostling for the best position.

Lit had taught him well. He handled the large crowd of high-profile reporters with grace and humour where only a few days ago he had difficulty being civil to two minor hacks from the local rag. She beamed proudly at him across the cobbled square, demolishing the last of her ice cream.

"Mmmm . . . That was delicious. You are a saviour, Pat Sullivan – even though technically speaking you are the enemy."

"You're welcome. Tell Maura I said hi." He fished in his pocket and pulled out a ragged edged card. He handed it to her sheepishly. "My number – in case it ever comes in handy. Nice to see you again."

He shook her hand firmly, grinned warmly and went off to rejoin the picket at the gates.

Finally Conrad broke away from the little cluster of reporters and joined Lit.

"Bastards! Nobodies!" he murmured in a low voice.

"Ssshh! They might hear you. How did it go?"

"How the hell do I know – what's that all over your face?"

Lit's hand went quickly to her face and she realised with horror that it was ice cream. She had enjoyed it so much, had found the half hour with Pat Sullivan such a pleasant interlude, that she had quite forgotten to check her face and mouth afterwards. Now she realised there was sticky stuff all over her mouth and chin. She laughed helplessly and dabbed at her face with a tissue. But Conrad did not see the joke. Lit understood. He was ruffled and upset from the enquiry. It was natural that he was a bit tetchy. She cleaned up as best she could and made her voice as soothing and comforting as possible.

"You must be relieved to have Day One over. Tomorrow will be easier. I think this will all work out fine."

"What would you know?" he snapped back at her. "Come on. We'll have dinner in my place."

He placed his hand firmly on her back and steered her towards the car.

In the car, his anger with her was unabated.

"What kind of PR consultant sits in the sun eating ice cream while her client is on the rack?"

"I wasn't allowed in," she said simply.

He glared at her. "Ten days. In ten days the development is set to be launched. It's not a time for basking in the sunshine and eating ice cream!"

She could have reminded him that strictly speaking she didn't have to be there at all, But she didn't. It wasn't the right time and she didn't want to get into an argument. The best policy was to let him get all the anger off his chest and then everything would be fine. In a way, it was a compliment to their relationship that he felt he knew her well enough to show his real feelings. His hand rested on the gear-stick and she patted it gently. He withdrew it immediately.

"Will I go over the plans for the launch?" she asked.

She wanted to appease him, take his mind off things. When there was no reply, she carried on anyway.

"Press releases, photos, video-clips are all sorted. A small brass band is organised. Some of the girls from Babes model agency for a bit of glamour, and of course a batch of well-known rugby players, courtesy of the IRFU, who are overcome with gratitude for your generous sponsorship. Catering, parking, stewards, crowd control, seating for the VIPs – it's all sorted."

He didn't seem all that impressed.

"So I haven't quite been sitting in the sunshine doing nothing," she added pointedly.

"Do you think I could buy a rugby team? I mean like Elton John or that cooking woman or the man who owns the greetings-card company?"

"Doubt it."

"Well, why not? I could buy one of the big Senior Cup teams – or Leinster – I could buy Leinster . . . they've done well this season with their new trainer. Or Munster – the cream. I could buy them. With my money they could concentrate on being the best – buy in the best players from the Southern Hemisphere."

He chatted all the way home like that, his good humour improving at the thoughts of his very own fantasy rugby league. The enquiry and the incident with the ice cream were totally forgotten.

In his penthouse, Conrad ordered dinner while Lit called home to Bonnie and Richie.

"Richie is dead keen to go to some party out in Enniskerry," Bonnie reminded her.

"It's a bit far away." Lit knew she should be at home with him. She'd promised to drive him out to Simon Fitzpatrick's house where the party was. Now there was no question of her taking him. She tried hard to suppress the nagging sense of guilt.

"I'll drive him out," said Bonnie. "I've nothing else to do this evening. And I'll collect him if you're not home. How's that?"

"That's great. But I'll definitely be home for ten. So you won't have to collect him."

She hung up, then kicked off her shoes and sank back into Conrad's great big sofa. She felt tired and drained.

"Drink?"

"Glass of white wine, please," she said, enjoying the cosy little moment of domesticity between them. He set the glass down in front of her and disappeared into the bathroom for a shower. By the time he re-appeared the food had arrived and the caterers had set up a small dining-table on the balcony.

Conrad held her chair and they sat facing each other across the table. She felt oddly ill at ease. She racked her brains for something interesting to say and found herself gabbling about the splendid view and the glorious weather, neither of which topics seemed to interest her host much. Mindful of the ice cream incident, she was most careful about her table manners and though normally when she felt this drained she preferred to curl up on the sofa with a fork and a plate of pasta, for Conrad's sake she sat up at table, her back rigidly straight, her legs tucked in under the table neatly, her elbows firmly at each side.

"The salmon is delicious," she said finally, as she dabbed her napkin at the corners of her mouth.

"Hhhmm," he replied.

"How's Angela?"

"What do you mean?" He flashed a little scowl at her.

"Just making conversation. You have to understand, I'm in an odd situation here."

"How so?"

She couldn't believe he didn't see it. "Well – you're still engaged to Angela. But you've said you love me. It's a bit awkward."

There was a brief reassuring smile, a fleeting flash of the deep, deep brown eyes, a momentary glimpse of the white teeth. "I told you. Don't worry. It's not a problem."

Lit picked her words carefully. She didn't want to make him angry again, but she didn't want to back down. "Conrad, please try to understand. It's not fair to either of us – not to Angela – not to me."

"Don't put pressure on me, Lit," he said brusquely. "I don't like that."

"But I'm not – I'm simply trying to explain – "

He flung his napkin aside angrily. "You women – you're all the same! You can't wait to nail a man down – that's all you want!"

Lit watched in amazement across the table. There was obviously some mistake, something she had forgotten to say, something he didn't realise.

"But I haven't tried to nail you – I kept cool. You were the one who – "

"I was the one who what? I told you I love you, but that doesn't mean I have to change my life this minute. I can't deal with it now. I have the enquiry, the development, and all that stuff. Just get off my back!" He took a quick swallow from a third glass of wine.

This wasn't fair. "I don't think it's too much to ask that you clear things up with Angela."

When he didn't reply, she rested her knife and fork quietly on the plate, placed her crumpled napkin on the table and stood up with as much dignity as she could muster. She was beginning to feel awful. She had a foolish urge to rush home to Dandy so that he would pat her on the head and tell her she was great and everything would be fine. She could feel tears burning up through the back of her eyes.

"I'd better go," she choked and retrieved her bag and briefcase from the sofa.

Suddenly he was by her side. He grabbed her by the shoulders, his face clouded in some fog of emotions that she couldn't fathom. "Please. I've had a tough day," he said, his voice softer than before.

"That's why I think I should go. We've both had a tough few weeks and I should really get home to Richie."

But even as she was saying that she should get home to Richie, she was paralysed by the feel of Conrad's hands on her shoulders, his breath on her face. Her whole body tingled with wanting him. The bag and briefcase dropped to the floor. Conrad bent and nibbled on her ear, then his hand slid up beneath her silk blouse and stroked her hardening nipples.

"Don't go! Please!" he said, his voice rasping.

She swallowed and could find no polite words to express the lava-flow of lust which was threatening to engulf her. But she wasn't sure if Conrad was the type of man to appreciate a woman who talked dirty so she said nothing.

He slowly undid her blouse, cupping her breasts in his hands and whispering in her ear what he wanted to do to her. Even hearing his words and imagining it all in her head, while he was still only at the stage where he was sliding her blouse down to the floor, made her want to scream "Now! Now! Do it now!"

But he didn't. He slid his hand down across her smooth stomach, gently brushing against her pubic hair and found her wet and swollen, screaming to be stroked and caressed and filled with the pleasure of him.

"You are so fucking sexy," he said, as he lay her on the bed and pulled every last stitch of clothing from her. Then he was naked beside her, his tongue flickering across her breasts, pressing himself rock-hard against her. His lips sought her out, parting her light pubic hair and pressing gently on her, then making tiny licks of his tongue until she was ready to scream out from the exquisite pleasure of it. At last he slid into her, hot and hard, almost roughly now, kneeling above her to drive himself more deeply into her. She was weak with the base animal sensation of it and gave herself up to precious quivers and shudders of orgasm as Conrad fell beside her sweat-drenched and sated.

By the time that Lit got round to looking at her watch it was almost midnight. She called home, but there was no reply. She showered quickly and dressed even more quickly. Conrad lay spread on the bed in delicious full-nude profile – like a tanned, naked gladiator. He looked like he might fall asleep at any moment. She sat on the edge of the bed and stroked his chest affectionately.

"About Angela," she said. "I'm sorry to keep bringing it up – but you must do something. I can't go on like this. It's wrong."

She half-expected more scowls and accusations about trying to snare him. But he said nothing for a while, then his face creased into a mischievous grin.

"What's so funny?" she asked. "It's hardly something to joke about."

She ran her fingers affectionately through his hair, anxious not to provoke another angry outburst.

"I suppose I'd better tell you."

She froze. "Tell me what?" That he had no intention of leaving Angela? That Angela was the mother of his love-child? That he was already secretly married to Angela? That Angela was really a man and that he was a closet gay?

"I made her up."

She thought she hadn't heard him right. "What do you mean?"

"I made her up. She isn't real."

"She isn't real? As in . . .?"

"As in, she doesn't exist."

She didn't believe it. She even giggled and poked him in the ribs and told him to stop being such a tease. But he didn't laugh, he didn't say anything, and an ominously long silence settled between them.

Lit felt obliged at last to consider the possibility – however daft. Only as soon as she began to think about it, suddenly it didn't seem daft at all. When had she ever seen Angela? There weren't even any photos of her around the apartment. Angela hadn't been able to make it to Lit's party. She didn't seem to play any significant role in Conrad's business life either. Lit had wondered why a fiancée would not be at her partner's side throughout all the trouble with the residents and the press, and especially now with him facing down a tribunal. Up to now, she'd simply assumed Angela had a busy life of her own.

But wait a minute! Hadn't she spoken to a woman on the phone when she'd called him the day after the party? Surely that was Angela? Wasn't it? And who did the Van Cleef & Arpels perfume belong to, if not Angela?

"But I spoke to her on the phone, didn't I? I borrowed her perfume, didn't I?"

"No. You just assumed it was her."

Her heart was sinking faster than the Titanic, plunging to some dark frightening place. She longed to end the conversation and escape. But she knew she had to go on – to find out the truth once and for all.

"Then who was it that I spoke to?"

Conrad frowned, his jaw tightening slightly. "Who knows? Damned if I can remember."

The casualness of the remark shot through her, frightened her. But now anger drove her on.

"You can't remember! You had a woman in your room, barely days after you and I . . . after we . . . and you can't remember?"

"It could have been my sister, for all I know. I don't keep a visitor's book! I see lots of people every day. As for the perfume – someone probably left it behind. But it certainly wasn't Angela – because she doesn't exist."

Then Lit remembered. Of course Angela existed! The engagement had been in the paper. Lit distinctly remembered seeing it one Saturday morning in *The Irish Times*, over a year ago. She remembered, because Bonnie was having coffee with her on the patio and they'd spent quite a while speculating about what Angela might be like.

"But I saw the announcement in the paper!"

"A fake," he said simply.

She ought to have been delighted, thrilled to have the way to his heart utterly clear without any obstacles, at last. But instead she felt deeply perturbed.

"Then I don't understand," she said at last.

He sighed patiently as though he was explaining something really quite simple to someone who really ought to understand. "I repeat! Angela doesn't exist. I am not engaged to anybody called Angela. I am not engaged to anyone. I don't know anyone called Angela."

She felt dizzy, her stomach churning horribly. Either he had lied to her before or he was lying to her now. Which was it?

And if he'd lied about this – what other lies had he told? What bigger deceits was he capable of? What Bonnie had said in the Cartagena Club flashed into her mind – that he was a crook, that he liked to get what he wanted, that he was always master of his own destiny.

She couldn't think straight any more, felt horribly nauseous and close to throwing up. She stood up shakily from the bed and walked out onto the balcony, bare-footed.

She leaned against the railing, barely noticing the delightful river view now.

Conrad had slipped into shorts and T-shirt and followed her. Now he was standing close to her.

"Lit, please! Hear me out at least. I never expected you to be so upset about this. I can explain it all."

He tried to put his arm about her, but she shrugged him away. Then she turned and faced him.

"Is it true?" she asked simply.

He nodded and suddenly she could feel a terrible rage bubbling up inside her, hot tears threatening to spill forth.

"Why?" She could barely utter the word.

"You want the truth?"

"It would be helpful at this point. Don't you think? In the end truth is always a gift."

He went inside briefly, poured two brandies and re-appeared. Lit held the drink in her hands, but didn't even take a sip. Conrad drained his glass in three sharp gulps.

"Because I was fed up to the teeth being touted in every newspaper and gossip magazine as 'Ireland's Most Eligible Bachelor'. The whole thing was getting out of control – like being a pop star or something. I couldn't go to a function without women launching themselves or their daughters, or their friends, or their friends' sisters' cousins at me. Don't get me wrong – it was fun for a while – but they're all so transparent, even the ones who think they're being incredibly subtle. I could nearly see the dollar signs light up in their eyes when they saw me coming. Have you any idea how many gold-digging, money-grabbing unattached women there are in this country?"

Listening to him, she almost understood his strange logic, almost found herself agreeing. Until she remembered that he'd deliberately misled her, allowed her to agonise over stealing another woman's man. Probably he'd got some perverse kick out of seeing her wrestle so violently with her conscience. She wouldn't put it past him. And what about the monumental arrogance of what he'd done? The sheer vanity of assuming that every woman who looked his way was after him, after his money, after his status?

"Poor you!" she said sarcastically. "My heart bleeds."

"Look, it really all started as a joke. Fergus Cunningham, my solicitor, was the one that suggested it and it was a joke that got a bit out of hand. A silly joke, and I should never have agreed to it. I realise that now. And then I met you. You didn't seem to care one bit about how much money I had and we hit it off. I was going to tell you when this whole stupid tribunal business was finished. You see, I thought we might have some sort of future together – I mean a long-term future. I've never even considered marriage before – but now . . ."

Lit stared at him, her jaw hanging in amazement now. She was gobsmacked.

"H-h-how dare you!" she stammered when she got her breath back.

"How dare I what?"

"How dare you make a fool of me like that! I've agonised over being involved with someone's else's fiancée, lain awake at night, wracked with guilt whenever I thought of it, worried about Angela and fretted about how she would cope with you going off with me. And you've let me worry and fret about it even throughout my father's death and funeral. Because your adolescent little joke got a little out of hand? How could you be so self-centred, so callous? And now you have the gall to talk about a long-term future together!"

Now it was Conrad's turn to be gobsmacked. "I don't

understand. I thought you'd be pleased and relieved."

"Pleased? At being made to look like a total fool? Of all the vain, selfish, deceitful, arrogant things to do! As far as I'm concerned, I never want to see you again!" She was shouting angrily now.

She struggled to regain control of her temper, but at the same time she wanted to punch him in the face. She placed her glass down carefully on the table, then retrieved her shoes from the dining-room. When she returned to the balcony, she felt strangely composed.

"Just tell me one thing before I go. How come some gossip columnist never figured it out?"

"That's the amazing thing. We waited and waited for someone in the tabloids to come sniffing around – but they never did. I didn't intend for it to go on for so long – you have to believe me . . ."

But Lit was heading for the door.

She arrived home in a state of blood-thumping rage – barely able to speak to Bonnie who was rustling up a late-night cup of tea in the kitchen.

"You took your time," said Bonnie. "I went and collected Richie in the end."

"Thanks."

"He's in bed."

"Grand."

"If I had known what sort of party it was – I wouldn't have taken him."

Lit felt a strong urge to consult horoscopes or scientific charts. Was this 'Everybody-act-bizarre-on-account-of-clusters-of-positively-charged-ions-in-the-atmosphere Day'? Bonnie Ballantyne was making sniffy remarks about parties which were unsuitable for Richie! As if it was even any of her business.

"I'm serious, Lit. Did you check this Simon person out?"

"Not in person – but Richie said he was OK – and after all I've had other things on my mind these last few days. You won't believe what Conrad has just told me!"

"Never mind Conrad. Your son is upstairs in his bed, out of his head on drink and heaven knows what else?"

"No! He promised – "

"Do you know there was cocaine at that party? That's the sort of person this Simon Whatsit is."

It was a rare enough occurrence for Bonnie to be really angry – but she loved Richie like he was her own son. After all, she'd been there with him since birth, watched him take his first steps, knew his favourite soccer team, always brought him back a box of his favourite chocolate-covered pretzels when she went to New York.

Lit froze. It was frighteningly well within the bounds of possibility that there would be cocaine at a teenage party. Once upon a time, a line of coke was something only super-rich models and fragile-egoed actors could get access to. But now it was as common as salt. It was dangerous too because dealers would cut all sorts of other stuff into it to get their money's worth. A few years ago, she'd been at a super glamorous party in Malahide and her host had tried to cajole her into snorting a few lines herself. It would, she was eagerly informed, get her in the party mood. She was mildly tempted, but when she heard one of the other guests saying that it was like sticking Andrews Liver Salts up her nose, Lit gave it a miss. When she had related the episode to Bonnie, she was horrified that Lit even considered trying it. "I mean think of it!" said Bonnie. "You would have just stuck something up your nose which in all probability made it into this country by being shoved up someone's bum. It's hardly glamorous now, is it?" They'd had a good laugh about it at the time.

But she wasn't amused now. "Did Richie . . . do cocaine?"

"No, he didn't. At least that's what he says. But who's to know for sure? He shouldn't be mixing with those people. You should devote more time to him. If you don't – you could lose him."

Lit shook her head. "Not Richie. He's too sensible."

Bonnie raised an eyebrow. After ten years of teaching them, she knew all about the unpredictable world of teenagers. "I see it happen every day of the week. And they're always the nicest kids. Because the nasty kids are too obsessed with throwing their weight around to go near drugs."

Lit sighed and fell into Dandy's old chair. She missed him so much now. He would know just what to say to Richie to steer him in the right direction. And she was angry with her son. He'd promised her never to touch drugs again, not to get drunk again. Now he'd broken the promise. And instead of being sympathetic to her plight, Bonnie was accusing her of neglecting him.

"I'll go up to him now," she said.

"That's not a good idea. Let him sleep it off if he can. But you need to talk in the morning. You need to find a way to spend more time with him. I mean it, Lit. If you don't – you will lose him. He's never needed you more that he needs you now – even though he doesn't show it."

Lit promised herself she would deal with it in the morning. In the morning she would make clear to Conrad that there was nothing further between them and then he would be nothing but a client. She had done all the important work on the Budd campaign, Matt could take it over now. Then she would select a number of other contracts and pass them on to Maura. She would cut down on her hours of work and have more time for her son. She knew she'd got her priorities wrong. But it wasn't too late to change.

"There were a few calls," said Bonnie. "Auntie Sheila asking if you'd found a bereavement counsellor." Bonnie laughed weakly . Lit couldn't even raise a smile. "Well, now – who else? Matt wanted to know if you needed company. Maura called to ask if you were OK and said to tell you she had sorted out the business with Barry Owens and his mother – whatever that meant?"

Ordinarily Lit's curiosity would have got the better of her and she would have called Maura on the spot. But she had enough troubles of her own right now.

"And Seán Tallon left a message."

"What did he want?" Lit shifted uneasily. She wasn't sure if she should tell Bonnie about the kiss on the beach.

"Just wanted to thank you for looking at the house with him."

"To be honest, I could have done without the hassle. I mean, I was doing him a big favour."

Bonnie bit her lip and said nothing. The plain facts of the matter were that Seán had any number of people who could have gone to see the house with him. Lit wasn't doing him a favour. It was exactly the opposite. Only she was too pig-headed to see it.

"Anyway," said Bonnie, her good humour completely restored, "what's this about Conrad. What did he tell you?"

Lit sighed and tried to find the words to tell Bonnie about Conrad.

It was barely more than a year ago that she'd sat in the garden with Bonnie, reading the engagements column in *The Irish Times*.

"Another one to cross off the list," Bonnie had murmured from behind the newspaper.

"Who is it this time?" Lit had asked, only vaguely interested.

Bonnie had heaved a large and world-weary sigh. "Angela Butler, from County Meath, whoever you are – I solemnly pledge to hate and despise your guts and gizzards for all eternity – "

"Who is it?" Lit cut in impatiently.

"Well, it appears that Angela Butler, whoever she is, has managed to do what half the women of Dublin have been failing miserably to do for almost a decade now."

"Jesus, Bonnie – I hate it when you spin things out. Give it here!"

Lit snatched the paper and scanned the engagements column. When she saw that Angela had managed to snap up Conrad, she remembered feeling vaguely curious and a little sad.

"I hope they'll be very happy together," she had said coolly.

"Yes, I hope so too," agreed Bonnie, "but, I have to say, it won't be easy for her."

"No, she'll have her work cut out and I don't envy her at all."

"Me neither. Not a bit. I. Don't. Envy. That. Poor. Girl. One. Bit!" said Bonnie adamantly. "I mean, take for instance the sort of people he mixes with – royalty, jet-setters – that will be hard for her coming from County Meath. Remember whatsername who took to vomiting and hiding the Mars Bars in shoeboxes when she married above her station and she was already an aristocrat

– so what tiny hope is there for Angela Butler?"

"True," Lit agreed. "And another thing I'd be really concerned about if I was her – and this is why I'm so glad that I'm not her – is that he's had so many beautiful women already – she'll have to be up at the crack of dawn to do her hair and her face and her nails and she won't be allowed to have a bad hair day or have water retention for a few days or get spots or anything – "

No! They hadn't envied Angela one little bit.

"So?" asked Bonnie now.

"He's just so arrogant," Lit replied evasively.

"Then why are you so low? That's Conrad. That's the way he is."

"Why do you keep saying that? 'That's Conrad.' It's really annoying."

Bonnie bit her lip and didn't answer.

"Angela doesn't exist," Lit said simply.

"So? That's great news. He's done the decent thing and sent her packing. Then the field is clear for you –"

"No, Bonnie – you're not listening. Angela *doesn't exist.*"

"Do you mean she's dead? Oh my God – but when –"

"She *never* existed. There is no such person as Angela Butler, dentist's daughter from County Meath."

"Then who was he engaged to if it wasn't Angela?"

"No-one! He was engaged to no-one."

"Yeah, right!" said Bonnie, looking at her friend oddly.

"Bonnie will you listen! Angela Butler doesn't exist. He made her up. He's not engaged to anyone. He doesn't know any Angela Butler!"

"Says who?"

"Says Conrad."

"What!" Bonnie gaped at Lit as the penny finally dropped. "But – but the engagement announcement –

the wedding plans – all the stuff – how – "

"Why is the question? Apparently to keep all the females pursuing him at bay."

Bonnie was rarely puzzled by anything – but now she had the look of a person who was utterly at sea and she did that strange thing that people do when they are puzzled – she made funny faces into the air at no-one in particular, her head shifting from side to side like a Siamese dancer.

"The chancer!" she exclaimed finally and squealed in girlish amazement. "The jammy dodger!"


# CHAPTER 33

A sudden and loud banging woke Lit abruptly from her troubled sleep. Her head was pounding and she felt disorientated. She was aware through a hazy mist, that some awful things had happened to her in the past few weeks, but for the life of her she couldn't remember them.

She sat swaying on the bed, trying to make sense of the digital numbers on the clock. Was it a one or a seven? Was it morning or evening? Why was she so sad? By the grey half-light she figured it was seven in the morning. She shuffled into the bathroom, splashed cold water on her face and dragged on a light cotton dressing-gown. The woman in the mirror was hardly recognisable – gaunt, expressionless, dead. She almost jumped with the fright.

Then she remembered Dandy and how he wasn't there any more and how the house felt melancholy and empty. He had filled it with his own brand of cantankerous wit and wisdom. His stubbornly direct slant on life, for all its contrariness, had been a bulwark against the shallow craziness of life in the fast lane. She had been annoyed and embarrassed by all his old-fashioned ideas, his prehistoric clothes, his refusal to rate anything that happened after 1960 (except one or two All Ireland Finals), his outrageous sexism and lecherous chauvinism. Now she missed all those things. There was nothing to kick against any more. Then she remembered Richie and the cocaine party and cold shivers of panic ran up and down her spine – the sort of cold shivers only a mother can feel – primeval, animal and quite fierce. Lastly she remembered Conrad. Conrad who said he loved her, Conrad who didn't seem capable of telling the truth, Conrad who had made a fool of her. She felt horribly numb and worse, a feeling she thought she'd left behind forever, left behind with her old moon boots and green leggings, left behind with Mary Dempsey and her surgical stockings, left behind with Harry Menton and his receding hairline. Lit felt deeply uncertain. The cool confidence which had carried her to the pinnacle of success had simply evaporated overnight.

She remained in front of the mirror, not because she was having a deep moment of insight, or an 'Oh my God, it's finally time for the facelift' moment, but because she couldn't think of what else to do. She knew she had to go to Richie and do or say something – but it was too early. He would still be asleep. And she was deeply afraid. Suppose he had taken cocaine. What next? Snorting heroin, then injecting the stuff into his fine young body. She couldn't bear to think of it, but she couldn't force the harrowing image from her mind.

She stood in a horrible trance until she heard the banging noise again. She couldn't think what it might be or what she ought to do about it.

It was her hands that began to tremble first, slightly to begin with and then almost uncontrollably. She tried picking up a toothbrush. She was able to hold it, but when she began spreading the paste, the tube shot out of her grasp and went flying into the toilet. Then the shaking spread to her legs and she thought she was going to buckle over. The rim of the polished granite counter provided some support as she tried counting to ten to calm herself. But she couldn't get past three. She felt light-headed, hot and cold at once, prickly all over, sweaty and parched at the same time.

Whenever Bonnie mentioned a panic attack, Lit always scoffed and remarked tartly that if only people would spend a little more time and effort planning and managing their time, if only they exercised regularly and went to bed at a reasonable hour, drank and smoked less – they wouldn't have panic attacks. In fact, Lit sensibly concluded – there were no such thing as panic attacks.

And of course this wasn't a panic attack as such. It was simply that her hands and legs were shaking and she felt like she was panicking – which was entirely different to actually having a panic attack.

She tried talking to herself in the mirror. It was a tacky, B-movie approach, but it might work.

"Pull yourself together! Pull yourself together now! Stop this nonsense and pull yourself together at once! You are going to pull yourself together now – this instant!"

She pointed her index finger at herself like in an army-recruitment ad – but her finger trembled like the palsied bony digit of an old Shakespearean witch. And each time she spoke her voice grew weaker and shakier.

In the distance, like the sound of faraway thunder, the knocking continued and she realised that it must be someone at the door. Somehow, she dragged herself to the top of the stairs. She had to take each step carefully because the stairs seemed to shift beneath her like quicksand and she held onto the curved mahogany banister with two hands like an elderly invalid.

She wondered if it might be Conrad at the door, begging for forgiveness, prostrate on the doorstep with shame and remorse.

But when she opened the door, it was not Conrad at all, and she realised that she had been hoping against hope it would be him. She wanted him to come and redeem himself. She would be icy to begin with, would chastise him and tell him that she would have to think long and hard about marrying him, would speak to him from the lofty heights of dignified sorrow and restrained indignation. That would put him through the hoops for sure. He'd eat out of her hand after that. She'd be sad and distant but noble and self-controlled.

Slouched in an expensive but baggy-looking linen jacket, leaning against the brickwork and sucking on a bruised cigarette like a condemned man, was Matt. He was unwashed, unshaven and smelt of a night's beer and stale tobacco.

"Matt!"

"Can I come in?"

She held the door open, shakily trying to make sense of a visit from her partner at seven in the morning. But she couldn't. Her thoughts became jumbled, disordered, her mind anxious and perturbed. He began telling her something, but she couldn't make sense of it. She watched in horror as words which she couldn't decipher came tumbling out of his mouth. He was drunk. There was no other explanation. His mouth was open, the sounds were escaping, but they made no sense.

"Lit! Lit! Are you OK?"

She nodded uncomprehendingly. Why was he asking her that? He was the one talking gibberish. The trembling and shaking began again in earnest and she cursed Matt for leaving the door open so early in the day. She opened her mouth to tell him so – but no sound came out. Instead the ground really did turn to quicksand this time and she sank down unconscious to the floor.

It seemed like only moments later that she woke and found herself stretched out on the sofa covered with Dandy's old Foxford rug that smelt of cigars, and surrounded by Bonnie, Matt and Richie.

"OK, Mum?"

She nodded weakly.

"Cup of tea?" suggested Bonnie.

Lit nodded again.

She eased herself up to a sitting position on the sofa. She wasn't feeling much better, but at least she was able to think a little more clearly, at least she could understand what people were saying.

"What was that all about?" asked Matt with casual concern.

"Panic attack," said Bonnie.

"Nonsense!" Lit snapped.

"What would you call it then?" asked Matt.

"It was just the shock of the cold air. Why didn't you shut the door? And what the hell are you doing here at seven in the morning anyway?"

Matt pursed his lips, scratched his head and reached for a cigarette.

"Please don't smoke. I'll get sick."

He rammed the squashed packet back into his pocket petulantly.

"Is there something wrong? Is it Conrad? Has something happened to him? Oh my God!" She threw the rug to one side and tried to stand up.

"Nothing like that," said Matt. "You're going to find out sooner or later so here goes. The Cornwells have done a bunk."

"Sorry?"

"Done a bunk – as in gone, scarpered, disappeared, the Bermuda Triangle, vamoosed, exeunt without a fanfare of trumpets. We're in trouble."

Trouble? A mere few months ago, she'd been careering along in red-BMW-I'm-rich-and-life's-never-been-better Heaven. Now the whole world seemed to be falling away in chunks around her.

"How bad?" She was wide-awake now – and still, very still. "I said – how bad?"

"Bad enough to have to go to the bank. They might decide to call in our loans if they don't have confidence in our ability to pay. If that happens we're very vulnerable. We're up shit creek in a leaky boat, without so much as a bucket, and the paddle will be totally redundant. Tallon tried to warn me – but I wouldn't listen."

"Seán tried to warn you? You never said."

Matt shrugged. It didn't seem important at the time. After all, the Cornwells were only one account. Shiels Doran could easily survive without them. But they were a big account and the company has invested a lot of its own money in putting together a campaign that would meet Dara Cornwell's stringent standards. Every bit of work done by the graphics company or the film company or even the bloke who composed the ghastly free-style flute music Dara insisted on using, had to be paid for – even if none of it was ever used. And now none of it would ever be used. Dara had disappeared into thin, organic and completely genetically unmodified air, taking the delightfully dippy Poppy with him. Matt wondered did she go or was she pulled?

"I have to go and meet the bank people. Who knows what they'll say, but my guess is that it won't be good. So we may as well prepare for the worst." He stood up and smiled down at her apologetically. "Sorry to be the bearer of more bad news."

"Maybe it won't be as bad as you think."

"Maybe," he said gloomily, his eyes hanging down at half-mast, his whole large awkward frame weighed down with worry.

Richie brought her a plate of hot buttered toast and more tea. Hot buttered toast was one of the great culinary inventions. If Lit was ever sent to a desert island, the thing she would most miss was hot buttered toast and piping hot breakfast tea. Nothing from champagne to caviare, from lobster to Lynch Bages came remotely near to toast and tea for soothing the palate.

Richie sat down hesitantly at the end of the sofa.

"Mum – about last night – "

Lit racked her brains. Now what was it the coping with adolescence experts said she should do with this youth on the verge of manhood that she was so utterly responsible for? Perhaps she should explain yet again about the dangers of drugs? Perhaps she should remind him of the down and out junkie story?

"Drugs can spoil your entire life," she began, ready to deliver the lecture. But one glance at his strained face stopped her in her tracks.

"OK. I'm listening," she said.

"I got drunk. I know I shouldn't have, but I did. Everybody at the party was much drunker than I was. I only had four cans of cider."

"Did you have anything else?"

"How do you mean?"

"I mean, did you take any drugs?"

He said nothing. He wanted to tell her all the things that kept him awake at night, like how he cried himself to sleep sometimes because she hadn't thought his father was good enough to marry. How he sometimes cried because he didn't have Dandy any more. Now she seemed to be friendly with Conrad Budd and had spent the evening with him instead of driving Richie to the party as she had promised. What if she married Conrad Budd? Then her whole life would centre around him and Richie would be left out, too young to go jet-setting around the world with them, too old and too independent to be taken care of by them. What if she decided to pack him off to boarding school for his final years in school? He had never felt lonely before, but since his grandfather's death large gaping holes were appearing in his life. This was supposed to have been his Summer of Love and Lazy Fun, when he would lose his virginity and hang out with his mates and chill in the easy and warm comfort of his own home, doing nothing in particular, before going to stay with his father in Berlin for a month. Instead, he'd had death and abandonment.

"If I tell you the truth, you'll only get mad at me."

"No! I promise. I won't get mad at you. Just tell me the truth. I love you and I care about what happens to you."

"Then here goes. I did."

"Did what?"

"Take something."

Lit swallowed hard. She pulled the rug over her, try-

435

ing hard to conceal the fact that her body was trembling uncontrollably again. She waited for the worst.

"Simon's big brother works in the music business."

She nodded to encourage him.

"Well, he gets all sorts of things – drugs, I mean. And Simon's parents are pretty laid back and cool about that sort of thing."

Simon's parents wouldn't be so laid back and cool by the time Lit was finished with them. Already she was preparing to drive out to Enniskerry and give them a piece of her mind. In her head, she imagined them as aging hippies who'd made a pile of money from selling leather belts in the seventies. They were probably the sort of parents who tried to be cooler and more hip than their own kids.

Richie shifted uneasily on the end of the sofa. "I wasn't going to take anything. I really wasn't. Then Simon said I would be a complete wimp if I didn't do a line of coke. I told him it had nothing to do with being a wimp and that I just wasn't interested. But he kept it up, following me around the house, slagging me in front of Barney and the others."

"Did Barney take anything?"

"He smoked a bit of a joint. That's all. He said he couldn't take any coke because it would react with the body-building stuff he takes for rugby and Simon believed him."

"So what happened then?"

"Then, just to get him off my back, I told him to set up a line and I'd snort it."

Her worst fears were coming true. She was full of rage at her son that he would be so weak and so easily bullied by his peers. But she was full of pity for him also. He was in an awful state.

436

"He set the line out on the table, showed me what to do and handed me the top of a biro tube. I sat down on the sofa and leaned forward with the tube in my hands. I really didn't want to, Mum. You must believe me."

What did it matter now if she believed him or not? Perhaps she should just book him into a clinic straight away – some place down the country where they would make him slop out and peel potatoes all day long?

"Go on. Just tell me the worst."

"I put the tube up to my nose and bent down. Then I couldn't help it. You know I get terrible hayfever. And I kept asking you where the hayfever remedy was and you kept telling me to look in the bathroom cabinet. Only it wasn't there. Anyway, I just sneezed and the powder went all over the place. Simon and his brother started calling me every name under the sun and all the other guys laughed and sniggered at me for being such a dork. Except for Barney and Dave who told Simon he was a stupid prick anyway. Then I tried to call you to come and collect me, but your mobile was off. In the end, I got through to Bonnie and she came and got me. I'm really sorry, Mum."

She felt a mixture of relief and anger. "I don't know what to say. You were going to take the stuff. It was just luck that you didn't."

"But only because they were slagging me. And the point is I didn't take it and I was really relieved. But it wasn't much fun being slagged."

"They don't sound like good mates to me – except for Barney and Dave."

"I won't go near them any more. Don't worry."

"I wish I could believe that."

"I promise, Mum. I really do."

"Don't tell me that wasn't a panic attack," said Bonnie later when Richie had gone off to work.

"Matt just left me standing in the cold – that's all. It was a brief and sudden chill and I'm fine now."

"Don't be ridiculous – you were barely coherent, a gibbering mess of nerves and panic."

"It's a bit early in the day for words like coherent."

"Whatever. Now you are going to lie here with tea and newspapers and Dandy's Foxford rug and you are not going to move until I see a bit of colour in your cheeks."

Bonnie pushed her back down on the sofa, plumped up a couple of cushions behind her head and tucked the rug around her legs. Lit thought of resisting, but found that she didn't have any strength. And it was nice to be mothered for a change, nice to be told to lie still and get better. She didn't do it very often. She couldn't remember the last day she had stayed at home sick, but it had probably been when she was working for Devlin Satchwell. Over the past few years, even if she was dying on her feet, she always dragged herself in to work.

"I'll lie here for three hours and then I'll go to work. Satisfied?"

"You'll lie there until I say so."

Lit sipped a little more of her tea and then sank back down into the cosy warmth of the rug. It was a great relief to discover that she could think straight again and that her mind wasn't a jumble or a tangled mess of disordered and frantic thoughts any more. On reflection, things weren't so bad. Richie's confidence was a bit bruised from the incident at Simon's party, which made her terribly angry and she would deal with it in due course. But otherwise he was fine. Matt's news wasn't good but the Cornwells was a setback rather than a disaster. She found herself thinking about poor Poppy Cornwell, dragged off to South America or somewhere and forced to wear clothes woven out of hemp and eat green bananas and swamp grass for the rest of her very compulsory natural life. Inside Poppy Cornwell was a normal woman trying weakly but desperately to get out. And now she never would. Instead she would spend the rest of her compulsory natural life meekly obeying Dara and gorging herself furiously on chocolate behind the palm-tree hut, like a naughty schoolgirl having a subversive puff of tobacco behind the bike-shed.

In the cold light of day, the news about Angela's non-existence didn't seem so catastrophic. It would be foolish to turn down the chance of long-term happiness with a man like Conrad, simply over a misunderstanding. She had to be sensible. She was thirty-five and men like Conrad didn't come along every day, especially not to thirty-five-year-olds.

It wasn't a frantic biological clock thing about having children. Richie was enough to be getting on with and she didn't lie awake at night fretting about babies or shrinking wombs. But in any circumstances, most women would give their eye-teeth to be marrying Conrad. He was the ultimate trophy husband. Though she didn't see him as a trophy at all. She loved him. The fact that she could forgive him for his callous behaviour was proof that she loved him.

As if on cue, the doorbell rang and this time it was Conrad.

When he saw her stretched out on the sofa, looking weak and frail, he almost broke down with shame.

"This is all my doing. I'm a bastard, Lit. I'm really sorry, but you don't have to forgive me. I'll understand. I'm just a sorry bastard."

He stood sheepishly on the Persian rug, hands shoved in his pockets, a look of abject shame and embarrassment on his handsome face.

She was too weak to say anything and anyway she didn't know what to say. Lofty indignation was all very well, but he was doing that little-boy thing of ducking his head and looking down glumly at his shoes, and occasionally pulling sheepishly at his earlobe.

"I'm not worthy of you," he added with hoarse contrition. "Please just tell me to go away and put me out of my misery!"

It wasn't how Lit had imagined this conversation. She was supposed to be tearing strips off him.

"I'm a nasty little shite," he added with disarming candour.

She was supposed to tell him to get lost. And here he was telling himself to get lost. She wasn't having that.

"Conrad, last night – well, it was a bit of a shock, that's all. I was very angry."

He looked up at her, a brief glimmer of hope in his deep, deep brown eyes which faded almost instantly. "No! No, I won't have that! There's no excuse for what I did. None! I'll understand if you never want to see me again."

Then Lit began to cry and beg him to let her forgive him, that he was being too hard on himself, that he must think little of her love for him when he wouldn't even allow that she would or could forgive him. She went to him and wrapped her slender arms around him, holding her head tight to his chest and pleading with him not to leave.

"I don't deserve a woman like you," he murmured finally, pulling away. Then he reached into his pocket and pulled out a little box. He sat her down on the sofa and placed himself beside her. "If you insist that I'm for-given, and you're determined to believe that I'm not a complete bastard, then I want you to wear this."

He lifted the lid of the box and inside was the most beautiful diamond ring Lit had ever seen. It sparkled and glittered and screamed to be on her finger. He took her hand in his and slipped it over her slender knuckle.

"Now it's official," he said and kissed her long and hard.

Lit felt her heart dancing in her chest. It was almost too much joy to deal with. She gulped and swallowed and sighed and couldn't think of a single thing to say. Given the choice, she could have lain on the sofa happily admiring her glittering new prize for the rest of the day. He beamed at her, a broad smile of admiration and love that she would happily have drowned in. Did ever a man smile so lovingly at a woman before, she wondered?

"I will make you happy," she gurgled. "Oh, Conrad, I will make you so happy and proud and we'll be the per-fect couple and there's so much to talk about – I suppose we'd better keep it quiet for now – but later when things have settled - whether I'll continue with the business – sorry, I'm babbling – I'm just so excited – "

He squeezed her tight and ruffled her hair affection-ately. "Whoah! Slow down – all in good time!"

But he was smiling and she could see that he was happy too. She felt a whole new bond of trust drawing them closer together, a deeper understanding and acceptance. It was, after all, true love.

Bonnie was predictably underwhelmed by the big ring. "Peanuts to a man like Conrad. He probably has a draw-er full of them at home."

"And congratulations – I hope you'll be very happy together – I'm so happy for you both – it's a match made in heaven – may you have a long and happy life together! Do none of those little phrases occur to you at all?"

Bonnie raised a quizzical eyebrow. "No. Not really. But – well done. You've got an engagement ring from Conrad Budd. It must make you feel a wonderful sense of achievement."

"Bonnie, please, just this once, don't be so cynical. There's genuine love between us."

"Is that so? Then where did that panic attack come from? What was that all about? You came back from his place last night looking like a week-old corpse – and it wasn't just about Angela. I hope you know what you're letting yourself in for. And I'm sorry I can't be happier for you. But I don't believe you love him. I think you're just flattered that he would pick you – and that's a different thing entirely. Entirely!"

Friends like Bonnie only came along once in a lifetime. Lots of Lit's friendships from the past had foundered because they were based on ridiculous premises to begin with.

But she and Bonnie were soul mates, different but similar, a good contrast and not a bad match either. Together they had travelled from childhood through adolescence to adulthood. And they often speculated about how they would be when they were old.

"We'll be on zimmer frames in some old people's home and we'll be arguing about the remote control and fretting about the wrinkles in our surgical stockings and the bumps in our dentures – and I'll probably have the hots for some ancient old rugby player who's bent double and got a chewed-up face from his years in the scrum. You'll probably be real religious and spend all your time praying and fasting and going to bed at six o'clock in the evening. God, Lit, I don't want to get old at all – do you?"

"Not much!"

"But we'll still be friends, Lit. I can't imagine ever not having you as my friend."

It was true – life without Bonnie would be unimaginable somehow and so Lit stopped herself from firing an apocalyptic thermonuclear scud straight to Bonnie's epicentre.

"You're wrong, Bonnie. I do love Conrad. And in the interests of a long and beautiful friendship, we're best not to talk about it any more. You'll just have to get used to the idea of me being Mrs Conrad Budd."

# CHAPTER 34

The next few days passed in a flurry of activity. Each afternoon Conrad faced the enquiry and emerged with a sphinxlike smile and a suitably bland comment for the reporters. Brendan Browne wheezed about in front of the camera too, ominously threatening to bring further, more damaging evidence before the enquiry. Each evening and morning, news bulletins and newspapers covered more excruciatingly boring revelations about who said what to whom and when and where and why they had said it.

Lit never had much interest in political scandals. Now, having to study one at close quarters, she knew exactly why. With rare exceptions, they were painfully tedious. Maura was in total agreement.

"What do them fellows in tribunals do when there

isn't a tribunal? Like can you train to be a tribunalist? It would make a good career – plenty of work. I suppose sooner or later, someone will set up a course in Tribunal Studies. They have courses in every other feckin' thing."

"They're a necessary evil," Lit countered weakly.

"Yes, but do we all have to read about them? Pages and pages of transcripts and questions and answers and records and photos of bald little men in suits carrying documents?"

"Conrad has to clear his name. It's important."

"They're not going to stop his big development now. Unless something completely awful happened. As for his name, who cares? Do you? Barry Owens has said loads of nasty things about me but do I care? I couldn't give a continental shite! Let him say what he likes. The little slimeball!"

"It's not quite the same. Conrad is – you know – high profile – "

"You're not worrying about him, are you?"

Lit nodded with a small degree of pride.

"Well, don't. Just you keep your mind on the priorities."

"Priorities?"

"The dress, the guest list, the ring, the reception, the best man – the private cruise round the West Indies – "

"Maura! Those are the last things on my mind!"

It was a barefaced lie and Maura grinned at her in disbelief.

"OK," said Lit, "let's change the subject. Why have you been so chirpy lately? What did you do to Barry Owens? What did you buy in the hardware shop?"

Maura's face lit up. She had thought Lit was never going to ask about her how she had got revenge on

Barry Owens and she hadn't wanted to mention it for the past few days because Lit had enough on her plate. She poured two coffees and set them down on the desk with milk and sugar. Then she reached into the drawer of her desk and drew out two long, plump and extremely creamy chocolate éclairs.

"Not for me thanks," said Lit primly.

"Go on! I dare you! When was the last time you had anything with chocolate in it? It's real important for releasing the pheromones, you know."

"Pheromones?"

"Or something to do with pleasure- zones – or natural euphoria-inducing thingies – or happiness chemicals in the back of the brain – I don't know – anyway when was the last time – "

"As a matter of fact only a few days ago someone bought me a ninety-nine."

"Who?"

"A guy – dishy – quite interesting, but a bit of a skirt-chaser, I'd say."

"Who?"

"Your friend Pat Sullivan."

"Why did Pat Sullivan buy you an ice cream?"

"Maybe he fancies me."

Maura frowned.

"Nope! Don't see it."

"Maybe I fancy him."

Maura frowned again.

"He's got a great body," Lit added mischievously.

"Never noticed."

"Sort of lean and muscular – bet he's a tiger in bed – could go at it for hours, I'd say."

Maura gave her a vaguely dirty look. "You're married. Well, practically. Leave Pat Sullivan alone."

Lit could see the realisation of something slowly dawning on Maura's face and she was getting quite a kick out of it. She persisted with the mischief-making.

"I'm not married yet. And he's got those sexy green eyes and chiselled cheekbones – and now that I think of it, I quite fancy one last fling."

Maura took a large and very deliberate bite from her eclair and chewed with great concentration. Then she fixed Lit with a vaguely warning look from her large brown eyes.

"I got his phone number as well," Lit added.

"So?"

"So nothing. Just thought you might have some use for it, that's all." She retrieved the battered card from her bag and set it down on Maura's desk. Maura glanced at it and tossed it in the bin.

"See? Like I said – no interest!" she retorted and quickly immersed herself in re-drafting a letter to a client, forgetting all about Barry Owens, hardware and revenge.

The phone on Lit's desk rang and she dashed into her office to answer it. It might be someone with word of Conrad's fate. But it was only a prospective client wanting her to outline in some detail the complete nature of the service they would be getting from the company. She listened patiently, explained at length. There were more questions.

"Did you not receive our brochure?" she asked tetchily at last.

Yes, but they wanted it all explained in more detail. She drew a deep breath. Would they like to pop into the office and chat face to face? No! It wasn't necessary. If she would only clarify a few final points.

In the outer office, Maura took advantage of Lit's

absence to retrieve Pat Sullivan's card from the bin. She took a deep breath and quickly dialled his number before her courage deserted her.

He answered almost instantly and she felt oddly queasy at the sound of his voice. To begin with, the conversation was a bit stilted and awkward – work, holidays, mutual friends.

"So," he said finally, "were you just calling for a chat? Or did you want to ask me out on a date?"

She was gobsmacked. "No way!" she said a little too strongly. "You've got a big head on you, Pat Sullivan – that's for sure. I was only enquiring about the Stoneyfield protestors – it's part of my job."

"I see. Well, since you ask – they're all keeping very well and thanks for asking."

"You know right well that's not what I meant! Anyway, I'm also ringing to thank you. What did you say to the crowd that day we were in the car?"

"I told them you were a lap-dancer, coming round to entertain them."

"No way! What did you say really?"

"Nothing much. I told them the truth – that you were a really good friend and that you were only with Conrad Budd because of your job."

"And they believed ya?"

"They let you through, didn't they?"

"Suppose so. Anyway, I hear you're swanning around Dublin Castle these days eating ice cream with all sorts of people."

"Oh, Lit, your boss. I see. Well, so what? This business with Stoneyfield has temporarily thrown us together and actually she's lovely."

"Yeah. But it's well for some. Some of us have to work for a living."

He laughed. "Maura – I didn't know you cared."

"Cared about what?"

"About me!"

"I don't care one bit about you and that's the truth." She was surprised at how unconvincing she sounded.

"So even if I asked you out – you'd probably say 'no'?"

"No! I mean yes!"

She felt all hot and flustered, confused, shaken and stirred. One time, they'd been great friends and once or twice even teetered on the brink of romance. Then he'd gone and got a girlfriend and she'd searched Dublin for the love of her life and found Barry Owens.

"Will you come out with me or not?" he was saying now.

Maura was the designated office sharpshooter. She generally had a quick answer for everything. But now she could think of nothing clever to say at all.

"Ah, quit feckin' around, Pat Sullivan. I'm not in the mood for that kind of thing at all!" She sounded a lot more bossy and in control than she felt.

"Maybe I could get you in the mood," he said, with a strange new huskiness she didn't remember. It made her feel odd – like she was melting inside. "Maybe we could go to a nice little restaurant and eat oysters and drink champagne and take a stroll in the moonlight."

"I don't know," she said, wavering.

Then the door from Lit's office opened and Lit reappeared.

"OK. That's grand so. We'll do that," Maura said quickly and slammed down the phone.

Lit rummaged disinterestedly through a few papers on the desk. Then she took another hearty bite out of one of the eclairs and reminded Maura about Barry Owens.

It took Maura more than a few moments to gather her thoughts. Something strange had happened on the phone with Pat Sullivan and she couldn't quite explain it. She felt unaccountably pleased with herself. And when he said the thing about getting her in the mood, she had felt a gorgeous little tingle of pleasure somewhere beneath her belly button. She took a deep breath, ran her fingers through her mane of long chestnut-brown hair and began her tale of revenge.

"Hell hath no fury like a woman scorned!" she pronounced in tones of gravity and moral retribution.

"So what did you do?"

"An eye for an eye and a tooth for a tooth – "

"Maura – get on with it. Please!" begged Lit.

"I'm just setting the scene – even as we speak, Mrs Owens is hiding out in her house, terrified to show her face in the neighbourhood. I hear she's having her groceries and everything delivered. And Barry – well, he's taken to the drink."

"Correct me if I'm wrong, but hadn't he reached that stage a long time ago?"

"Yeah, but this time it's really bad – he has to have two cans of special-brew lager before he can even pass the front door."

"But tell me! What did you do?"

"Did you know that Barry Owens is a Chelsea supporter? Well, he is and his mother is too."

"And?" Lit was halfway through the eclair by now. She could leave the other half, but what was the point? She might as well scoff the rest. "Well, Chelsea are crap."

"In what way?"

Maura couldn't really think of an answer. "They just are. Believe me."

"OK. So Chelsea are crap. Go on!"

"Right – I have this friend who paints murals for a living – don't say this too loud, but he used to make a fortune up north during the troubles – he'd do grand paintings of King Billy on a horse on the gable ends of Protestant houses for the Loyalists and then he'd do tricolours and Wolfe Tone and that stuff on the gable ends of Catholic houses. Sometimes he'd have to work at night so the security forces wouldn't catch him. Well, one night he drank too much and got a bit mixed up – he went and painted King Billy on the Falls Road – and you can guess the rest. Well, he had to get out after that –"

"Maura, you know the oddest people!"

"Anyway, the reason I had to go to the hardware store was because he had given me a shopping list – twenty gallons of bright red paint – fifteen gallons of brilliant white – ten of yellow – "

"I'm not sure I like the sound of this."

"The Owens live in a nice, respectable housing estate – you know, all red brick and cobble-locked driveways. If one house gets a new front door with stained- glass panels or a weather-glaze porch – they all have to get one. They have competitions in the road for who has the best-kept window boxes and the most imaginative mixed borders. His mother always wins. She talks to her plants, you know."

"No wonder he's such a sad specimen."

"Anyway, last week Mrs Owens had to go down the country to visit her sister who's sick and Barry drove her. So the house was empty. I called Ian, told him the job was on, and he went there in the dead of night and did up the front of their house for them – in red and white – and bright yellow."

"What – in stripes or something?"

"No! Not stripes! The Manchester United Crest!"

450

"That's a crime!" Lit was horrified "What if you're arrested? And the neighbours and the lovely window boxes and the beautiful doors with the stained-glass panels – no wonder she's hiding out in the house!"

Maura smiled with blissful satisfaction. "If I have to go down for ten years – it will all have been worth it," she said, beaming with childish delight.

In the afternoon, and spurred on by Maura's dazzling success on the revenge front, Lit took time out to visit Simon Fitzpatrick's parents. Bonnie came along for moral support.

What all the Coping With Adolescence books had singularly failed to mention was what type of lethal weapon one should arm oneself with, when setting out to confront a pair of trendy liberal my-son-is-my-best-pal-type parents – people who had been responsible for putting her son through temptation, pain and deep humiliation. Lit gave it considerable thought. Bonnie felt that a bucket of slurry would be just the thing for a nice mock-Tudor front doorstep in Enniskerry, but where did someone living in Dublin 4 lay their hands on slurry?. Anyway, it was too disgusting. Maura offered her the leftovers of the Barry Owens Paint Project. Somehow Seán Tallon had got wind of the story too, and he called to say that he knew a very good barrister who would have Simon Fitzpatrick's parents up in court for supplying drugs to minors if she wished. But she didn't wish. She didn't want to do anything which would embarrass Richie further or cause him any pain or put him in an awkward position later with his friends.

An hour later, her car pulled up outside a vast mock-Tudor mansion about two miles from the village. The house stood in its own grounds and bore plenty of signs and hints to the passing public that these people had really 'arrived'. There were massive black and gold electronic gates and a long cobble-locked drive flanked with every gardening experiment from Japanese Tranquillity to Sunny Mediterranean terracotta pot jungle. On their own, each of these horticultural statements might have been quite appealing. But altogether they looked pretty disastrous.

"Oh, my God!" said Bonnie. "Look at that!" She read from an elaborately carved wooden placard. "The Oasis Garden!"

It was a circular patch of lawn, flanked by a path of sand and featuring three palm trees and a few cactuses. The pièce de résistance was a lifesize statue of a camel standing woodenly in the middle.

Bonnie was furious about the social inequality of it all. "Why is it always people with no taste who have the money to live in places like this?"

Lit barely heard. Her mind was focused on one thing only – savaging the leather-fringed, boho-chic, kaftan-wearing pair of imbeciles who were the parents of Simon Fitzpatrick.

"Wait here," she told Bonnie.

"No way! Richie is almost my kid too. We're in this together – whatever it is."

Lit rang the doorbell which chimed an appallingly clangy bit of classical music. She was mildly surprised that it didn't play a doleful tune by some long forgotten hippy group from the 1970s.

"Hang on a minute," said a disembodied but vaguely familiar voice over the intercom.

Auntie Sheila often said that it was a long road that had no turn in it, but until this moment Lit had never really understood what it meant. Now she knew. It meant – what goes around comes around. And what had gone around finally came around for Lit. Standing before her, in a helmet of stiffly laquered auburn hair, flicked out in Barbie-doll style, with not a flower or a boho-chic leather-fringed pair of boots in sight and wearing enough make-up to put Lily Savage in the shade, in a sheath of a tight-fitting black suit and heels to match – was her old sardonic friend with the laundry company – the acerbic Alice Madigan.

"Lit!"

"You!" was all she could think of for now.

"Come in!"

Speechless with amazement and rage, Lit stepped into the cavernous atrium that brimmed with elaborate stat-ues and bits of ethnic furniture from the four corners of the globe: Buddhas, Easter Island statues, Godess Kalis, Sile-na-gigs – the lot. There was not a bean-bag in sight.

"Can I offer you a drink?" said the svelte Alice, barely able to move in her tight black trousers and heels as high as the flick in her auburn hair.

"No. I'll get straight to the point," said Lit. "I'm here about the party the other night."

"Oh? Yes. I think they all enjoyed themselves."

"Oh, do you? Well, I have only one thing to say to you, Alice Madigan. If you or your son or any of your family as much as look at my son again, I'll have you up before the courts for supplying drugs to minors!"

"Oh really," said Alice with traces of her old acidity, "you're just like Simon's father – he doesn't agree with it either. But I say – hey – you know – at least the kids are experimenting in a safe environment. And there wasn't much of anything. We're not that stupid."

"Simon's father?"

"Yes. We don't live together any more. I moved here with my new partner a couple of years ago. He's not Simon's real dad."

"I'm not interested in your sleeping arrangements. And I'm not interested in your phoney liberal philosophy on life either. Just keep away from my son. And keep your son away from my son." Her voice cracked and wobbled with anger.

Alice laughed her crooked smile. "We'll see about that!" She started up the stairs. Then she turned back to Lit and Bonnie and added chattily, "He's just back from a long business trip. Let me tell him you're here."

Moments later, Lit and Bonnie heard the murmur of her voice filling her partner in on the situation. Then she came down again, swaying on the dangerously high heels.

"Here he is!" she said.

He descended the stairs in a short-sleeved pin-stripe shirt and casual trousers wearing his easy, unassuming smile. Lit noted that his receding hairline had almost completely disappeared, replaced by a very expensive and carefully tended hair-piece – complete with greying temples.

"Lit – what a charming surprise!" said Harry Menton. "So good to see you!"

He held out a hand which she ignored.

"So what is all this nonsense about?" He was charm personified, casually mixing drinks and gracefully accepting their refusal. He talked warmly about living in Enniskerry, the people, the golf courses, the food, the scenery, how after all he was a true son of Ireland.

In spite of being on a mission to avenge her son's humiliation, Lit would happily have turned and run at that point, except that Bonnie was blocking the door and flexing her hands as though she was planning to reach for a poker or something.

"Don't you dare leave, Lit Doran!" Bonnie hissed menacingly as they listened to Harry waffle on about being a true son of Ireland.

Alice leaned against the massive pine mantel, gleefully observing the unfolding drama. She had slipped out of her black jacket and was now proudly displaying a slightly flabby midriff beneath a cropped T-shirt. Her belly-button protruded over the rim of her tight black trousers. Bonnie regarded it with some horror.

Lit barely noticed the offending navel, not even when Harry ran his hand affectionately over it.

"I think I'm going to be sick," said Bonnie.

Lit took a deep breath. She had a number of choices – rant and rave, scream and shout, return after dark with malicious intent like Maura had done, hiss and spit venom, rage and scorn at the pair of them, smash a few vases, slash a few paintings, knock the heads off a few ethnic statues, burst into tears and tell Harry how much he'd hurt her, call him all the names to his face that she'd only ever called him in her head . . .

At last, when she'd gotten over the shock of finding out that he was back and living with Ireland's answer to the puff-adder, she got her second wind. She coolly surveyed the pair of them and realised that they were a match made in some place – not quite heaven – but they were a match all right.

"I'd appreciate it if you remove Simon from the school before the start of the new academic year."

"That's my Lit Doran!" murmured Bonnie.

"That's ridiculous," smirked Alice, clasping Harry's hand to her midriff. "You can't make us."

"No, of course not. But I imagine Simon will be asked

to leave anyway when the principal finds out that you allowed him to pass around a class A drug in your house."

"That's not fair!" said Alice, her jaw dropping way past her belly-button to the rim of her trousers.

"That's the way of the world, Alice. It's not a very fair place – as I expect you and your partner Harry here already know."

She turned to go, barely glancing at Harry.

"Oh, and by the way, if Richie ever hears one inkling of our conversation today – you'll have to hire the best barrister in town to keep you out of prison. That wouldn't be too good for the dirty-laundry business, now would it? Bye!"

Matt had spent the morning with the bank manager and he was a very chastened man when he slouched through the door of the office later in the afternoon.

"How did it go?" Lit asked in her most bright and breezy voice. It was essential to keep an air of optimism about the place.

He pulled a face, poured himself a coffee and led her into the inner office.

"We can't recruit any more staff. We'll have to postpone some of our plans – no move to a bigger premises – no company cars. They asked about the value of your house and my apartment . . ."

"And?"

He slurped the hot coffee. "And nothing. Just stuff about assets and what might happen if we couldn't pay our bills – you know, like the Cornwells. We're motoring. No worries. I had a chat with Tallon."

"What does he think?"

"He says, just wait and see what happens. He says not

to do anything drastic. Let the dust settle."

"That's it! That's what they pay him hundreds of thousands of euros for – dust settling! Did you find out anything more about the Cornwells?"

"Totally bankrupt. Owed money all over the place to suppliers. Dara misread the trends, and against Poppy's advice invested heavily in expensive organically grown produce and found that he had been undercut by all the major supermarket chains who have latched onto the organic thing. Couldn't get rid of the stuff. The backers called in hefty loans and the company collapsed overnight. House in Dalkey seized – everything gone overnight. Poor Poppy!."

"A tale for the times. The destructive power of market trends."

"Nothing to do with market trends. Cornwell was a man on a mission. It tends to colour the judgement."

Conrad called to tell her he was too tired to meet her for dinner as planned and that he was going home to have an early night. She tried not to sound hurt and rejected. But it felt like he didn't really need her at all. People who loved each other should be able to give support and understanding in times of trouble. Wasn't that what love was all about? Why did he want to marry her if he didn't want to share his sorrows as well as his joys with her? She called Bonnie for a chat and told her about Conrad being all cool and distant again. She had to bite her lip really hard when Bonnie said yet again, "That's Conrad for you."

At home, she made a seafood pasta with frozen sea food, white wine, dill and cream and she and Richie sat to table in the kitchen. She'd always sworn that when Dandy was no longer there, they would dine every evening in the elegant dining-room with the jade silk curtains, which looked out onto the back garden. But now she couldn't bring herself to eat there. She felt that if they kept on eating in the kitchen as always, it would feel like her father was still with them in some way.

They made a glum pair. Richie was much chastened by what had happened at the party and though she was bursting to regale him with the story of Alice Madigan's jaw dropping to her belly-button at the mention of barristers and court, she knew she had to hold her tongue. Richie must never know how she had rowed in to avenge and protect him. So they sat chewing quietly, lost in their own thoughts for a while.

"So exciting times in Stoneyfield?" Richie said after a while.

Lit nodded, preoccupied.

"Don't suppose there's any point in me trying to get you to ask Conrad about the crane?"

"The crane?"

"You remember – I want to climb it. I told you ages ago and you said you'd ask him and then you never did. But now that you two are engaged . . ."

"Not officially and besides now is not a good time, Richie – for lots of reasons. Anyway it's a silly, dangerous idea. I'm sure Conrad wouldn't agree to it. So just put it out of your head for good."

He wanted to remind her that she was going back on her word, but he was hardly in a position to argue that one. And as for being a silly dangerous idea, it didn't seem half as silly or dangerous as getting engaged to a man like Conrad. Richie was eager to climb Conrad's Lampson crane – but he didn't actually like Conrad, or the way he had so quickly and dramatically taken over Lit's life. He didn't like the way his mother was sporting Conrad's engagement ring now without having even

458

talked it over with him first. In fairness, when she'd found the time a few days later, she'd carefully explained everything to him and said that if it made Richie unhappy, she'd send Conrad packing in an instant. Richie didn't really believe that – but he felt completely powerless in this newest phase of his mother's life. If she wouldn't help him now in a simple matter of climbing a silly crane, then he might be forced to take matters in his own hands. After all, he was off to see his dad in a few weeks. Time was running out.

His mobile buzzed.

"Oh, hi Zoe. What's up?"

His face didn't exactly light up – but he didn't seem all that irritated by her call either.

"I'm not sure. I'll have to check with my mum. I'll call you back."

He was invited to a movie – a gang of them were going. And then they were going for a pizza afterwards. They might all go on to Zoe's house for a while.

Lit agonised about it. Twice in recent weeks, she'd trusted him to go somewhere and each time he'd let her down in some way. How could she trust him again? She could offer to collect him after the film, but that would be embarrassing for him. And supposing he actually had a date with Zoe? She didn't want to spoil that either. What was the right thing to do?

The doorbell rang and Richie went to answer it. Lit was less displeased than usual to discover that it was Seán. In fact, she even smiled at him and he smiled right back at her.

"Good timing," she said to him when Richie had left the room.

"How do you mean?"

She explained briefly about the party and the cocaine

and her visit to Simon Fitzpatrick's home.

"Now I don't know if I can trust him again. I don't know what to do."

At this point, if Seán Tallon was being true to himself, he should have been leaping in with ring-binders full of helpful suggestions. But he was oddly silent. She waited. Perhaps he needed time to think. Without even noticing, she put a plate of seafood pasta and a glass of white wine on the table in front of him.

"This looks good," he said, tucking in.

While she waited for his Unsolicited Advice Menu to flap down, she hooked up the sprinkler-hose to a tap outside the back door and began watering her tubs. The Ali Baba tub with the black bamboo needed shifting. She tried to ease it across the patio. But it was large and heavy. Still she persisted and had shifted it about two inches when a pair of strong arms appeared out of nowhere and took hold of the rim of the pot.

"I'll need Richie to shift this," he said.

Lit watched in amazement as Richie, whose idea of helping in the garden was to tell his mother the lawn needed mowing, and Seán slowly and carefully moved the tub into its new position.

"That's thirsty work," Seán said.

"I'll get you another glass of wine. Richie? A beer?"

"OK. Thanks, Mum."

When she reappeared they were sitting in easy chairs admiring their handiwork. Richie was telling Seán all about the crane on the Stoneyfield site and how it was the biggest of its kind and how more than anything he would love to just climb it and have a go at the controls.

"Richie, are you still on about that?" she said disapprovingly.

"When I was a young fella I climbed to the top of this

massive tree near our house," said Sean. "My mother didn't speak to me for a week afterwards."

"I'm not surprised," said Lit.

"A tree's different. Cranes are safe, Mum. Even in storms they're safe. They have to be. Actually that would be cool – being way up there in the cabin in the middle of a really big storm. I love storms. Even when I was a kid. I used to make tidal waves and tempests in the bath – remember, Mum?"

"Yes, I do." She smiled fondly.

"So, Mum, the next time there's a big storm, you know where to find me . . ." Richie winked conspiratorially at Seán.

"Oh, stop teasing me, Richie – I'm not really in the mood," she said.

Seán deftly changed the subject to golf and Richie quizzed him about his handicap and challenged him to a game. Once or twice she caught Seán's eyes coming to rest on her fabulous engagement ring, but he didn't pass any comment. The one thing he didn't talk about was what she should do about Richie. If he didn't say something soon, she might be forced to ask him for his advice.

"So what's the story, Mum? About tonight?"

"I don't know, love. I mean – after the other night . . ."

Richie tried not to look glum. He knew he should never have gone to Simon Fitzpatrick's party. They weren't even mates. Simon was a notorious bully and quick to rat on his mates. He wondered how long it would be before his mother would trust him again. Had she called his father in Berlin? His father would be horrified and deeply disappointed to hear what had happened. If he had to choose between being grounded and his father finding out – he would much prefer to be grounded.

Lit looked to Seán for some guidance, but he just sipped his wine and said nothing.

"What about coming home straight after the pictures?" she said.

Richie hung the lip. He'd quite gotten over his aversion to Zoe and was looking forward to going back to her house for a while. But he knew if he pushed it, Lit might dig her heels in and not allow him to go out at all.

"So where are you off to?" Seán asked him finally.

Richie told him.

"I have an idea, if your mother agrees," said Sean. "Why don't you call me when you're finished in Zoe's and I'll drive you home. That way you get to spend more time with your friends and Lit won't be worried about you."

"Sounds good," said Richie with his habitual shrug. He glanced at his mother, waiting for the resounding 'No!', the 'you've blotted your copybook once too often' speech. He felt mildly resentful at being subjected to all this sudden scrutiny about his comings and goings, could even feel a grumble coming on. But he decided to play it cool. "What do you think, Mum?"

"OK. But if you let me down again, I'll have to get on to your dad about it."

She hadn't told his father! Richie almost danced for joy. Except it would have been a highly uncool sort of thing for a sixteen-year-old to do. He showered and splashed on the Ralph Lauren aftershave, put on his Ben Sherman shirt and his jeans and loafers, and headed off to Barney's house, leaving Lit on the patio with Seán.

Seán insisted on watering the rest of her plants and she went upstairs to have a shower and change.

When she returned he'd finished watering the plants and was stretched out in a chair, basking in the warm evening sun.

They chatted easily, the house in Laraville being a comfortable topic of conversation for a while. He was closing the deal in a few weeks and hoped to move in the spring when the builders had finished working on it.

"What are they doing?"

"Some minor repairs around the place – floors, pipes, that sort of thing. The central heating system needs to be replaced. And the kitchen will be bigger – much bigger. The builder is a brother of the man who owns the bar where we ate."

At the mention of the bar, Lit couldn't help remembering the evening stroll on the beach and then she blushed. Up to that moment, she'd quite forgotten about the kiss. She twiddled her fabulous engagement ring, hoping he'd get the hint that there was to be no more kissing. Because in any case she wasn't the slightest bit interested in any further kissing.

"This wasn't really just a social call," said Sean suddenly. "I have another reason for being here."

Her heart sank. It was going to be one of those tedious awkward moments, she could tell. He'd say he fancied her something rotten and she'd have to explain that she felt nothing at all for him and besides she was –

"I was thinking about that business with the Cornwells."

Phew!

"It should be OK if you both keep your nerve. Of course, you'll have to make sure the rest of your clients are cast iron for the next couple of years."

"I suppose that makes sense."

"And if there's any way I can help – "

"That's good of you."

He shifted uneasily in his chair and leaned forward.

The evening sun shone directly into his face and reflected in his eyes.

"Um . . . but that's not really why I came by . . . the thing is . . ."

She knew he was about to say something personal.

She had to stop him.

"If it's about what happened on the beach the other day, I think we should both forget about it, don't you?"

"What? What beach? Oh, yes, I see what you're talking about. Don't worry! I'd completely forgotten about that. I was only going to ask if I could watch the golf. I don't have the cable channels at my place."

He'd completely forgotten about it! How dare he completely forget about it! Nobody kissed Lit Doran and completely forgot about it! She had a good mind to lean over and kiss him again, just to remind him that he hadn't completely forgotten about it. He grinned impishly at her, daring her to challenge him.

"Golf? Sure," she said and led the way into the sitting-room.

Tiger Woods was winning his latest tournament and there was all sorts of excitement on and off the fairways.

Gradually she forgot her annoyance and became quite engrossed in it all, sitting on the edge of her seat for those last vital putts, cursing as a ball slid tantalisingly past the little hole on the green. When the golf finished, he wanted to watch a rugby match from Australia and she was soon hurling abuse at the referee and cheering on whoever was racing towards the try line. She sipped wine and he stuck to mineral water and they both tucked into a bowl of black olives and the time passed easily. She couldn't believe it when he told her it was time to go and collect Richie.

"Unless there's a problem, I'll just drop him at the end of the road. I've got one hell of a busy day tomorrow. Thanks for a lovely evening."

He kissed her very briefly and fraternally on the cheek.

"Thanks for collecting Richie."

He shrugged and disappeared into the night.

Not long afterwards Lit's phone rang. Auntie Florence had passed away.

# CHAPTER 35

These were nail-biting days for Gearóid Magill. His reputation as chief community activist stood or fell on whether he could defeat Budd. And of course being chief community activist was a mere stepping-stone. Gearóid had his eye on high office, a Dáil seat, a place in the cabinet, even higher things maybe. It was why he chose to live on the North Side. He had noticed over the years that it was often northsiders who made it to the highest office in the land.

He thought that the bribery business would at least have stopped the development, if not even put Budd in jail. But somehow it wasn't that simple at all. Budd was holding his own far too well at the enquiry, making smooth and elegant talk about integrity and the strong man helping the weak man when he's down. The bottom line seemed to be that the cheques to Brendan Browne didn't in fact prove anything.

So Geraoid was in a foul mood. In the little office, he hissed orders at Fidelma like a Reichsführer. She dashed about frantically, sorting papers, looking for vital pieces of information, trying to soothe him whatever way she could.

"Don't worry, Gearóid," she said, trying to console him. She rubbed him gently on the back of his neck.

"Can't you see I'm busy?" he snarled in his rich western accent.

The natives were getting restless and now he had to face them all in the Stoneyfield Community Centre. There was a palpable sense of anger and disappointment and Gearóid was hurt and enraged by their ingratitude. Did they not realise that he was working on their behalf? Did they not know the personal sacrifices he was making to destroy Budd? Most of his teaching friends were off in Australia for the summer, while he, Geraoid Magill, had stayed behind to defend his people from the worst ravages of the Celtic Tiger.

Still, he was a man of greater substance than all these people. He had leadership, charisma, a determination to succeed where others failed. He was, in short, born to lead. He chanted a little mantra to himself: "Let me assure you all that I have a mental shield and no-one can make me feel bad without my permission."

The words soothed him and restored his equilibrium. Calmed and ready now to lead the people to victory, he took his place at the long table in front of the assembled crowd. He noticed with some annoyance that Pat Sullivan was sitting in the front row, head bowed, flicking through a bunch of notes. When he saw Fidelma smiling down at Sullivan and giving a little flirty wave of the fingers, he quickly decided it was time to call the meeting to order.

"We are into the final stages of this battle and we will win! We will fight to the end and we will win! Let us have no fear of that," he began like Winston Churchill.

There was a bit of muttering and grumbling from the back rows. "Let me reassure you all that we have right on our side and that we will destroy Budd. We will expose him for the conniving, law-breaking crook that he is. The man will never show his face in this town again!"

"He doesn't look too bothered to me any time I see him on the telly!" shouted Declan Byrne, the editor of the local paper.

"What for you get all these hopes of these peoples rising up only to make disappointment?" shouted Alesandro, the new scientist from Corbawn Street.

"Aren't you a bit out of your league, Magill?" chipped in Joe Corcoran the owner of the Cobblers.

Gearóid listened earnestly to a few such comments. It was wise to let the more disgruntled people have their little moan. When he sensed the anger dying down, he raised his hand to address them once more.

"My fellow Stoneyfield Residents, I feel your anger and your disappointment. And I am happy that we live in a community where we are all free to express our views in such a fine democratic manner. For if Conrad Budd were to have his way, this vital sense of community would slip away. Do we really want Tristram from Tunbridge Wells, or Helmut from Frankfurt telling us how to run our lives? Do we really want Porsches and Ferraris speeding up and down our cosy little streets, putting the lives of our children in danger? Do we want our children in schools where the illustrious mother tongue of the nation is not treasured and nurtured? Above all, do we want this monstrosity looming over us all like some horrible pestilence from outer space?"

'Horrible pestilence' was good. He knew he was a great speaker. The crowd, who had been angry and baying for his blood only moments before, now listened intently, silently soaking up the awesome power of his words.

"People of Stoneyfield, we do not!"

"Hear, hear!" they shouted.

"And that is why I am glad to inform you all that I now have the certain means to put a stop to it all!"

"What is it? Tell us!" they shouted.

He looked down at them, his eyes making contact with each and every one of them, except, that is, for Pat Sullivan who was still flicking laconically through papers and occasionally jotted notes.

Gearóid held up a jiffy-bag. Slowly and with perfect dramatic timing he withdrew from it a video cassette.

"Conrad Budd – " He decided they were ready for a joke. It would spin out the tense atmosphere of expectation which had suddenly filled up the little hall. "And incidentally, did you know that Budd or 'budh' is the Irish for – prick? I wonder is there a connection?"

The crowd laughed and clapped in spontaneous applause. Gearóid bowed humbly in the face of their adulation.

"But seriously," he went on as the laughing subsided, "this is security-camera footage of the carpark of a prominent Dublin hotel. It shows Conrad Budd handing over money to Brendan Browne."

Gearóid was glad to see that even Pat Sullivan was impressed. He lifted his head, looked curiously at the tape for a moment and returned to his notes.

"Get a video screen and recorder!" someone shouted. "Let's watch it."

But Gearóid was adamant. "No! You'll all just have to wait until tomorrow. And I can guarantee you one thing. It'll be on the evening news. It will be the most exciting security footage in the history of the State."

"What will happen then?" asked Tom McNally the retired bus conductor. "What should we do?"

"Right. Now listen very carefully, everyone. A copy of this tape will be viewed at the enquiry tomorrow morning. I imagine the outcome is a foregone conclusion. The procedure then will be an emergency court injunction against Budd. A file will be brought to the DPP and there will be a court case at some point in the coming months. If Budd is found guilty he will go to jail and his assets will be frozen pending further investigations. We must anticipate and plan. I, of course, will continue as spokesperson for the group and will deal with the reporters tomorrow. The pickets and demonstrations which I have organised will continue in an orderly and lawful fashion."

He looked down triumphantly at Pat Sullivan.

"Cometh the hour, cometh the man," he whispered proudly to himself.

"So you're going to marry Lit Doran?" Jack Kennedy enquired of Conrad with some amusement.

But Conrad wasn't in the mood for talk. "No time for idle social tattle, Kennedy."

"Of course. I only meant – well, congratulations. A great man needs the help of a fine woman."

"Indeed."

"Like JFK and Jackie – "

"Quite." Conrad withdrew into a deep and impenetrable silence, sitting in his leather swivel-chair, running his fingers over the large detailed site map that rested on his desk.

"The money's in the bank, Conrad," Jack said finally.

"Good!" his boss replied distractedly.

"Yep! It's all there. Diamond have come up trumps.

And I was thinking . . ." He waited for Conrad to show some interest, but he didn't so Jack continued on regardless. "I was thinking, only thinking mind, that since we don't actually have to pay out anything much for another few weeks, we could use the money to do a bit of careful buying and selling and then still have it with a profit to pay the bills."

"Nothing risky?"

"Conrad! You know me better than that. Have I ever lost you a single penny?"

It was true. He had the personality of a trout, the looks of a gnat, all the social skill of a mole. But he had the brain of about ten NASA computers.

"What did you have in mind?"

"Property? Blue-chip shares?"

"No risks, mind! No risks at all!"

"Great! I'll get working on it straight away."

He set off across the marbled hall to his office and just missed Fergus Cunningham who arrived from the Four Courts, looking slightly stressed.

Conrad picked up on the change in his solicitor's demeanour straight away.

"What is it?"

Fergus sighed and threw himself into a big comfortable leather armchair. "Any chance of a drink?"

"Of course."

Conrad poured him a whiskey and watched as the solicitor took several good gulps to restore himself.

"Right! The shit may have hit the fan."

Conrad half-sat on the edge of his desk, his hands shoved in his pockets, and waited.

"They've got a video – some sort of security-camera footage."

"I see."

"You're on it. So's Browne."

"Have you seen it?"

"Not until tomorrow. But it sounds like it might be tricky."

"Is there anything we can do?"

Cunningham laughed grimly. "Short of breaking into the court and stealing it, I can't think of a damn thing. Every reporter in town is down there sniffing around. We are in the arms of fate, my old friend."

When Lit arrived at Conrad's office with the running order for the official opening of the site, she found him sitting silently at his desk, like a condemned man waiting for death to come for him.

She kissed him lightly on the cheek and sat beside him. There was silence for a while and then he told her about the tape. She shifted uneasily, felt the need to escape, to get away from the sordid business of corruption. But she couldn't now. She was bound to him, not just professionally, but personally. Instead, she told herself that the tape wasn't important, that it was a last desperate attempt by Brendan Browne to destroy Conrad, that it would prove nothing.

"I'm sure it will all turn out fine." She couldn't think of anything else to say. "Why don't we talk about the opening? It might take your mind off things."

"No, thanks."

"Where would you like to have dinner?"

"I've changed my mind. I need to be alone tonight."

"You don't have to be alone. It might help to talk to me and – "

"Leave it. Leave me. Go home. I'll see you tomorrow."

She felt rejected but, if Conrad needed to be alone, then she wasn't going to force herself on him. It didn't mean he didn't love her. He was just one of those men who needed to go into his cave and think things out.

"Right. Bye then!" she chirped. "Call me if you like."

# CHAPTER 36

An air of palpable expectation buzzed among the journalists and reporters who clustered in little groups outside Dublin Castle in the searing, sticky heat. A TV news reporter was speaking very earnestly to camera, trying to catch the mood of the moment.

"Is this at last to be the day of judgement for Conrad Budd? The prospect inspires mixed emotions in many people. Both the envy and the inspiration of many, he has for several years cut a dashing swathe through the world of international finance and business, has dared to build his vision of a new Dublin, casting aside in his swashbuckling way the scorn and contempt which lesser men and sometimes even greater men have heaped upon him. Love him or hate him, Budd has been a hero of the times – almost Shakespearean – a visionary, inspirational in his efforts, handsome, fearless, generous and modest. It is widely expected today that evidence will be produced which will may result in the immediate cessation of building on the Stoneyfield site. Budd has invested heavily in this project and it could be a fatal blow to his business interests if it fails. Of more immediate concern is the possibility that he may have to stand trial and if found guilty could be sentenced to a minimum of three years . . ."

A large crowd had gathered alongside the Stoneyfield pickets and the Gardaí had erected barriers in an effort to contain them. When Conrad's sleek black Mercedes pulled up at the gates, the crowd surged forward.

"Give us a kiss, Conrad! You're only gorgeous!" shouted one woman.

"Conrad Budd for Taoiseach!" yelled someone else.

"You're a star! You've made us the proudest little city in Europe."

Others had less complimentary things to say.

"Parasite! I hope they skin you alive! You won't push the people of this city around any more with your big fat wallet!"

"Go back to the filthy rugby pitch you crawled off, you dirty big flanker!"

"The lads in the Joy will sort the likes of you out!"

Conrad, looking taller and more handsome than Lit had ever seen him, wearing a fine dark grey Italian suit, with a crisp white shirt and a sober maroon-coloured tie, moved charismatically through the crowd, attended by Jack Kennedy, Fergus Cunningham and Lit. If he was worried or nervous, it didn't show on his face. He looked calm and dignified, a giant among pigmies. He smiled at some of his well-wishers and shook their hands, pausing at one point to exchange a few words with a very elderly lady who had come along to offer her support.

Then he passed beneath the pillared entrance to learn his fate.

Lit felt a terrible sense of helplessness as she watched her man going into battle for his life. She wasn't sure whether she felt proud or ashamed. She was a great believer in the truth and straight dealings, but at the same time, it wouldn't exactly suit her on a number of counts if Conrad were to face trial, if his business were to fold.

She stood about aimlessly, carefully avoiding the inquisitive looks of reporters. This time, there was no nice Pat Sullivan to buy her an ice cream and she had to endure the attentions of Jack Kennedy.

"So how do you see it?" she asked finally.

"Looks bad for the boss and no mistake. I'd say he's frigged. Definitely frigged. We're all frigged. Stoneyfield is frigged. Dublin is frigged."

"You have a gift with language," she retorted tartly.

The sudden realisation that she might have to spend the next four hours with Jack Kennedy spurred Lit into action. She made a hasty excuse about having some stuff to do at the office and left.

At home, Bonnie, who was as good a cook as Lit was hopeless, had baked a delicious honey-glazed ham and what everyone called Bonnie's sexy mashed potatoes. The mash included olive oil, lardons, butter, cream, rosemary and salt and pepper. One mouthful of it would floor a man into undying love and devotion.

"How's Conrad?"

"Bearing up, I suppose."

Lit was perturbed to find that she was almost dreading being alone with him. She might even make some excuse to get out of it. Whatever the outcome, he would be angry and tired and she would be a convenient target to lash out at. It wasn't meant to be like that. She was meant to be his support and comfort in times of trouble. He was supposed to find peace and contentment with her. But that was not the way between them. Conrad's way of dealing with stress and trouble was to lash out at the nearest target. That was what had happened before. Wouldn't it most likely happen again? Of course she loved him, but she was just a bit afraid of him. And he wasn't the sort of man that could just be told to go and take a run and a jump for himself.

She changed the subject. "What have you been up to?"

"Booked a little holiday – a week on Lake Como – bit of opera, wine, food, sex – that sort of thing."

"Lucky you. Wish I had time for a proper holiday. Maybe when this launch is over – who knows?"

Bonnie smiled a secretive, mischievous smile. "Seán Tallon is taking me to the Horseshow Ball."

"Go way! He wouldn't get in. That's only for handsome, rich, dashing men of breeding like Conrad."

"He's taking me to the ball because he said he wants someone beautiful, witty and intelligent to spend the evening with."

Lit felt unaccountably peeved for a number of reasons. Who did Seán Tallon think he was, going to the Horseshow Ball? It was way out of his league. And what was he doing kissing her on a beach and completely forgetting about it when, all the time, he was planning to bring Bonnie to the ball? And why hadn't Conrad thought of inviting her? She knew he had gone last year because his photo was splashed all over *Social & Personal*. She remembered the caption: *Billionaire Irish Businessman Cuts a Dash at the Ball*. It was unthinkable for them not to go. It would be the perfect place to show off her new engagement ring. She would have enough time in the morning to get her hair done and buy a gown.

While she was considering this latest turn of events, she glanced at her watch and shot out of her chair in horror. "Oh my God! The enquiry! Bonnie – he'll kill me if I'm not there."

## CHAPTER 37

Outside the Castle, the crowd was muted. Gearóid Magill stood to the fore of his troops, already strutting the triumphant strut, smiling the magnanimous, triumphant smile.

"When Budd comes past, I want the press to see victory written in all your faces! But remember – magnanimous in victory!"

"You must be feeling pretty pleased with yourself, Gearóid," said Pat Sullivan who had turned up with some of the residents.

Gearóid cocked his head to one side and grinned smugly. "Carpe Diem, Pat. Seize the moment!"

Pat nodded and smiled briefly before turning away in disgust. He was not greatly impressed by the motley crowd which Magill had assembled at the gates of the Castle. They were mostly the disordered rabble to be found outside any pub on a Saturday night. These weren't the people he grew up with in Stoneyfield, the people he liked, the old people who had struggled through hard times, the decent young couples rearing their families and holding the community together as they had always done, the teenagers in the soccer club, the GAA club, the guards, the priests, the shopkeepers, the publicans, the labouring men, the teachers.

He had no interest in watching a man being publicly humiliated, hounded, scorned and villified. He stubbornly clung to the view that savaging a man's reputation was not the way to bring about change. And so as the doors of the Castle swung open for Conrad and his advisors, Pat had already left the scene.

Lit arrived panting and flushed. She had to park miles

away in a hotel carpark and then run like the clappers in her kitten heels. She just about made it in time to see the doors open and Conrad, followed by Fergus Cunningham, step hesitantly out into the sun. She tried to read his face, but it was blank, inscrutable.

Instantly the reporters were upon him, thrusting microphones at him and hurling the usual questions.

"Mr Budd, Mr Budd – any comment – is it true that –"

Fergus Cunningham stepped forward and raised his hand.

"A statement will be issued in due course, gentlemen. Thank you."

"Will there be a trial?"

"Mr Budd has no further comment at this time. Thank you."

Conrad swept forward through the group, making his way towards the gates and the pickets. Lit caught up with him.

"Is it bad?"

"Depends on your point of view," he said and gave the briefest of smiles.

Behind them the reporters stood around in some confusion. They had expected something different – a shocked Conrad, looking grey and drawn from the humiliation of facing a group of twenty or so inquisitors. His solicitor might have remained behind and made some cryptic comment to them about 'further legal action' or asked them to respect Conrad's 'right to privacy at this difficult time'. But now they were flummoxed, in disarray. They had waited all day in the stifling heat, knowing that a major scandal was about to break before them, sure that they would see one of the most influential heads in the country roll. Some had even written his obituary.

The great gates swung open and Conrad made his way regally past the picket line.

"Your ass is grass!" shouted one of Gearóid's men.

Conrad stopped in his tracks and turned to face the man. Jack Kennedy tried to lay a restraining hand on him, but it was no use.

"What's that you said?"

"I said – your ass is grass!"

"Ha! Ha! I like it. Your ass is grass. And tell me – is it so, do you think?"

"Nothing surer."

"Ah! Well, now that's where we differ. Good day to you, gentlemen."

He sat into the car, waved genially at them and was gone out of their sight in an instant.

Inside the gates the reporters pounced on a spokesman who had emerged from the enquiry. They struggled to make sense of his brief summary of the day's events.

"Not enough evidence – fifteen-second delay in frames on most security cameras – no evidence of Conrad Budd actually giving money to Brendan Browne –"

"But surely – "

"The inquiry into allegations of corruption against Budd Construction and Property Holdings is at an end. A full transcript will be issued in due course. No further protests or demonstrations will be permitted in or around the Stoneyfield site."

The crowd were worse than disgruntled – they were angry and baying for blood. Not only had Budd got off scot-free, but the reporters were virtually ignoring them, didn't seem to even care what happened to them or their homes. They watched in disgust as Gearóid Magill forced his way in front of a few stragglers and stumbled through a hastily written press statement. And since a baying crowd must have someone to bay at, they turned on him.

"This is all your doing, Magill! Now we're worse off than we ever were – you thick culchie!"

"Bear with me, friends! This is just a setback."

"We're not your friends. You're full of shite!. At least Pat Sullivan tells it like it is."

"This is not the end – I assure you. And if Sullivan was still in charge, you wouldn't even have got this far."

"Pat Sullivan is right. Nothing good ever came out of the ruins of a man's reputation. Go on! Feck off home to wherever you came from! Stoneyfield is better off without the likes of you!"

Gearóid felt deep personal pain. When he considered all the time, the energy, the investment of himself and his talents in the cause of defeating Budd, it struck to the very core of his heart to be so shabbily treated. It was a moment of tragic insight.. He had discovered that people would always be ungrateful. People didn't deserve or appreciate great leaders. The greatest leaders in the world ended up crucified or assassinated or villified. It was maybe time to rethink the whole notion of a career in politics.

Back in Conrad's penthouse the champagne flowed as a small crowd of his closest friends and associates assembled to celebrate his victory.

"We're invincible, boss. Invincible!" crowed Jack Kennedy.

"I have to hand it to you, Budd. You are one lucky bastard!"

Conrad allowed himself a smile of satisfaction. Things had turned out even better than he had hoped. In four days, he would preside over the opening of the largest and most ambitious development in the country. The politicians would be there, his rivals in the property world, international financiers, the media, resentful but acquiescent. He put his arm absentmindedly around Lit's shoulder and hugged her.

"It was a tough one."

"Another ten seconds either way on that tape, and you were history."

"You can't keep a good man down, eh Conrad?"

Jack Kennedy beamed with admiration. He was on his best behaviour now with Lit, standing aside so she could be next to Conrad, complimenting all the helpful advice she had given which had paid off so well. In fact, for a brief moment Lit even began to think that Jack Kennedy was tolerable – until he told his whale joke, out of the blue and totally unprovoked, and to the mirthful delight of everyone in the room except herself.

"The brother in Philadelphia e-mailed me a great joke."

"Good man! I'm just in the mood for a joke," said Conrad.

This was a new dimension to his character. Up to now, whenever Lit had been with him, it was either business or romance. She hadn't thought that he might have his 'one of the lads' moments like any other man. She never considered that a man of his wealth and influence might enjoy that unique brand of male camaraderie that goes with the telling of spicy jokes.

"Right," said Jack, slipping into joke-telling gear, a dirty champagne-induced leer spreading across his face as he launched his little gem. "A male whale and a female whale were swimming off the coast of Japan when they noticed a whaling ship. The male whale recognised it as the same ship that had harpooned his father many years earlier. He said to the female whale, 'Let's both swim under the ship and blow out of our air holes at the same time, and it should cause the ship to turn over and sink.' Well, they tried it and, and sure enough, the ship turned over and quickly sank.

Soon, however, the whales realised that the sailors had jumped overboard and were swimming to the safety of the shore. The male was enraged that they were going to get away and said to the female: 'Let's swim after them and gobble them up before they reach the shore!' At this point, he realised that the female was reluctant to follow him. 'Look,' she said, 'I went along with the blow job, but I absolutely refuse to swallow the seamen!'"

Conrad, Fergus, Jack and most of the others collapsed into high-spirited mirth, like boys on a school bus outing.

"Here, I've got one," said Fergus when he'd finally stopped belly-laughing. "A man buys a load of sheep –"

"I should be going," said Lit.

Lit had no desire to stay for a smutty joke-fest. She felt a curious sense of anti-climax, a worrying feeling of not wanting to be there at all, as though all their high-spirited celebration was in bad taste somehow. She hadn't really given it much thought before, but she couldn't help thinking of Pat Sullivan. How was he feeling now? The gentleman in him would be relieved to see that a man's reputation had not been destroyed, but it meant the certain end of his beloved old Stoneyfield, the place he was born and reared in.

She tried to dismiss the thoughts. They were ridiculous. It wasn't healthy to stand in the way of progress. Did Pat Sullivan and people like him want Dublin to return to the dark ages? Yet she couldn't get the thought out of her head. She had an image of getting up in the morning in her own sunny bedroom with the big south-facing bay window, the sun beaming in and the trees clearly visible from her bed. Then she pictured what it would be like if there was a huge monstrous development right behind it. It would be dark always. There would be no trees, no birds, no squirrels. Office people would be able to see into her room. Her treasured privacy would be at an end. All her carefully bought and nurtured sun-loving plants would die off.

"Stay a while," said Conrad, hugging her like a prime piece of property.

"No. I don't want to spoil your fun. Enjoy your celebration. I have stuff to do."

She hugged and kissed him back. It was best to go.

But Conrad was frowning now. "I want you to stay."

There was that cold, ominous tone of voice again.

In an instant the atmosphere in the room changed and the warm champagne-induced glow evaporated.

"No, really. It's your celebration."

He caught her arm and led her away to the balcony.

"Don't make a fool of me in front of my friends," he said vehemently.

"But I'm not – I don't feel – "

"You're staying – and that's final."

At this point a number of options would normally have suggested themselves to Lit. The first one would have been a resounding 'Fuck off! I'm not one of your regular prize bimbos'. Or she might have gone for the less direct option and said, 'I'm not keen on being told what to do'. Or the no-nonsense 'stop being such a bully'. She could have just raised one withering, glacial eyebrow, lifted her chin and sent him reeling across the room with the impact. But the coolness had all but deserted her now. Perhaps it was nerves. After all, the prospect of being married to him would frighten anybody. It was only natural to be a little apprehensive, especially in front of his gathered friends most of whom she'd never met before. When she reasoned with herself, she realised she was being foolish. Of course, her place was at his side, sharing the highs and lows of life with him.

"Of course I'll stay if you want. I didn't want to be in the way, that's all."

"Right," he said, his good humour restored in an instant.

"Jack, order some transport. We're going out on the town – it's a long time since I've been clubbing and I deserve a bit of fun."

Three hours and several bottles of wine later, Lit found herself sitting in Puerto Libre with Jack Kennedy drunkenly expounding on the greatest deceased Irish-American in the history of Irish Americans.

Beside her on the other side was a very mannerly, very shy and very drunk engineer from the Glens of Antrim, who kept on saying in most apologetic terms: "I'm bloody proud of my Unionist roots and my heritage." Lit told him she wasn't really bothered about his Unionist roots since her grandmother had been a Protestant from County Down.

Jack asked her out to dance and proceeded to prance about like a daddy-long-legs on ecstasy. He made silly exaggerated faces at her and mouthed along ostentatiously to the words, whenever he recognised a song. When the DJ played a slow song, Jack slithered in like an oil slick and pressed his body close to hers. She had to grin and bear it. There was no sense in offending him.

But she made a mental note never to be in the same room at the same time as Jack Kennedy, a DJ and a slow number, ever again.

Conrad was propped at the bar, his tie shoved in his pocket, his shirt pulled open, his dark hair slightly ruffled on top. A pair of very pretty, slim, dark and gorgeous young girls hung onto his every word and gesture. Whenever he spoke, they threw their heads back with smiles of frank admiration. They stood, they swaggered, they strutted their stuff, they touched him lightly on the forearm and clasped their hands behind their backs coyly. They pouted and fluttered their eyebrows and flicked their hair and waved their magnificently manicured hands under his nose. Occasionally they cast furtive looks in Lit's direction. Conrad lapped it all up.

Was this something she would have to learn to live with? Could she learn to live with it? What man could resist that level of temptation? Most of all Conrad, who could and did make his own rules. Would she spend evenings at dinner parties and gala balls being chaperoned by the obnoxious Jack Kennedy, as Conrad topped up his ego-tank with the string of younger, prettier girls who were even now quite happy to engage with a man who was clearly not available? By nature, Lit was not a particularly jealous person. Even in the days with Harry Menton, when other women tried to move in she was not fazed, took it almost as a compliment that the man who loved her was desired and coveted by lots of other women. But now, looking at the gleam of vanity in Conrad's eyes as he soaked in their admiration, she wasn't so sure.

She decided to join him and was cross to discover that she felt anxious about it – anxious about joining her own fiancée, her future husband, as though she would be disturbing him or spoiling his fun.

She took a deep breath and walked over to the bar. "Conrad, won't you introduce me to your two beautiful friends?"

"If you insist. Ladies – do you have names?"

They laughed and did coltish things with their legs and did the coy, shy thing with the eyelids.

"I'm Laura and this is Fiona," one giggled through frosted-pink lips, virtually ignoring Lit.

"It's so nice to meet you," she said. "What pretty dresses! I'm Conrad's fiancée, by the way."

She waited for him to say something complimentary, something which would set her apart from all the other women in the room.

"Ladies – meet the ball and chain," he introduced her laddishly.

To give him his due, he put his arm around her and kissed her fondly on the cheek, but Lit did not take to the notion of being anyone's ball and chain. Next, he would be calling her the trouble and strife, 'er indoors, the missus, She Who Must Be Obeyed and other such highly original titles.

All she could do was make a few polite enquiries about where they had bought their dresses and nod coolly as they each spoke in exaggerated faux distress about how they looked sooooooooo fat and how the dresses were sooooo expensive and they were sooooo broke and couldn't afford food until they got paid at the end of the month and ohmyGod it was sooooo embarassing . . .

"That should help with the weight control," she said, smiling her most charming angelic smile.

After what seemed like a tedious millennium of

'sooooooo's' and 'ohmyGod's' she managed to drag Conrad away, but only when she promised to stay overnight in the penthouse. That meant a phone call to Bonnie.

"It's all under control, honeybun. Don't worry! You stay out all night if you want to – "

"Bonnie, are you sure – I really want to come home but – "

"It's fine. I've cracked open a bottle of Sancerre and we're playing Boggle."

"Bonnie – will you be my bridesmaid?"

"Ask me when you're sober. Have fun. See you in the morning."

Conrad was very drunk. Lit had never seen him so drunk. You couldn't exactly tell by looking at him, for he still held himself straight as a die and walked as steadily as a tightrope walker. But his face was sort of distorted and red, and the deep, deep brown eyes were glazed and slightly unfocused.

As they drove home in the taxi, he slouched up against her, grazing on her ear and neck, mumbling and muttering what might have been extremely sexy and suggestive remarks. It was just that she couldn't understand them. Once inside the penthouse, he pulled her to him, plastering her with kisses and working his hands around her breasts like a baker kneading dough.

She was tired and not in the mood. What she wanted more than anything was to climb into bed, have a nice cuddle and fall asleep in his arms. As his hands kneaded incessantly, she thought about telling him. After all, he loved her – he would understand, wouldn't want to tire her even more. And what pleasure was there in making love to a woman who was tired? He must be tired too. He'd had a long and harrowing day. She wondered how he could even think about the pyrotechnics of sex.

"You must be very tired," she ventured at last.

"Never too tired for sex," he murmured huskily.

She squeezed his hand and suppressed a tiny yawn.

Then she chanced a bigger yawn.

"I'm so tired I can't even think straight," she offered in the bedroom.

"No worries. That's the great thing about sex. You don't even have to think."

No escape then. No understanding offer of a nice warm cuddle instead. It was time, she realised, to act for Ireland, to breathe heavily for Ireland, to moan with abandon for Ireland, to whisper naughty urgent words for Ireland, to writhe steamingly for Ireland – in short, it was time to fake for Ireland.

She led him to the bed, rubbing herself suggestively against him, provocatively sliding out of her skirt and blouse, playfully teasing him with her short black slip and panties. She licked him, bit him playfully, kissed him hard all over.

"That's more like it," he said like a coach scolding a lazy player.

She climbed on top. She rolled her eyes, licked and bit her lips lasciviously, and finally when the time was right she faked – the biggest, most orgasmic fake orgasm she could conjure up. It was Oscar-winning stuff. And all the while, she was busily occupied planning the new herbaceous border that she wanted at the side of the garden – white – all white – white African Agapanthus – "Yes – yes!" – white clematis – "Oh, God, yes!" – a white wistaria on the redbrick wall – "Now – now!" – and white jasmine – "Yes, there!" – white cranesbill –

delphinium – "Oh my God! Yes! Yes! Yes! Yes!"

Conrad was so convinced, he fell asleep on the spot.

# CHAPTER 38

Two days later, in a tight-fitting, silk, russet-coloured evening gown, with her boobs perfectly displayed in a state-of-the-art balcony bra, and with her gleaming black hair piled up in a confection of curls and tiny bows, Bonnie descended the stairs to join Seán Tallon. He was leaning against a wall, watching her descend. She looked the picture of voluptuous elegance against the sweeping mahogany banister of Lit's staircase.

"You look great," he said, suppressing a non-PC wolf-whistle.

"I aim to please."

"You'll be the prettiest woman there. I'm afraid it's going to be a bit of a bore. We'll be with company people – clients – don't expect too much excitement."

"Don't worry. I'll provide the excitement."

"Look, if you get stuck with anybody boring or any-thing, we better have a signal – so that I can come and rescue you. I know – just tug at one of the bows in your hair – and I'll bail you out."

"I don't get bored – well, except with boyfriends. We weren't allowed to be bored as kids – my mum used to say there were no such things as boredom, being bored and boring people – anyway, thanks for the offer."

"Great – let's be off then."

He held the door open for her and glanced briefly back at Lit who was watching the scene from the kitchen doorway. It was an odd sort of glance and for a moment

Lit could think of nothing to say.

"Have a lovely night," she called after them eventually.

They certainly made a handsome couple: a handsome, prosperous and successful couple on their way out to join all the other handsome, prosperous and successful couples in the city. She felt so happy for them, Bonnie smiling the flashy white-teeth smile in anticipation of a fine night out, Tallon, more relaxed than Lit had ever seen him. He seemed almost pleased to be going out on the town.

She was so happy for Bonnie. They would have a lovely night. Perhaps, in spite of himself, Tallon might even fall in love with Bonnie after tonight. Yes, that was it. He would fall in love with Bonnie, sweep her off her feet and marry her. Then they would have a lovely white wedding surrounded by their families and friends and all the trimmings and they would live very happily ever after in that big old rambling house in Laraville. They'd have a few kids and they'd do ordinary stuff like going for mucky, wax-coated, welling-tonned walks in the woods on Sunday mornings, and planning scary, witch-infested Hallowe'en parties for the children, and having long and chaotic dinner parties with a wide circle of friends at the weekends. On Saturday mornings all the children would clamber into their big warm bed and they would share hot buttered toast and tea and he would read Harry Potter to the children who would all snuggle up against him, while Bonnie slept on. Sometimes Bonnie would feel sad about growing old and he would joke and whistle and tell her she was still the sexiest woman in Ireland. And every year on her birthday, he'd whisk her off to some-where romantic and buy her another diamond ring.

Yes, Lit was very happy for her friend.

Wait a minute . . . she wasn't a bit happy. She was as mad as hell. Was she going to spend life married to Ireland's answer to Donald Trump, just waiting for the day when he would ditch her for a younger model, while Bonnie got to live happily ever after? Was she going to live forever on a diet of pureed cucumber in a fat-free dressing, while Bonnie got to gorge herself on succulent Sunday roasts, and deep-fried parsnips and sticky toffee pudding with double clotted cream? And on Saturday mornings would she be up at the crack of dawn, cutting a frenetic dash from the hair stylist, to the beautician, to the manicurist, to the gym, so that when Conrad awoke, he would find her perfectly gorgeous, firm and pouting body ready to satisfy his every need – and all this while Bonnie snored on in blissful oblivion?

Then she stopped herself. What an idiotic thought – to be jealous of anybody marrying Seán Tallon! Of course, Conrad was a little tactless and perhaps a trifle selfish, and had a tiny tendency to want to control everyone but, all in all, she couldn't do much better. After all, she was a successful, independent woman in her own right. It would take more than marriage to Conrad Budd to destroy that hard-won independence and control of her own destiny. Conrad was kind too when he wanted to be, and considerate and sensitive to a woman's needs. So what if she had to fake a few orgasms here and there? So what if she could never eat an ice cream cone again? So what if she had to spend the rest of her days looking stunningly beautiful from morning to night. She knew that if she really needed his support or his understanding, she would most certainly get it. He was, in short, a perfect catch.

She pushed thoughts of Seán and Bonnie from her mind.

Tomorrow was the big day and a clear, uncluttered head was needed to focus on that. A long checklist held her attention for a while, but she'd done her work so well that there was nothing left to do. Even the clothes she planned to wear were hanging in her wardrobe, freshly cleaned and pressed.

Richie was on the phone to his dad in Berlin, making the final arrangements for his holiday. He would be gone for almost a month and already the loneliness was taking hold of her. It would be his first time away for longer than a week. It would be her first time ever being alone in the house. No Dandy now to carp about the absurdities of life, to throw icy water on the trappings of her glamorous, glitzy lifestyle. Conrad was to be her helpmate, of course, but he was terribly busy and a man of perpetual motion. He would not be the sort to put his feet up and keep her company during Richie's long absence.

She sat into her father's chair and tried to draw some comfort from the memories of his presence there. Could he be right? Was her life an absurd and shallow thing? For a brief moment the dreadful word 'meaningless' hovered somewhere on the outer edges of her subconscious. But just in time Richie ambled into the kitchen and asked her if she'd like to go to the pictures with him. She tried not to looked shocked or pathetically grateful. But inside she was very definitely both of those things. Luckily, he didn't notice or he might have withdrawn the offer.

So for the first time in years Lit and her son went to the movies. Only this time he took her and paid out of his own wages. He bought the best seats in the house,

insisted she have a bucket of popcorn and even subjected himself to the latest romantic chick-flick, though he
was really much keener on seeing Ghoulishly Scary
Teen Horror Flick 2 – The Total Nightmare Returns.
Afterwards, they rambled along the new boardwalk on
the river and had a late-night snack in a little Italian
place down some old cobbled steps in Temple Bar.

Sitting at the tiny table, looking across at him in the
half-light, she felt staggeringly proud of her son. He was
turning into a handsome young man, polite to the
waiters and with lovely table manners. He chatted away
easily with her about all sorts of interesting things, even
his plans for the future. Of course she knew that those
plans would change a thousand times over the next
couple of years, but it didn't matter. At least he had
plans.

"Mum?"

"What?"

"Do you like your work?"

"What a question! Of course I like my work. And it
allows us to have a very comfortable lifestyle."

"I suppose."

He didn't seem convinced.

"And do you love Conrad?"

"Richie! Of course I do."

He wasn't very convinced by that either but, though
he wasn't happy with her answer, he knew that pursuing the matter would have spoiled a perfect evening.

The following morning she was in a state of high
anxiety at the breakfast table, nibbling nervously on
toast, sipping piping hot breakfast tea and putting the
finishing touches to her toenail polish at the same time.
The kitchen was a bustling powerhouse. Matt fussed

about with the coffee machine and ducked in and out to the garden to smoke, Bonnie flossed her teeth and drank tea at the same time and checked her airline tickets and her passport for Italy.

"Great night at the ball," she said through the floss.

Lit nodded dismissively. Hearing about yet another brilliant night out on the town from Bonnie was something she didn't have time for right now. She especially didn't want to hear any details about Seán Tallon.

Richie sat in the middle of it all, lazily stirring scrambled egg in a saucepan.

"So, big day, Mum," he grinned at her.

Lit nodded absently as she waved her polished toes in the air.

"What are you going to wear?" asked Bonnie.

"Fitted raspberry linen suit – black slingbacks. Tonight – a strapless olive-green shot-silk sheath – "

"What shoes will you wear with the green dress?"

"Haven't a clue," she snapped, wriggling into the skirt of her suit.

There wasn't time to sit around discussing fashion statements with Bonnie. She had more important things on her mind – a hundred and one things to worry about. Would everything be in place? The stands, the catering, the glossy brochures, the music – would the right people turn up – would the speeches be all right? Then there was the minister who had a reputation for tactless jokes and for rambling on endlessly about himself . . .

"Why don't you just move in here?" Richie observed as Bonnie hauled her holiday suitcase down the stairs. "There's plenty of room and you spend most of your time with us anyway."

"It's a nice thought."

The taxi waited patiently as she dished out hugs and

kisses to Richie and Lit.

"I wish you were coming with me. Good luck with the launch."

Pat Sullivan was feeling quietly pleased with himself, not least because he had spent the previous night with Maura. They had met for a drink and then a meal in a little Thai restaurant a few yards up the street from his house. Over tasty little seafood delicacies, Maura told him about painting Barry Owens' house with the Manchester United crest. He laughed so much when he heard the story that people sitting at the cramped little tables nearby turned around and stared at him peculiarly.

"And what team do you support?" she asked slyly.

"Oh no! You won't get me that handy. And if you ever send someone to redecorate my house, do you know what I'll do?"

"What?" she asked with horrified curiosity.

"I'll send someone back to plaster a giant poster of Daniel O'Donnell across the front of yours!"

"There's nothing wrong with Daniel O'Donnell and anyway I live on the third floor of an apartment block."

"I'll think of something. Hey, Maura?"

"What?" she said between mouthfuls of chicken in coriander and coconut.

"Give's a kiss – I'm dying to kiss you."

"Feck off! I'm eating."

"Very well then. I must take matters into my own hands."

He leaned across the table, held her face lightly between his two hands and planted a brief kiss firmly on her lips. In spite of herself, Maura shivered. She remembered what Lit had said about him being all lean and athletic and it was true. He wasn't a big hunk of lardy meat, but she thought it was nice the way his chest kind of bulged out and there was no telltale little layer of flesh hanging out over the top of his trousers. And the muscles on his upper arms were nicely rounded.

"Stop it!" she said half-heartedly. "I never eat when I'm kissing."

"Don't you mean kiss when you're eating?"

"Whatever. Just don't think that you can just buy me dinner and assume that I'm just one of those girls that's up for anything after the third glass of wine. Because I'm just not."

Some hours later, in the big untidy, but essentially clean and cosy mess that was Pat Sullivan's bed, Maura heaved a throaty sigh of satisfaction. Pat sat up, leaned on his elbow and looked down at her.

"What'll we do at the weekend?"

"How do you mean?"

"I mean – you and me – what about a walk by the sea – a film – I don't care – "

"OK – "

"Next week, we could fly to London for the weekend. There's this great play on."

"Now, wait a minute – don't mess with me – I'm very vulnerable right now."

He leaned forward and kissed her on the forehead. "You don't get it, do you? I've been waiting ages for that prat Barry Owens to get off the scene."

"I never knew! I mean, you never said – I mean, you didn't exactly make it obvious."

"Why would I risk being turned down? Besides you couldn't take your eyes off him. You wouldn't have even noticed."

"Well, I don't know what to say to that."

"Nothing. Maura, you're dead sexy, dead straight, have a wicked streak and you scare the hell out of me! I love you as a matter of fact– "

"You do?"

She was amazed at how easily he'd said it. Barry Owens had said it once when he was drunk and wanted to do something disgusting with a jar of massage oil – but that was all. And the funny thing was, Barry Owens had – well, he didn't have – he didn't have much – what he had was like a small marker-pen with a squishy tip or one of those bumpy broad bean pods. Perhaps that was why he needed the massage oil. Pat Sullivan needed no such embellishments.

At six in the morning, Maura sat bolt upright in the bed and stuck her elbow sharply into Pat's side.

"I have to go. Why didn't you wake me?"

She had to poke at him a few times before she got a coherent response.

"You never asked. Where are you going at this hour anyway?"

She dashed around the room, hastily retrieving her clothes. Her bra was draped across a very serious-looking book and Maura smiled when she remembered how it had got there. It began when she teased Pat about his house not needing any walls because he had so many books.

"What are they all about? I mean you haven't actually read them all, have you? Like, is there anything useful in them?" She had rummaged around through the books, pulling one out at random. "So what's this one all about?"

"*Deus Ex Machina* – it's Latin for when something you haven't been expecting sorts out a difficult situation for you . . . like in a book or a film. Say if you were drowning in the sea and out of nowhere a boat comes along and you're saved."

"I get it. Or if you're stuck on a lousy date with some nerd and a giant nerd-eating monster appears out of nowhere and gobbles him up?" She eyed the book with barely disguised scorn. "That's Deus Whatsisname, is it? Well, sod him," said Maura and whipped off her bra, draping it seductively across the front page. It was a completely silly thing to do, but the funny thing was that Pat laughed his head off.

"So where's the rush?" he said now, with the new huskiness in his voice that she liked.

"The site – the opening – I've got to get to Lit's house – "

His face fell in an instant and he sat up dejectedly.

"I'm sorry," said Maura. "It was stupid of me to mention it."

He turned and looked out his front window. Across the street was a high blue and gold hoarding. Along the hoarding were tasteful artists' impressions of the slick urban landscape which would soon rise up behind it. There were delicate little trees, children playing in perfectly contained, colour-coordinated playgrounds, sprightly old ladies feeding ducks at sparkling ponds, surrounded by landscaped shrubs and flowers. But it was like one of those magic-eye pictures and only if you stared hard could you really see the background for what it was – not a serene blue and grey haze of cloud and sky, but a cluster of glass and steel buildings so large that everything in sight was dwarfed almost to invisibility. He pointed out at it.

"This is what your company is selling to the world."

"We have to take the business where it comes. It's a

market economy. It's easy for university lecturers to be high and mighty about sleazy commerce – "

He hung his head. He didn't want a fight – least of all with Maura. If he was angry at all, it was with himself. How was it he could be so well read and so incapable of action? He had all the history books ever published in the world, stories of people who had got up off their backsides to change the world for good or ill, but he didn't have the guts to do anything. Yet Gearóid Magill, who never read anything more challenging than *Buy & Sell*, could drum up a political storm in a matter of hours. It didn't really matter that Magill's misguided foray had failed miserably. At least he had tried.

Later, Pat dressed in T-shirt and shorts and went out walking the perimeter of the site one last time. It was almost three miles long and by the time he reached the entrance, he was bathed in sweat. All was quiet there, no protesters, no reporters, no Magill shouting from a soapbox. The huge gates were open and inside he could see hundreds of men clambering about like ants, lifting, hauling, climbing, shouting, digging. He passed through the gates and waved to Tommy in the hut.

"How's it going, Pat? Haven't seen you in a while. Time for a quick cuppa?"

Pat nodded and stepped inside Tommy's hut. After all, he hadn't much else to do.

"There was a military coup. I was overthrown by Magill," he said taking a mug of steaming hot tea between his hands.

"Wants his head examined, that Magill fella. Thinks he's Eamon De Valera or someone. Hey, Pat, not that it matters any more, but what would you have done with this place anyway?"

"A park. That's all most people ever wanted here. The

nearest decent green space is the Phoenix. That's miles away if you don't have a car or you're old or you're pushing a buggy."

"True enough."

They stared out at all the activity on the site for a while until Pat finished his tea.

"That was just the job, Tommy – thanks. Mind if I look around? A fond farewell to dreams and all that."

"Work away."

A large area had been levelled, cleared and covered with artificial grass – just for the day. A bandstand had been erected, emblazoned in blue and gold with the letters CB done out in a tasteful crest. Sound engineers and cameramen busied themselves in preparation for the day's spectacle. Some classy-looking blue and gold marquee tents housed food and drink and provided shelter in the unlikely event of the day turning wet.

He looked up at the sky, wishing that God or whoever would rain down a mighty deluge and wipe away all trace of Budd Development from Stoneyfield. But it seemed that God or whoever was preparing to make his torrential downpours somewhere else in the universe today, because the sky was cloudless and the air dry and sluggish.

He strolled over to the massive Lampson crane and, despite himself, marvelled at the feats of engineering which must have gone into designing and building it. He could barely see to the top, and the base was large enough to accommodate a fine-sized house. Way above his head, Charlie Long, the driver, sat proudly ensconced in his cabin, swinging the jib across the broad expanse of the site. Pat watched mesmerised as the long cable dangled precariously in the air, waiting to hook up its load. Charlie had been sent to the States to get special training and some of the younger lads on the site regarded him as a special sort of hero. There was even an underground bet going as to who would be the first to climb up to the cabin in secret and drive the crane when Charlie wasn't looking.

Pat stood around watching for a while, then walked away. There wasn't anything more he could do. There was no sign of a *Deus Ex Machina* to deliver the people of Stoneyfield.

The limousines arrived, disgorging wealthy passengers at the gates who walked across layers of thick disposable red carpet which led to the viewing stand. A bevvy of unbelievably gorgeous girls from Babes Modelling Agency passed among the guests, smiling radiantly and handing out glossy brochures and commemorative packs. A group of young rugby players decked out in the IRFU development colours stood about in the midday sun. They idly watched the girls from Babes and half-heartedly studied the glossy brochures.

Neatly costumed waitresses and waiters dispensed champagne and canapes. A small brass band played bright and breezy tunes. People joked and laughed and looked about approvingly. They gasped in astonishment as they browsed through the brochures and saw the breadth of Conrad's vision, the imaginative grandeur of the world he was about to create for the people of Stoneyfield.

Lit, Maura and Matt bustled about, welcoming and seating the important guests, distributing name-tags, sorting out inevitable last-minute hitches.

Conrad entered the gates on foot, flanked by Jack Kennedy and Fergus Cunningham. He made his way directly to Lit and kissed her lightly on the cheek.

"All under control?"

"That's what you pay us for. No hitches so far. The minister is due in five minutes."

"Great. The media?"

"No major problems. Though word has it *The Mail* are going to do a hatchet job."

Conrad smiled crookedly. "Does it matter? Let them bellyache all they want. Nothing they say can make a difference now."

"Conrad?"

"What?"

"Don't be arrogant with them – especially now that you've won. It looks bad."

"I'll be any way I damn well like!"

Lit bit her lip. "I need to see someone," she said and departed hastily to talk to Cormac O'Dea the rugby player. He was to make a short speech of thanks on behalf of the IRFU to Conrad.

"Speech all sorted?"

"I'm no orator. But I'll do my best." He passed his notes to her for approval.

Lit was used to sports people who insisted they were bad at speaking in public. She reassured him. "It's great. You'll be fine. I saw you give a speech once – short and sweet. Most people get what I call 'FMF syndrome' when they get a microphone into their hands."

"FMF?"

"Fifteen Minutes of Fame syndrome. A chance to relate their childhoods, discuss their golf handicaps, share their gift for stand-up comedy, reminisce about the old days, expound on the decline of civilisation as we know it."

"Have no worries about me on that score." He smiled at her reassuringly.

Jack led Conrad into one of the tents. "Just some ideas on your speech, boss."

"Don't bother me now, Jack."

Jack persevered. "How about – that one from Shakespeare – 'I have done the state some service' – or 'Conrad Budd – the state's servant – but Stoneyfield's first'. Or I have some good rugby jokes –"

"Nothing worse – the last resort of a desperate man. I will simply thank the minister, the backers, and the people of Stoneyfield and declare the site officially open."

It was just as well that Conrad was a man of few words, because the minister had many thoughts, jokes, anecdotes and observations which he was anxious to share with his audience.

He began with key vote-catching phrases. "Rejuvenation of the city – unprecedented growth of the nation – the Celtic Tiger – commitment to environmental issues – 98per cent employment – fanfare for the common man – Ireland taking its place among the nations of the world – "

"Jesus, this guy should be in the Guinness Book of Cliches," Matt muttered under his breath to Lit.

The minister leaned his ample frame forward onto the podium. "'All this will not be finished in the first one hundred days. Nor will it be finished in the first thousand days – nor even perhaps in our lifetime on this planet. But let us begin.' The words of the great John F Kennedy, your excellencies, ladies and gentlemen. This is a historic moment. It must be celebrated, lauded, marked and remembered in years to come – and when I look down at those fine young men there, specimens of Irish manhood, I'm reminded of my own time as a rugby international. Indeed, one of my favourite jokes

502

goes back to the time we played the Fijians – "

Lit noticed that the workmen were becoming restless. The TV cameramen were busy shooting the pretty marketing assistants. The young rugby players glared sullenly into the middle distance, unimpressed by the minister's rugby joke. The girls from Babes examined their cuticles and picked particles of site-dust from their clothes. And still he droned on.

". . . asked how they celebrated their victories – 'Simple,' said the Fijian captain. 'The winners eat the losers!'"

Everyone squirmed. It was about as tasteless and tacky a joke as Lit ever heard. It was so bad that she almost forgave Jack Kennedy his whale joke.

"So without further ado, I give you a fine specimen of the present Irish crop of players – who will ever forget that stunning try against the French last year? – Cormac O'Dea!"

Cormac stood awkwardly to attention and tugged at the knot of his tie a couple of times. His shoulders strained beneath the stiff fabric of his suit. He began hesitantly, spoke simply for forty-five seconds, then sat down to heartfelt applause from the crowd.

It was oppressively hot and, during the speeches, Lit noticed a peculiar stillness in the atmosphere. Now a slight southerly breeze was beginning to raise little eddies of dust from the dried earth on the site. Looking down at the low-flying dust, she thought of Dandy and how he would know what the little eddies of low-flying dust meant.

Soon the ceremony was all over, the speeches, the presentation of the cheque to the IRFU, the turning of the sod.

Matt was the first to seek Lit out.

"Don't think this entitles you to more than fifty per cent – because it doesn't. Well done, partner!" He hugged her warmly and patted her on the back.

"Thanks. It went well, I think."

"Couldn't have worked out better. Couple of guys over there from Allied Provincial Banks – want to meet us to discuss – well, you know – stuff. They had a big share thingy that all went pear-shaped. Looking for help with their image."

Seán Tallon joined them and shook Lit's hand. "Not bad," he said, looking straight into her eyes with what she thought might be some sort of glint. The glint was quickly followed by a brief smile. "Champagne though," he went on, "no expense spared – "

His eyes glinted again.

Would she rise to it? Would she hell! She fixed him with her frostiest smile. It should have turned him to stone.

But instead he laughed. Oh my God – a teeth laugh and a warm smile, full of something very nice – but what was it? She couldn't get her head around it at all.

"Excuse me. I must join Conrad," she breezed and walked away.

In the distance there was a faint rumble of thunder, like an empty lorry trundling past in the early morning stillness. The wind seemed to veer around to the east. The air cooled and she felt goose-bumps on her skin, as though the heat which had enveloped the city for the past six weeks was now suddenly and rapidly draining out of the atmosphere. Then she felt the first tiny drops of rain on her skin.

# CHAPTER 39

Suddenly it was cold, an almost forgotten sensation, and the familiar greyness and sheets of sticky, wet rain quickly returned. People in the streets took on a pale, pinched look – almost instantly their eyes scrunched up, their faces grimacing against the sharp cold wetness. The wind howled banshee-like and blew litter along the pavements and flattened arrogant plants which had brazenly flaunted themselves in the heat.

At home, Lit gazed grimly through the French windows at her back garden. Everything was tossing about madly or beaten down already with the driving rain. Delphiniums dropped cravenly on the spot. Cranesbills put up a more spirited fight – but it was only a matter of time before they too succumbed. The South African daisies had shut up shop in disgust, closed their faces and huddled to the ground. They had not been bred to endure such indignity.

As she kicked off her mud and water-stained shoes, Lit realised that all this rain could mean only one thing. The slugs, who had temporarily migrated to the wetter climes of the north, would return with a vengeance. Even now they were probably massing on the border, like returning migrants, their passports checked, their visas stamped, their luggage cleared through customs, ready to chomp mercilessly through her hostas and oriental poppies, graze callously on calendulas, nibble cynically on her fritillaries.

She thought of donning the old blue track suit which hung at the back door for gardening emergencies, making a mercy dash into the wind and the rain, and spreading enough slug-pellets to cause a global slug catastrophe. But she didn't have time. As it was, if she didn't get a move on she'd be late for the big celebration in the Shelbourne. She showered and dressed hastily in the olive green sheath dress and made herself up. She surveyed herself in the full length mirror. With her corn gold hair swept back from her face and her slender shoulders bared – she looked – not bad at all. And the dress clung flatteringly in graceful curves.

Downstairs in the living-room, Richie's lean frame was draped across the sofa.

He looked up at her, cast a casual eye over her dress.

"Well," she asked, "do I pass the Richie Doran test?"

She waited for some scathing comment about sad middle-aged people trying to cling pathetically to their youth, but he said:

"You look just great, Mum, as always."

"Thanks," she replied, unreasonably chuffed.

"And, Mum . . . I love you."

"I love you too."

"And, Mum . . ."

"Yes?"

"I know it's a big night and everything, but if you get a chance – will you ask Conrad about the crane – please? It's something I really want to do. Other people want to do far more dangerous things – parachuting, bungee-jumping, white-water rafting . . . come on, Mum – is it really such an unreasonable thing to ask?"

She rubbed a tense hand across her forehead, suppressed her irritation and forced a laugh. "I thought you'd forgotten all about that silly business and I really don't have time to discuss it now."

She expected a hostile shrug or a petulant sigh at the very least. But instead he simply smiled at her.

"OK so," he replied easily. "I was only thinking – tonight would be deadly for being up there – what with the storm and everything. Can you imagine?"

Lit shuddered. "Yes, I can. It would be absolutely terrifying. Richie, you're being very childish. What a notion!"

"Oh, forget I even mentioned it. Have a good night."

"Don't wait up. I might be very late."

The ballroom in the Shelbourne heaved with people – glitzy, glamorous, monied, young, handsome and beautiful people. Lit took the stairs in elegant little steps. She had hoped that Conrad might escort her to the hotel, and lead her proudly into the ballroom on his arm, but he was far too busy. Instead, she arrived in the limousine he'd sent for her, quickly dashed through the wind and the rain to the main door, and made her way past the crowds in the foyer, quite alone.

At the base of the steps, she bumped into Seán Tallon.

"Oh!" was all she could think of saying.

"Looking for someone?"

"Yes. Conrad."

"Haven't seen him. Drink?"

"Thanks."

He steered her towards a quiet little alcove of comfortable armchairs. He grabbed two glasses of champagne from a passing waitress and sat beside her.

"Cheers!"

"Yes. Cheers."

"You look very beautiful."

"Em – ah – em – you look fine in that suit."

Silence. Where was Conrad?

"How's Richie?"

"He's great. Thanks for asking."

He stood up suddenly and she noticed his glass was empty.

"Have another?" he asked.

"Not yet."

He sat down again.

"So – you're going to marry Budd."

"Yes."

"Good! Good plan! Sound choice. Excellent strategy."

"I think so!"

"Yes. Do you – do you . . . but it's really none of my business."

"Do I love him or am I just marrying him as a sound financial investment?"

"Not exactly – "

"Yes, I love him."

"Then congratulations. He's a lucky guy," he said a bit sharply. He stood up and tried to straighten his bow-tie. "A very lucky guy. Damn! Excuse me."

He stalked off across the room and left Lit clutching her champagne glass in a state of pulverised shock.

When she finally got over the shock of Seán Tallon saying not one, but two complimentary things to her, Lit stood up, straightened the hem of her dress and went in search of her fiancé. She found him at the bar, but instantly wished she hadn't. Once more he was surrounded by a clutch of fresh gushing oestrogen and once more he was leaning rakishly on the counter, lapping it all up. He didn't even see her. One of the girls stood on coquettish tippy-toes and whispered something in his ear which brought on the familiar dirty smile and low gravelly laugh. And for a moment, she felt she imagined the next bit. It was possibly the champagne, or the shock of Seán Tallon's compliments, but she almost thought she saw Conrad nibbling the girl's ear and kissing her shoulder. Then she thought she imagined his hand sliding down the girl's back, squeezing her bum and discreetly rubbing his hand along the curve of her thigh.

Then she knew that she wasn't imagining it. She watched in horror as his hand roved about while the girl just laughed and wriggled.

As usual a number of strategies suggested themselves: 'the glass of champagne over the girl's head' trick; 'the knee in Conrad's groin' trick; 'the screaming harridan-bitch from hell with a broken glass in hand' strategy; the noble 'Take your ring back, you selfish cad, you don't deserve me!' strategy. Bonnie would have walked over, blitzed the girl with a comment about it being so important to get your bikini-line done when you wear a short skirt – then she would turn to Conrad and say something like: 'Put her down, darling. You don't know where she's been. Besides, you forgot to take your viagra pill.'

But for Lit none of those things were worth doing. The thought uppermost in her mind was that she couldn't live with the constant spectre of infidelity – ironic considering she had once felt OK about it with married Harry Menton.

In the entire history of Lit Doran she never achieved such a high level of drunkenness so quickly. She set about it with her usual ruthless professionalism. Standing with Matt in the foyer, she knocked back two glasses of champagne in about two minutes flat. Not having eaten anything since breakfast, that helped the situation enormously.

"In the party mood? Celebrating the engagement! Goodonya!"

"Fuck off, Matt!" she said and tossed back a third glass.

"What's up – old buddy – old pal?"

"Mind your own fucking business!" she spat as she surveyed the people in the room with a look of withering contempt.

"Hey! This is not like you – hey, hey – this is Matt here –

He put his big pudgy arms about her and led her reluctantly to a quiet corner.

"Now you are going to tell me what this is all about."

She couldn't speak. She was all choked up inside, humiliated, belittled. She was the ball and chain, 'er indoors, the future trouble and strife, the old bag – all the things she had dreaded.

"Conrad . . ." she sobbed.

Matt hugged and squeezed her and she bawled away to her heart's content.

"He wasn't for you," he said finally. "Anyone could see that."

"How do you mean?"

"He's a jerk – handsome, very – rich, no question there – charming, certainly – but that's all there is to him. Pry beneath the glossy wrapping and there's nothing. I mean, just picture this. It's a cold dark windy night in November, too miserable to go out anywhere. Besides, you're very tired. You've got a massive dose of PMT. You look like shite. You just want to curl up in front of a big log fire and read a good book or paint your nails or look at baby clothes – Conrad senses your mood, pours two glasses of wine, hands you one, pats your bloated PMT tummy, kisses you, sits in the chair opposite, wearing his old slippers. Then he smiles across at you and says 'Darling, you look beautiful. You've made me the happiest man in the world'. Can you picture it?"

No, she couldn't! Matt was right. But she didn't intend

to think about it right now. Was it time to reflect on yet another failed relationship, time to confront the inadequacies that drove her into the arms of unsuitable men every time, time to look deep into her psyche and be brutally honest with herself for once, time to face at last the ominous spectre of a world full of younger prettier women?

Was it hell! "Less talking, more drinking is what I say!"


Lit faced Conrad across the large round banquet table. It was heavily laden with all manner of silver, china, fine wines and pretty little floral displays. She was seated between Seán Tallon and Jack Kennedy. Conrad held court between Fergus Cunningham's wife and yet another attractive model from Babes. He hardly noticed Lit. She tossed the champagne back, glass after glass of it, and each mouthful seemed to rip away at the facade of the man she thought she was in love with. Behind the deep, deep brown eyes, behind the rugged, handsome face, the broad shoulders, the ample thighs, she found – nothing. At least nothing she particularly liked. He hadn't turned into a fat, balding man with nasal hair and a breath problem. He had become something far worse – a vain, self-seeking, selfish, bullying, insensitive, predatory, manipulative control-freak.

By the time the main course arrived, she was barely capable of focussing on the small but perfectly formed lamb chops in a rosemary and redcurrant sauce. Slowly and with great care she lifted up first a fork and then a knife. She speared the fork into one of the tiny chops and both fork and chop skidded across the plate. The metal on the china made a screeching sound and

Conrad glanced across at her disapprovingly.

"There you are, Conrad!" she said loudly with a stupid grin. "It's me! Can you see me? Yoo-hoo!"

The disapproving glance became a hostile glare.

Seán Tallon leaned forward ever so slightly so that almost no-one could see and mumbled something which sounded like 'karaoke'.

She straightened herself up with exaggerated effort and turned to him. "Karaoke? Are you drunk?"

"I said – are you OK?"

"Oh, I thought you said 'karaoke'! Isn't that funny? Yes, I'm OK! The finest. The absolute and uttermost, completely and utterly, the finest! Pass the wine there, Android!"

Seán filled up her glass.

"I propose a toast." She held up her glass in the air. "No, wait a minute. I have a riddle instead – or is it a joke? Anyway – what do you call a man – no, listen, everybody – what do you call a man who's engaged to one woman and puts his hand up a young one's skirt?"

Conrad turned away to talk to Fergus.

"No, Conrad! Listen! This one's for you – especially for you . . . you call him d-d- d- d-disengaged – howsat? Disengaged!"

She stood up unsteadily and glared across at him as she wrestled the massive ring from her finger. She flung it across the table and it landed in the exquisite little mound of basil mash on his plate.

"There! See! Disengaged! Now if you'll all excuse me – I need to use the baroom."

She keeled over onto Seán Tallon's shoulder and remained there for a few precarious moments, grinning apishly across the table at Conrad. She tried to straighten herself up. But her legs wobbled, jelly-like and she was in imminent danger of sliding inelegantly to the floor in her lovely shot-silk dress. But luckily a pair of firm hands appeared from somewhere and led her stumbling from the room.

She found herself propped on a bench in a quiet side street. It was raining heavily, the thick downpour flattening her hair and making a dark pattern in the green shot silk. The trees in front of her seemed to dance and sway and move about. It was quite amusing, like something out of a Disney film. She watched them through half-opened eyes for a while, almost expecting them to break into a cheerful little ditty about all being shiny happy trees dancing together in stormy weather.

Then she felt her stomach take a turn. In fact, it wasn't so much a turn as several complete circular rotations and a few somersaults. Something was inside trying to get out. Was she at last in a Stephen King novel, her body taken over by some Tummyknocker? It sure felt like it. This Tummyknocker kept on banging and tapping and pushing around inside, nudging his way up her intestines until he found an exit. Then she felt him gushing up through her chest, into her throat, until she could hold him no longer and he shot out in the direction of the trees.

"That got you – bastard Tummyknocker . . ."

She felt slightly less drunk now, though still far from well.

She sat up straight and watched the trees for a moment. She realised now that they weren't dancing at all. She was in the middle of a gale-force wind. And the turmoil inside her stomach wasn't a Tummyknocker at all. Lit Doran, Ice Queen, founder of the International Withering Eyebrows Federation, rich, successful, independent single mother, Lit Doran – had puked her miserable drunken guts out in a dingy side street. She felt a terrible emptiness and it wasn't just because the Tummyknocker had escaped. So this was what despair felt like. She'd sometimes wondered, but could never get her head around it. Despair as a concept didn't make sense. People who felt despair were miserable failures – self-pitying misery-guts who needed to get a life. It was the worst sin of all.

Then she felt a hand on her shoulder, an arm about her and a kind voice, a voice that she recognised.

"Are you OK?"

She nodded.

"Best thing is to get it out. You'll be fine now."

Then a coat was draped across her shoulders and a glass of water was held out in front of her.

"Drink it."

She was thirsty. Her mouth felt like the inside of a vacuum-cleaner and when the cool water hit her parched tongue she gulped back greedily. In a matter of seconds, the glass was empty.

"Do you want some more?"

She shook her head and they sat in the downpour without saying anything for a while, watching the trees gyrating in the gale.

"Perhaps we'd better go back in. You'll catch a chill."

"I think I'd like to go home."

"Would you like me to take you?"

"That's OK," she snapped, in a desperate attempt to salvage some tiny shred of dignity.

The waves of drunken nausea which had shot through her only moments earlier, were nothing compared to the horrible waves of shame and embarrassment which were engulfing her now. Why of all the people on the planet did it have to be Seán Tallon who witnessed her final sickening degradation?

"Why don't you just leave me alone? I'm perfectly all right."

"But I – "

"I suppose you get some sort of malicious pleasure in seeing other people make eejits of themselves!"

"No – I –"

"Just leave me alone! Go away!"

She buried her head in her hands. When she finally looked up, he was gone.

She made her way gingerly back inside the hotel and slunk into the secluded comfort of the lady's rest room. The attendant there had seen all sorts of drunkenness before and took pity on Lit. Out of a little cupboard, she produced a tube of toothpaste and disposable toothbrush still in its wrapper. "Brush your teeth, love – you'll feel loads better after it." Lit hovered unsteadily, but did as she was told, then washed her hands with scented soap and splashed cold water on her face. The attendant made her sit in the large armchair in the corner, then fetched her a black coffee. By the time Lit emerged back into the foyer much later, though her hair was a flattened mess, she was cleaned up and not completely but almost sober.

All around her were dazzling, glitzy, fabulously dressed, smiling, happy people. But she wanted nothing more now than to go home and be with Richie. She asked the doorman to call her a cab. He told her it would take a while so she ordered another black coffee and waited in the foyer. Suddenly she needed to be with Richie more than anything else in the world. She decided to call him and say she was coming home early after all. She wanted to tell him that it had all been a big mistake with Conrad, that she'd completely lost the run of herself, been foolish and selfish and forgotten to consider her son. She wanted to apologise for being such a neglectful mother, to try and rebuild the close, easy relationship they'd once had. She and Richie had an awful lot to talk about.

She tried calling him, but there was no reply from home or his mobile. Perhaps he was in bed already. She hoped he hadn't decided to go out. The storm was worsening by the minute. She tried his number again without any success.

Then out of the corner of her eye, she saw Jack Kennedy. He sidled up to her in a state of high anxiety.

"The boss was looking for you everywhere."

She was about to make some cutting reply when she recognised genuine panic in Kennedy's face. "Why? What's wrong?"

"A problem on the site. The big crane. It's swaying dangerously."

Was that all? Just as well she'd never agreed to Richie going up on the damn thing.

"What's it got to do with me anyway?"

"He just wanted you to know he's gone to the site to sort it out. The light is on in the cabin. They think someone might have tried to climb up the crane for a prank, or maybe even sabotage. You know youngsters – up for all that dare-devil stuff. The site engineer is in Donegal and Charlie Long the crane operator is into his seventh pint."

She didn't really have the energy to become embroiled in this latest drama of Conrad's. She felt emotionally mangled, needed to be in the peace and calm of her own home, to lick her wounds, to be with Richie. There was still no sign of the taxi. She excused herself and ducked into the restroom once more to try and fix her hair.

"Feeling better, love?" asked the kindly attendant.

"Yes, thanks," she said.

Then a sudden icy chill shot through her.

Richie!

He'd been unusually cheerful and relaxed when she'd left him. He'd asked about climbing the gigantic crane and took it surprisingly well when she'd once again dismissed the idea. Now she couldn't reach him. He wasn't answering his phone. Dear God – would he do anything that stupid? She'd treated him so carelessly over the past months that she barely knew him any more, could hardly guess what went on in his head.

Trembling with a primal fear, she bolted back through the foyer and prayed that the taxi had arrived.


# CHAPTER 40

There was still no sign of the taxi.

She made a frantic call to Conrad and warned him about Richie.

"Damn fool!" said Conrad brusquely, and hung up.

Lit could vividly picture the massive crane swaying in the gale, rocking on its foundations. She imagined the long braced jib swinging about uncontrollably in the wind. When he was a child, Richie used to take his toys into the bath and put them through all sorts of tempests and tornadoes. She'd sit on the toilet seat next to the bath and watch him, totally absorbed in play. Anything was possible – tidal waves, alien invasions, attack of the Killer Bath Foam, Giant Slimy Green Flannel Thing gobbles up nuclear submarine. Sometimes he would set up

517

his crane in the bath and dangle the jib out over the edge. He would hang a little Playmobil man with a hard hat on the end of the cable and then set a tidal wave in motion, tossing and swaying the crane until the man fell off or the crane toppled over into the water.

She rang the house, tried Richie's mobile again, sent a text message. But there was no response. Her sense of panic and dreadful foreboding increased with each unanswered call, each undelivered text message.

At last the taxi arrived and she clambered in quickly, ordering him to drive quickly to the Stoneyfield site, that her son's life probably depended on it. She made frantic phone calls, firstly to Conrad for any news, but he wasn't answering, to Richie himself, to his friends, to Matt, but got no reply from anyone.

The horrific weather added to Lit's sense of impending doom. She would never cope with the grief of losing her son. Suicide would be the only option. She busied herself planning how she would go about it. Hanging – ugh – too gruesome. Drowning – too cold and too wet. Drinking a bottle of whiskey and driving her car at a brick wall at nine hundred miles an hour? But what if she survived and was in a wheelchair for the rest of her life? What if she didn't survive and went to hell and ended up next to Alice Madigan? She just couldn't think about it right now.

Conrad probably had a number of reasons for climbing the crane that night. First, there was the possibility that Lit's son might be engaged in some dare-devil prank, in which case he would have to be rescued. There was the crane itself, millions of pounds' worth, crucial to the successful excavation and construction of the site. In its present position, dangling out over the houses, it might keel over and kill a resident. That could set the development back months, if not years. Finally, and perhaps the real reason, in spite of everything Conrad was an engineer by training and inclination. If things were broken or not working properly, he tried to mend them. He had always been far happier with things that had mechanisms, than with people or paper. Paper was nothing. Ideas were nothing until put into practice. But there was a certainty about a thing with a mechanism – a car, a computer, a digger or a crane – it would do what it was designed to do, and if it didn't, it could be adjusted or repaired. Spurred on by the challenge of putting the crane to rights he slipped and clambered his way up the wet ladder in the gathering storm.

Pat Sullivan had intended having an early night. Maura was all excited about the Celebration Ball in the Shelbourne and had invited him to join her. But it would have been unthinkable for him to be there. It would have all sickened him – the smugness, the greed, the self-satisfaction.

He watched the news which was mostly coverage of the sudden and ferocious storm. In Wexford, roofs had been ripped from houses. In Wicklow, a summer house had been washed off the cliffs and into the sea. Rivers were bursting their banks at an alarming rate! Towns, villages and fields flooded and farmers fretted over livestock. Pat was glad he didn't have an outdoor job.

He ran a hot bath, poured himself a glass of Barolo brought back from a spring trip to Italy and slid into the steaming water, clutching a paperback copy of *The Decline and Fall of The Roman Empire*. It was as good a book as any to lift his despair. He might someday write a book called *The Decline and Fall of The Celtic Tiger*. But it wouldn't be for a while yet.

He sank down into the bath, sipping from his glass and listening to the wind and the rain. The fate of the Roman Empire could wait. He knew the ending anyway. He began to nod off into a pleasant steam and wine-induced snooze. His thoughts scattered and ambled about at random. He was a Roman attending the baths, waiting for news from the Senate. He was dressed in a toga and stood about looking statesman-like, holding important scrolls in his hands. He might have made something interesting of the dream, but he was startled from his torpor by a very loud creaking noise – like the sound effects in the film *Titanic*. Very loud, very sinister, creaking noises.

He jumped out of the bath, water and wine splashing everywhere, then hastily wrapped a towel around his midriff. He peered through the window and the driving rain that streaked down in rivers. He could see nothing. The blue and gold hoarding was still intact. Then a movement in the air caught his eye and he looked up.

"Oh, fuck!"

He dressed quickly in jeans and a frayed woollen jumper. Then he threw on an old hiking jacket and boots and ran out to alert the neighbours, banging on doors, shouting at them to get out of their beds. With his mobile phone, he called the local garda station and the fire brigade.

Lit sat in Tommy Russell's hut, peering out at the crane. There was an air of unreality about it all. Just hours ago, she was engaged to Conrad, believed herself to be in love with him, Richie was safe at home and the building site was awash with sunlight and wealth and optimism.

Now life seemed to be disintegrating at an alarming

rate. High up in the darkness, she could just about make out the figure of Conrad climbing into the dimly-lit cabin. It was a classic cliffhanger situation. Would Richie be in the cabin? Could Conrad save him? Much to her relief, it was the briefest of cliffhanger moments. Tommy Russell's mobile flashed and it was Conrad calling from the cabin.

"Tommy – there's no-one here. Tell Lit there's no sign of Richie. Maybe the storm triggered the light-switch. I'm going to swing this thing away from the houses, and see if I can steady it somehow."

There was a loud knock on the door of the hut. Tommy was not surprised to see that it was a drenched and very concerned Pat Sullivan. He'd called a couple of ambulances on stand-by, he said, in case they were needed and the Gardaí had cordoned off the area and were trying to move the residents whose houses were in danger into the local national school, well out of harm's way. But it was all taking too long. It was late at night and people had to be woken from their sleep.

Lit felt punch-drunk, too tired, dazed and confused to even feel relieved that at least Richie hadn't been daft enough to climb the crane. But it still left the question of his whereabouts. She dialled home again and this time he answered.

Relief flooded through her, tears sprung up and coursed down her cheeks. She sank down into a chair and tried in vain to compose herself.

"Hi, Mum, what's the story?"

She choked, beyond speech, beyond even coherent thought.

"Where the hell have you been?"

"Here!"

"Why didn't you answer the phone?"

"Didn't hear it."

"And your mobile? Why was it switched off?"

"No credit. Pointless having it on when there's no credit."

Some day soon, she thought with a mother's perverse logic, I'll kill him!

"How could you? I've been through hell worrying about you."

"What hell? What did I do? Think you're having another one of them panic attacks, Ma."

"There is no such thing as a panic attack and don't call your mother Ma! I've been worried sick about you. I thought you were – I thought you were – "

"You thought I was what? At an all-night drugs party? I told you that's definitely not my scene."

"No! I didn't think that."

She tried to frame an explanation which would make sense to him. But how could she explain that while he was comfortably stretched on the sofa, with the telly turned up too loud and a bowl of popcorn in his lap, she was imagining him mangled to bits and gone forever.

"I don't know what I thought," she said finally.

"Right – see ya – have to go. Celebrity Death Match is on."

Tommy Russell and Pat were peering out through the rain-streaked window at Conrad trying to swing the crane away from the houses. Tommy kept up a mumbling commentary on his mobile, mostly about shifting levers and gears and 'swinging her round'. Lit almost expected him to shout 'Lock hard!' up at Conrad.

But suddenly Tommy's expression changed to one of horror.

"Oh, Jesus!" he said with startling clarity.

## CHAPTER 41

An ambulance arrived on the scene in a matter of minutes and Conrad was whisked away, his life hanging by a thread. The crane had buckled in the violent winds, and seemed certain to tumble down on those residents who hadn't yet vacated their houses. But somehow, with a combination of engineering skill and foolhardy determination, he'd managed to steer it in the opposite direction so that it crumpled and crashed to the ground landing with a tremendous clanging noise on an enormous pile of steel girders. But Conrad had been injured, his head crushed against the steering column of the crane.

By now, Lit felt like she'd done ten rounds with Mike Tyson. No-one had chewed off her ears, but the rest of her was pulverised, vaporised, shattered, scattered and battered. She wasn't allowed to travel with him in the ambulance, his injuries were too serious. So Pat Sullivan and Maura (who had arrived as soon as she'd heard the news) drove her to the hospital and they all waited outside the intensive care ward for hours for news of Conrad. It was almost mid-morning when his mother and a brother arrived, shocked and grief-stricken. And Maura at last dragged Lit away. There was nothing more she could do.

At home, she slid into a hot bath and stared blankly at the marble-tiled wall. When the water became uncomfortably cold, she climbed out, pulled on a pair of cotton pyjamas and a dressing-gown. She barely knew what she felt about Conrad. Though he had treated her appallingly, she couldn't deny that his life hung in the balance because of his strange impetuous heroism, couldn't forget that he had gone willingly to the top of

523

the crane to rescue Richie, partly at any rate. She found it too difficult to untangle the complex web of feelings that engulfed her now when she thought of Conrad. But there was one person she could deal with.

She went downstairs to confront Richie about his despicable behaviour.

He was in the kitchen making an everything-sandwich for breakfast. She straightened herself up and vowed to pin her index finger to the inside of her pocket so that it wouldn't pop out and start wagging at him. But she would tear strips off him – make no mistake.

"Now listen here, Richie!" she began. "Your behaviour last night – "

She stopped. What had he done wrong? Apart from slouching on the sofa and not hearing the phone, he'd done nothing. She decided to let it rest.

"No offence, Mum, but you look awful." He gave her one of his casual hugs.

"It's been a tough night," she said, close to tears.

She told him about Conrad, the accident, left out the little incident with the engagement ring and the episode in the alleyway, admitted she'd had a panic attack and apologised for shouting down the phone at him.

Richie was still hungry. He digested the news about Conrad as he made himself a microwave chip buttie, spreading lashings of ketchup on the chips – not that he was heartless or anything, but he was just as upset about the destruction of the crane. All the same, certain things about his mother's behaviour the night before didn't add up.

He sat into Dandy's old chair and stared out the window, vaguely trying to make sense of her.

At last, when he'd packed away the last of the bread

and chips he asked: "Why were you so angry with me last night?"

"Just forget it now. I made a mistake, that's all."

He stood and edged up beside her, his tall, lean frame dwarfing her.

"Ah, go on! Tell me," he said, briefly draping his arm around her shoulders.

She poured herself a cup of coffee, took a deep breath and looked up at her son. She flicked a lock of hair back from his smooth forehead.

"I thought you'd gone up in the crane. I thought . . . well, you weren't answering the phone . . . then you were always going on about that stupid thing. You even brought it up last night before I went to the Shelbourne."

Richie nodded, mildly confused. Weren't mothers strange creatures really! He reached into the bottom drawer of the freezer and pulled out a tub of ice cream.

"Go on," he said, digging the stainless steel scoop into the frozen tub.

"You can't eat ice cream for breakfast!"

He ignored her.

"Remember when you were little and you used to make up all those big dramas in the bath with cranes and planes and big battleships . . . you even told Seán Tallon about it . . . well, they thought at first that someone was up in the crane and I got it into my head that . . . well, that it was you . . ."

He sat at the table, then poured maple syrup on the ice cream and swirled it around in the bowl to soften the mix.

"That I'd gone up the crane," he said matter-of-factly as he spooned the ice cream and syrup mix into his mouth.

"Well, yes. Exactly."

He scoffed to himself. The very idea! As if he'd worry her like that! As if he didn't know his mother would tear him limb from limb if he ever did such a thing! As if he'd really go out on such a godawful night! As if he'd risk catching his death of cold! As if he'd risk putting his own life in danger! When Mettalica were playing on MTV and Barney Ryan was calling over with this brilliant new Playstation game and Zoe was dropping by with a Chinese takeaway?

"I've more sense than that," he said, burying his head in *Kerrang* magazine. "I've got more sense than you if that's what you thought! Anyway, when he was driving me home from Barney's the other night, Seán Tallon said that if I ever went up in that crane without your permission, that I would have to answer to him and that he would inflict some sort of dire punishment on me."

Lit raised an eyebrow. "And what did you say to that?"

"I told him he was an eejit, of course." He returned to his magazine.

She patted him affectionately on the shoulder and took herself out into the garden on slug patrol. They'd returned with a vengeance and entirely chomped through a large clump of white and delicate pink poppies. All that remained now were a few hideously mutilated stalks.

Later she called the hospital for news of Conrad. But there was none – only that he was unconscious and that he was being monitored carefully and the doctors would assess his condition in the evening. She desperately needed to talk to someone, to explain the peculiar deluge of feelings which swamped her whenever she thought of Conrad. In fact, she desperately needed Bonnie. But she wouldn't be back from Lake Como until the following day.

She tried to snatch a few hours' rest, but sleep wouldn't come. With Conrad at death's door, she felt horribly guilty about her drunken outburst at the table the night before. Yes, he'd treated her appallingly, but it was hard to be angry with him now, because he was hovering at death's door, because he'd done such a heroic thing. What a complex man, she thought, ruthlessly buying his way into Stoneyfield on the one hand, carelessly risking his life on the other, to protect the lives of those very people who despised him.

But something else was dancing about, waving frantically at her from the far borders of her subconscious. What was it? Some niggling thing that would not let her rest. Try as she might, she could not identify it.

She spent the rest of the evening slumped on the sofa, calling the hospital at hourly intervals, gazing at the TV screen, and dozing off, then waking suddenly. Richie cooked her up a Spanish omelette. It looked like he'd thrown everything into it – cheese, red peppers, onions, tomatoes, lardons of bacon, slices of frankfurter sausage, slices of potato. But it tasted surprisingly good and, discovering that she was absolutely starving, she wolfed down the lot. At last, when she couldn't bear to gaze at the TV screen any longer, she took herself off to bed. She tossed and turned all night, but the hours passed and once more she found herself listening to her old friend – the bird whose job it was to wake all the other birds. This time, he seemed even jollier. Probably he was thinking about all the extra worms that the rain had brought.

She went for a run in the park. There was a nice cool breeze now and everything looked pleasantly drenched. She stopped for a few minutes to talk to Mrs O'Greaney who was walking her little Yorkshire terrier. It was just homely neighbourhood talk – about old neighbours leaving and new ones arriving, about the new coffee shop around the corner, about the O'Connors' new grandchild.

"Why don't you call in for a cup of tea some time? I'd love the company," the old lady said.

Lit was about to list the hundreds of really important things she would be doing over the next few weeks and say that, of course, when she found a moment, she would love to visit and she would file a reminder on her mobile phone about it this very morning.

"Thank you. I'd love to," she found herself saying instead.

The run and the chat cleared her head a little and when she stood under the shower to freshen up, she smiled at her own foolish panic over Richie, then laughed out loud as she thought of Seán Tallon threatening her son with dire consequences. She realised with a start then what had been dancing and waving on the far edges of her subconscious. It was the realisation that she had misjudged someone terribly, been nasty to a good and decent and fine person. She would have to apologise. He might not even accept her apology. He had every right to tell her to get lost. It was nothing more than she deserved.

Seized with a sense of purpose, she picked up the phone and dialled his number. Her heart thumped loudly as she waited for him to answer. She knew that her heart was thumping only because she was about to say the two second-hardest words in the English language: "I'm sorry!"

She was both disappointed and relieved when there was no reply. Several more attempts yielded the same result. She called his office to be told he was away for a few days. At last, she called Matt who knew nothing either. And now it would have to wait because she ought to go to the hospital to be at her ex-fiancé's side. She could write a letter, but what would she say? Dear Seán, I'm very sorry for being rude and for having misjudged you. Thank you for issuing my son with dire threats. Yours sincerely, Lit Doran . . .

No way! She'd done her best to find him. It wasn't her fault if he was away. And she congratulated herself that at least in principle she had been fully prepared to apologise humbly and sincerely to him.

The women of Ireland – those who had thought him a cross between Anthony Quinn and George Clooney – with the merest hint of the oriental about his eyes and a slight dash of Gregory Peck thrown in, those who had admired his thighs in many a scrum, those who had longed to rest their heads on his broad shoulders and chest, those who had yearned to drown in his smouldering, deep, deep brown eyes – those women were mightily relieved to learn that there wasn't a mark on Conrad's body or his face, when the firemen cut him from the mangled cabin. There was merely a slight dinge in the back of his skull.

In the Intensive Care Unit, his life hung by the finest of threads. For days on end, he lay in bed, tubes passing in and out of his body, his chest rising and falling with the help of a ventilator, his head heavily bandaged where it had collided with the steering column.

The people of Stoneyfield already mourned his passing. They spoke of his heroism, how he had saved lives, his essential decency in the end. Maybe he had offered bribes. Maybe he was a crook. But he was someone to look up to, a man with the common touch. And at least he'd had a bit of vision and got things done.

But Gearóid Magill was jubilant and the Shakespearean quotations rolled from his fluent tongue. "Hoist with his own petard! And good enough for him!"

"What are you on about?" asked Fidelma.

"Killed with his own poison, blown up with his own gunpowder!"

"And you'd know all about that!" she snapped in disgust. She'd completely fallen out of love with him.

Jack Kennedy was inconsolable. In his pantheon of heroes, Conrad had ranked second only to JFK. In his desolation, he turned to funeral arrangements. Conrad must be buried in style. His coffin would be carried along the quays on a gun-carriage. There would be a twenty-one-gun salute. The cranes of the city would dip their jibs in respect. And in the church, the world's rich and powerful would congregate to mourn his passing.

Even the newspapers bowed their mastheads in sorrow. Scandals forgotten, they hoped and feared for him. They called on people to forget his indiscretions, to forgive his transgressions. He was after all, one of the founding fathers of the Celtic Tiger.

Tycoon's Life Hangs In The Balance . . . Brave Tycoon Averts Catastrophe . . . Lifes Saved By Quick-Thinking Tycoon . . . Conrad Budd Hero Of The Nation . . . A Flawed Genius . . . Doctors Hold Out Little Hope For Budd . . .

But a knock on the head is a strange thing. As a lad, Conrad had lain at the bottom of many a pile-up on the rugby pitch. Often he was concussed, several times rendered unconscious. Once his mother had sent for a priest and he had been given the last rites. That time, he imagined a shadowy presence standing at the end of his bed which melted away as his strength returned. Now the ominous figure stood quietly at his bedside once more, that same shadowy presence that had stood in his penthouse bedroom a couple of months past. Deep in his subconscious, Conrad wrestled with all his might, straining every muscle in his body. Death the Leveller could piss off and level someone else.

Outside in the plush reception area of the luxurious Blackrock Clinic, Bonnie, freshly tanned and returned from Lake Como, held Lit's hand.

"Don't worry. He's a tough nut."

Lit shook her head and said nothing.

"I'm sorry I said you didn't love him. Maybe I was just the teeny weensiest bit jealous. And I'm sorry I wasn't here for you," Bonnie said, her own eyes filling up with tears.

"You were right. As usual, Bonnie Ballantyne – you were right. I don't love him. Not in the slightest. I couldn't live with him for even a minute. I finished with him the night of the accident and now I just feel guilty."

"Guilty? What for?"

"If he dies – I'll have it on my conscience for ever that I was horrible to him and then in spite of my awful behaviour, he went to his death, nobly trying to save my son."

"Don't be daft," said Bonnie. "None of that's your fault."

"And think of the scandal – if the papers get hold of it – just imagine the headlines  – Tycoon's Girlfriend Breaks Off Engagement On Night Of Fatal Accident . . . Tycoon Driven To Death By Callous Girlfriend . . ."

"Don't feel guilty about being tough on a guy like Conrad. That's all he ever understood. Treat him mean – keep him keen – remember? He doesn't – didn't understand sensitivity and kindness. He occasionally did good things like going up the crane when it suited him, but mostly it suited him to be ruthless, arrogant and self-serving.""

"Maybe so."

"Why did you finish with him anyway?"

"I saw him with a young one and they were all over each other like a rash."

"That's Conrad."

"Why do you keep saying that? As though you know something I don't? It's very annoying."

Bonnie bit her lip. She looked even more ravishing now, tanned and glowing healthily after her pleasant little trip to Italy. But inside she was sadder than she'd ever been. Perhaps it was time to tell Lit the truth.

"Remember when Richie was small, and you had no social life and the height of excitement was finding the plastic toy in the cornflakes box, or deciding what you were going to make out of the big Pampers boxes."

Lit strained to remember. Richie's childhood was just a blur now and only the oddest moments remained frozen in her memory: the time he ate the cigarette, the time he went missing in Dunnes, the night he had camped out in the garden and she and Dandy had stayed awake all night watching over him, the night he was ill and wouldn't stop laughing at an invisible man in the corner, the day he picked one of Mrs Kelly's prize dahlias for her. The rest was filed in her subconscious, a warm unreachable glow in her heart.

"I had a little thing going with Conrad then."

Lit looked into her best friend's face, to see if she might, on the off chance be joking, fantasising, perhaps a bit of wishful thinking.

No, she was clearly not joking!

The look in her eyes told of something much stronger and deeper than any fantasy or bit of wishful thinking.

"But you can't have! It's impossible! I would have known! You've never kept any secrets from me! I know about every single man you've ever even fancied."

Bonnie smiled ruefully. "I never told anyone about Conrad. He was my perfect little secret."

It was clear from Lit's face that she felt hurt.

"Of course I was tempted to tell you, but what was the point? Apart from Richie, the only male you showed much interest in was Thomas the Tank Engine. Anyway – it ended. I told him to get lost."

Lit was still gobsmacked that Bonnie had managed to keep the biggest romantic secret of her life under wraps for years.

"But how? When? Where?"

"I bumped into him at a night club one night. I'd only started teaching and didn't have much money. He was there splashing the champagne around – he was just beginning to make serious money in those days. I went over and started chatting to him, teased him about the champagne lifestyle a bit, I suppose . . . then, at the end of the night, he asked me out . . . six months it lasted."

"Then what happened?"

"Other women. He said they just threw themselves at him and what could he do? He said he often thought of faking his own marriage just to get them off his back. So I suppose that's where the fake engagement to Angela came from. Anyway we went our separate ways – and we didn't really meet again until the night of your party."

"Oh my God, Bonnie Ballantyne!"

Lit stood up and stared at her dearest closest friend in amazement. It had never even entered her head, though the signs were there if only she had read them – Bonnie's knowing comments about Conrad, how lately she seemed to have silly arguments with Bonnie over nothing, the fact that Conrad and Bonnie barely even spoke to each other when they met – not even to discuss the weather . . .

"You love him! Don't you? You sly, sneaky – and you never once said a word."

Bonnie shrugged. "The past is history and all that," she said, her lower lip quivering horribly.

Then she began to cry in earnest. Lit had never before seen Bonnie cry – except at *The English Patient* and that didn't really count. Certainly Bonnie had never shed a tear about a man in her entire life. She simply wasn't made that way. After all, Bonnie was the one with the embroidered use 'em and lose 'em cushion. Bonnie didn't love men. She used them – for excitement, for glamour, for getting into the top bashes, for sex. She'd never actually mentioned loving any of them.

"You must have really hated me!" Lit said, realisation continuing to dawn.

"Well – you're a pain in the fanny sometimes, Lit Doran," Bonnie said through her tears," – you're prissy, smug, self-righteous, superior, self-absorbed – obsessed with money – don't know your arse from your elbow . . ."

"That bad?"

"Just lately. But it's nothing terminal. I predict changes – I look into my crystal ball and I see big changes coming –" She cupped her hands around an imaginary ball. "Oh, yes – Laetitia Doran is about to find love, happiness and contentment and children – yes – I see children several . . . and a cure for that awful splitting thing that happens to the skin on your thumbs in winter – "

They giggled like schoolgirls, the tearful moment past, until a passing nurse eyed them with saintly disapproval. Anyway, it wasn't right to be laughing while Conrad lay in a coma only metres from them. They returned to their gloomy vigil of silence, leafing half-heartedly through newspapers, with an occasional burst of enthusiasm for the crossword which might last all of five minutes. They walked the corridors, drank endless cups of coffee, kept hunger at bay with bags of Tayto and chocolate muffins in the hospital cafe. Told each other silly doctor jokes which neither of them laughed at.

"Doctor, doctor, sometimes I think I'm a teepee and sometimes I think I'm a wigwam . . . You're two tents."

"Doctor, doctor, I think I'm turning into a vampire . . . Necks please – "

Sitting in the café depressed them. It was full of cheery, healthy-looking men who had come through triple bypasses and lively, determined women who were trying out their new hips. They even spotted Dee Dee Caulfield lurking in the corner with a brand new nose.

"Much good will it do her," said Bonnie. "Not unless she gets the chin, the eyes, the lips and the botox injections in the forehead as well."

They chortled half-heartedly, but even honest-to-goodness bitching couldn't lift their spirits and they returned to their station outside Conrad's room.

George Clooneys came and went, each time bearing more ominous tidings.

"It's looking bad."

"It's not good."

"Stable but critical."

"Critical but stable."

"Not dead – but in the next cabbage patch . . ." Bonnie

was appalled to overhear one young intern whispering to another.

"Why do they always bring fruit and vegetables into it?" Lit commented.

His family came and played him tapes of his favourite music, held up photos of him as a little boy, reminded him of childhood toys and pranks. His mother wept and prayed and kept her own counsel. Friends came and recited tales of the old days, all-night drinking sessions, lap-dancing clubs, lost weekends in Paris, London, New York. A video of Conrad scoring a try for Ireland was played over and over again with the roars of the crowd cheering him on. A string of beautiful women visited his bedside, calling wistfully to him, hoping that they would be the one to bring him back from the brink of death. Nothing worked. He didn't stir.

"We're turning off the life-support machine. There's no hope. No hope at all," said one of the George Clooneys.

Bonnie and Lit cowered in the corridor, clinging to each other in despair. Their faces were pinched and drawn from sleepless nights, their eyes sunken and dull, their shoulders sagging defeatedly.

"Can we see him one last time?"

George nodded gravely and led them into the darkened room.

They sat and held his hands, stroked his forehead, kissed him lightly on the cheek and wept silently. Lit told him she was sorry and that he wasn't to die because she couldn't live with the guilt. She told him how brave he was, how clever, how handsome, how wonderful. She told him it was a privilege to have known him and that she deeply regretted the fact that she didn't love him, that she had entirely forgiven him for all his transgressions.

"You jammy bastard! Don't you dare lie there and die! If you die, I'll kill you – I swear!"said Bonnie.

Lit stepped out of the room. If Bonnie loved Conrad, then she ought to be alone with him one last time.

Alone with Conrad, Bonnie stroked his hand, rubbed his forehead, ran her fingers through his hair. She kissed him on the forehead, on the cheeks, on the lips, whispered words of true affection in his ear. He lay on in deep sleep, nothing moving except his chest rising and falling with the ventilator. Then, in a moment of inspired genius (she would later boast) and because she couldn't resist doing it for old time's sake, Bonnie slipped her hand beneath the sheet and gently ran her hand across his broad, magnificent chest. Tears welled up as her fingers grazed over the smooth ripples of his stomach and the bullet-hard muscles of his thighs. She fell into a reverie of sweet memories of this man who was for her The Holy Grail of Manship – in her eyes, in spite of all his faults, The Only Perfect Man In the World.

So deep in thought was she, that she didn't at first notice the faint flickering of his fingers, the merest little stirring of his eyelids. She didn't notice a thing until a firm hand locked onto her slender wrist.

"Bonnie, is that you?"

"Of course it's me! You big girl's blouse! It's about time you woke up."

So Conrad survived and almost the first thing he did on regaining consciousness was to summon Jack Kennedy to his bedside.

"Kennedy . . . get that Sullivan bloke from the Residents' Association in here in a few days – I want to talk to him."

537

"What for?"

"That's my business. I want to see him, that's all. Now leave me."

When she heard that Conrad had summoned Pat, Maura urged him to be cautious. There was no knowing what a man like Conrad Budd could get up to. Pat, on the other hand, was quite unruffled by the summons.

"People like him don't scare me," he said easily.

"I'm just saying he might only want to offer you a bribe or something," she said now as they made their way along the hospital corridor to Conrad's plush suite.

Maura waited outside, as Pat rapped lightly on the door and Conrad told him to come in.

Pat hesitated in the doorway for a few moments. Conrad was sitting up in bed, engrossed in a pile of papers that lay in front of him.

"Take a seat, Sullivan," he said, without looking up.

Pat sat down and waited. His feelings about Conrad were even more complex than they had been before. Now, he felt an odd mixture of disapproval and admiration.

"You survived," he said matter of factly. "It was a brave thing you did."

"Yes, I suppose people will see it that way," Conrad replied absently.

It was clear he didn't want to talk about the accident with the crane, or even make polite conversation about the weather, clear above all that he had no time for Pat and his airy-fairy world of parks and community spirit. Pat had a good idea why Conrad had summoned him. Conrad was suddenly a hero in Stoneyfield. As far as the people there were concerned, he could build what he wanted now. And he probably wanted to spell this out, to ensure that there were no further protests or disturbances at the site. Which was fine by Pat. He'd had enough of protesting anyway. Only the previous day, he'd gone to an estate agent for a valuation on his little house in Corbawn Street. The agent's eyes had lit up when he saw the address. Pat would sell the house at enormous profit – could buy himself a roomier house in an area like Ranelagh – where there would be no massive developments, where he could settle down to finishing his research and get on with his life, and hopefully that would include Maura.

"Mining . . . that's where it's at . . . " said Conrad absently after a while.

"I wouldn't know," Pat replied.

"The thing is, Sullivan – I have a low boredom threshold and Stoneyfield bores me now."

"We're talking about people's lives – it's not your place to be bored by them."

"I can be bored with whatever I damn well please!"

Pat could feel anger rising in his chest, at Conrad's arrogance, at his careless disregard for the rest of mankind. He opened his mouth to speak but Conrad cut him short.

". . .and I've had it with Stoneyfield. We'll clean up on the sale of the site. The government will buy it and the people will get their park. Who cares? I certainly don't."

Pat frowned and pulled at his ear in some confusion. He wasn't sure if he'd heard right. Perhaps Conrad Budd had suffered a more serious injury to the brain than was reported in the papers.

"I'm not sure I understand," he said to Conrad.

"And I thought you were the brainy one," said Conrad, a trace of the old cocky superiority in his voice. "Put it simply – I'm selling the site. Insurance will cover my losses. You'll make sure the people get the park they seem to need . . . now go away. I'm tired . . ."

When Pat finally got over the shock, when he'd asked a few more questions to make sure Conrad wasn't just raving in the head, when he'd seen that the papers resting on Conrad's lap were to do with the sale of the site, he finally stammered out his thanks.

"I knew you had a noble streak in you, Conrad. And you won't regret this, I promise you."

Conrad waved his hand dismissively. "Don't kid yourself, Sullivan. Nobility has nothing to do with it. I leave nobility to people like you. Good-bye."

# CHAPTER 42

Dublin Airport was thronged and Lit, Richie and Bonnie ploughed their way through the suitcase-hauling, backpack-wielding crowd. At the departure gate, Lit suppressed the several buckets of tears which were threatening to burst forth and hugged her son. Bonnie hugged him too and told him he was so handsome that all the German girls would fancy him rotten. He blushed and turned back to his mother.

"I'll call you tonight, Ma."

"Say hi to your dad for me. Take care and have a wonderful time." She handed him an envelope. "Spend it on something nice."

She gave him another hug and watched him disappear into the crowd, her young man on the threshold of life, going off into the world with all its adventures and uncertainties.

At work things were quiet. At home, it was even quieter. Truly alone in the house in Harwood Park for the first time, Lit finally had the time to take stock of her life. It had been a rough few months, but she'd come through. She'd made some bad mistakes, particularly with Richie. She'd lost sight of family, friends and even her own happiness for a while, dazzled as she was by success and then blinded by Conrad's awesome charm. But now she had the chance to put things right. Slowly but surely she came to terms with the loss of Dandy. She would focus now on helping to make Richie's path into manhood clear and smooth as it should or could be. And she taught herself to think of Conrad without regret or bitterness.

Richie returned from his dad's for the new school year, looking quite grown up. And they settled into life in Harwood Park with just the two of them. Winter came and with it a lonely but a peaceful Christmas. Lit cooked a massive turkey on Christmas Day with all the trimmings. They were joined by Pat and Maura and Matt and Bonnie and they felt sure that Dandy was there in spirit.

In spring, Maura became a partner in Shiels Doran and moved into Pat's little house in Stoneyfield. Pat was busier than ever now. At Conrad's suggestion, he was spearheading the development of the Stoneyfield site into a magnificently landscaped park with stately trees, glimmering lakes and tennis courts and an expansive playground for the children. Conrad was not yet fully recovered from his injuries and Bonnie spent many hours with him, alternately bossing and coaxing him back to health. Matt occasionally wondered about Poppy Cornwell, but otherwise carried on as he had always done, smoking too much and drinking more than was wise.

One Saturday morning in late spring, on the spur of the moment, Lit whisked the painting of Chatham Harbour, Cape Cod, from its place in the hall, then jumped into her car and drove away from the city, heading out past the prosperous suburbs into the lush, wooded Wicklow hills. She turned off to the left and drove along the narrow winding road until she came to Laraville.

A repentant visitor should bring a gift of food, she thought, as she noticed a new food shop in amongst the little cluster of rose-washed houses in the village. The window displays looked fresh, appetising and very inviting. Inside was a treasury of jams and preserves, home-cooked moussakas and lasagnes, fine cheeses, freshly baked breads and glistening fresh vegetables and fruit. A large wooden sign above the counter displayed the name of the shop – The Organic Food and Wicked Chocolate Shop. Sure enough, as she looked to her right, there was a counter displaying every kind of rich and indulgent chocolate confection ever invented. It was an odd combination, she thought – organic food and wicked chocolate.

"Can I help at all?" said a sweet, tremulous voice from behind.

Lit turned and came face to face with Poppy Cornwell.

Poppy seemed very different. She glowed with self-confidence and warmth. She insisted on bringing Lit into her kitchen, making tea and plying her with chocolate, and relating how she'd ended up in Laraville. It turned out Dara had not only liked the plump, luscious fruits of South America. He'd developed a taste for plump, luscious Latino lasses as well. Poppy, delighted to escape from the tyranny of his love at last, used some inherited money to come home and start up the shop.

She'd only been open a month, but already it was doing well.

"How's Matt?" she asked, blushing slightly.

"Ask him yourself," said Lit with a mischievous smile, and gave Poppy Matt's card.

"Oh, I couldn't do that!" said Poppy, carefully placing the card in a jar on the mantelpiece.

An hour later, Lit left the shop, laden down with a variety of suitable edible gifts – a basket of ripe purple plums, a box of rich cream-filled chocolates, a fine wedge of crumbly cheese from West Cork and a bottle of vintage Burgundy wine. Poppy said even one sip would cast a warm glow on any situation.

She drove to the gates of Sweetbriar House, her heart thumping mightily. Someone had cleared away all the weeds around the little churchyard and cut the grass. A workman was busy resetting parts of the crumbling chapel wall.

The avenue stretched ominously in front of her. She could turn around now, drive away and never come back. No-one would know the difference. After all, it wasn't such a big deal. She was only here to apologise. Perhaps she should just leave the things she'd bought with the workman. Before she had fully teased out that idea, she found that the car had driven through the gateway of its own accord and was making its way very steadily along the curved avenue towards the lovely old rambling house. The woods about the house were peaceful and she admired the gentle valley sweeping away into the distance. The car seemed to park itself outside the front door which was wide open. Inside she could see evidence of restoration work, workman's tools, ladders, paint.

The trees rustled softly in the light wind. Birds called

out sweetly to each other. The scent of a climbing rose wafted towards her as she made her way up the two stone steps to the door. Every muscle in her body was tense with expectation. She felt like a girl again, hesitating at every moment, fearful of what the meeting with Seán might bring. But what was the worst he could do? Tell her to get lost? She wasn't afraid of that. Then why was she so rigid with fright and expectation, so much so that she could barely breathe?

"Hallo," she called or rather croaked out.

There was no response. Somehow she managed to propel herself forward through the house and into the kitchen. It too was empty. A glass of tap water failed to steady her nerves and even stern warnings to herself to stop being ridiculous didn't help. Deep breaths didn't work and neither did a brief little sit-down on one of his old kitchen chairs. The little waving figure on the far edge of her subconscious was shouting a word at her now and that word began to drum louder and louder in her head.

When she realised what the word was, she shot out of the chair as though she'd been struck very viciously by lightning.

"Love!" she said out loud to herself. "Don't be ridiculous. I never heard such nonsense!"

At that moment she glimpsed him through the kitchen window. He was mending an old garden seat, leaning over a bench and sanding a plank to replace the old rotted one. She'd never seen his naked torso before and a hot little gasp of pure lust sent her reeling back to the tap for more cold water. She gulped and gulped and wished herself a thousand miles away. But there was no escape now. She had to admit that she missed his glinting steely grey-eyed deadpan sense of humour. She missed the way he always watched out for Richie. She missed the way he couldn't help shooting his mouth off sometimes. She missed how they were such equal sparring partners. She admired how he liked to live a simple life. She loved how she never needed to be on her best behaviour with him. He was honest, decent and humble – and glancing out at him through the window again – achingly sexy besides.

But she also saw that it was all hopeless. He didn't love her. That was obvious. Why would he love her? She was a single mother, a drunk, a woman who didn't know her arse from her elbow, prim, prissy, cold, rude and ungrateful. She gathered up her things and made her way back quickly through the house, darting out through the front door before he got the chance to see her. She bolted across the gravel to her car and rummaged frantically for her keys, thinking of how narrowly she'd escaped making a complete fool of herself. At last she found the keys and pulled the door open hastily.

Too late.

She heard footsteps on gravel.

"And where do you think you're going?"

She froze, the colour rushing to her face and draining out again.

She felt she could almost hear his warm ironic smile behind her.

She turned naked before him, no withering eyebrows, no cutting remarks, no Scudmissiles, no barriers of any kind, nothing that she could hide her love behind any more. Her cornflower-blue eyes looked up into his.

"I – just brought – " She pointed foolishly at the painting and the food from Poppy's. "To say sorry – that I – anyway, I'll be off. See you."

"Wait," he said, reached out and took her into his arms. He smelt of soap and sweat. His breath smelt of apples. He looked down into her eyes.

"How about you and me start again?"

"Start again?"

"I mean, we got off to a bad start."

"I suppose so."

"Well, let's take it from the beginning then and see if we can be more civil to each other."

She nodded, feeling vaguely disappointed. She didn't really envisage going right back to the day when he'd walked into the office and given her the lecture about the London Underground.

"Of course . . . we could try something else."

He pulled her closer, his warm breath now on her face. She was rapidly becoming a mass of fluttering, pulsating, throbbing jelly. He bent down and planted a moist kiss right on her lips.

"We could, I suppose," she managed to croak.

He lips were on her hair now, her ears, her neck.

"We could just cut all the usual crap," he said softly.

"We could."

"Right, here goes," he said, standing back abruptly and taking her hand in his.

"Will you, Lit Doran, promise never to steal deep-fried scallops from my plate again?"

"No!"

"Will you swear to never ever make a cutting remark to me again?"

"No way!"

"Will you promise faithfully to heed all the un-solicited advice I give you in the years to come?"

"Certainly not!"

"Great! Well, at least that's sorted!" he said, grinning

at her in the warm spring sunshine.

He pulled her slowly towards him and kissed her again.

"Do you have any idea how much I love you? How long I've loved you?" he murmured into her ear.

"I had no idea . . . I didn't think . . ." she said, her breath returning at last.

She could feel her body melting into the hardness of his chest, her heart soaring, her soul settling at last.

"Do you have a bed at all?" she asked, murmuring happily into his ear.

THE END